FIASCO

FIASCO
IMRE KERTÉSZ

TRANSLATION BY
TIM WILKINSON

 MELVILLEHOUSE

BROOKLYN, NEW YORK

FIASCO
Originally published in Hungarian as *A kudarc*
© 1988 Imre Kertész
Published by permission of Rowohlt.Berlin Verlag GmbH,
Reinbek bei Hamburg
Translation © 2011, Tim Wilkinson from *A kudarc*,
(2nd edition) Századvég Kiadó, Budapest, 1994
First Melville House printing: February 2011

Melville House Publishing
145 Plymouth Street
Brooklyn, NY 11201

www.mhpbooks.com

ISBN: 978-1-935554-29-5

Printed in the United States of America

1 2 3 4 5 6 7 8 9 10

Library of Congress Control Number: 2011922454

CONTENTS

The old boy was standing in front of the filing cabinet. He was thinking. It was midmorning. (Relatively—getting on for ten). Around this time the old boy was always in the habit of having a think.

He had plenty of troubles and woes, so there were things to think about.

But the old boy was not thinking about what he ought to have been thinking about.

We cannot know precisely what he was thinking about: all one could see was that he was thinking, not what he was think-ing. It could be that he was not thinking at all. But then it was midmorning (relatively—getting on for ten), and he had got used to being in the habit of having a think around this time. By now the old boy had acquired such a routine of having a think that at these times he was capable of giving the impression of having a think even when he was not thinking, and perhaps even when he imagined he was thinking. That's the honest truth, not to put too fine a point on it.

So the old boy stood thinking (absorbed in his thoughts) in front of the filing cabinet.

At this juncture we can hardly avoid saying something about the filing cabinet.

The filing cabinet was a direct descendent of one of those corner bookcases the two wings of which occupied the southwest corner of a west-facing room, precisely from the southern edge of the longitudinally north-south window surface to the corner, and from a chest of drawers placed along the line of the longitudinally east-west wall to the same corner, against a roughly 50-inch-wide protrusion of the wall the purpose of which no one had ever been able to establish and which was covered over (out of bashfulness, so to speak) by a glued-on (and very messily glued-on at that) wooden board (an appurtenance of the bookcase, as it were), if not quite up to the ceiling, then at least to the full height—a good six feet, in other words—of the bookcase.

If we are going to go into this level of detail, we cannot pass over the fact that the above-mentioned bookcase itself had been put together from the linen drawers of two former *divan-beds* through the ingenuity of a neighbourhood carpenter, whereas a more distant upholsterer had fashioned from the upholstery of the divan-beds two modern *sofas*, which were still standing, re-covered to be sure, in the western and eastern corners of the room's north-lying wall.

It may be recollected that it was in the midmorning (relatively—getting on for ten). We are now in a position to supplement that with further details: it was a splendid, warm, slightly humid but sunny late-summer (early autumnal) morning.

While the old boy at this relatively midmorning hour—getting on for ten—was standing in front of the filing cabinet and thinking, he was fleetingly subject to a temptation to close the window.

He didn't have the heart to do it, however, because the warm, slightly humid but sunny late-summer (early autumnal) morning outside was so splendid.

It was as if a pale azure-tinted bell jar had been overturned onto the old boy, standing and thinking in front of the filing cabinet, and his wider environs.

That simile, like apt similes in general, is aimed at heightening sensitivities through the associations it evokes. For what we must also imagine are the countless sources of noise and smells in a very busy street under a tightly sealed bell jar, because that was the sort of street overlooked by the window, slightly to the south of which— or to the left, if we stand facing him—the old boy was standing and thinking in front of the filing cabinet.

It was an odious street.

The Slough of Deceit, as the old boy called it.

In reality it was just a side street. (Officially speaking).

Nonetheless, jammed as it was between two main thorough-fares, the side street was very busy coping—how could it not have been?—with the traffic from the two main thoroughfares.

On the kerbs of the sidewalk, which ran in a longitudinally north-south direction, were mounted various signposts (so many flagrant symbols of futility), whereas the southern debouchment of the street, at the junction of one forking main thoroughfare and three converging side streets, was closed off by a traffic lamp, which behaved as if the street were indeed a side street, so that out of the herd of cars of every conceivable size, from midget minicars to the giant towing units of heavy-goods vehicles (along with the corresponding exhausts and harmonics) (the latter sometimes in surprising discrepancy, yet more often than not proving to be pro-portionate, to the size), which honked, vroomed, and tremulously fumed before it, its permitting a mere two or three at a time to proceed before changing back to red.

Officially no trams ran along the street.

Unofficially, however, all trams travelling to or from one par-ticular depot along one of the two main thoroughfares in point of fact effected their route, as if it were nothing to make a fuss about, by progressing via this side street jammed between the two thoroughfares.

A bellowing, rattling, grinding, rattling, screeching, and unbridled tumult boiled up from the Slough of Deceit as from the depths of a bubbling cauldron, among exhaust gases that were sometimes blackly louring, sometimes merely grizzling, whereas after the onset of evening (before the onset of winter) (for thus far we have not seen fit to so much as mention the chimney stacks) turning more a torpid bluish—until toward the dawn hour of 3:30 the first harbinger of the swarms of buses that would be emerging from their garages made its appearance (and with it a fresh day's fresh black gases), hurtling at breakneck speed and twitching its empty rearend like a mare in heat, at the northern debouchment of the street.

This street, running in a longitudinally north-south (or south-north) direction, was lined by not more than ten or fifteen buildings, yet an entire historical epoch had stamped its mark on even that relatively small number of buildings—a mark which, curiously enough, found chronological expression, going spatially in a south-north longitudinal direction.

The first half of the Forties had fallen on the middle of the street's eastern side.

Those years had been characterized by the war, its buildings by an urgent investment of capital and the attendant corner-cutting and wartime material shortages.

The old boy lived in one of these buildings, in a second-floor flatlet (a bed-sitting room with hallway, bathroom, and kitchenette, 28 m² in all, rented council property, at a monthly rental which had grown, in line with the general inflation of rents, from 120 forints to currently still just 300 forints), registered temporarily for decades by right of marriage (since his permanent residence permit was valid, by right of his being an immediate family member, for his mother's apartment, though he never lived there, not even temporarily, but seeing that it was ultimately inevitable that the old lady, for all the hopes that she would carry on to the extreme limit of human life…) (in short, on being left vacant as a consequence of this ultimately inevitable event, the apartment would, by virtue of this subterfuge, pass on to the old boy) (provided this subterfuge, as could be anticipated on grounds of customary law, was respected by the competent authority within the council) (and despite the fact that it too was just a single room, albeit a large room with all amenities and in the green belt, on account of which this apartment where the old boy was registered as a permanent resident, though he never lived there, not even temporarily, was undoubtedly more serviceable, if only as the basis for a swap).

Since the furnishings of the flat—the one in which the old boy lived permanently, albeit registered only as a temporary resident—had been kept to the bare necessities from the first, one may confidently hope that those items that we shall pick out below as the most necessary of the bare necessities are at least not unnecessary in the context of our story.

The hallway running in the east-west longitudinal direction (from the entrance), which led, on opening a hammered-glass door bisected at its middle by a painted wooden strip (or, to be more precise, on sidestepping the door, since it was always open in view of the hallway's airlessness), to the living room, was bounded on its south side by doors to the kitchenette and, to the west of that, the bathroom, with the remaining approx. 30 inches of wall still farther to west providing space for a hall stand (with hat rack).

The northern wall of the hallway was covered along its entire length, from doorframe to doorframe, by a curtain made from an attractive print of manmade fibre, behind which a clever system of racks and shelves strove to efface the memory of two ungainly, disparately-sized wardrobes that had once stood there, long defying the steadfast antipathy of the old boy's wife, and which, as is allegedly the wont of materials, did not disappear but were merely transformed into said clever system of racks and shelves; indeed a

5

3 × 3 inch chunk originally from one of the wardrobes (noteworthy for the wax seal that was visible on it) (though the inscription on the wax seal had been rendered almost illegible by a yellowish-white layer of paint from repeated decoration) could still be found, at the time of our story, in one of the old boy's boxes of papers (though which one, even he didn't know).

This brings us to the hammered-glass door bisected at its middle by a painted wooden strip on opening which (or, to be more precise, on sidestepping which, since the door was always open in view of the hallway's airlessness) we can enter the living room.

In the southeast corner of this room (which faced westward on the street side) was a tile stove, and both north and west of the stove, allowing for adequate gaps, were single armchairs (of the Maya II model, constructed from beechwood, nitrocellulose lacquer, HDP straps, foam rubber, furnishing fabric, quality in compliance with the specifications of Hungarian Standards 8976/4/72 and 8977–68, PROTECT FROM DAMP!), between the armchairs (slightly north-west of the stove) a sweepingly curved standard lamp (its shade changing roughly every five years) and, a little farther to the northwest, a tiny, rickety thingamajig, resting on stick legs, which according to its Quality Certificate was a child's mini-table, 1st-class special ply of 1st-class sawn hardwood, but which in regard to its actual function was more a kind of tiny smoker's table.

After the armchair to the north of the stove (allowing for an adequate gap) was another gap, and then the hammered-glass door—or to be more accurate, since the door was always open due to hallway's airlessness—a door-sized aperture, then the hammered-glass leaf of the hammered-glass door, behind which was a gap and, after the gap, in the northeastern corner of the room, the narrower side of one of the sofas, then the corner itself, after which came—now along the northern wall—the longer side of the sofa, space, a low chest of drawers, space, and finally the second sofa, the longer side of which snuggled up to the west wall, stretching north-to-south right under the window where, still more to the south, there was a space, then a table (to be more precise, *the* table, the only real table in the flat) stretching farther southward, almost to the southwest-ern corner of the room, the sole obstacle to reaching which was an item of furniture standing in this corner, and which by now should certainly no longer be entirely unfamiliar to the observant reader.

Our job is a good deal easier if we start from the armchair standing to the west of the stove (allowing for an adequate gap) and proceed along the room's southern wall, because here there is just another gap then, more to the west, a low chest of drawers (an exact copy and pair of the chest of drawers opposite it), with a gap beyond which was the wall protrusion (the purpose of which no one had ever been able to establish), and lastly, in the southwest corner of the room, that hybrid, the bookcase–filing-cabinet centaur (if such a catachresis may be entertained), before which, one splendid, warm, slightly humid but sunny late-summer (early autumnal) morning—which spilled over him and his wider environs like an impenetrable bell jar—the old boy was standing and thinking.

To guard against any definitive fixing of notions which no doubt have already begun to form, our hitherto neutral use of words probably calls for some clarification at this juncture.

Just as the filing cabinet, for example, was not really a filing cabinet, or, to take another example, the old boy's side street (the Slough of Deceit, as the old boy called it) was not really a side street, the old boy was not really old.

He was old, of course (for why else would we call him the old boy). Still, the old boy was not an old boy for being old; that is to say, he was not an old man (though he was not young either), (for why else would we call him the old boy).

In all probability it would be simplest just to say how old he was (if we were not averse to such exceedingly dubious specifics, changing as they do from year to year, day to day, even minute to minute) (and who knows how many years, days and minutes our story will arch) (or what twists and turns that span may span) (as a result of which we might suddenly find ourselves in a situation where we may no longer be able to vouch for our rash assertions).

So, for want of better, let us fall back on an observation, though in itself it is by no means a particularly original one:

If a person is weighed down by a good half-century, then he either sinks under the burden or somehow withstands it, comes to a standstill (on the hook of time, as it were) (a hook which may, of course, drag and pull him ever further into the wasteland of the other shore, into a shadowy, desiccated abstraction amidst succulent colours and palpable forms), and an enduring moment supervenes which is as if it were not even here, or in other words, tempts us with the deceptive appearance of something still not having been definitively decided (whether or not the rope is strong enough, so to speak) (why wouldn't it be? nevertheless we are all aware of the circumstance that, for sake of a more secure grip, it gives a little may, in itself, give rise to misconceptions) (above all in the sort of person who has already succeeded in severing the rope once) (but let us not anticipate our tale).

If in what follows we continue to maintain—and we shall—that the old boy was old, obviously we shall have to find another way of justifying this usage (which neither the old boy's appearance nor even the superior knowledge of a registry office official peeking beneath the surface of things puts in our mouth).

Nothing easier.

For the old boy thought of himself—we can hardly dispute that he had every reason to do so—as old, as someone to whom nothing more could happen, nothing new, whether good or bad (with a proviso for the far from consubstantial chances of the just slightly better or slightly worse) (although this made essentially no difference to the essence), as someone to whom everything had already happened (including what might still happen or might have happened), someone who had outwitted—transiently—his death, lived out—definitively—his life, gained his modest reward for his vices and strict punishment for his virtues, and had long been a permanent figure on that grey list that is kept, who can tell where, and in accordance with what sort of promptings, of those who are excess to headcount; someone who, despite all that, wakes up day after day to the fact that he still exists (and doesn't find it so unpleasant at that) (as he might, perhaps, have felt) (if he always took everything into consideration) (which he did not do at all).

For that reason, then, there are no grounds at all for us to believe that these were the things being thought when the old boy was standing in front of the filing cabinet and thinking.

No, all that's at issue is that it was midmorning (relatively—getting on for ten), and that around this time the old boy was in the habit of having a think.

That was how he ordered his life.

Every day, when ten o'clock (or thereabouts) came around, he immediately started to think.

This was an upshot of his circumstances, since before ten o'clock he would not have been able to start thinking, whereas if he only set about it later on, he would have reproached himself for the lost time (which would have only led to further loss of time, or held him back even further, if not—in extreme cases—completely obstructed him from thinking).

Thus at ten o'clock (or thereabouts), so to speak automatically and quite independently of the intensity of the thinking, or even of whether or not he thought at all (the old boy was so much into the routine of thinking that he was sometimes capable of creating the appearance of being in thought even when he was not thinking, possibly even when he himself might have imagined he was thinking), the old boy stood in front of the filing cabinet and thought.

For at ten o'clock (or thereabouts) the old boy was left alone in the flat (which for him counted as a precondition for thinking), as his wife would earlier have set off on the long journey to the bistro on the city outskirts where, as a waitress, she earned her bread (and occasionally the old boy's as well) (if fate so willed it) (and it certainly did so will it more than once).

He had also done with his ablutions.

He had also drunk his coffee (in the armchair to the west of the tile stove) (allowing for an adequate gap).

He had also already smoked his first cigarette (pacing back and forth between the west-facing window and the closed entrance door to the east) (sidling a bit in the constricted space formed by the curtain made from an attractive print of manmade fibre covering the north wall of the hallway and the open bathroom door) (a door which was constantly open, for purposes of ventilation, since the bathroom was even more airless than the airless hallway).

These were the preliminaries, if not reasons (though most certainly preconditions), for the old boy to be standing in front of the filing cabinet and thinking at ten o'clock (or thereabouts) on this splendid, warm, slightly humid but sunny late-summer (early autumnal) morning.

The old boy had plenty of troubles and woes, so he had something to think about.

But the old boy was not thinking about what he ought to have been thinking about.

Yet we cannot assert that his most topical care—that is to say, the one he ought to have been thinking about—had not so much as entered his head.

Indeed we cannot.

"I'm just standing here in front of the filing cabinet and thinking," the old boy was thinking, "instead of actually doing something."

Well certainly, the truth is—not to put too fine a point on it—that he should long ago have settled down to writing a book.

For the old boy wrote books.

That was his occupation.

Or rather, to be more precise, things had so transpired that this had become his occupation (seeing as he had no other occupation).

He had already written several books as well, most notably his first one: he had worked on that book (since at the time writing books had not yet become his occupation and he had written the book for no obvious reason, just on an arbitrary whim, so to say) for a good ten years, but had subsequently seen it into print only after a fair number of vicissitudes—and the passage of a further two years; for his second book just four years had proved adequate; and with his other books (since by then writing books had become his occupation, or rather—to be more precise—things had so transpired that this had become his occupation) (seeing as he had no other occupation) he merely devoted the time that was absolutely necessary to get them written, which was essentially a function of their thickness, because (since things had so transpired that this had become his occupation) he had to aim to write books that were as thick as possible, out of carefully considered self-interest, since the fee for thicker books was fatter than that for slimmer books, for which—since they were slimmer—the fee was correspondingly slim (proportionate to their slimness) (regardless of their content) (in accordance with MoE Decree No.1/20.3.1970 concerning terms and conditions for publishing contracts and authors' royalties, as issued by the Ministry of Education with the assent of the Treasury, the Ministry of Labour, the president of the National Board of Supply and Price Control, and the National Trades Union Council).

Not that the old boy was burning with longing to write a new book.

It had simply been quite some time since a new book of his had been published.

If this were to continue, his very name would sink into oblivion.

Which, in itself, would not have concerned the old boy in the slightest.

Except that—and there was the rub—he had to be concerned about it in a certain respect.

In not so many years he would reach the age at which he might become a retired writer (in other words, a writer who had earned enough from his books not to have to write any more books) (though he could do, of course, if he still had the wish to).

That, then—if he stripped away all the vague abstractions, and he was a stickler for the concrete and tangible—was the real goal of his literary labours.

But in order not to have to write any more books, he would still have to write a few more.

As many more as he could.

For if he were not to lose sight of the real goal of his literary labours (that is, that he might become a retired writer, or in other words, a writer who had earned enough from his books not to have to write any more books), then it was to be feared that the degree of oblivion into which his name was falling might affect—to wit, adversely—the factors determining his pension (about which factors he had no precise information, but he reasoned, perhaps not entirely illogically, that if a bigger royalty was to be expected for a thicker book, then more books should yield a bigger pension) (which, in the absence of more precise information, as has already been indicated, was just speculation, if not entirely illogical speculation, on the old boy's part).

So that was why the old boy had to be concerned, even if in other respects he was not in the slightest bit concerned about the fact in itself, that his very name was sinking into oblivion.

Consequently, despite not burning with any longing to write a new book, he ought to have settled down to it long ago.

Only he had no clue what. (This, incidentally, had already happened to him on other occasions, though only with any regularity since writing books had become his occupation (or rather—to be more precise—since things had so transpired that this had become his occupation) (seeing as he had no other occupation).

And yet it was a just a question of a single book.

Any old book, just so long as it was a book (the old boy had long been aware that it made no difference at all what kind of book he wrote, good or bad—that had no bearing on the essence of the matter) (though as to what he meant by the essence the old boy either knew only too well or had no idea at all) (at least we are forced to this conclusion by the fact that, standing and thinking in front of the filing cabinet as he was, this thought, among others, was running through his head, though he gave not the slightest sign of wishing to clarify the essence of this notion—of the essence—if only for his own purposes).

But the old boy did not have so much as a glimmer of an idea, little as that may be, for the book he needed to write.

Despite having done truly everything in his power as far as he was concerned (for, as we have seen, at this very moment he was standing in front of the filing cabinet and thinking).

In recent days he had already gone through every one of his old, older, or still older ideas, sketches and fragments, which he kept in a folder furnished with the title "*Ideas, sketches, fragments,*" but either they had proved unusable or else he had understood not a word of them (even though he himself had been the one who noted them down some time before, or some time before that, or still further back in time).

He had even undertaken lengthy walks in the Buda hills (contemplative walks, as the old boy called them).

All to no avail.

Now, with his ideas, sketches, fragments, and walks (contemplative walks, as the old boy called them) in turn, one after the other, all having come to nought, all that was left was his papers.

It had been a long time since he had seen his papers.

Not that he wished to see them.

He had even hidden them in the farthest depths of the filing cabinet in order to avoid somehow catching sight of them.

So the old boy had to be in a very tight spot indeed to be driven, for once, to place his ultimate trust—if previously it had been on a stroke of good fortune (which, for known reasons, we might better amend to the virtually impossible), then on the his ideas, sketches, fragments and his contemplative walks—in his papers.

But at this juncture it is to be feared that if we do not break away a bit from the old boy's train of thought, we shall never get to see in the clear light that is indispensable to what follows the subtle, but not inconsequential, difference between ideas, sketches, and fragments, on the one hand, and papers, on the other.

It may be that we shall not be forced into too lengthy an explanation.

Specifically, ideas, sketches, and fragments are only produced by someone who is driven to those resorts by imperative and pressing reasons; someone—like the old boy, for instance—whose occupation happens to be writing books (or rather, to be more precise, for whom things had so transpired that this had become his occupation) (seeing as he had no other occupation).

Papers, on the other hand, everybody has. If not a number of them, then certainly one: a scrap of paper on which one noted down something at some time, presumably something important that was not to be forgotten and was carefully put away—and then forgotten about.

Papers which preserve adolescent poems.

Papers through which one sought a way out at a critical period. Possibly an entire diary.

A house plan.

A budget for a difficult year ahead.

A letter one started to write.

A message—"Back soon"—that may later have proved to be portentous.

At the very least a bill, or the washing instructions torn off some undergarment, on the reverse side of which we discover minute, faded, unfamiliar and by now illegible lettering—our own handwriting.

The old boy had a whole file of such papers.

As we have perhaps already mentioned, he kept them in the farthest depths of the filing cabinet in order to avoid somehow catching sight of them.

Now that he wanted the exact opposite—namely, to catch sight of them—he first had to lift out of the filing cabinet his typewriter, several files—among them one labelled "*Ideas, sketches, fragments*"—as well as two cardboard boxes which held a miscellany of objects (both necessary and unnecessary) (at all events only the occasion of the particular moment could assign a firm ascription to those designations) (as a result of which the old boy could never know for sure which of these objects were necessary and which unnecessary) (a distinction that became all the more unclear, as years might go by without his opening the lids of the two cardboard boxes and so casting even a single glance over the variety of objects, necessary and unnecessary alike).

This, then, was his way of ensuring that he caught sight of the ordinary, grey, standard-sized (HS 5617) box file containing his papers.

On the grey file, as a paperweight, so to say, squatted (or swaggered) (or sphered) (depending on the angle from which one looked at it) a likewise grey, albeit a darker grey, stone lump; in other words, a stone lump of irregular shape about which there is nothing reassuring that we might say (for instance, that it was a polygonal parallelepiped) (anything, in fact, that can soothingly reconcile the human soul to the world of objects, without its ever truly comprehending them, insofar as they at least match a familiar construct, thus allowing the matter to be left at that), seeing that this particular lump of stone, by virtue of its still extant or already worn-down edges, corners, roundings, bumps, grooves, fissures, projections, and indentations was as irregular as any lump of stone can be about which one cannot tell whether it is a mass from which a smaller lump has been broken off or, conversely, the remnant small lump of a larger stone mass, which in its turn—like a cliff face to a mountain—was in all certainty part of a still larger stone mass (but then every lump of stone instantly entices one into prehistoric deliberations) (which are not our aim) (difficult though they are to resist) (most especially when we happen to be dealing with a lump of stone which diverts our failing imagination toward ulterior) (or rather primordial) (beginnings, ends, masses and unities, so that in the end we retreat to our hopeless) (though it is at least invested with the alleged dignity of knowledge) (ignorance regarding which, for this lump of stone as for so many other things, one cannot tell whether it is a small lump broken off from a larger stone mass or, conversely, the remnant small lump of a larger stone mass).

The situation pertaining at the start of our story, to which we have consistently adhered all along—not at all out of obstinacy, merely due to the ponderousness of the old boy's decision-making process—has now been modified as follows:

The old boy was standing in front of a wide-open filing cabinet, in whose half-emptied upper drawer only a grey box file, upon which, as a paperweight, so to say, a likewise grey, albeit a darker grey, lump of stone is visible, and was thinking:

"I'm afraid," he thought, "I'm finally going to have to get my papers out."

Which, by the way, is what he proceeded to do.

And then, out of orderliness (for what other reason might we discern) (unless we take the shortage of space into consideration) (or perhaps as a way of setting a seal on the irrevocability of the decision), he tidied the typewriter, several files—among them one labelled "*Ideas, sketches, fragments*"—as well as the two cardboard boxes back into the upper drawer of the filing cabinet.

It may be found to be more than sheer prolixity if we were now to report, as briefly as we can, on a further modification to the situation pertaining at the start of our story, already modified as it is:

The old boy was standing in front of the filing cabinet and reading.

> "*August 1973*
> What has happened, has happened; I can do nothing about it now. I can do as little to alter my past as the future implacably ensuing from it, with which I am as yet unacquainted…"

"Good God!" the old boy uttered aloud.

> "…Yet I move just as aimlessly within the narrow confines of my present as in the past or the time which is to come.
> How I got to this position, I don't know. I simply frittered away my childhood. There are no doubt deep psychological explanations for why I should have been such a poor student in the lower classes at grammar school. ("You don't even have the excuse of being dumb, because you have a brain, if only you would use it," as my father often stressed.)

Later, when I was fourteen and a half, through a conjunction of infinitely inane circumstances, I found myself looking down the barrel of a loaded machine gun for half an hour. It is practically impossible to describe those circumstances in normal language. Suffice it to say that I was standing in a crowd which was sweating fear, and who knows what scraps of thoughts, in the narrow courtyard of a police barracks, the one thing which all the individuals had in common being that we were all Jews. It was a crystal-clear, flower-scented summer evening, a full moon beaming up above us. The air was filled with a steady, low throbbing: obviously Royal Air Force formations flying from their Italian bases and headed for unknown targets, and the danger which threatened us was that if they should chance to drop a bomb on the barracks or its environs, the gendarmes would mow us down, as they phrased it. The ludicrous connections and imbecilic reasons on which that rested were, I felt then and also since then, absolutely negligible. The machine gun was mounted on a stand rather like the tripod of a cine camera. Standing behind it, on some sort of platform, was a gendarme with drooping Turanian moustache and impassively narrowed eyes. Fitted onto the end of the barrel was a ridiculous conical component, rather like the one on my grandmother's coffee grinder. We waited. The drone's rumbling grew louder and then again faded to a low buzz, only for each quiet interval to give way to a renewed intensification of the rumbling. Would it drop or wouldn't it, that was the question. Gradually the gendarmes let the deranged good humour of gamblers take control of them. Is there any way I can describe the unforeseen good spirits that, after I had got over my initial surprise, coursed through me as well? All I had to do to be able to enjoy the game, in a certain fashion, was to recognize the triviality of the stake. I grasped the simple secret of the universe that had been disclosed to me: I could be gunned down anywhere, at any time. It may be that this…"

"For fuck's sake" the old boy suddenly broke off his reading at this point as he lifted himself partway from his seat to reach over to the filing cabinet.

The reason for this curious development lay in an event that, although it had not been anticipated, could not be categorized as unexpected (because it occurred regularly, practically every single day), but even the frequent repetition of the event had not robbed it, as we have seen, of its original, elemental impact on the old boy (indeed, quite the opposite, one might say).

Obviously, it would be wrong for us to hold back on providing a satisfactory explanation.

Still, this obligation undeniably puts us somewhat at a loss.

It hardly serves as sufficient explanation for the words which erupted from the old boy's mouth, for the mild cramps which constricted his stomach, or for the ever-so-slight nausea that shot up with a hurtling and a dizzying jolt, like some kind of elevator, through his chest and throat to slam against the back of his neck, for us merely to say—sticking to the bare facts—that a radio had been switched on above his head.

It is not without purpose (indeed, we are admittedly thinking of easing our task as narrator) that we now leave the old boy's papers where they are and, in their stead, open a not overly bulky book with a green half-cloth binding that the old boy had been leafing through frequently, and to great advantage, in recent days, evidencing especially appreciative relish for the following lines (on page 259 of the volume) (at which page, incidentally, the green half-bound volume fell open, almost as if by pre-arrangement, once the old boy had lifted it down from the bookshelf occupying the northeast corner of the room) (although, as a further safeguard to unerring location, the yellow bookmarking ribbon of artificial silk had also been inserted at the same page) (on which page the following lines) (for which the old boy evidenced especially appreciative relish) (may now be read by us too, bending over his shoulder, so to speak):

> *There exists a creature which is perfectly harmless; when it passes before your eyes you scarcely notice it and forget it again immediately. But as soon as it invisibly gets somehow into your ears, it develops there, it hatches, as it were, and cases have been known where it has penetrated even into the brain and has thriven devastatingly in that organ, like those pneumococci in dogs that gain entrance through the nose.*
> *This creature is one's neighbour."*

True enough.
Oglütz is what the old boy called it.
The Unsilent Being.
Not female, not male, not beast, least of all human.
Oglütz is what the old boy called it.
Whether due to unlimited listening to radio and television or as a consequence of some hormonal imbalance (the explanation for which imbalance lay, perhaps, in unlimited listening to radio and television) (though a copious intake of foodstuffs should not be overlooked), the Being proliferated not only in the old boy's brain but across the entire 28 square metres above his head.
The old boy lived below a female Cyclops which fed on noise. (Although this particular Cyclops had two eyes, two tiny rhino eyes.)
All day long the old boy was helplessly tossed about on the heavy swell of its sounds. He heard the appalling slam of the door each time it got back to its lair; a burst of quickfire thuds and rumbles, perhaps (the old boy conjectured) through dumping the haul

of spoils that it had brought back home; a broken, jarring rhythm of heavy bumps—training bears, as the old boy was in the habit of commenting; and soon enough the bellowing wild beast of some broadcast service or other, either the radio or the television.

Oglütz is what the old boy called it.

Nothing could be done about it.

One had to resign oneself to it.

Some time long, long ago, at the beginning of time, the old boy had willy-nilly surrendered himself into admitting that the noises disturbed him (indeed, had requested that they be moderated). Since which time it had kept an unremitting watch above his head.

He had got to know its habits.

It waited for him to strike the first key on the typewriter keyboard.

It sensed infallibly when he was in the habit of standing in front of the filing cabinet and having a think.

Nothing could be done about it.

One had to resign oneself to it.

The course of long years had built up a set of automatic defence reflexes in the old boy (rather like, for instance, opening his umbrella when it rained).

The above-cited lines from the not overly bulky, green half-bound volume (for which the old boy evidenced especially appreciative relish) may likewise be classified as one of those defence reflexes.

This wholly spiritual consolation and source of strength would have been to little avail, however, without his considerable collection of earplugs of fusible-wax, which took up almost the entire left rear—southwest—corner of the lower drawer of his filing cabinet (as it was not always possible to procure them, since they were of foreign manufacture) (OHROPAX Noise Shields, VEB Pharmazeutika, Königsee) (on account of which, during periods when they were procurable, the old boy laid in such a stock of them, that his earplugs) (like Josef K.'s shame) (would in all likelihood outlive him), from which stock a pair of wax balls, in a cylindrical glass phial, lay constantly ready for use at the front of the next drawer up in the filing cabinet, so that in the event of need (and the need almost always arose, with clockwork regularity), after a certain amount of preparatory softening work with the palm of the hand, they could be instantly inserted into the old boy's ears.

During the preparatory softening work, the old boy was in the habit of reciting, in an undertone, yet another longer or shorter text—more in a mechanical sort of manner, sacrificing, as it were, the vital emotion which had once provoked the words (just as, with frequent repetition, the essence dwindles even from the ritual of prayer, making way for dutiful distraction)—the length, or short-ness, of which longer or shorter text varied with the season: in winter he recited a longer text than in the summer, which finds a simple explanation in the physical fact that wax softens more rapidly in the warmth than in the cold.

And so it was that on this splendid, warm, slightly humid but sunny late-summer (early autumnal) morning, all that the old boy intoned, unhurriedly and syllable by syllable, was "You fucking miserable, scummy, old Nazi bag...", while carefully shaping the by now softened wad between his fingers as he crammed it into his ear, thereby placing himself beyond the reach of Oglütz, the Slough of Deceit—the entire world in effect (by virtue of which the modified situation is once again modified a bit, insofar as the old boy now carried on with his reading with two wax plugs in his ears):

> "...the simple secret of the universe that had been disclosed
> to me: I could be gunned down anywhere, at any time. It may
> be that this, by the way not particularly original, perception
> disturbed me a little; it may be that it left a deeper impres-
> sion on me than was justified, for how many countless oth-
> ers went through exactly the same mass justice, whether on

the same spot at the same time or at other times and other places in the big, wide world. Perhaps I was an oversensitive child, and even later on was unable to rid myself of my subtlety: possibly some sort of short-circuit occurred, a disturbance in my normal metabolic relationship with my experiences, even though I could only lay claim to essentially the same normally grubby experiences as any other normal being. Many years later—and many years before now—I knew that I would have to write a novel. At the time I happened to be hanging around, completely indifferently, in some indifferent office corridor when I heard an indifferent sound—of steps. The whole thing was over in a trice. In recollecting that moment, which I am otherwise incapable of recollecting, I have to suppose that if I had been able to preserve within myself its lucidity, some kind of distillate, as it were, of its content, then I would probably be able to grasp the thing that was truly always of greatest interest: the key to my existence. But moments pass and do not recur. I therefore supposed that I ought at least to remain faithful to its intimation; I started to write a novel. I wrote one and tore it up; I wrote it afresh and again tore it up. Years went by. I kept on writing, writing until I felt that I had finally hit upon a possible novel for me. I wrote a novel, in the meantime producing dialogues for musical comedies, each more inane than the last, in order to obtain a livelihood (hoodwinking my wife who, in the semigloom of the theatre auditorium at "my premieres," would wait for me, wearing the mid-grey suit specially tailored for such occasions, to take my place before the curtains in a storm of applause and would imagine that our beached life would finally work free from the shoals after all); but I, after assiduously putting in appearances at the pertinent branch

of the National Savings Bank to pick up the not inconsiderable royalties due for my claptrap, would immediately
sneak home with the guilty conscience of a thief to write
a novel anew, and in the years that I have just put behind
me this dominating passion grew to be an obstacle even to
my being able to present my public, avid for entertainment,
with fresh comedies and myself with renewed royalties ..."

"Well now," the old boy got up and began, with the pliable wax
plugs in his ears muting the sound of his tread to the velvety glide of
a panther, to pace up and down between the west-facing window and
the closed entrance to the east (sidling a bit in the constricted space
formed by the curtain made from an attractive print of manmade
fibre covering the north wall of the hallway and the open bathroom
door) (a door which was constantly open, for purposes of ventilation, since the bathroom was even more airless than the airless hallway), "It starts off as if it were aiming to be some sort of confession,"
he muttered. "Not bad as such, but it can still go off. The trouble is that
it's honest. Not the happiest sign. Nor the subject either."

Well indeed, if he had to write a book (any old book, just so
long as it was a book) (the old boy had long been aware that it made
no difference at all what kind of book he wrote, good or bad—that
had no bearing on the essence of the matter), at least let it be a book
on a happy subject.

Certainly his subjects so far had not been too happy.

As the old boy saw it, the reason for that—on the rare occasions he gave it any thought—was that he probably had no fantasy
(which was quite a disadvantage, considering that his occupation
happened to be writing books) (or rather, to be more precise, things
had so transpired that this had become his occupation) (seeing as
he had no other occupation).

As a result—for what else could he have done?—he drew his

subjects, for the most part, out of his own experiences.

That, however, always ruined even his happiest subjects.

On this occasion he wanted to be on his guard.

"It was dumb of me," he mused, "to get out my papers. Best pack them away again."

"Only," he mused further, "they've got my interest now."

"I feared as much," he added (musing).

Rightly so, because for once we can now report the restoration of an earlier situation, itself only temporarily modified by the pacing back and forth: the old boy was sitting in front of the filing cabinet and reading.

...with the guilty conscience of a thief... to present my public... and myself with renewed royalties—

But this is getting me nowhere. In the final analysis, it is just a story; it may be expanded or abbreviated but still explain nothing, like stories in general. I can't make out from my story what happened to me, yet that is what I need. I don't even know if the scales have just now fallen from my eyes or, on the contrary, are just now dimming them. These days, at any rate, I am caught off guard at every turn. Take the flat in which I live. It takes up twenty-eight square metres on the second floor of a comparatively not too ugly Buda apartment house of fairly human proportions. A living room and a hallway that lets on to the bathroom and the so-called kitchenette. It even has belongings, furniture, this and that. Disregarding the changes that my wife held to be necessary every now and then, everything is just the same as yesterday, the day before, or one year or nineteen years ago, which was when..."

"Nineteen years!" the old boy snorted.

"...or nineteen years ago, which was when we moved in, under circumstances that were not without incident. Yet, recently some sort of perfidious threat issues from it all, something that makes me uneasy. At first I had no idea at all what to make of this since, as I said, I see nothing new or unusual in the flat. I racked my brains a long time until I finally realized that it's not what I see that has changed: the change comes just from the *way* I see. Before now, I had never properly seen this flat in which I have lived for nineteen years..."

"Nineteen years," the old boy said, shaking his head.

...and yet there is nothing puzzling about that if I think it over. For the fellow with whom I was once, even just a few months ago, identical, this flat was a fixed but nevertheless provisional place where he wrote his novel. That was this chap's job, his express goal, who knows, perhaps even his purpose; in other words, however slowly he might actually have done his job, he was always rushing. He viewed objects from a train window, so to speak, in passing, as they flashed before his gaze. He gained at best a fleeting impression of the utility of individual objects, taking them in his hands and then putting them down, going through them, pulling them, pushing them about, bullying them, terrorising them. Now they no longer feel the power of the controlling hand they are having their revenge: they present themselves, push their way before me, reveal their constancy. How indeed to take account of the panic which grips me on seeing them? This chair, this table, the sweeping curve of this standard lamp and the shade, scorched in the areas near the bulb, that hangs submissively, so to speak, from it—each one of them now jostles me and surrounds me with sham meekness, like forgiving, mournful nuns after some king of drubbing. They want to convince me that nothing has happened, though as I recall it, I have lived through something with them, an adventure, let us say—the adventure of writing, and I supposed that in pursuing a certain path to its very end my life had altered. But nothing at all has altered, and now it is clear that with my adventure it was precisely the chances of altering that I forfeited. This twenty-eight square metres is no longer the cage from which my imagination soared in flight every day, and to which I returned at night to sleep; no, it is the real arena of my real life, the cage in which I have imprisoned myself.

Then there is another thing: the strangeness of mornings. There was a time when I would awake at dawn; I would restlessly watch the light prising the cracks in the window blinds, waiting until I could get up. Over breakfast tea I exchanged only a few obligatory words with my wife; subconsciously I was just watching out for the time when I would finally be left to myself and, having completed the indispensable ablutions, be able to devote myself to the stubbornly waiting and perpetually recalcitrant paper. These days, however, out of some peculiar compulsion, it seems as if all I do is excuse myself; at breakfast I talk to my wife, and she is delighted at the change, not suspecting its cause; and when she leaves I catch myself anxiously following her in my thoughts…

At this point, the old boy thought that he might have heard the telephone ringing, but, having loosened one of the pliable wax plugs, ascertained that it was merely the noises from Oglütz as well as The Slough of Deceit swirling about him, perhaps just at a somewhat higher frequency than usual; and this bit disturbance may explain why he had to search for the continuation, and also why—as the lack of this continuity indeed demonstrates—he must have skipped a few lines of the text at this point:

I sense all kinds of traps opening up beneath my feet, I compound one mistake after another; every perception I make, everything that surrounds me, serves only to attack me, to cast doubt on and undermine my own probability.

I wonder when it was that these nuisances began. I don't know why: it seems a person finds it reassuring to discover a starting point, some possibly arbitrary reference point in time that he can subsequently designate as the cause. Once we believe we have discovered a cause, any trouble appears rational. I suppose I never truly believed in my own existence. As I have already hinted earlier, I had good, sound, one might say objective, reasons for that. When I was writing my novel, this deficiency paid remarkable dividends as it became practically a work tool for me; it was worn down in the course of my daily activity, and when it had tired of my converting it into words, it did not bother me further. The trouble only started up again when I had finished my novel. I can still remember how those last pages were written. It happened three a and half months ago, on a promising May afternoon. I sensed that the end was within my grasp. It all depended on my wife. That evening she was due to visit one of her woman friends. During dinner I was tensely alert to whether she might be tired, not in the mood ... I was lucky; I was left on my own. A sudden attack of diarrhoea delayed me from setting to the paper straight away. I had to ascribe this annoying symptom to a *motus animi continuus*, an onward sweep of the productive mechanism in which, as we know from

Cicero, the quintessence of eloquence resides. That spirit is nothing but a certain state of excitement, but it can have an effect—with me, at any rate—on the entire body, including in all likelihood the digestive system. I finally sat down at the table, after all, and then finished off the text just as speedily as I was able to glide pen over paper. I got the last sentence down as well: finished. For days after that I kept on tinkering with it, scribbling in something here and there, correcting some words, deleting others. Then there was nothing more that could be done: that was it, the end. I was overcome by a somewhat idiotic feeling. Suddenly, something that had been a rather good diversion over many long years had folded, it seems. I only came to realize this later on. Up till then I had presumed I was working and had set to it, day after day, with a corresponding, contrived fury. Now that had been drained from me. The daily hard slog had been transfigured into a heap of paper. Now I was left with empty hands, plundered. All at once I found myself confronting the immaterial and formless monster of time. Its gaping mouth yawned witlessly at me, and there was nothing I could shove down its maw.

"Did you get any work done?" the old boy's wife enquired after she had returned from the bistro where, as a waitress, she earned her bread (and occasionally the old boy's as well) (if fate so willed it) (and it certainly did so will it more than once).

"Of course," the old boy replied.

"Did you make any progress?"

"I pushed on a bit," said the old boy.

"What do want for dinner?"

"I don't know. What's the choice?"

His wife told him.

"All the same to me," the old boy decided.

A little later the old boy and his wife sat in front of the filing cabinet to eat their dinner (with due regard, naturally, to the circumstances that have already been touched upon) (thus when we say that the old boy and his wife sat in front of the filing cabinet to eat their dinner, this should be understood to mean that although the filing cabinet was facing them, in reality they were seated at the table, to be more precise, *the* table, the only real table in the flat) (and eating).

The old boy's wife had got into the habit during dinner of relating what had happened to her in the bistro.

They would be making stock check soon; the managers were afraid that shrinkages would show up (not without reason, as they pilfered far too much) (and most unprofessionally at that, most notably the Old Biddy) (the chief administrator, to give her her official title) (though certain members of staff were no better) (but then there was much greater opportunity for the managers) (most notably the Old Biddy—the chief administrator, to give her her official title—who wanted to make up all the shrinkages through the tap beer and, more especially, the lunch menus) (what in the waitresses' jargon was dubbed "pap") ("pap" being the meals consumed mainly by children whose parents, not wanting, or possibly not being in a position, to cook for them, paid a weekly sum to the bistro for the lunch menu, or "pap" in the jargon) (although, as the old boy's wife never omitted to remark, she had yet to meet the parent who checked up on what their children ate, or whether they even ate at all) (despite which the children did put on weight and, in time, would indisputably grow up into adults, who quite possibly would condemn their own children to lunch menus for want of time to fuss about with household chores) (that being the way of the world, what one major but highly suspect mind called eternal recurrence) (about which, as about many other things, he was mistaken, let it be noted): in short, veiled hints and open insinuations were already being expressed on the matter of the prospective stock check.

"Apart from which," the old boy's wife added, "blood is being spilt over the shift rota."

The point was that the old boy's wife always worked the morning shift.

The bistro, on the other hand, stayed open until late at night (during which late-night hours the bistro was frequented by an army of customers who, by the late evening hours, were transformed into exceptionally generous, open-handed beings).

In accordance with the worthy, fair-play rule of equal opportunity, which was also enshrined in law as a labour right, the bistro's employees shared alike the clientele for the lunch menu in the mornings and afternoons (pap-eaters in the jargon), as tight-fisted as their time was rushed, and the late-night clientele who, by the late evening hours, were transformed into exceptionally generous, open-handed beings.

Nevertheless, the old boy's wife, at her own request, as confirmed by signature, only ever worked in the mornings (so that the old boy would also be able to work in the twenty-eight square metres during the mornings) (and also because she could not abide the late-night clientele who, by the late evening hours, were transformed into exceptionally generous, open-handed beings but at the same time mostly drank themselves stupid or to the point of causing a nuisance).

Thus the late-night shift hours (as well as the by no means inconsiderable benefits that went with them) to which the old boy's wife would have been entitled on the worthy, fair-play rule of equal opportunity, which was also enshrined in law as a labour right, were almost automatically assigned to a certain colleague called Mrs. Boda; however, most likely as a result of long habitude and also, perhaps, the greater inclination that human nature shows toward what, no doubt, is—if we may put it this way—a more instinctive attitude to legal practice than the worthy rules of fair play (even when also enshrined in law as a labour right), this certain colleague called Mrs. Boda (whose first name was Ilona) had already long regarded the benefits that had been assigned to her not as assigned benefits but entitlements.

One must take all that into account in imagining the effect produced by the announcement made by the old boy's wife that very day that from now on she too wanted to work in the evenings.

"Why?" the old boy asked.

"Because as things are I hardly earn anything, and now you are not going to earn anything because you have to write a book."

"That's true," said the old boy.

That evening the old boy declared, "I'm off for a walk."

"Don't be too long," said his wife.

"All right. I need to think a bit."

"There was something else I meant to tell you."

"What was that?" The old boy paused.

"It's slipped my mind for the moment."

"Next time write it down so you won't forget."

"It would be nice if we could go away somewhere."

"Yes, that would be nice," the old boy said, nodding.

On returning from his walk (his contemplative walk, as he called it), the old boy asked:

"Did anyone call?"

"Who would have called?"

"True," the old boy conceded.

"That tin-eared, clap-ridden, belly-dancing bitch of a whore…" the old boy intoned, unhurriedly and syllable by syllable, while carefully shaping the softened wad between his fingers as he crammed it into his ear, thereby placing himself beyond reach of Oglütz, the Slough of Deceit—the entire world in effect.

…Yes, if I had been consistent I might never have

finished my novel. But now I had finished it none the less, and it was inconsistent of me to be surprised that it stood ready. But that was how it was. I'm not suggesting I was unaware that, if I were to write a novel, then sooner or later a novel would come out of that, since over long years I had striven for nothing else than that. So as far as being aware is concerned, it's not a question of my being unaware; it's just that I forgot to prepare myself for it. I was too preoccupied with writing the novel to reckon on the consequences. So there it lay before me, more than two hundred and fifty pages, and this pile, this object, was now demanding certain actions on my part. I had no idea how to get a novel published; I was totally unfamiliar with the business, I knew nobody; as yet no prose work of mine, as it is customary to call it, had been published. First of all, I had to get it typed, then I stuffed it into the one and only press-stud file I possessed, which I had acquired by not altogether inno-cent means during a visit to my mother at the head office of the export company where the old lady supplemented her pension by doing shorthand and typewriting for four hours a day. Then, with the file under my arm, I called on a publisher I knew was in the business of publishing nov-els by, as it was phrased, contemporary Hungarian authors, among others. I knocked on a door marked Secretariat and enquired of one of the ladies working there, who emanated that mysterious, so hard to define aura of being in charge, whether I might leave a novel with her. On her giving a positive response, I handed the file over to her and watched her place it among a stack of other files on a table at the back of the room. After that I made my way straight to the open-air swimming pool...

"My God!" exclaimed the old boy.

...straight to the open-air swimming pool, as I hoped—and was not disappointed—that the weather, being sunny but cool and windy, would deter the crowds from flocking to the pools that day, and I swam a twenty lengths with long, leisurely strokes in the cold water."

"My God!" exclaimed the old boy.

Subsequently, a good two months later, I was sitting with a chap who was something or other at the publisher's. I had already paid a visit on him a week previously since, according to the lady in the secretariat, "he will answer any enquires about your novel." As it turned out, he had heard neither about me nor about my novel.

"When did you submit it?," he asked.

"Two months ago."

"Two months is not so long," he assured me. The chap was grey-faced, with a gaunt, harassed, neurotic look about him, and silvered sunglasses. On his desk there were piles of paper, books, an appointment diary, a typewriter, a manuscript bundle covered with scribbled corrections—manifestly a novel. I fled. For preference I would have gone straight to the open-air swimming pool ...

"My God!" exclaimed the old boy.

...but now that it was the height of the heat wave I had no hope of being able to have a swim.

On the next occasion he showed himself to be more talkative. By now he had heard both about me and about my novel, though he personally had still not read it. He offered me a seat. Fascism, (he turned toward me and away from his typewriter, in which I could see he had inserted a sheet of the firm's headed letter paper) was a huge and ghastly subject about which there had already...

"Aha!" the old boy exclaimed aloud as he started to rummage agitatedly in the file until he spotted a sheet of headed letter paper among his papers.

It was an ordinary, neat business letter, with fields for date (27/JUL/1973), correspondent (unfilled), subject (unspecified), reference number (482/73), and no greeting:

"Your manuscript has been assessed by our firm's readers," the old boy started to read,

> On the basis of their unanimous opinion ... We consider that your way of giving artistic expression to the material of your experiences does not come off, while the subject itself is horrific and shocking. The fact that it nevertheless fails to become ... the main protagonist's, to put it mildly, odd reactions... While we find it understandable that the adolescent main protagonist does not immediately grasp what is happening around him (the call-up for forced labour, compulsory wearing of the yellow star, etc.), we think it inexplicable why, on arrival at the concentration camp, he sees... More passages in bad taste follow... It is also incredible that the spectacle of the crematoria evokes in him feelings of ... "a kind of student jape," as he knows he is in an extermination camp, and his being Jewish is sufficient reason for him to be killed. His behaviour, his gauche comments ... annoyed ... the novel's ending, since the behaviour the main protagonist has displayed hitherto ... gives him no ground to dispense moral judgements...

"Aha!" the old boy commented aloud.

The old boy was now sitting in front of the filing cabinet and thinking.

"I ought to read the book again," he was thinking.

"But then again," he continued his thought, "why would I do that? I am not in the mood for reading about concentration camps."

"It was dumb of me," he mused, "to get out my papers," he added (mentally).

Upon which the old boy sat in front of the filing cabinet and resumed reading:

> ...was a huge and ghastly subject ... a sheet of the firm's headed letter paper ... (he turned toward me and away from his typewriter, in which I could see he had inserted a sheet of the firm's headed letter paper) was a huge and ghastly subject about which there had already been much written by many authors. Yet, he added, as it were reassuringly, he was by no means suggesting that the subject had been completely exhausted. He then informed me that it was the publisher's normal practice to have three readers assess a manuscript "before a decision is made about its fate." He was a little coy: they were not in the habit of initiating authors into the publisher's affairs, but he did not exclude the possibility that he might be the third reader for my novel. He fell silent.
>
> "Isn't it a trifle bitter?" he suddenly asked.
>
> "What?"
>
> "Your novel."
>
> "Oh, indeed," I replied.
>
> My response manifestly threw him into confusion.
>
> "Don't take what I said for granted; it's not an opinion, as I haven't even read your novel yet," he explained.

It was now my turn to be confused: the indications were that, to the extent he might feel my novel was bitter, it would probably not be to his taste. This would obviously be a black mark and might set its publication back. Only then did I see that I was sitting opposite a professional humanist, and professional humanists would like to believe that Auschwitz had happened only to those to whom it had happened to happen at that time and place; that nothing had happened to the majority, to mankind—Mankind!—in general. In other words, the publishing man wanted to read into my novel that notwithstanding—indeed, *precisely* notwithstanding—everything that had happened to happen to me too at that time and place, Auschwitz had still not sullied me. Yet it had sullied me. I was sullied in other ways than were those who had transported me there, it's true, but I had been sullied none the less; and in my view this is a basic issue. I have to recognize, however—how could it be otherwise?—that anyone who takes my novel in his hand in good faith and innocently starts to read it will thereby, it is to be feared, also be dragged a little bit into the mire.

I can therefore readily understand why my novel might irritate a professional humanist. But then, professional humanists irritate me because they seek to annihilate me with their cravings: they want to invalidate my experiences. Yet something had happened to those experiences through which, I was taken aback to perceive, they had suddenly turned to my disadvantage, for in the meantime—somehow or other—they had been transformed within me into an irrevocable aesthetic standpoint. The difference of views between me and this man plainly arose from differences in personal convictions between us; but the fact that my novel lay between us, at least symbolically, spoilt everything. I felt that my personal opinions, which my novel exposed utterly, were starting to look inauspicious from the viewpoint of my concerns. On top of which, those concerns, which happened to be embodied in the objective form of the novel, were attached to other factors, less prominent certainly but not negligible for all that—among which were my financial prospects…

"Aha," the old boy brightened up.

…the question of my future, my social status, if I may put it that way.

"Ha-ha-ha," the old boy chuckled.

I suddenly found myself in the fairly strange and—through my lack of foresight—surprising situation of having become a hostage to that two-hundred-and-fifty-page bundle of paper that I myself had produced.

"To be sure," the old boy said aloud.

…I myself had produced.

"To be sure," the old boy said aloud once more.

…I don't believe that I saw distinctly then what even…

The telephone.
This time the old boy had no doubt about it. Nevertheless, he did not get up straight away but merely loosened the wax plug in one ear.

Indeed it was.

"No, of course you're not disturbing me," the old boy declared (by now into the telephone).

The old boy was standing in the southeast corner of the room, next to the child's mini-table, 1st-class special ply of 1st-class sawn hardwood (which in regard to its actual function was more a kind of tiny smoker's table), and holding a telephone conversation.

"…and I immediately thought of you," he heard a muffled female voice through the loosened wax plug. "The book is just right for you; only four hundred and fifty pages, and you would have a six-month deadline. If you really want, you could go two months over that."

In point of fact, the old boy also undertook translation work.

He was a translator from German (German being the foreign language that he still did not understand the best, relatively speaking, the old boy was in the habit of saying).

The money for translating might not be a lot, but at least it was dependable (the old boy was in the habit of saying).

Right now, however, he needed to be writing a book.

On the other hand, it's true, he also needed to earn some money (maybe not a lot, but at least dependable).

Besides which, the old boy did not have so much as a glimmer of an idea, little as that may be, for the book he needed to write.

If he were to accept the translation, he could kill two birds with one stone: he would earn some money (maybe not be a lot, but at least dependable) and also he wouldn't have to write a book. (For the time being).

"Yes, of course," he spoke into the telephone.

"Then I'll send you the book, along with the contract," he heard the muffled female voice through the loosened wax plug.

"Yes, of course. Thank you," he heard his own muffled voice (through the loosened earplug).

"It was stupid of me to accept," he mused afterwards (stuffing the wax plug back into his ear).

"But now I've gone and accepted it," he added (mentally) (as if there were no choice in the matter) (though we always have a choice) (even when there is none) (and we always choose ourselves, as one may read in a French anthology) (which the old boy kept on the bookshelf on the wall above the armchair standing to the north of the tile stove that occupied the southeast corner of the room) (but then who chooses us, one might ask) (justifiably).

> …and—through my lack of foresight … I suddenly found myself in the fairly strange and—through my lack of fore-sight—surprising situation of having become a hostage to the two-hundred-and-fifty-page bundle of paper that I myself had produced.

"To be sure," the old boy said.

> …I don't suppose that I could have seen distinctly then what even today is not entirely clear to me—what sort of trap, what an amazing adventure I had let myself in for. To the best of my recollection, I made do with a fleeting suspi-cion. It seems my character is such that I am only able to free myself from one captivity by instantly throwing myself into another. I had barely finished my novel and I was already scratching my head over what to write next. Nowadays at least I have an idea of what purpose it all served: it was my way of avoiding worries about tomorrow's looming proxim-ity. As long as I succeed in arranging a fresh set of home-work for myself, I can again confuse the passage of my time and the events which occur within it with the will that I have harnessed to the yoke of my goals. In this way infinity

can once again open up before me, even though all I have done is conjure up refractions of light in a real perspective.

But I still did not know what I should write. I ought to have seen that as a suspicious symptom in itself. To tell the truth, in not one of my lessons that might be counted as such did I manage to sense that significance—what one might call the necessity which sweeps every sober consideration before it—in the way that I did then in that novel; but that, I knew, albeit with a certain sorrow, was by now behind me, once and for all.

In the end, the spur was given by a trifling street incident. I have always been a believer in long walks, since they allow me to organize my thoughts as I go along. For these purposes I favour cheerful, meditative surroundings such as the banks of the Danube or the hilltops of Buda, where I can yield in delight to the enchantment of each unexpectedly unfolded panorama that brings me to a halt. Before me a hazy blue vista: the built-up flat terrain of the Pest side; here and there a high-rise building, a dome, a glinting roof, or row of windows; in the mid-ground the gleaming ribbon of the river with the arches of the bridges over it. Behind me the grey-green compactness of a hillside, villas, building blocks, the contentment of tranquil homes, the distant television tower. The day in question, as I recall, was humid and stifling hot, the sun beating down viciously on the back of my head out of a white sky. I was bathed in sweat by the time I had crested a highway with a strip of grass running down the middle. The exasperation I felt from the heat, a dull headache, and my indecisiveness had been wound to exploding point by a thousand little things en route: the abrupt switching-on of a screeching siren just as an ambulance had drawn alongside me; the inexplicable outburst of rage from a dog which unexpectedly hurled itself at the railings as I passed by, its demented, hoarse, rancorous barking, which unremittingly accompanied my steps; a half-wit in a boater, short-sleeved shirt, and, dangling on a leather strap that reached from his neck to his belly, a pocket radio which appeared to be equipped with every gadget that a modern radar-detector vessel might need, the crackling howl from which I didn't seem able to get rid of; my choking and sneezing and my eyes stinging in the dense, black exhaust cloud from a truck that rattled past—in short, the sort of impressions which are inconsequential of themselves but which collectively, and coupled with a degree of mental turmoil, take such a hold on people in big cities as to drive them to unpredictable excesses, individual perversions, anarchistic thoughts, bomb throwing. I had just cut obliquely across the street—quite against the regulations, as a matter of fact. I could hear a bus at my heels, but having got the worst of so many indignities already, I was overcome with an unusual fit of obstinacy: "Screw you! Either pull out or just run over me," I thought to myself. A blast of the horn, a screeching of brakes: I leapt like a grasshopper which is just about to be trampled on. A torrent of curses broke over my head from the door which opened next to the driver's cabin. I screamed back. We filled the impartial air with an unproductive cacophony of foul language. I suspect it did us both good: it gave us a chance to vent our accumulated impersonal venoms.

Once I had been left to myself by the roadside, I came to the cheerily satisfying conclusion that I was a cheat, as I had only dared to take the risk because I had complete trust in the driver.

Of course, he could have run me over—through a

mechanical fault, let's say. But I fully appreciate that bus drivers have excellent road skills. He might also have run me over because the law would have been on his side: I was crossing the road illegally. On the other hand, without being personally acquainted with this particular one, I am well aware that bus drivers are loath to kill people under certain circumstances. Driving over a limp body— that is the privilege of tanks. Murder is something else, and mass murder something different again. In that way I was reminded again of an earlier idea of mine: a plan for a dissertation, on a not too ambitious scale, concerning the possibilities for an aesthetic mediation of violence.

"Now we're talking," the old boy nodded.
"It was stupid of me…"

…on a not too ambitious scale, concerning the possibilities for an aesthetic mediation of violence…

"For Christ's sake!"
"You ought to get out for a bit."
"I shall," the old boy replied, placing back in the filing cabinet the grey file, and on top of that the likewise grey, albeit a darker grey, lump of stone that served as a paperweight, so to say.

At the same time, he took out the cylindrical glass phial from the front of the third drawer down in the filing cabinet and loosened the pliable wax plugs from his ears.

Oglütz.
"That…," the old boy started to say.
"It's not worth it, I'm going out anyway," he reflected. In the series of the various stations of torture the old boy had passed beyond that transitional state when a person attempts to rise above

43

his situation by propounding universal theories. At one time he had decided that Oglütz (and the old boy's starting to call Oglütz Oglütz may have dated from this decision) embodied a qualitatively new form of being, namely, a visual (or auditory) (or audio-visual) being (which differed radically from, for instance, the) (nowadays in any case barely realisable) (art-loving being, in that Oglütz's watching) (or listening) (or watching and listening) (habits both in prose and music were confined exclusively to the products, so to speak, of the light-entertainment genre, quiz and game shows, gala evenings, current-affairs programmes, advertisements, or at most, natural history documentaries); and if it is questionable whether this form of existence is satisfying in every respect, there can be no doubt that it is extremely comfortable, because instead of our having to live a many-sided life, it constantly swarms before our eyes—true, only on a screen, and all we can do is be diverted or angered by it, but not influence it, guide it, intervene in it or accept its consequences—yet in that respect, and in that respect alone (not in what happens on the screen), does it not resemble some of our lives? and as a last resort the old boy would even have been able to imagine a pure visual (or auditory) (or audio-visual) being in the shape of someone who has spent decades in front of the screen, so that even in its last moments, when death arrives to summon it, it does not question that it leaves behind a rich, action-packed and varied life...

"Did you get any work done?"

"Of course."

"Did you make any progress?"

"I pushed on a bit."

"There was something else I meant to tell you."

"What was that?" the old boy paused.

"It's slipped my mind for the moment."

"Next time write it down so that you won't forget."

"Did anyone call?"

"Who would have called?"

"True."

...As a matter of fact—and this was my point of departure—
the composite notion of blood, lust and the demon has
always upset me in the form that one encounters it in certain works of art. The image that these works of art present,
in connection with certain historical periods and events,
of some sort of extraordinary, unbroken witches' Sabbath,
incompatible with human nature in general and dolled up,
so to say, with a festive character, simply does not tally at all
with my own experiences. Murder in some degree, over a
certain time span and beyond a given number, is after all tiring, systematic, and harrowing work, whose daily continuity
is not vouchsafed by the participants' likes or dislikes, bursts
of ardour or onsets of disgust, enthusiasm, or antipathy—in
short, the momentary mood, or even cast of mind, of single
individuals, but by organisation, an assembly-line operation, a self-contained mechanism which does not permit
so much as a moment's time to draw breath. In another
respect, there can be no doubt about it, that is what put paid
to tragic representation. Where would personalities who
are grandiose, exceptional, and extraordinary even in their
awfulness fit in? Richard III wagers that he will be evil; the
mass murderers of a totalitarian regime, by contrast, take an
oath on the common good.

On the other hand, I pondered further, we have impassive, cool, objective reporting of bare facts. Except that this
does not really bring us any closer to the subject either. The
problem with facts, however important they may otherwise
be, is that there are too many of them and they rapidly wear
fantasy down. Instead of our coming to terms with them

and mingling in their world—ultimately an indispensable requirement for an aesthetic mediation—we are ever more alienated as we gawk at them. Cumulative images of murder become just as lethally tedious and discouragingly tiring as the attendant work itself. How can horror be the subject of an aesthetic if there is nothing original in it? In place of exemplary death, the facts can only serve up mountains of corpses.

At that very time I happened to be reading about the deaths of 340 Dutch Jews in the stone quarry at Mauthausen. On the arrival of the contingent, Ernstberger, the camp's second officer, made it clear to political prisoner and block clerk Glas that the order was none of them should remain alive more than six weeks. Glas objected: he was sentenced to a beating of thirty lashes, then replaced by one of the criminals. The next day the Dutch Jews were herded off to the stone pit. Instead of using the 148 steps, hewn into the rock, which led down to the bottom, they were forced to slither their way down over the naked stone rubble of the precipitous rock walls. Down at the bottom boards were loaded on their shoulders, onto the boards, massive boulders, and they had to carry these at the double up to the top— albeit this time by way of the 148 steps of the stairway. At times the boulders would slide off the boards with the first few steps on the stairway, crushing the feet of those pressing behind. An accident meant a beating. Already on the first day a number of the Dutch Jews threw themselves into the stone pit from the edge of the rock face. Later on, groups of nine to twelve were to leap together, holding hands, into the chasm. The civilian employees at the quarry put in a complaint to the SS: the shreds of flesh and brain tissue which were clinging to the rocks, they objected, "afford too gruesome a sight." The rocks were hosed down by a labour squad with powerful water jets: from then onwards prisoner functionaries were posted to stand guard and deal out exemplary reprisals on further offenders. Death wishes, one might say, were here punishable by death. Any of them who did not wish to die with the rest were also killed. It took only three weeks, instead of six, to dispose of them.

I closed the book and put it aside with the feeling that this fact, which I came across at random among 400 pages of further facts (which in themselves are but a modest fraction of a complete list of facts which would take up who knows how many tens of thousands of pages), that these 340 deaths on the rocks, for instance, might rightly find a place among the symbols of the human imagination—but on one condition: only if they had not occurred. Since they did occur, it is hard even to imagine them. Rather than becoming a plaything, the imagination proves to be a heavy and immovable burden, just like those boulders in Mauthausen: people do not want to be crushed under them. That, however, leaves us at risk of falling behind our times: we live our lives without being enriched by the experiences of our era. Yet maybe, I pondered, it is the obsessive monotony of those experiences with which the imagination wrestles ineffectually. At the time I was reading a novel published under the title *The Long Voyage*, and in it came across Sigrid, the beautiful blond fashion model who, I read, was

> …*there only in order to make us forget the body and face of Ilse Koch, that straight, stocky body planted solidly on her straight, sturdy legs, that harsh, sharp, incontestably German face, those fair eyes, like Sigrid's eyes (but neither the photographs nor the newsreels taken at the time,*

and since used and re-used in certain films, enabled any-
one to ascertain whether Ilse Koch's fair eyes were green
like Sigrid's, or blue or light blue or iron gray—more
likely iron gray), Ilse Koch's eyes fixed on the naked torso,
on the bare arms of the deportee she had chosen as her
lover a few hours before, her gaze already cutting out
that white, sickly skin along the dotted lines of the tat-
too which had caught her attention, her gaze already
picturing the handsome effect of those bluish lines, those
flowers or sailing ships, those snakes, that seaweed, that
long female hair, those pinks of the wind, those sea
waves and those sailing vessels, again those sailing ves-
sels deployed like screaming gulls, their handsome effect
on the parchment-like skin—having, by some chemical
process, acquired an ivory tint—of the lampshades cov-
ering every lamp in her living room where, at dusk, she
had smiled at the deportee brought in first as the chosen
instrument of pleasure, a twofold pleasure, first in the
act of pleasure itself and then for the much more dura-
ble pleasure of his parchment-like skin, properly treated,
the colour of ivory, crisscrossed by the bluish lines of the
tattoo which gave the lampshade its inimitable stamp,
there, reclining on a couch, she assembled the officers of
the Waffen-SS about her husband, the Commandant of
the camp, to listen to one of them play some romantic
melody on the piano, or something serious from the piano
repertory, a Beethoven concerto perhaps...

I stopped reading. There it was, blood, lust, and the
demon encapsulated in a single figure, indeed, a single
sentence. Even as I read, it offered definitive forms: I can
fit them with no trouble at all into the ready-made tool
box of my historical imagination. A Lucrezia Borgia of

Buchenwald; a great sinner, worthy of Dostoievsky's pen, settling up with God; a female example of Nietzsche's horde of splendid blond beasts, prowling about in search of spoils and victory, who "go *back* to the innocent conscience of the beast of prey..."

Yes, indeed yes, our thoughts are still held captive by the delusions of dove-conscience intellectuals, a more balanced era's simple-minded visions of the daring grandeur of depravity, although they never pay the required attention to the details. There is some kind of unbridgeable discrepancy here: on the one hand, drunken paeans to the first blush of dawn, a revaluation of all values, and a sublime immorality, and on the other, a trainload of human cargo which has to be disposed of as rapidly—and most likely as smoothly—as possible in gas chambers that never have enough capacity. What business does lacerated, devil-may-care intellectual toil have here? Too solitary, too fussy, too passive, too far-from-average, unherd-like, uncorporate—just too *immoral*: what is needed here is an ethic—a straightforward, easily understandable, readily usable *work ethic*. "'And does Herr General Globocnik not think,' ministerial counsellor Dr. Herbert Lindner poses the highly practical question to SS-Brigadeführer Globocnik, 'that it would be more prudent to burn the corpses instead of burying them? Another generation might take a different view of these things!' To which Globocnik replies, 'Gentlemen, if there is ever a generation after so cowardly, so soft, that it would not understand our work as good and necessary, then, gentlemen, National Socialism will have been for nothing. On the contrary, we should bury bronze tablets, saying that it was we who had the courage to carry out this gigantic task!'"

Yes, I wove my thoughts further, maybe the demon is lurking hereabouts: not in the fact that man kills but that he proclaims its indispensable virtues into a world order of killing. I took down a documentary compendium from my bookshelf and leafed through it for a photograph of Ilse Koch. The face, though it may once have been steeled with a hint of female allure, was certainly here ordinary, sullen, doughy-skinned, piggish—quite incapable of convincing me that I was beholding a figure of a stature who was grand even in her excesses, someone who had transcended good and evil and whose life had run its course in terms of a ceaseless, implacable challenge which spurned all morality. For Ilse Koch had not, in truth, opposed a moral order; quite the contrary, she herself epitomized it—and that is a big difference. Nor did I find in that documentary compendium any evidence that she took a special pleasure in music—Beethoven in particular—or that she had given herself to prisoners. She picked her lovers from the staff-officers—the camp doctor, Dr. Hoven, nicknamed 'Handsome Waldemar,' and *SS-Hauptsturmführer* Florstedt—as befitted her logic. Manifestations of her inventiveness were restricted to customs that were practices of the time. Shrunken heads and decorative articles of tanned human skin ornamented the villas and office desks of many officers in Buchenwald, and Ilse Koch too possessed a number of these. Possibly more than others, but then that would only have been her right—after all, she was the camp commandant's wife, the "*Kommandeuse*." She generally owned more of everything than the wives of subordinates: bigger villa, more opulent household, more privileges. Giving free rein to her fantasy—bolstered by who knows what kinds of reading matter just a few years before, when she was just a stenographer in a tobacco and cigarette factory—took her as far as bathing in Madeira wine and having a riding hall of four-thousand-square-metres constructed for her own use, none of which bears the least stamp of a solitary moral renegade. It is unlikely it ever crossed her mind that if there was no God, then everything was permitted; on the contrary, she needed a god above all else—more specifically a god who would set down in writing everything that he permitted her. Indisputably, the moral world order offered by Buchenwald was one of murder; but it was a world order, and that was good enough for her. She never went beyond the bounds of its logic: where murder is a commonplace, a person becomes a murderer out of zealotry, not revolt. Killing can become just as much a virtue as not killing. The spectacle of so many corpses, and so much torture, no doubt had its reward, now and then, in an exceptional moment of elation about existing, and simultaneous gratitude and pride in service.

But wasn't that its *function*? I continued to brood. Is it not possible that a predetermined state of affairs—the state of affairs of a camp commandant's wife—goes together with, so to say, predetermined feelings and actions that are prescribed in advance? That one and the same state of affairs—give or take a little, perhaps—could have been filled by essentially *anybody* else with similar feelings and actions, or would that person suddenly find himself in some other, likewise ready-made state of affairs, like political prisoner Glas, who was unwilling to conform to his state of affairs in 340 stony deaths, and for that reason ended up in a pun-ishment brigade? One state of affairs created Buchenwald; Buchenwald—among numerous other states of affairs—created a state of affairs for the camp commandant's wife;

that state of affairs created Ilse Koch who—let us put it this way—gave her life for that state of affairs, and thereby she too created Buchenwald, which now is no longer imaginable without her. How many more states of affairs were there just in the totalitarian world of Buchenwald alone? I hardly dare pose the question that lurks, seemingly inescapably, in my mind: whose handiwork, in the end, were those skull paperweights, the lampshades and bookbindings of tanned human skin?...

I laid Ilse Koch's photograph aside. I shall never know what she herself thought about her own life as '*Kommandeuse.*' Since she kept silent about it, she barred herself from interpretability. I shall not become acquainted with her mundane experiences and grey everydays among the bondsmen of murder. I shall be unable to discover whether it was libido or boredom, fulfilled ambition or irksome minor frustrations which preponderated in her emotional balance, unable to unravel her wholly personal neurosis, her compulsive psychosis—in a word, the secret of her personality. I can view her as a humdrum sadist who found a home for herself in Buchenwald and was at last able to give free run to her repellent instincts. Or, if I want, I can also imagine her to have been a more complex being: perhaps she only tried to order her unexpected and incomprehensible state of affairs with even more unexpected and incomprehensible gestures simply to make it cosier, more habitable for herself, and see the proof, day by day, of how it is possible to live the unliveable, how natural the incredible...

None of this is a bit important. Ilse Koch fits a mean that can be extracted between her and her state of affairs, a formula in which she herself is not necessarily present. Yes, her character is only interpretable if we abstract her, look at her separately, so to say, from herself. The greater we imagine her significance, the more we downgrade what surrounded her: the reality of a world equipped for murder, because the essence that we would be attributing to her could only be abstracted by taking it from that reality.

Perhaps it is this, I speculated, this lack of essentiality, which is the tragedy. Except that, from another angle, this dashes to pieces any attempt at interpretation which insists on imposing figures. Because tragic figures live in a world of fate, and tragedy's perspective is infinity; the world of violence of totalitarian systems, by contrast, is a circumscribed and insuperable world, whereas their perspective is merely the historical time for which they happen to endure. How, then, could one hope to interpret an experience that cannot, and does not even wish to, transmute precisely as experience because the essence of their states of affairs— states of affairs that are at once all too abstract and all too concrete—is an inessential and at any time exchangeable figure which, in relation to the state of affairs, has no beginning, no continuation, and no analogy of any kind—and in relation to reason is thus improbable? Perhaps, I mused, one should construct a device, a revolving machine, a trap; the characters who fall into its grasp would scurry about ceaselessly, just like electronic mice, on tracks that look labyrinthine but are actually always unidirectional, pursued by a single automaton. Everything would be wobbling, rattling, everyone trampling on one another, until the machine suddenly explodes; then, after a pause for startled, dazed astonishment, they would all scatter in every direction. That still leaves the secret, figuring out the principle on which the machine operates, which is both too simple and too humiliating for them to listen to, and that is the mechanism for the pursuing automaton utilizes the energy derived from their own rushing about...

But I had better break off here before my pen runs away with me, as they say. Why am I poking around, anyway, in those exercise books which I put aside long ago, that impressive-looking pile of dog-eared notes? Why am I copying out the outline of this never-to-be-completed essay? As a symptom, a characterisation of my state at the time. I had just then started to think these things over, but to publicize the mere fact that I was thinking had never even crossed my mind until then. Obviously, I had written my novel out of some sort of conviction, but not with any aim of convincing anyone about anything. I had written my comedies without any conviction at all, yet was paid money for them. But now a theoretical work: to pore over things, to form an opinion with knowing superiority and self-confidently step forward with that opinion—to do that I also had to possess the added conviction needed to convince others. And so I have to suppose that after finishing my novel some sort of change has taken place within me, or at least the proclivity for such a change was present within me.

Yes, carefully disguising my goal, bit by bit, cunningly and surreptitiously, I set about making definitive preparations for a delusion. I can discern a motive for it, in the end, if I think about it. Plainly, I wanted to forge some necessary consequence from a now irremediable act—the writing of a novel—that had swallowed up irreplaceable years of life, but meanwhile I had quite overlooked the possibility that my very uncertainties might have brought the novel itself into existence through me. I have the feeling I was almost beginning, at least secretly, to consider my destiny as a writer's destiny; even if I did not overtly reckon with it, I was almost beginning to invest my thoughts with some kind of property which sustained an unconditional need for their communication by me and for their reception by others.

Who could know where all this would have led. During that period I may have felt myself ready to regard my future life as an inexhaustible source of ideas for public display; to set down the fruits of my reflections straightaway onto paper; to call on editorial offices and publishing houses with duplicate copies of this triumphant act; and to watch out for signs on people's faces, or even in their lifestyle, of changes wrought by the influence of those ideas. Amidst a deafening fanfare of portentous pronouncements, authoritative views, and unappealable opinions, I too would have blown on my own toy trumpet. Once released on the mirror-smooth surface of paper, my hand would have glided at breakneck speed on the skate-blade of my ballpoint pen. I would have written as if I were seeking to avert a catastrophe—the catastrophe of not writing, obviously. In other words, I would have written for fear that, God forbid, I wouldn't write; I would have written so as to kill every minute of time and to forget who I am: an end-product of determinacies, a maroon of contingencies, a martyr to bioelectronics, a reluctant surprised party to my own character.

The old boy was sitting in front of the filing cabinet and doing nothing.

He was not thinking.

He was not even reading.

"It was stupid of me to get those papers out," he eventually thought to himself.

…In this respect, and in just this one respect, the letter

I received two days after the last visit I had paid to the publisher chap arrived at a fortunate moment.

"Aha!" the old boy exclaimed, picking up the ordinary, neat business letter (with the firm's letterhead and fields for date—27/JUL/1973, correspondent—unfilled, subject—unspecified, reference number—482/73, no greeting) that he had already once picked up and scanned cursorily, but which we too, bending over his shoulder, as it were, may now read in full:

> Your manuscript has been assessed by our firm's readers. On the basis of their unanimous opinion we are unable to undertake publication of your novel.
>
> We consider that your way of giving artistic expression to the material of your experiences does not come off, whereas the subject itself is horrific and shocking. The fact that it nevertheless fails to become a shattering experience for the reader hinges primarily to the main protagonist's, to put it mildly, odd reactions. While we find it understandable that the adolescent main protagonist does not immediately grasp what is happening around him (the call-up for forced labour, compulsory wearing of the yellow star, etc.), we think it inexplicable why, on arrival at the concentration camp, he sees the bald-shaven prisoners as "suspect." More passages in bad taste follow: "Their faces did not exactly inspire confidence either: jug ears, prominent noses, sunken, beady eyes with a crafty gleam. Quite like Jews in every respect."
>
> It is also incredible that the spectacle of the crematoria arouses in him feelings of "a sense of a certain joke, a kind of student jape," as he knows he is in an extermination camp and his being a Jew is sufficient reason for

him to be killed. His behaviour, his gauche comments repel and offend the reader, who can only be annoyed on reading the novel's ending, since the behaviour the main protagonist has displayed hitherto, his lack of compassion, gives him no ground to dispense moral judgements, call others to account (e.g. the reproaches he makes to the Jewish family living in the same building). We must also say something about the style. For the most part your sentences are clumsy, couched in a tortuous form, and sadly there are all too many phrases like "…on the whole…," "naturally enough," and "besides which…"

We are therefore returning the manuscript to you.

Regards.

…The letter at least granted me a morning charged with emotions; I recall it even today with a certain sense of nostalgia. If I was surprised, it was no more than the way a person is surprised to bang his head on a protrusion in the wall he had long ago noticed was too low, and he would undoubtedly bang his head on it sooner or later. At least I would encounter a certain amount of passion and perspicacity, albeit only the perspicacity of anger and injustice—at any rate sentiments and senses worthy of the subject!

Then, as I recall, I was exceedingly amused, for instance, by the gesture, that self-assured, firm dismissive wave of the hand, with which the purpose of an endeavour I had undertaken, for motives which were problematic, and far from clear even to myself, was being expropriated, so to speak, only to be immediately destroyed; because the letter presumed, if I was following it correctly, that my sole reason for writing the novel was for it to end up in a publisher's office where decisions are taken about these sorts of commodities. The comic aspect of this absurd loss of proportions was enough to set even my diaphragm aquiver. For I could not deny it, in the end I had taken my novel to the publisher. But that had been intended purely as a temporary resting place in a whole chain of events, which since then had already been overhauled by time and further events occurring within that time—such as this letter that had been delivered to me. "And so?" I ask myself, "Does that somehow obliterate what I have accomplished?" On the contrary, it has set a seal on it, because—and this fundamental factor had not escaped my watchful eye—that dismissive motion is, at one and the same time, also the first real, one might say, authentic proof that my novel actually exists. Yes, I may have told myself, the unstructured time which now lies behind me has gained its definite outlines precisely in the light of this letter; until now I have never seen my situation so simply—as one that, in point of fact, can be summarized in a single clear sentence: I had written a novel, and it had been rejected, presumably through ignorance and lack of courage, as well as evident spite and stupidity.

It may be—indeed, as I now know, it is quite certain—that I made a mistake when I left…

"Was that the doorbell?"
The old boy loosened the pliable wax plug in one ear.
"I already rang once before!" the old boy's mother complained indignantly as she traversed the east-west axis of the hallway with brisk (and somehow martial) steps which belied her advanced age and, after swerving to avoid the hammered-glass door (which was now, as always, open, in view of the airlessness of the hallway), popped up in front of the filing cabinet (with due regard, naturally, to the previously described surroundings) (which it would therefore be superfluous to describe again here) (so let us merely make it clear

that when we say the old boy's mother popped up in front of the filing cabinet, this should be taken to mean that although she was, indeed, facing the filing cabinet, she actually popped up in front of the table—or, to be more precise, *the* table, the only real table in the flat) and (exchanging her street glasses for her reading glasses in a lightning-quick movement) was reading.

The old boy didn't like it when other people started dipping into his manuscripts.

"I don't like it," he said, "when other people start dipping into my manuscripts."

"Why?" the old boy's mother asked. "Are they secret?"

"Well as a matter of fact…" the old boy scratched his head.

"I can see you are busy again with your private affairs," his mother declared.

"Yes," the old boy conceded.

"Did they reject your novel?" his mother enquired, no doubt more out of stringency than malice.

"I haven't even written it yet," the old boy muttered.

"But I see here that you wrote a novel and they rejected it!"

"That was another novel. Wouldn't you be more comfortable in an armchair?" the old boy ventured.

"And what's this?" The old boy's mother picked up from the edge of the grey file the likewise grey (albeit a darker grey) lump of stone that served as a paperweight, so to speak.

"It's a lump of stone," said the old boy.

"Even I can see that; I'm not senile yet, thank God. But what do you need it for?"

"I don't exactly need it, if it comes to that," the old boy muttered.

"Well then, what's it for?"

"I don't know," said the old boy, "It just is."

The old boy's mother was seated in the armchair situated to the north of the tile stove, behind the 1st-class special ply contraption of

1st-class sawn hardwood (child's mini-table) (which in regard to its actual function was more a kind of tiny smoker's table):

"There are some things," she said, "I could never understand with you."

"Would you like a coffee?" the old boy ventured.

"Yes, I would. For instance," his mother swept a glance around the room, from the bookcase-filing-cabinet centaur (if such a catachresis may be entertained) standing in the southwest corner, which had been created from a bookcase assembled from the base of a former linen drawer, across to the (relatively) modern sofa occupying the northeast corner, "you are capable of giving up every demand you have just to avoid having to work."

"But I do work," the old boy remonstrated (though not with an entirely clear conscience) (since he should have sat down long ago to writing a book now his had become his occupation) (or rather, to be more precise, things had so transpired that that had become his occupation) (seeing as he had no other occupation).

"That's not what I mean," said his mother, "But why don't you find yourself a proper job? You could still easily go on with the writing."

"But I'm no good at anything; you forgot to get me trained in some well-paid profession."

"You always were the comedian," his mother said.

"There was a time when that's what I lived off," the old boy reminded her.

"Why don't you still write comedy pieces now instead?" his mother asked

"Because I don't want people to laugh. It makes me envious."

"That rubber seal needs to be changed," the old boy thought to himself as he was percolating the coffee.

"Aren't you going to ask why I came?" his mother asked.

Indeed, the old boy's mother was not in the habit of calling at his place; rather it was he who was in the habit of visiting her (more specifically, once a week, between seven o'clock and half past nine on Sunday evenings) (the weekly intervals being complemented by daily telephone conversations during which the old boy was able to keep abreast of his mother's state of health as well as the) (important or not so important) (but in any case significant) (events which had happened to her) (as well as to her personal belongings or household objects) (which current events gained significance precisely because it was to her) (or her personal belongings or household objects) (such as water heater, wall hangings, kitchen tap, etc.) (that they happened).

"Well, anyway," the old boy's mother continued, "I finally got a serious response to my advertisement."

The old boy's mother had, in fact—as may be gathered from this announcement—placed an advertisement in the newspaper.

Through the advertisement she had dangled the prospect of a room (a big room, however, in the green belt and with all mod cons) in exchange for an undertaking to look after her.

For the old boy's mother had to make ends meet (or rather, to be more accurate about it, she was unable to make ends meet) from her pension.

To supplement her pension, the elderly lady did shorthand and typewriting for four hours a day at the head office of an export company.

But now, with the passage of time, not only the old boy but also his mother was getting old (albeit more slowly, to a lesser degree, and more reluctantly, than the old boy) (although she had been forced to acknowledge its symptoms nevertheless) (such as the backache she got while typing) (on account of which she had given it up—the typewriting, that is to say).

Nevertheless, the hard fact of the matter—namely that the old boy's mother needed to find an extra two thousand forints a month (to supplement her pension)—remained unchanged.

And the old boy did not have two thousand forints a month extra (indeed, there were times when he was that much short).

Which was why, through an advertisement, and in exchange for an undertaking to look after her, she had dangled the prospect of a room (a big room, however, in the green belt with all mod cons) (which is to say the apartment where the old boy was registered, by right of being an immediate family member, as a permanent resident, though he never lived there, not even temporarily) (and from which he would now have to transfer to the apartment where he had been temporarily registered, by right of marriage, even though he had been permanently resident there for decades) (thereby yielding place to a caregiver who, by right of being the caregiver, would be permanently registered but, on the basis of the agreement, would not reside even temporarily in the old boy's mother's apartment) (patiently waiting in his or her present place of residence, which presumably did not meet his or her requirements, for the ultimately inevitable fact that the old lady, for all the hopes she would carry on to the extreme limit of human life...) (in short, on being left vacant as a consequence of this ultimately inevitable event, the apartment would pass on to him or her) (which for both of them, caregiver and cared-for alike) (after careful weighing up of the expected costs and the number of years that might come into consideration) (and bearing in mind the end-result, might yet prove, on human reckonings, to be a rational and mutually profitable business transaction).

"So you will have to arrange to be deregistered," his mother said.

"Fine," said the old boy.

"As soon as possible; not the way you generally arrange your affairs," his mother added.

"Fine," said the old boy.

"You surely can't be expecting me to do without in my old age."

"God forbid," the old boy said.

"It's not my fault," his mother carried on, "You ought to have ordered your life differently."

"No question about it," the old boy acknowledged.

"I wanted to leave the apartment to you."

"Don't worry about it, Mama," said the old boy. "Was the coffee all right?"

"Your coffee is always too strong for me."

"Well, that's my day gone already," the old boy thought to himself after his mother had left.

"I ought to change that rubber seal on the coffee percolator," he continued his train of thought.

"But where the hell are the seals?" he then puzzled (not finding them in their usual place) (that is, the place he imagined to be the usual place for the seals).

Thus it was that the old boy came to be standing in front of the filing cabinet and holding in his hands a flat, square-shaped piece of wood.

This chunk of wood, about 3 × 3 in. in size, rough on one side and on the other covered with a layer from multiple daubings of white paint (which had yellowed over time), had come to light from one of the old boy's two cardboard boxes in which he kept a miscellany of objects (both necessary and unnecessary), among which, or so he imagined, he might chance upon the rubber seals needed for the coffee percolator.

Instead of them, however, he came across the remaining original piece of one of the two ungainly, disparately-sized wardrobes which had once stood there, long defying the steadfast antipathy of the old boy's wife (and noteworthy for the wax seal that was visible on it) (though the inscription on the wax seal had been rendered almost illegible by the yellowish-white layer of paint from repeated decoration).

"So much for their saying care would be taken to spare the wax seal," he fumed (mentally).

For which reason, at this point in our story—as the old boy was standing in front of the filing cabinet and holding in his hands a piece of wood (noteworthy for the wax seal which was visible on it)—out of the group of letters arranged in a circle only the fragments SE, ST, and, in front of that, a dot-shaped nubble, as well as—further on, with a bit of imagination—TY could be made out from the original inscription (SEALED BY • STATE SECURITY AUTHORITY), the purpose of which inscription, as its sense suggests, was to keep the doors of the hallway wardrobe under seal (not, however, ruling out the possibility that the plywood sheet which formed the back of the hallway wardrobe might be prised open) (which, incidentally, is what happened) (because, whatever the subsequent, by then patently obvious evidence, what else would have explained the fact that when, one summery evening, the old boy's wife) (at a time when she was not yet the old boy's wife) (and the old boy was not yet old) (indeed, they had not yet met each other) (anyway, on that summery evening the old boy's wife-to-be had tried fruitlessly to open the door to her own apartment with her own key and thus, since she saw a light on inside, was reduced to ringing the doorbell) (what else would have explained the fact that the unknown, short, stocky, somewhat piggish-looking woman who opened the door to the ringing was wearing a dressing gown, shortened and altered to fit her own figure, which belonged to her, the old boy's wife-to-be—a fact which did not escape the old boy's wife-to-be even in the brief minute while she introduced herself to the unknown woman, who then, after an indignant exclamation) ("What's this?! You're still alive?!") (immediately slammed the door in her face) (in consequence of which, there being nothing else she could do, the old boy's wife) (who at that time was not yet the old boy's wife) (and as far as meeting him goes first met him only somewhat later) (faced with the unappealing prospect of spending a summer's night on the street) (and an even more uncertain tomorrow) (before long returned to the place whence she had set off for her apartment) (that is to say, the State Security Authority) (where she was obliged to ask the officer who had released her earlier, accompanied by the official paper, to provide her with accommodation for the night—if nowhere else, then in her old cell, where the old plank-bed and blanket were certainly still waiting) (a request that it turned out to be impossible to fulfil now that she had been released, accompanied by the official paper) (so that the officer had only been able to offer the leather couch in the corner of his room, while he himself went off duty for the whole night, accompanied by the official papers, and in the morning) (worn out, dehydrated, gaunt, and nicotine-stained from his whole night off-duty) (like one of the countless cigarette butts which had overflowed his ashtray in the course of off-duty nights) (set off with her to the housing office of the competent local authority in order to discover how they could have allocated an apartment that the State Security Authority had sealed off) (a matter that in itself was to be treated as a *state secret*) (consequently there were grounds for suspecting that behind not just the procedural irregularity, but also the very leaking of the address there no doubt lay a criminal act of bribery) (though in the end no light was ever thrown on that) (and only after a year of litigation was the apartment itself restored to the rightful ownership of the old boy's wife) (whom we may now refer to as the old boy's wife without reservation) (even if the old boy was not at all old at the time) (and his wife was not yet his wife) (but by then they at least knew each other) (indeed, they were sharing a household) (insofar as their joint household could be called a household, that is).

This, then, was the reason why even today, at this late point in our story, the old boy was fuming that—contrary to all the advance warnings he had given—care had not been taken to spare the wax seal (which the piece of wood in his hands preserved).

"After all, a memento is a memento," he continued to fume.

"And this piece of wood is the only thing that's left of it all," he carried on fuming.

"It was rather embarrassing," his face suddenly brightened (as if touched by some memory) (a memory which was evidently bound to the humorous) (yet rather embarrassing) (though the two are by no means mutually exclusive) (indeed their simultaneous presence is the spice of all genuinely funny episodes) (assuming one is capable of valuing the funny side of a rather embarrassing episode) (as when it turns out, for instance, that one actually has no objective proof of any kind for an event that one has held to be so decisive in one's life, and thus it exists purely in one's unverifiable memories) (so in short, the brightening of the old boy's face was evidently bound up with this episode which was simultaneously humorous and rather embarrassing).

For in point of fact, years later—and now years (many years) before the present moment—the idea had struck the old boy that his wife should in any event (and here the word should be understood in the strict sense, which is to say an event that may be pure supposition, but it does no harm to be prepared for it) (if it holds logical water to be prepared for something we haven't the faintest idea about), so in any event should apply to get her name cleared (as is only right and proper) (if we do not wish that the mere fact of our having been punished is to be held against us as a crime that we have committed).

They were visited by a detective.

He introduced himself.

He sat down (not in one of the armchairs placed to the north and west of the tile stove) (since those armchairs did not yet exist at that time) (but presumably in the rush-bottomed chair, the rush strands of which were severed at the wooden frame, which, along with two backless seats with similarly severed rush bottoms and a stripped-wood colonial table, two sofas) (one of them padded out with books at its centre, where the spring had gone) (and two blankets, as carpeting on the floor, constituted the apartment's furnishings at that time).

He asked to see the release paper.

This was when the abovementioned simultaneously humorous and rather embarrassing episode ensued, which was characterized by the helpless glances of the old boy (who was not yet old at that time) and his wife, a hasty pulling out of drawers, an agitated rummaging under bed linen until it was discovered that the sole authentic proof of release (and above all the committal to detention which had preceded it)—namely, the release paper—had, every sign indicated, been mislaid in one subtenancy or another (or perhaps along one of the routes from one subtenancy to another).

No problem, said the detective (a burly but kindly chap in a raincoat), he would look into the matter and track down the files.

A few days later he (the burly but kindly chap in the raincoat) duly turned up: he had found the files.

He sat down.

He was troubled.

"Madam," he said, "it looks like you were innocent."

"Of course," the (as yet not old) old boy's wife agreed.

"There isn't even a record of any interrogation," the detective continued, "only of regular extensions of the period on remand. They never laid charges against you."

"No," the (as yet not old) old boy's wife agreed.

"Not even, if I may put it this way … well, not even false charges."

"No."

"To say nothing of any sentencing."

"No."

"But that's where we have a problem, madam," fretted the detective (a burly but kindly chap in a raincoat). "Because … how can I put it?... We can only clear someone's name if a trial, sentencing or at least a preferment of charges has taken place. But in your case ... please try to understand what I am saying ... in your files there is no trace of any of that, you aren't suffering any consequences, you don't carry a criminal record ... in other words, there is simply nothing to be cleared."

"And what about that one year?" the (as yet not old) old boy's wife asked.

The detective spread his arms and lowered his gaze: it was evident that he took the issue as a matter of conscience.

He sat for a short while longer on the rush-bottomed chair with the rush strands severed at the wooden frame.

"We had trouble consoling him," the old boy cheered up (mentally) at the memory.

...so simply—as one that, in point of fact, can be summarized in a single clear sentence: I had written a novel, and it had been rejected, presumably through ignorance and lack of courage, as well as evident spite and stupidity.

It may be—indeed, as I now know, it is quite certain—that I made a mistake when I left the assessment at that. I should have pushed on further to a final conclusion which brooked no going back. If I had grasped and embraced the role inherent in the situation, I would never have got to where I am today. For a writer there is no more ornate crown than the blindness that his age displays toward him; and it carries yet one more gem if that blindness is coupled with being silenced. But then, although I had written a novel, and meanwhile would have been unable to entertain the idea of my having any other occupation, in reality I never thought of it as my occupation. Even though that novel was a greater necessity for me than anything else, I never succeeded in persuading myself that *I* was necessary. It seems I am incapable of going beyond the bounds of my nature, and my nature is temperate, like the climatic zone I inhabit. My feelings recoiled from the precarious glory of failure. All the more because that place was already occupied by something else, a feeling which proved a good deal more determined than any enthusiasm of a purely abstract kind: the guilt I felt when I also showed the letter to my wife.

"Perhaps that bit ought not ..." the old boy winced.

...This shift was so unexpected that even I was surprised. I couldn't decide where it came from. Did I have a guilty conscience because my novel had been rejected, or because I had written a novel in the first place? In other words, to be more precise, would I still have had a guilty conscience if the publisher had happened to inform me that my novel had been accepted? I don't know, and now I never shall find out; but I was taken aback that subversive processes were under way in some deep recess of my brain, as if battle positions were being drawn up behind which ramifying arguments were being concentrated in order to swing onto the attack at a designated point in time. But my wife, with wordless self-control ... I know that little, silent smile of hers ... No whisper of an assuaging reproach that ... I felt the importance of every novel and publisher in the world, as well as my own self-justification, fading away. I was deeply offended; dinner was consumed sullenly.

It could be that already then I suspected what I had lost. Now, with the benefit of a wider perspective, I can measure more precisely not just how right I was, but my comfort too. As I say, it all depended on whether I would grasp or repudiate the role inherent in the state of affairs. To repudiate it would have been at once to repudiate destiny by opening the door to time and ceaseless wonderment. While my destiny was with me—which is to say, while I was writing my novel—I had no experience of these kinds of concerns. Anyone living under the spell of destiny is liberated from time. Time still marches on, of course, but its duration is irrelevant: its purpose is solely to accomplish that destiny. One is not left with much chance: all that's needed is to know how to be ruined and to wait. And I knew. Once I had received the letter, it should just have become even easier for me: my time was up—if you like, there was nothing further for me to do. Destiny—since that's its nature—would have robbed me of any future which was definitive and thus could be contemplated. It would have bogged me down in the moment, dipped me in failure as in a cauldron of pitch: whether I would be cooked in it or petrified hardly matters. I was not circumspect enough, however. All that happened was that an idea was shattered; that idea—myself as a product of my creative imagination, if I may put it that way—no longer exists, that's all there is to it.

Yet that is not the way I had planned it. Oh, the plan was simplicity itself; I saw nothing irrational in it. If I have now regained my freedom, I want to pass judgement on my novel myself, to decide its true quality, good or bad—that was what I thought. The exercise seemed practicable enough. The next morning, when my wife had set off for work, I took out the press-stud file and set it down in front of me then, brimming with cheerfully disposed and somewhat cere-monial expectations, I opened the cover to read my novel. After about an hour and a half of resolute struggling, I had to admit that I had taken on an impossible task. To start with, I was pleased at each well-fashioned sentence, each apt epithet. But all too soon I caught my attention wandering, and my having to leaf back incessantly because my eyes were just grinding through pages that were divested of sense, devalued into emptiness. I reproved myself, tried to concentrate, but perversely I relaxed, made myself a coffee, took a break. Nothing helped; I was overcome by irresistible bouts of yawning. I had to admit that I was bored: at every line I knew what would follow on the next; I could anticipate every twist, knew in advance every paragraph, every sentence, indeed every word, while the train of thought offered nothing new for me, nothing surprising. One can't read a novel that way.

Since then I have racked my brains a lot over this phenomenon. I fell into a trap, there is no question. In order to make an objective judgement, I would have needed to see with a stranger's eyes, so I tried reading it with someone else's eyes—without even a thought that this other, imagined scrutiny was just my own. I tried cheating, but it didn't work. It seems I am unable to trick myself into soberly examining, with adequate detachment, the shadow that I cast on the reaches beyond me. Which means I shall never know whether my novel is good or bad. Fine, I can live with that. In truth, I came to realize, it doesn't even matter to me. The novel is the way it is, and it's that way because it could be no other way—that much, at least, I had understood while I was reading: it is the way it is, and in that capacity is a finished and ready article that I am unable, and probably it is not even possible, to alter any more.

The big stumbling block, though, is why is that article no longer *mine*? To put it another way, if I am incapable of looking at it with a stranger's eyes, why am I unable to read *my own* novel with *my own* eyes? Within the novel, for instance, a train is moving toward Auschwitz. Crouched in one of the wagons is the subject of the story, a boy of fourteen and a half. He gets up and in the crush squeezes a place for himself by a window slit. Just at this moment the summer sun climbs red and balefully into the periphery of his field of view. While I was reading, I recalled precisely how much difficulty and racking of brains both this as well as the passage which follows it had caused me. Somehow the events of that sweltering summer morning just would not unfold under my hand onto the paper. It was abnormally gloomy here inside, in the room, as I toiled over the text; from the table I looked out on a foggy December morning. There must have been some traffic disturbance on the roads, as the trams were constantly rattling by beneath my window. Then all at once, with astonishing suddenness, the sentences fell into place and enabled the train to arrive and the subject of the story—the fourteen-and-a-half-year-old boy—finally to leap out of the stifling gloom of the cattle truck onto the blazing hot ramp at Auschwitz. As I was reading this passage, these memories came alive within me, and at the same time I was able to verify that the sentences fitted together in the organic sequence I had envisaged. That was all very well, but why had not what existed *before* those sentences, the raw event itself, that once-real morning in Auschwitz, come to life for me? How could it be that those sentences for me contained merely *imaginary* events, an imaginary cattle truck, an imaginary Auschwitz, and an imaginary fourteen-and-a-half-year-old boy, even though I myself had at one time been that fourteen-and-a-half-year-old boy?

So what had happened here? What is it what the

publisher's readers had referred to as "your way of giving artistic expression to the material of your experiences"? Yes, what had happened to "the material of my experiences," where had it vanished to off the paper and from within me? It had existed at one time, indeed it had happened to me twice over: the first time, improbably, in reality, the second time, with much more reality, later on, when I recollected it. Between those two time points it had lain in hibernation. It did not so much as cross my mind at that certain moment when I knew I had to write a novel. I had laboured with various types of novels, only to scrap them one after the other; not one of them had turned out to be a possible novel for me. Then all at once it had popped up within me, from some obscure place, like a brain wave. I suddenly found myself in possession of a body of material which at last offered a definite reality to my agitated, but until then constantly disintegrating, vision and which, solid, pliant, and shapeless, started forthwith to ferment and swell within me like a yeasty dough. A strange ecstasy took hold of me; I lived a double life: my present—albeit halfheartedly, reluctantly, and my concentration-camp past—with the acute reality of the present. My readiness to immerse myself in it almost scared me; even now I could not give a reason for the voluptuous feeling which attended it. I don't know if memory itself is attended by that delight, irrespective of its subject, since I would not say that a concentration camp is exactly a bowl of fun; yet the fact is that during this period the slightest impression was enough to hurtle me back into my past. Auschwitz was present here, inside me, sitting in my stomach like an undigested dumpling, its spices belching up at the most unexpected moments. It was sufficient for me to glimpse a desolate locality, a barren industrial area, a sun-baked street, the concrete pilings of a newly started building, to breathe in the raw smell of pitch and timber, for ever-newer details, input, and moods to well up with something like the force of actuality. For a time, I awoke each morning on the barrack forecourt at Auschwitz. It took a while for me to realize that this perception was evoked by a constant olfactory stimulus. A few days before, I had bought a new leather strap for my wristwatch. At night I put the watch on a low shelf directly by the bedside. Most likely that characteristic smell, reminiscent of chlorine and a distant stench of corpses, had lingered on the strap from the tanning and other processes. Later on I even used the strap as a sort of sal volatile: when my memories flagged, lay low inertly in the crannies of my brain, I used it to entice them from their hiding places—smelling them to pieces, so to speak. I shrank from no means and no effort in waging my battle with time, wresting from it my due right. I crammed myself with my own life. I was rich, weighty, mature, I stood at the threshold of some sort of transformation. I felt like a wild pear tree which wanted to bear apricots.

However, the more vivid my memories, the more abjectly they were caught on paper. While I was remembering, I was unable to write the novel; but as soon as I started to write the novel, I stopped remembering. It's not that my memories suddenly vanished, they simply changed. They transformed into the contents of some kind of lucky-dip tub into which I would reach, at the intervals that I deemed necessary, for a negotiable bank note. I would pick and choose among them: this one I needed, that one, not. By now the facts of my life, the so-called "material of my experiences," only distracted, confined, and hampered me in my work of bringing into life the novel for which that life had originally provided the conditions for life and had

74

nourished from first to last. My work—writing the novel—actually consisted of nothing else than a systematic atrophying of my experiences in the interest of an artificial—or if you prefer, artistic—formula that, on paper, and only on paper, I could judge as an equivalent of my experiences. But in order for me to write I had to look on my novel like every novel in general—as a formation, a work of art composed of abstract symbols. Without my noticing, I had taken a run-up and made a big leap, and with a single bound I had suddenly switched from the personal into the objective and the general, only then to look around me in astonishment. Yet there was no reason to be surprised; as I know now, I had already completed that leap as soon as I made the start on writing my novel. It was no use my trying to plod back to the intention, no use that my original ambition had been directed solely at this one novel and did not so much as squint at anything beyond it, did not extend beyond the pages of this manuscript: by its very nature, a novel is only a novel if it transmits something—and I too wanted to transmit something, otherwise I would not have written a novel. To transmit, in my own way, according to my own lights; to transmit the material that was possible for me, my own material, myself—for, overloaded and weighted down as I was by its burden, I was by now longing like a bloated udder simply for the relief of being milked, being interpreted ... however, there was one thing that, perhaps naturally enough, I did not think of: we are never capable of interpreting for ourselves. *I* was taken to Auschwitz not by the train in the novel but by a real one.

That's right, I had failed to reckon on just this one small matter. Meanwhile, while I withdrew into my private, indeed most private, life (my "private affairs," as my mother used to say); while I was shutting myself off from everything and everyone else in order to be able to grub around peacefully in my own world of thoughts; while I did my utmost to insure that nobody else would be able to interrupt me in my solitary passion, I had started innocently, and with a heartfelt diligence, to write—for others. Because, as I now see clearly, to write a novel means to write for others—among others, for those who reject one.

Yet I could not reconcile myself to that notion. If that had been my goal, I had committed a huge blunder; I ought to have written something else, a more saleable commodity—a comedy, for example. But that had not been the goal, as I keep on asserting; it had only became that in the course of implementation, without my knowledge or consent, so to say, indeed without my even noticing at all. What did I care about those others for whom I may have written my novel but who did not so much as enter my head while I was writing it?! What kind of chance was it—and even as a chance, what kind of unforeseeable, inconsequential, idiotic chance—if our common business, my novel and their entertainment, happened to chime?! And however absurd, in practice—and purely in practice—that is precisely what I had been striving for; so now I have to declare that I did not achieve my goal—the goal that was never my goal. But in that case, what had been the original sense of my goal, my undertaking? I swear I don't remember; it could be that I never thought about it; and now I shall never know, because that sense had become mislaid somewhere—who knows where—in the course of the undertaking.

I get up from the table. Almost involuntarily, like an automatic reflex, my feet start moving around the apartment. I cross the room, through the wide-open door into the hallway, strike my right shoulder on the open-door to the bathroom, and reach the end of the apartment. Here I turn about, skirt the open door to the bathroom, strike my right shoulder on the hallway wardrobe, cross the room and reach the window, turn again. A distance of about 23 feet. Relatively commodious for a cage. Up and down, up and down; turn at the front door, turn at the window. This had once been a regular habit of that fellow, the novel writer, the chap with whom once, just a few months ago, I had been identical. Those were the times when his most notable ideas sprang to mind. *I* didn't have anything to think about. Yet slowly something nevertheless was taking shape inside me. If I distinguish it from the mild dizziness caused by walking and from other contingent impressions, I discover a definable feeling. I suppose my state of affairs was materialising in it. It would be hard for me to put it into words—and that's exactly the point: it settles itself in spaces that lie outside of words. It cannot be couched in an assertion, nor in a bald negation either. I cannot say that I don't exist, as that is not true. The only word with which I could express my state, not to speak of my activity, does not exist. I might approximate it by saying something like 'I amn't." Yes, that's the right verb, one that would convey my existence and at the same time denote the negative quality of that existence—if, as I say, there were such a verb. But there isn't. I could say, a bit ruefully, that I have lost my verb.

I have had enough of my walk; I sit down. I snuggle down, nestle deep into the armchair, adopting a curled-up posture as if in some Brobdingnagian womb. Maybe I am hoping I shall never have to emerge from here, never go out into the world. Why should I? And then I am also a bit afraid of the stranger who will nevertheless struggle to his feet out of here in the end. In a certain sense, it will be someone other than the person to whom I have grown accustomed until now. Nor can it be any other way, for he has completed his work, fulfilled his purpose: he had flopped utterly. He had transmuted my person into an object, diluted my stubborn secret into a generality, distilled my inexpressible truth into symbols—transplanting them into a novel I am unable to read; he is alien to me, in just the same way that he alienated from me that raw material—that incomparably important chunk of my own life from which he himself had originated. I shall miss it, and perhaps ... why deny it, perhaps I shall also miss the person who brought it all off. Yes, as I sit in the armchair a startling feeling suddenly passes through me: a bleak and chilly feeling of some irrevocable occurrence, a bit like the feeling when the last guest has gone after a big party. I have been left alone. *Someone* has departed, leaving an almost physical void in my body, and this very instant, with a malicious smirk on his face, is waving a final farewell from the far corner of the room. I stare impotently after him, I do not have the strength to detain him. Nor do I even wish to: I harbour a feeling of mild but firm resentment toward him—let him go to hell, he tricked me...

"That he did," said the old boy, "that he did, the numbskull!"
"Did you get any work done?"
"Of course."
New development in the bistro: the Old Biddy (the chief administrator, to give her her official title) had made a surprise assault on the bar counter and snatched away the order chits from the spike (checking up on the old boy's wife) (as to whether, in point of fact, she had passed through the charges for all the meals on her tray) (as if, let us say, she was not always in the habit of doing so) (in

proof of which postulate the risible) (and equally futile demonstration could end up showing nothing else than that the old boy's wife had on this occasion) (as ever) (passed them through).

"If I really wanted to steal," the old boy's wife said indignantly, "she could scrabble after my orders as much as she wants. I could carry off half the kitchen under her nose without her noticing it."

"I'm sure," the old boy agreed. "So why don't you do that?" he enquired almost absent-mindedly as he was spooning his soup.

"I don't know. Because I'm stupid," his wife said.

In any case (his wife said), that was evidently the sole result of today's announcement (to the effect that from now onwards she too wanted to work in the evenings); and if one can perhaps also discern in it some explanation for the peculiar (yet for all that by no means logical) logic, as an outcome of her colleague, Mrs. Boda (whose first name was Ilona) recently taking, instead of greeting her, to looking the other way, for the harder (in fact, totally impossible)-to-understand reason why the Old Biddy (the chief administrator, to give her her official title) shared that grievance (unless, perhaps, the key to the mystery was to be sought in the bedlam of those wild hours when the Old Biddy would find urgent barrel-tapping and other tasks for the bartender to attend to in the cellar) (right at the height of the evening rush) (at which times, with obvious magnanimity and shrinking from no pains, she herself, in her white coat, would stand in at the bar) (like the captain of a ship at a hurricane-lashed helm) (at which times the colleague who was called Mrs. Boda was obliged, like her other colleagues, to pass through the orders for draught beverages directly to her) (if indeed she passed them through) (the only way of establishing which fact beyond a shadow of doubt would be to snatch the order chits right away from the spike) (the right to do which, however, was the sole prerogative of the Old Biddy—the chief administrator, to give her her official title).

"So that's why there's a deficit," the old boy commented (shrewdly). "They're pilfering."

"That may well be," his wife said.

"I'm going out for a little walk," the old boy declared later on.

The old boy was sitting in front of the filing cabinet.

It was morning.

(Again.)

He was translating.

He was translating from German (German being the foreign language that he still did not understand the best, relatively speaking, as the old boy was in the habit of saying).

antwortete nicht—the old boy read in the book (from which he was translating).

did not answer—the old boy tapped onto the sheet of paper that had been inserted in his typewriter (onto which he was translating).

"For Chrissakes...!" the old boy stretched out his hand, half-rising from his seat, toward the filing cabinet.

"...That hairy ape of a tree-dwelling Neanderthal and all its misbegotten breed," he (the old boy) said, stuffing the carefully formed plugs into his ears.

"I ought to change these ear plugs," the old boy mused.

"They're old," he (the old boy) continued his musing.

"Dried out," he mused further.

"They're pressing too tight in my ear." He fiddled with the plug in one ear.

"But then if it doesn't press tight enough I hear everything," he chafed.

"There, that's it, perhaps..." the old boy stopped his fiddling.

The old boy was sitting in front of the filing cabinet and listening out for whether he could hear anything.

He couldn't. (Relatively speaking.)

"Wonderful." His face beamed.

"Come on now, this is no way to make a living." His face darkened.

The money for translations might not be a lot, but at least it was dependable (the old boy was in the habit of saying).

By doing the translation he could kill two birds with one stone: he would earn some money (maybe not a lot, but at least dependable) and also he wouldn't have to write a book. (For the time being.)

Besides which, the old boy did not have so much as a glimmer of an idea, little as that may be, for the book he needed to write.

...antwortete nicht.

...did not reply.

"That's it,' said the old boy approvingly.

He had not looked at his papers for days now. Nor did he have any wish to look at them.

He had tucked them away at the very bottom of the filing cabinet in order to avoid any chance of catching sight of them.

Sein Blick hing an den Daumen, wie festgesogen.

"Festgesogen," the old boysaid, scratching his head.

Der Blutfleck unter dem Daumnagel hatte sich jetzt deutlich vorwärts bewegt. Er war von Nagelbett abgelöst, ein schmaler Streifen sauberes neues Nagelhorn hatte sich hinterdreingeschoben.

"What on earth is 'Nagelhorn'?" The old boy would have reached for the dictionary (if he had known for which dictionary he should reach, as he had two of them) (or to be more accurate, three of them) (namely, the *Concise Dictionary*, at hand to the right of the typewriter, for which he scarcely ever had to reach) (but then it usually did not contain the word he happened to be after) (as well as the *Unabridged Dictionary*, in which he usually managed to find it in the end) (and thus pure considerations of economy would have advocated his reaching straight away for the latter) (except that this required him to perform an awkward twist of the upper part of his body, given that, alongside the book that was to be translated, the piles of blank as well as already typed paper, the typewriter, and the *Concise Dictionary*, there being no space left for the two volumes of this dictionary colossus, together weighing at least ten lbs., on the table) (to be more precise, *the* table, the only real table in the flat) (they found a place on the 1st-class special ply contraption of 1st-class sawn hardwood from the southeast corner of the room, which, its actual function being thus modified during periods of translating work, stood beside the old boy's chair) (for which reason, when searching for a word, the old boy usually consulted both dictionaries) (if not all three volumes) (as he did on this occasion, when, having tried to find "Nagelhorn" first of all, hopefully, in the *Concise Dictionary*, then, more exasperatedly, in the first, A–L volume of the *Unabridged Dictionary*, he finally, and thoroughly incensed, picked up the second, M–Z volume—incidentally, without coming across it in any of them, after all, let it be noted) (which may have infuriated the old boy but did not succeed in embittering him, since the meaning of the word was perfectly obvious) (if he thought a little bit about it) (but until it was left as a last resort that did not enter into the old boy's head) (most especially when he was in the middle of translating).

Sein Blick hing…—the old boy read.

His gaze—the old boy tapped—*was fixed on his thumb as if*

"Festgesogen," the old boy said, scratching his head.

it were incapable of moving away.

"Hardly inspired," the old boy said, scratching his head.

"And anyway not even accurate." He kept on scratching.

"His gaze held fast to his thumb as if transfixed to it," the old boy deliberated. "That might be more accurate."

"The image is mixed up," he deliberated further. "On the other hand, it's more expressive—" he hesitated—"but then it's rather forced," he decided.

"Anyway, I've written it down now."

"I ought to erase it and type over."

"Not worth it."

Der Blutfleck…

The blotch of extravasated blood had visibly moved further forwards. By now it had separated from the nail bed and in its stead a fresh, narrow crescent of clean nail was emerging from the root.

"That'll do," the old boy deliberated.

"A little more long-winded than the original," he deliberated further.

"But that's the compactness of the German language for you," he continued his deliberation.

"And anyway they pay by the word," the old boy concluded his deliberations.

Die Natur. Etwas von mir, repariert sich. Langsames Wachstum, unbeirrbar. Löst sich ab, wie die Zeit, wie Nichtmehrwissen. Was vorher wichtig war—schon wider vergessen. Ebenso: leere Zukunft—das auch. Zukunft: was niemand sich vorstellen kann (wie mit dem Wetter) und was doch kommt.

"At least this bit is easy," the old boy cheered up. "I don't need a dictionary here," he determined (almost gloatingly).

Nature—he tapped out briskly—

Something of me, a part of me, is restored again. A slow, unwavering advance. It works itself loose like time, like forgetting,

no-longer-knowing. What was important previously—already
forgotten. Just like the empty future—that too. The future: the
thing that nobody can envisage (as with the weather) but which
comes to pass all the same.

"Not a bad text at that," the old boy enthused.

"The novel too."

"A professional job," he thought enviously.

"That's the way to write novels," he carried on enviously, "with secondhand material, objective formulation, a well-honed technique, three steps back, no autobiography, nothing personal, the author might as well not exist."

"An issue of general interest, a guaranteed moneymaker." His envy intensified.

Just like the empty future
that nobody can envisage
comes to pass all the same.

The old boy's gaze held fast to text as if transfixed.

"Hang on a second!" The old boy leapt up from his place without any apparent (that is to say, external) reason (unless it was something inapparent) (that is to say, internal) (that impelled him to do this) (such as something which suddenly sprung to his mind), and he snatched off the bookshelf on the wall above the sofa occupying the northeast corner of the room a not overly bulky volume in a green half-cloth binding (the very same as the one that in recent days) (as we have already had occasion to recount in the proper place) (the old boy had been leafing through frequently, and to great advantage, in which the old boy evidenced especially appreciative relish for certain lines on page 259 of the volume) (which we have likewise not passed up the opportunity of quoting in the proper place, so that repetition would be superfluous) (all the more so because at this point in our story the old boy) (leafing like greased lightning) (was evidently searching for something else in it, evidently on some other page) (though which one evidently he himself did not know).

"*And even today writing comes hard to me because I have already had to write a lot of letters so that my hand is tired,*" the old boy read.

"*The future stands firm, dear Mr. Kappus, but we move in infinite space.*"

"That's it," the old boy enthused.

"*As people were long mistaken about the motion of the sun, so they are even yet mistaken about the motion of that which is to come,*" the old boy read on further (or, to be more exact, further back) (since the latter line stood before the previous one).

"*it must only just then have entered into them, for they swear,*" the old boy read on further (or, to be more exact, further back)

"*in their bewildered fright*"

"*It is necessary.*"

"Here we are," the old boy said.

> "*It is necessary—and toward this our development will move gradually—that nothing strange should befall us, but only that which has long belonged to us. We have already had to rethink so many of our concepts of motion, we will also gradually learn to realize that that which we call fate goes forth from within people, not from without into them. Only because so many have not absorbed their fates and transmuted them within themselves while they were living in them have they not recognized what has gone forth out of them; it was so strange to them that, in their bewildered fright, they thought it must only just then have entered into them, for they swear never before to have found anything like it in themselves. As people were long mistaken about the motion of the sun, so they are even yet*

*mistaken about the motion of that which is to come. The future
stands firm, dear Mr.. Kappus, but we move in infinite space."*

The old boy stood firm, book in hand. After some time he moved
after all (if not in infinite space, at least to put the book back in its
place) (on the bookshelf on the wall above the sofa occupying the
northeast corner of the room).

"I have the awful feeling," he reflected in the meantime, "that
I'm going to get my papers out again."

"That would be really stupid," he reflected further, now standing
in front of the open door of the filing cabinet in the upper drawer
of which (from which he had earlier removed the typewriter to
work on the translation) could be seen several files—among them,
one entitled "*Ideas, sketches, fragments*"—and two cardboard boxes
which held a miscellany of objects (both necessary and unnecessary),
behind which was a grey box file on which, like a sort of paperweight, was a likewise grey—albeit a darker grey—lump of stone
(not visible).

"There's still time to have second thoughts about this," he continued his reflection (as if he could really have second thoughts) (that
is to say, like someone who still has a choice) (but all the while knows
full well that he doesn't) (even though we always have a choice) (and
we always choose ourselves—in the words of the French anthology
to which we have already referred) (which the old boy kept on the
wall bookshelf above the armchair standing to the north of the tile
stove occupying the southeast corner of the room) (for this is what
our freedom amounts to) (although one might ask in what manner
such a choice could be said to be freedom) (if in point of fact we can
make no other choice than ourselves).

On account of which the old boy was soon rooting again
among his papers and, what is more, on this occasion sitting on the
sofa occupying the northwest corner of the room—perhaps partly

to emphasize the transience of this activity, the deferment for a merely fleeting interval of his more important work, but partly also because he was unable to take his proper place in front of the filing cabinet (or to be more precise, at the table) (or to be even more precise, *the* table, the only real table in the flat), it (which is to say *the* table) being covered with the accoutrements of his more important work (the book to be translated, the piles of blank as well as already typed paper, the typewriter, and the *Concise Dictionary*):

...This turn of events ... sitting in the ar ... irrevocable ... I was left alone ... robbed ... I therefore face what stands before me without my past, without a destiny, without heartwarming delusions, robbed of everything I had. I see a billowing, grey, impenetrable bank of cloud and sense that I must force my way through it, though I have no idea in which direction I should strike out. No matter, in that case I won't move and it can come to meet me, force its way over me, and then pass on, leaving me behind. This is time, what they call the future. Sometimes I scrutinize it anxiously, at other times I wait trustingly for it as for sunshine in foggy weather. Yet I am well aware that it's all an illusion, and even now I am only deceiving myself, I am fleeing in just the same way that I once launched myself into infinity on the rocket of my goals: it's not the future which is waiting for me, only the next instant, because there is no future, it is nothing other than the ever-continuing, eternal present. Not a single minute can be omitted, or at most only in stories. The prognosis for my future—that's an attribute of my present. Yes, the time passing is me; and that—me—is exactly what I am least sure about.

If only I could say I made a mistake! Only I don't know if it is not I myself who is the mistake. Now and again, my feet set me off on my accustomed meditative journeys—and not just in my apartment. I take an interest in nature—what else can I do? I contemplate autumn's destruction with gloomy satisfaction, breathe in deeply the sparkling aroma of decay. The other day, I was just making my way down the hillside when I saw two old men. They were standing at the foot of a stone wall, faces turned toward the languorous warmth: they were sunbathing. They were snuggled up so closely to the no doubt lukewarm stone that at first I took the two grizzled heads jutting out from the grey wall to be stones too, unusually lifelike reliefs. It was only on coming closer that I saw they were alive. One had a long, ovine face with eyes like molten aspic and a red tip to his sheep's nose; the other face was somewhat rounder, but a curving mouth, drawn into a half-smile under his square, grey moustache, lent him too a bit of the air of a faun. I don't know why they fascinated me so much. I fancied that I discerned some indefinable yet completely identical expression on the two faces, an involuntary expression which was not tied to the moment, nor even to their words—they might have been talking about anything at all—but sprang from somewhere deeper, from some conduit of their existence, bubbling far below. When I passed by them they fell silent, as if they had some kind of secret—no, on the contrary, as if they had something to say, and it was precisely that which they were keeping secret, but it had already moved to their faces like the ruins of some defeat that they were reluctantly obliged to display to their fellow human beings, in part as a warning, in part out of weakness, somewhat maliciously and at all events improperly, yet beseeching a little attention.—Well indeed, if death is an absurdity, how can life have any meaning? If death is meaningful, then what is the purpose of life? Where did I lose my redeeming impersonality? Why had I written a novel and, above all, yes, above all, why had I invested all my trust in it? If I could only work that out…

I pay regular visits to my mother. I sometimes hear her tell stories about a young woman who had a little boy. On these occasions I usually listen politely, discreetly hiding my boredom. Yet nowadays I find myself paying attention to her, even watching out for what she says; I listen as if I were increasingly expecting her to suddenly unmask a secret. For in the end, the child in question once upon a time had been me. As the saying goes, the child is father to the man. Maybe I shall manage to catch out this sneaky brat, so passively ready to adapt to every circumstance, expose a word, a deed, anything which would hint at his future activity—writing a book. Yes, that's how far it has gone with me, how low I am stooping, if you will; I would make do with anything—my astrological chart at birth, the critical DNA sequences of my genes, the mystery lurking in my blood grouping, anything, I tell you, to which I might give a nod of assent, or at least reconcile myself that this was the way it had to be, this was what I was born to be, as if I were not perfectly aware that we are not born to be anything but, if we manage to live long enough, we cannot avoid becoming something in the end.

I take a book down from the shelf. The volume exudes a musty smell—the sole trace that a finished work and a completed life can leave behind in the air: the smell of books. "*It was on the 28th of August, 1749, at the stroke of twelve noon, that I came into the world in Frankfurt on the Main,*" I read. "*The constellation was auspicious: the Sun was in Virgo and at its culmination for the day. Jupiter and Venus looked amicably*

upon it and Mercury was not hostile. Saturn and Mars main-
tained indifference. Only the Moon…" Yes, that is the way to
be born, as a man of the moment - of a moment when who
knows how many others were likewise born on this globe.
Only the rest of them did not leave a book smell behind and
so they don't count. The cosmic constellation arranged the
lucky moment for a single birth. That is how a genius, a great
creative figure, sets foot on earth—like a mythical hero. An
unfilled place longs yearningly for him, his advent so long
overdue that the ground is practically moaning out for it.
Now all that has to be done is to await the most favourable
constellation, which will assist him just as much through
the difficulties of birth as through the uncertain beginnings,
the years of hesitancy, until that shining moment when he
enters the realm of recognition. Looking back from the pin-
nacle of his career, there will no longer be room in his life for
any contingency, since his very life has assumed the form of
necessity. His every deed and every thought is important as
a carrier of the motives of Providence, his every declaration
pregnant with the symbolic marks of an exemplary development. "A poet," he pronounces later, "should have an origin,
he must know where he springs from."

I suppose he is right: that truly is the most important
thing.

Well then, at the time I came into the world the Sun
was standing in the greatest economic crisis the world had
ever known; from the Empire State Building to the Turul-
hawk statues on the former Franz Josef Bridge, people were
diving headlong from every prominence on the face of the
earth into water, chasm, onto paving stone—wherever they
could; a party leader by the name of Adolf Hitler looked
exceedingly inimically upon me from amidst the pages of

his book *Mein Kampf*, the first of Hungary's Jewish laws, the so-called *Numerus Clausus*, stood at its culmination before its place was taken by the remainder. Every earthly sign (I have no idea about the heavenly ones) attested to the superfluousness—indeed, the irrationality—of my birth. On top of which, I arrived as a nuisance for my parents: they were on the point of divorcing. I am the material product of the lovemaking of a couple who did not even love one another, perhaps the fruit of one night's indulgence. Hey presto, suddenly there I was, through Nature's bounty, before any of us had had a chance to think it through properly. I was a healthy child, my milk teeth broke through, I started to burble, my intellect burgeoned; I began to grow into my rapidly proliferating materiality. I was the little son in common of a daddy and mummy who no longer had anything in common with one another; a pupil at a private institution into whose custody they entrusted me while they proceeded with their divorce case; a student for the school, a tiny citizen for the state. "I believe in one God, I believe in one homeland, I believe in the resurrection of Hungary," I prayed at the beginning of the school day. "Rump Hungary is no land, reunified Hungary the heavenly land," I read from the caption on a wall map outlined with bloody colour. "*Navigare necesse est, vivere non est necesse*,"[1] I parroted in Latin class. "*Shoma Yisroel, adonai elohenu, adonai ehod*," I learned in religious instruction. I was fenced in on all sides, my consciousness taken into possession: they brought me up. With a loving word here and stern warnings there, they gradually ripened me for slaughter. I never protested, I endeavoured to do what was

---

[1] Plutarch: "It is indispensable to sail, it is not indispensable to live."

asked of me; I languished with torpid goodwill into my well-bred neurosis. I was a modestly diligent if not always impeccably proficient accomplice to the unspoken conspiracy against my life.

But enough. It is not worth searching for my origins: I have none. I landed in a process that, thanks to my inborn sense of mistiming, I took for a beginning. Like everybody else, I have one or two anecdotes and a few personal memories, but what do they signify? At the right temperature, they dissolve without trace into the communal mass, unite with the inexhaustible material churned out in general hospitals and disposed of in mass graves or, in more fortunate cases, in mass production. In hunting for my origins I see nothing but a packed and never-ending queue, my century on the march. Blinded, now staggering, now breaking into a trot, I too stumbled along in the soporific warmth of the herd. But at some point—who knows why—I stepped out of the line: I did not go on further. I sat down beside the ditch and my glance suddenly fell on the stretch of the way I had put behind me. Could this be what literary men call "talent"? Hard to believe it. I had given no sign of any talent in a single act or word or other manifestation—unless it was in managing to stay alive. I did not dream myself into invented stories; I did not even know what to do with the things that had happened to me. Not once had my ears resounded to the biddings of vocation; the totality of my experiences could convince me only of my superfluousness, never of my importance. I was not endowed with the redeeming word; I was not interested in perfection or beauty, not even knowing what those are. I regard notions of glory as the masturbation fantasies of senile old men, immortality as simply risible. I didn't start on my novel in order to have a verifiable occupation. If I were an artist, I would entertain or teach; my work would be of interest to me, not the reason why I had produced it.

Having got that off my chest, I can discern only one possible explanation for my stubborn passion: maybe I had started writing in order to gain my revenge on the world. To gain revenge and regain from it what it had robbed me of. Perhaps my adrenal glands, which I managed to preserve intact even from Auschwitz, are hypersecretors of adrenaline. Why not? After all, representation contains an innate power in which the aggressive instinct can subside for a moment and produce an equipoise, a temporary respite. Maybe that is what I wanted. Yes, to grab hold, if only in my imagination and by artistic means, of the reality that all too really holds me in its power; to subjectivize my perpetual objectivity, to become the name-giver instead of the named. My novel was no more than a response to the world—evidently the sole way of responding as best I can. To whom else would I have been able to address this response if, as we all know, God is dead? To nothingness, to my unknown fellow human beings, to the world. It did not turn out as a prayer but as a novel.

But let us not exaggerate: that is already literature. In the end it may yet transpire that I do, indeed, have some talent for writing, which would make me truly sorry since I did not start writing because I have talent; on the contrary, when I decided I would write a novel, evidently I also decided, by the bye, that I would become talented. I needed it; there was a job to be done. I had to aim to write a good book, not out of vanity but in the nature of the beast, so to say. I could not do otherwise: by some mysterious means, the necessity to give a response condensed within me into freedom, like a gas subjected to very high pressure. What was I supposed to do with this unformed and intolerable feeling? Freedom sometimes becomes purely a question of expertise. Even a bad novel can be freedom—it is just that the freedom is unable to reveal itself, precisely because the book prevents it. At least now I know it is no use my tugging at the halter of the writer's fate; its diabolical irony will keep me in harness. Whatever my original motive, I can only justify the character of this personal business if I also offer others something at the same time. All of a sudden, I found that the aggrieved hand which had been poised to strike was holding a novel, and now with a deep bow I was trying to place it as a festive gift under everybody's Christmas tree.

So that is how it happened. Lacking in certainty to the degree that I was, I somehow had to convince myself that I existed after all. I responded to the preserved murder attempts—both real and symbolic—now with neurasthenic apathy, now with aggression. However, I recognized fairly quickly (I am a rational creature, after all) that I was more vulnerable than the outside world. In the end, out of weakness and impotence, as well as out of a certain desperation and a sort of vague hope, I began to write. That's it, it's done: here is the answer to my question. And here I could also bring these remarks to a conclusion.

It is just that something inside me bristles against finishing. My remarks are at an end, but I carry on. I am running out of letters, and once again I shall be left standing at a loss for what to do with the seconds, hours, and days as they succeed one another. As you see, what should I pick again but exactly the same therapy, and again with exactly the same result as when I set to work on writing the novel. It's not as if I were seeking a solution—I am well aware that there is no solution for life—but I find that a mere listing of symptoms is not enough. A medical report does nothing to help me: as the patient, it's the pain that interests me. Not the diagnosis, but the process, the active disease. 'The details. Above all, the details,' as Ivan Karamazov, the instigator, says as he interrogates Smerdyakov, the killer. Just don't finish, since nothing ever comes to an end: I have to continue, carry on writing, yes, confidentially and with sickening talkative-ness, like two killers chatting. Yet what I have to say is as bleakly impersonal as a murder reduced to the soulless, to just another statistic which is just as super…

"Teleph…?"

"…fluous as writing a book…"

"For the love of…!"

"I was beginning to think you weren't home!" the reproachful voice of the old boy's mother drilled like a laser beam into mashed potatoes (a simile which cannot be said to be either graphically or logically apposite) (since what would a laser beam be doing drill-ing into mashed potatoes) (but in the heat of the moment that was what sprang into the old boy's mind, and we have no right to concoct a better one in its place) (let alone a worse one) (insofar as we wish to remain faithful chroniclers of his story) (and what else might be our goal) into the plug of fusible wax.

"Where else would I be?" the old boy snapped.

"Who can tell with you?!… Guess what has happened. The little glass shelf on which I keep my cacti has broken. The pots fell as well, and one of them is smashed, the earth is all over the floor. What should I do now?"

"Sweep it up," the old boy suggested.

"I'm not exactly clueless!" the next laser beam pierced the old boy's skull. "What I want to know is, where I am going to find a new glass shelf!"

"From a glazier," hazarded the old boy.

"A glazier! It's not as if the neighbourhood is crawling with glaziers!... You wouldn't happen to know of a good one, would you?"

"No," the old boy said.

"Of course not. When did you ever know anything?!"

"If you put it like that..." said the old boy indignantly.

"Aren't you even going to ask me how the accident happened?"

"Yes, of course," answered the old boy hurriedly.

"I wanted to dust the picture which hangs above it, but I got up on the chair so awkwardly that my housecoat snagged on the corner of the glass shelf. I think that ripped too ... I didn't even look yet..."

"You shouldn't be climbing on chairs at your age," counselled the old boy.

"You don't say!" a hand grenade exploded in the old boy's auricle. "I don't need others to tell me what I can and can't do at my age ... but since I've had my backache and can't go into the office, I can only afford a cleaning lady once a week. It's no use my asking you to come over and dust for me!"

"You could be right about that," acknowledged the old boy.

"There you are! Did you arrange to be taken off the register yet?"

"No," quailed the old boy.

"You've had so much else to do the whole week, I suppose?"

"There's been enough," the old boy bristled. "I'm working to a deadline; I have a translation to do."

"You're slipping lower and lower. You started off writing plays, then a novel, and now it's translating."

"And I'll be a typist before too long," the old boy remarked in annoyance.

"What you choose to make of yourself is your own affair, but you're running out of time to decide. You're not getting any younger either."

"That's nice of you," the old boy muttered.

"But you have to get yourself off the register double-quick so I can get the maintenance contract signed."

"All right," said the old boy.

"I know your 'all rights' by now. You always put things off till the last possible moment. That's exactly what got you where you are today," was the parting shot from the old boy's mother.

"That's today shot to pieces," thought the old boy.

"I ought to pack it in," he pondered further.

"The whole thing, I mean," he continued to ponder.

...I packed it all in...

"There you are." The old boy cheered up (a little).

...I decided to go for a walk...

"Very sensible," the old boy approved.

...which was how I came to be on Margaret Island...

"Big mistake," thought the old boy peevishly.

...Who should I see at a table in one of the open-air restaurants, under the rustle of the languidly drooping leafy boughs, but Árpád Sas, with another fellow...

"Worse luck," muttered the old boy.

...two exotically plumed male parrots under the

horse-chestnut trees, two coloured shirts, two distinguished, elegant heads. I was about to give them a wide berth…

"Uh-huh," the old boy perked up.

…but it was too late: Árpád Sas had already spotted me…

"He would, wouldn't he," gloated the old boy.

…invited me over to the table with an insistent wave of the hand:

"Aha! the prince of life! Come on and join us, my arch-duke, the very man we were waiting for!"

"Why don't you go to hell?" I enquired in my friendliest fashion as I clambered over the flower tubs which enclosed the terrace. He did not reply to this but glanced in discreet triumph at the other fellow, who on my arrival had got to his feet by the table and was smiling broadly. He was tall and spindly, his hair flecked with grey, his spectacles round-framed, and at the sight of his yellowing big teeth between dark moustache and minute beard, long-deposited scraps of memory began sluggishly stirring within me, like grounds at the bottom of a cup of coffee.

"So? So?" he enquired with a slightly foreign accent.

"Hellfire and damnation!" as Jules Verne's English sea captains say.

"Mijnheer Van de Gruyn, the Dutch cocoa planta-tioner!" I exclaimed.

"You idiot!" guffawed Gerendás Van de Gruyn, who was called Grün when he came into the world. "You haven't changed a bit in seventeen years!"

That was debatable but this wasn't the right moment to point it out. Instead I emitted a medley of sounds, ranging from joyous amazement to chummy familiarity. I immediately slipped into my role as into a long-discarded and unexpectedly rediscovered pair of slippers. I played myself, or to be more precise the good old pal whose image Gerendás had sustained. God knows who he was; God knows what possessed me to try to live up to an old photograph that, even in those days, was probably not faithful: perhaps it was that permanent fear we have that our image will in the end fade away forever.

Fortunately, I was not uninformed. Sas, whom I would run into every once in a while—in the street, at the cinema, at a bridge evening, but most often at the open-air pool—always kept me up to date: Grün's success on Dutch television; the humorous articles Grün had published, one after the other; the West German production of a film with a screenplay by Grün; Sas, on the way home from a trip to London, stopping over at Grün's villa in one of Amsterdam's suburbs, where he cultivated tulips in his garden. Sas's face at these moments displayed both pleasure and malice—the pleasure was meant for Grün, the malice for himself and, of course, no less for me. Sas had devised for himself a metaphysical view of life from which the metaphysics had been extracted, since he believed in consumer goods rather than in God. In his scheme of things, he himself lived in the Vale of Tears, albeit out of his own free choice, having condemned himself to it, probably through defeatism, but it comforted him greatly that, even if the chance had been blown for him, there nevertheless existed a more glittering other world in which he could have an occasional fling—whenever possible at the state's expense.

"Of course, you never travel," he was in the habit of reproaching me.

"Not I," I would reply, sticking to the truth.

"Why not?" he would enquire.

"It's not possible to get away from myself," was one of the things I would say at this juncture.

Or else: "One can learn about the world even in a prison cell; indeed, one learns most of all there."

Or yet again: "I don't like it when the world from which we have been excluded is constantly portrayed as if it were ours."

"You're talking double Dutch. And I say Dutch because that's the only language I understand not one word of."

But I can see that he is nettled, and that's enough for me. Sas, by the way, is a columnist for an illustrated weekly magazine, covering the major European languages as translator and discreetly, slyly, sensitively, and knowledgeably promoting the national line as feuilletonist and leader-writer for the inner pages. He had mentioned that Grün would be coming and wanted to see me as one of the relics of his former life. They had just happened to be discussing whether to call me by telephone.

To their great delight, I ordered a black coffee. I then rattled off a string of questions that I supposed one asks on such occasions. Mijnheer Van de Gruyn affected modesty: he had achieved a thing or two, to be sure, but he was not yet what one would call a big name. Sas let out a sharp guffaw at that. Family? Yes, a wife and a five-year-old daughter.

"Didn't I tell you?" asked Sas.

"Of course you did. Just checking," I tried to extricate myself. I was dismayed to sense that I was starting to run out of questions. Fortunately, Grün took over: he had heard from Sas that I was having success writing comedies, so he would like to see one of them.

"None of them is running at the moment," I apologized.

Well in that case he would read them, he said.

"It's not worth it," I tried to talk him out of it. "They're no good." Grün let out a protracted guffaw at this and slapped me heartily on the back with his bony hand. He plainly thought I was joking.

"He hasn't changed a bit," he gurgled happily.

"There isn't another person between the Yellow Sea and the Elbe who has sorted out his life as well as he has," Sas bragged on my behalf with a paternalistic smile.

"The same for yourself," I offered no less charitably.

"My dear chap," Gerendás said, turning serious, "there's a big demand for good comedies back in the West."

Only then did I realize that I was sitting right in the middle of a farcical misunderstanding.

"I don't write comedies any more," I said.

"What then?" enquired Mijnheer Peeperkorn. The devil knows what got into me, but it seems the wish to open up got the better of me. Maybe I did it out of perplexity; after all, I was sitting among colleagues. But it could be that what fleetingly crossed my mind was Goethe's good counsel that in order to preserve our poetic works from starvation, it behooves us to converse with well-intentioned connoisseurs about their origins, thereby bestowing historical value on them.

"I've written a novel," I announced modestly.

"Aha!" enthused Van de Gruyn.

"And you didn't say a word about it to me?!" Sas gave me an offended look.

"When is it due to be published?" Gerendás put his finger on the practical aspect of the matter.

"That's just it: it won't be published," I said.

"What do you mean?"

"The publisher rejected it."

"Oh, I see, *zo*," Mijnheer Gruyn remarked with a slight foreign inflection, his face meanwhile assuming a noncommittal expression.

Sas, by contrast, seemed to liven up: which publishing house had rejected it, and why, he wanted to know. I replied that I didn't know the reason, but I had received a preposterous letter from which it was clear that they had either not understood, or not wanted to understand, the novel because, I explained, it seems they ascribed any marks that it hit as down to pure luck, its audacity to clumsiness, its consequentiality to deviation.

"What is the novel about?" Sas asked.

Whatever the reason, there was no denying my embarrassment.

"What any novel is about," I said cautiously, "it's about life."

Sas was not one to be thrown off so easily:

"Let's drop for once the high-flown philosophical expositions you normally give us," he warned. "What I wanted to know is what, specifically, your specific novel is about. Is it set in the present day?"

"No," I said.

"Then when?"

"Oh ... during the war."

"Where?"

"In Auschwitz," I whispered.

Slight silence.

"Of course," Van de Gruyn remarked with grudging commiseration, as if he were speaking to a half-cured leper, "you were in Auschwitz."

"Yes," I said.

"Have you taken leave of your senses?" Sas had recovered from his initial astonishment. "A novel about Auschwitz! In this day and age! Who on earth is going to read that?"

"Nobody," I said, "because it's not going to be published."

"Surely you didn't suppose," he asked, "that they were going to fling their arms round your neck?"

"Why not? It's a good novel," I said.

"Good? What do mean by good?"

"What else?" I stuttered. "Good means good. A self-explanatory whatsit ... that is to say ... good *an und für sich*, if I may put it that way."

"*An und für sich*," Sas glanced at Gerendás, as if he were interpreting my words, then slowly turned his elegant, narrow, sharp-beaked head back toward me, his half-closed eyes and the yellowish sideburns framing his ruddy face reminding me of a sad and sleepy, widely experienced fox. "*An und für sich*," he repeated calmly. "But good *for whom*? What is anybody going to make of it?! Where are you living? Which planet do you think you are on?" he asked with growing distress. "Not a soul in the trade has ever heard of you, and you go and send in a novel, and to top it all one on a subject like that..."

"That Sas," Mijnheer Gruyn attempted to smooth things over, "he hasn't changed a bit. He was always such a ... what's the phrase ... smart-arse, *azes ponem*," he gleefully hit upon the words he had been seeking. "Do you remember when..."

But by now there was no holding Sas back; me neither, for that matter.

"In other words, I'm not entitled to write a good novel!" I heard the angry yelps of my own voice.

"That's it exactly." Sas was jubilant. "I couldn't have put

it better myself. No one is looking for a good novel from you, old chap. What evidence do you have that you can write a good novel? Even if we suppose that it really is good, where's the guarantee for it? No expert, my dear chap, is simply going to believe the evidence of his own eyes! Your name is unknown," he kept count of the points on his fingers, "You have no one behind you, the subject isn't topical, no one is going to deal you the ace of trumps. What do you expect?"

"But what if," I asked, "someone were to submit a brilliant novel?..."

"You're obviously talking about yourself," Sas pronounced.

"Let's suppose," I conceded.

"First of all, there's no such thing as a brilliant novel," Sas patiently enlightened me. "Secondly, even if there is, so much the worse. This is a small country; what it needs is not geniuses but honest, hardworking citizens who..."

"Yes, all right," Van de Gruyn took pity. "But now that he's gone and finished a novel ... Possibly," he ventured cautiously, "you could give it to me ... I'm staying for another two weeks, I might be able to zip through..."

"That's it!" I said, "You translate it and publish it in Holland!"

Mijnheer Gruyn seemed thunderstruck:

"I don't have anything to do with translating," he said, "I sometimes have need of help myself with the language." In his agitation, his Hungarian was deteriorating. "That's a complete ... what's the word ... absurdity!... Anyway," he rallied gradually, "even back in the West it's no pushover for novels. There you have top pros, you see, and they know what's what. To make money with a subject like that, well you need to have something! With Anne Frank the Dutch have already got that particular subject, what d'you call it..."

"Sewn up," I hastened to his assistance.

"Not quite that, but if you can't bring anything new ... add something ... and even back in the West a publisher's rejection slip is hardly a letter of recommendation for a novel ... unless of course," a pensive expression appeared hesitantly on his face, "the author is the sort of personality who just happens..."

"I'm not going to get myself banged up just for the sake of becoming a five-day wonder where you live!" I said.

"Some hope!" Sas gave speedy reassurance. "These days it's not so easy to get slammed into prison for a book."

"Whereas in the good old days!" Mijnheer Gruyn chortled in relief. "Do you remember when..."

"Nowadays they deal with those matters in a much more civilized manner here," Sas carried on unruffled.

"Yes, so I hear everyone say," the Mijnheer butted in. "Things are going very well here. The shop window displays are attractive, the people well-dressed ... but where are all those classy Budapest women there were in the old days?"

"They're still here," said Sas, "it's just you who doesn't notice them. You're not the dashing hussar of seventeen years ago either, old fellow..."

In short, the matter of my novel was finally drawing to a close, like a boring record. Sas offered a few more pieces of advice: I should write short stories and try to get a foothold in the literary magazines; that way they would grow used to me and might even start mentioning my name. Then I should join some literary group or other; it didn't matter which one, he said, because those things were always unpredictable.

"A literary group," he patiently instructed me, "is like a wave: now cresting, then crashing down, but it always carries the alluvium with it, whether on the swell or in the trough, and in the end washes it up in some harbour." He referred to the examples of several authors who had come safely to port that way, some quickly, others more slowly. Some had dropped out of the queue in the meantime, becoming suicides or giving up or ending up in a psychiatric home; but others had made it and, after thirty or forty years, it transpired that they were great writers and, what is more, precisely on account of works to which nobody had paid the slightest attention. From then on, if they were still alive, it was all nicknames, celebrations, and pampering, and there was as little they could do to alter that as they had been able to do about their previous neglect.

"Or else," he continued, "you have to hit the jackpot. In other words," he said, "you have to keep an eye open for the issue, which is, so to say, just breaking the surface at the time. In that case it can happen that a previously unknown writer comes into vogue, because," Sas said, "your book comes along at just the right time for someone, or somebodies, and they can make use of it either pro or contra, as a whipping-boy or a banner."

The Mijnheer related that it was not much different in the West, although there was no question that the market gave a free run to success. But then the tricks one had to devise in order to get it to surrender to "the besiegers." One person had stripped naked at a reception for the queen, others set new speed records, or they were constantly divorcing and then remarrying, or they joined suspicious sects, or had themselves carted off to hospital with a drug overdose—all just to get their names into the newspapers. He himself, Mijnheer Van de Gruyn, was fed up with funny stories and with constantly having to repeat himself. He had a subject for a serious novel and had even announced it to his agent. The agent had not raised a single word of objection but had simply placed two contracts before him. One was for the usual humorous pieces, except that the fee was one-third higher than usual; the other was for a novel, for starvation wages, and with the additional rider that the agent retained the right, on being shown the first half of the finished manuscript, to break even this miserable contract.

"I'm not saying that I won't sign one day, but right now I can't afford it."

"That's the way it is," Árpád Sas noted, "One can't always do what one would like."

"Or else you have to pay the price," added the Mijnheer. They had stopped speaking to me long ago. The two clever and worldly-wise men communed agreeably over the head of the mug sitting between them.

By then I was no longer paying much attention to them either. The restaurant terrace had filled up, the autumn sunlight seemed just as languid and distraught as my straying concentration. Other scraps of sound began to mingle with the blur of conversation from Sas and Gerendás. Plates clattered, outside on the street a bus roared past now and again. On my left an elderly fellow with a d'Artagnan moustache and a resolutely bright-patterned necktie was sitting opposite a well-preserved lady with a ready smile.

"I like some pictures," the bloke said with a deeply meaningful glance, a sausage sandwich in his hand.

"Ai laik djor myusik," said the lady in fractured English

with a smile that went far beyond the content of her utterance.

"As I recall, two parcels were packed together," a yapping voice came to my ears. It belonged to a diminutive old man in a circle of primped-up old ladies: with his enormous ears, his withered face, and the thin strands of hair twined into a crest on the crown of his head he resembled an irate hussar monkey.

Meanwhile I overheard just in passing that Sas had invited himself to Amsterdam for the coming spring.

"That may be precisely when I shan't be at home," said the Mijnheer. "Some time in the spring I have to fly to America. But of course one of the guest rooms…"

The d'Artagnan moustache was taking a dip in the foaming white bubble bath of a glass of beer.

A shrill cackling rose up at the old ladies' table:

"You always know best!" one of them shrieked, her faced flushed and trembling with indignation.

"Indeed I do, I'm precisely informed about everything!" yelped the aged head male. The old crones suddenly settled down and fell silent. The old codger snorted loudly as he looked around at them, his lower row of dentures popping up threateningly before finding its place again.

At our table, in the meantime, the discussion had passed on to Sas's English minicar, which very likely needed some spare part or other. In the ensuing conversation the suggestion came up that he would try to translate one of Gerendás' non-political humorous volumes and find a publisher for it:

"At least I'll learn some Dutch: I've already done translations from Norwegian. If I get stuck, you can help me," he declared merrily.

I looked about. Everything around me was seething and bubbling, a chirping twitter of voices from all sides, as if carried by invisible telegraph wires on invisible telegraph poles; ideas, offers, plans, and hopes jumped across like flashing electric discharges from one head to another. Yes, somehow I had been left out of this vast global metabolism of mass production and consumption, and at that moment I grasped that this was what had decided my fate. I am not a consumer, and I am not consumable.

"I have to go," I stood up.

They did not try too hard to detain me.

"Now I sit here at home."

"The end," the old boy registered surprise.

"There's nothing more."

"And yet they did publish me in the end."

"Two years after that."

"4,900 copies."

"18,000 forints."

"Did you get any work done?"

"Of course."

"Did you make any progress?"

"I pushed on a bit."

"What do you want for dinner?"

"I don't know. What's the choice?"

His wife told him.

"All the same to me," the old boy decided.

Dénouement at the bistro: the guessing is going on as to who will go and who will stay, the old boy's wife related.

The stocktaking was over now: there was a surplus rather than a shortage (which was generally praiseworthy, except when the surplus went beyond a certain surplus which was grounds for a reprimand at the very least) (since a surplus of that magnitude could not come about from anything other than practising systematic fraud on consumers over a protracted period).

The Old Biddy—or the ex-chief administrator, to give her her official title—had already put in an urgent request for what was in any case a long-overdue retirement, which the Company had immediately accepted (in a spirit of general equity) (and also in the hope of suppressing wider publicity) (which—the wider publicity, that is—would undoubtedly be more damaging for the Company than any surplus over and above a certain surplus) (which—the surplus, that is—was a profit after all) (it just had to be entered into the accounts) (of course).

Now the regular consequence of the not exactly rare cases of this kind (when a chief administrator falls, that is to say) was that the staff too were transferred to other business concerns, usually to worse ones, occasionally to similar ones, and exceptionally to better ones (even though the majority of the staff) (as is clearly stated in labour law as enacted) (bore no responsibility for the inventory; indeed, were not supposed to have any knowledge of what it comprised) (nevertheless the long shadow of crime is cast on everybody) (most especially on those who have committed none).

And so it was no more of a surprise than it was a secret that the tall, impassive, tight-lipped, blonde lady—the new chief administrator, to give her her official title—enveloped in scented clouds of perfume subtly blended with cherry brandy, a cigarette constantly dangling loosely from the corner of her mouth, was already preparing a blacklist in the office; and it was all the less a secret since she herself had declared in the presence of others, including the old boy's wife, that she was "not going to work together with a bunch of thieving employees," on account of which everything was uncertain, the only certainty being that the colleague known as Mrs. Boda (Ilona by first name) would be staying, whether thanks to the unpredictability of personal sympathies or to some more predict-able factor (for instance, foresight on the part of the—by official title—new chief administrator for a time when fate might decree that she) (the—by official title—new chief administrator) (might likewise accumulate a surplus, in which case) (just possibly at the very height of the evening rush) (she too might take over in a white coat at the beer taps) (in the spirit of that way of the world—but by no means an unconditional necessity, let it be noted—that the earlier-cited highly dubious mind called eternal recurrence) (which naturally) (we must hope at least) (life always belies).

"So now I'll have to look out for where I'm going to end up," the old boy's wife closed her words (in conclusion, so to speak).

"Oh yes," the old boy said later on, "my mother telephoned."

"What did she want?" his wife asked.

The old boy outlined the situation.

"So we no longer have any hope of eventually exchanging apartments," his wife said.

"Not much, that's for sure," the old boy said, "For the time being," he added (hastily).

"We are going to live our entire life in this hole," said his wife.

"What can I do about it?" the old boy said. "I'm going out for a bit of a walk," he also said besides that (later on).

The next morning, the old boy's wife was sitting tousle-haired, in her night-dress and slippers, on the sofa occupying the north-west corner of the room and, with a look that was still somewhat unsteady from an abrupt awakening, made the following statement:

"I had an odd dream."

"Not that I remember it precisely in every detail," she continued.

"The main thing was that I was working in a huge catering complex. It was six storeys high and built of red brick, like a—hang on … like a prison. Yes, of course. Music was blaring out on every floor, mainly gypsy music. I was assigned to the roof terrace. It was packed. I was carrying dishes, those heavy Pyrex ones, I couldn't get the twelve bottles of beer off my tray. The kitchen was on the ground floor; everything had to be carried up from there, and there were hardly any staff. We were behind with the orders, the people at the tables were bawling their demands, the ashtrays were full of cigarette butts, a lot of drink had been spilled on the grease-spattered tablecloths and was dripping onto the floor. There was such a peculiar reddish light, like you sometimes see at twilight in the summer. I was rushing from one customer to another, sweat was pouring off me, but at the same time I had the feeling that somehow none of it had anything to do with me.

"Mrs. Boda dashed by me in some Hungarian costume—red waistcoat, a cap on her head, a skirt in the national colours over that enormous backside she has. The tray she was carrying was so big that she was almost collapsing under the weight. 'So how do you manage all this with a winter snowstorm chucking it down?' she pants. 'That's your problem,' I tell her. Only then do I notice that her cap has slipped almost down to her ears, sweat is pouring out beneath it and has washed the rouge and mascara from her face. I started laughing so hard that I had to put my tray on the floor and sit down. I unlaced my shoes—I was wearing my usual high-cut work pumps—because something was pressing hard into my feet. Well if it wasn't a ten-forint coin which must somehow have slipped into the shoe in the commotion. A fellow then starts bawling at me: 'Just you wait, I'll get some order around here. I'm going to put your name down in the complaint book!' I knew that he was a deputy commander but not what sort of commander he was a deputy for. I say to him: 'You would be doing me a favour, sir. I've already been given my death sentence,' and show him the paper. He takes it and reads it, but while he is reading it his eyes start to boggle in a really odd way, as if they were going to drop out. 'That's different!,' he said. He suddenly sprang to his feet, clicked his heels and seemed about to salute but instead gave a resigned wave of his hand. While he was doing this, he even winked at me, though it was somehow more in sadness.

"At that point the new, blond chief administrator popped up from somewhere, her face white as chalk, a cigarette dangling from the corner of her mouth, and she hissed in my ear 'You can't resign! I have no staff and you have to keep going to the end of the day!' I could even smell the stench of cherry brandy on her breath, just like in real life. I say to her: 'And you can do me exactly the same favour. I'm free now, I already have my sentence!' I took my apron off and hurled it at her feet along with the money that was rattling in the pocket. I was aware that this meant the ball was over. I had never in my life felt as light as I did then. I stepped over to the guardrail. I could see a vast crowd of people swarming down below, all wanting to get in to eat and drink. They were streaming along in long black lines, like ants, even in the far distance. It was already getting dark. The whole building was bustling and humming like a beehive; music was playing, people eating and drinking, and here and there some were already tight and warbling drunkenly. The staff was running ragged among them, slapping down the food and the drinks and then quickly disappearing down the stairs into the invisible kitchen. The food was flowing out from there faster and faster, and the oddest thing about it was that I knew all along that there were no staff in the kitchen, and it would only carry on until the bosses had cooked all the surplus…

"I can't tell it the way I would like to…

"I've already forgotten many of the details…

"I have to get dressed or I'm going to be late after all that…

"It was actually a bad dream, but not as bad as having to wake up," the old boy's wife closed her words (in conclusion, so to speak).

A little later the old boy was standing in front of his filing cabinet and thinking that today he would not think.

In order to accomplish this plan (if, indeed, one may speak about a negative intention as a plan, and its occurrence as an accomplishment) (and what is more an intention which did not require any particular exertion on the old boy's part since) (as we may already have mentioned)

(he had acquired such a routine of having a think that at these times he was sometimes capable of creating the impression of being in thought even when he was not thinking, and even when he himself might have imagined that he was thinking) he produced from the back right—northwest—corner of the lower drawer of the filing cabinet a small box of sorts, a case with a beige-coloured, pockmarked surface, seemingly of pigskin.

On an outer (undoubtedly at one and the same time also the upper) surface of the small, beige-coloured (pockmarked) box, in the middle of a round, embossed, stylized seal, in a beige darker than beige (one could say brown), the letter cluster MEDICOR could be made out (possibly the expedient abbreviation for a manufacturer of pharmaceuticals or medical instruments) (if we may place any reliance on pure logic, though) (in the absence of a more appropriate point of reference) (since the old boy himself had not the slightest idea when, why, or how it had come into his possession) (we can hardly do anything else), while its two inner compartments each contained a pack of regular playing cards (one blue and one red pack, each pack of fifty-two) (thus a total of one hundred and four) (red or blue playing cards) (each playing card bearing on its back surface a round, stylized seal, in a darker blue or red than that blue or red, in the middle of which was the letter cluster MEDICOR) (invariably in the matching colour) (it goes without saying).

The old boy took out the blue pack (since that had been used less).

After a brief shuffling the old boy laid out four sets of thirteen (thus a total of fifty-two) playing cards—dealing them singly and always right to left—before him on the table (to be more precise, *the* table, the only real table in the flat).

This activity intimated, however surprising it may seem, that he was preparing to play bridge.

For to play bridge one needs four people (no more and no less).

Bridge is an English mental exercise, the old boy was in the habit of saying (for the sake of weaker spirits).

Its essence (one might say, its specific feature) is that two partners sitting across from each other play against two other partners who also sit across from each other (which is why the English call it bridge) (though this altogether too simple explanation) (along with the English origin of the game) (has been placed in question) (by recent investigations in Hungary) (in accord with others abroad).

As a result of which—for what else could he have done?—the old boy by himself represented the other three missing persons; in other words, all the players in the rubber or, to use the technical terminology, both the declarer and the defenders, which had its own undeniable advantages—for instance, it significantly reduced the obstacles to understanding between partners—though one drawback which might be raised is that the open cards made it awkward for the old boy; this may have accounted for the fact that, after announcing as declarer an otherwise easily achievable contract of four hearts he relied on outscoring rather than on finessing the red cards—a tactic whose success could be predicted—and thus ended up losing on the black cards anyway (although, as partner, he had been aware of this well in advance), as a result of which one remaining issue was left to be decided—namely, whether he would rather identify with the losing declarer or with the winning defenders (after brief vacillation the old boy decided in favour of the winning defenders) (yet he was still annoyed at not achieving the easily achievable four hearts)—before he could put the pack of cards back in the small box, and the box in its place (the back right—northwest—corner of the lower drawer of the filing cabinet), shut the filing cabinet and allow his arms—now idle—to fall, by virtue of which what, in the end, was actually a well-established, customary—indeed, one might say, very nearly ritual—position was all at once restored, which is to say:

The old boy was standing in front of the filing cabinet. He was thinking. It was midmorning (relatively—getting on for ten). Around this time the old boy was in the habit of having a think.

He had plenty of troubles and woes, so there were things to think about.

The truth is—not to put too fine a point on it—he should long ago have settled down to writing a book.

Any old book, just so long as it was a book (the old boy had long been aware that it made no difference at all what kind of book he wrote, good or bad—that had no bearing on the essence of the matter).

So with a gesture of irritation (as though he now truly did not have too much time to squander) he snatched the folder furnished with the title "*Ideas, sketches, fragments*" from the upper drawer of the filing cabinet and then tugged out from roughly the centre of the pile of paper scraps and slips and scribbled sheets, practically at random (as though it did not matter to him whether he drew the ace of spades or the two of clubs) (or perhaps more accurately, as though he were well aware that he would not be able to draw either the ace of spades or the two of clubs, since he had shuffled the pack himself) (which already predetermines the strength of the cards that can end up in our hand) (with allowance for the far from consubstantial chances of the just slightly better or slightly worse) (and thereby leaving at least some scope, after all, for the action of the instantaneous planetary constellation) a sheet of note-paper that had already somewhat yellowed at the edges.

On the sheet of note-paper (already somewhat yellowed at the edges), written with a green felt-tip pen (a type he had not used for some time), he read the following note (idea, outline, or possibly fragment):

> Köves had twice submitted a passport application and three times they had it turned down. Although it was obvious there must have been an administrative error, Köves nevertheless discerned a symbolic significance in the occurrence, so that he finally made up his mind: now he had to leave whatever might happen.

"So there it is," the old boy muttered to himself.

"Just my luck.

"I remember.

"I didn't have any job recommendations.

"That was a long time back," he wandered away from the subject (mentally).

"But what in hell's name can I make out of this?" he returned again to the subject (mentally).

"Although," he thought a bit, "it's not such a bad idea at that.

"There are some interesting elements in it.

"I could make a start with this.

"One can make a start with anything.

"What matters is what you aim for.

"So then what is Köves aiming for?"

The old boy sat down in front of the filing cabinet and pondered (evidently on the question he had posed himself, which) (as we have cited above) (was what Köves was aiming for).

"What could Köves have been aiming for, anyway?" was the next question the old boy posed to himself (and from the expression that gradually lit up his face it seemed he was beginning to guess the answer as well).

The upshot of which was that he got out the typewriter (from the upper drawer of the filing cabinet) (thereby leaving in the drawer only a few files, two cardboard boxes, and behind them a grey box file, on which there was, as a paperweight so to say, a likewise grey—albeit a darker grey—lump of stone), and at the head of the sheet of paper that he fed in, set in the middle, in uppercase type (as a person customarily does) (by general convention) (when writing down the title of something) (his book, let us say), he tapped out the following:

FIASCO

and beneath that, after some further pondering, he tapped:

CHAPTER O

"For fuck's sake!" The old boy abruptly broke off his typing at this point, while raising himself halfway from his seat as he reached toward the filing cabinet.

"Let the old goat shove all seven turns of that rigid corkscrewed poker…" the old boy intoned, unhurriedly and syllable by syllable, while carefully shaping the softened wad of fusible wax between his fingers as he crammed it into his ear, thereby placing himself beyond reach of Oglütz, the Slough of Deceit—in effect, the entire world.

CHAPTER ONE

Arrival

Köves came to with a buzzing in his ears; he had probably fallen asleep, almost missing that extraordinary moment when they descended from starlit altitude into earthly night. Scattered flickers of light showed on the borders of a horizon which tilted constantly with the turns of the aircraft. For all he knew, he could be watching a bobbing convoy of ships on the dark ocean. Yet below them was dry land; could the city really present such a pitiable sight? Köves' home came to mind, the other city—Budapest—that he had left. Even though he had already been flying for sixteen hours, it now caught up with him for the first time, like a slight tipsiness, the certainty of the distance which separated him from the familiar bend of the Danube, the lamp-garlanded bridges, the Buda hills, and the illuminated wreath of the inner city. Here, too, he had glimpsed a faintly glistening band down there, more than likely a river, and above it the odd sparsely lighted arch—those were presumably bridges; and during the descent he had also been able to make out that on one side of the river the city sprawled out over a plain, while on the other side it was set on hillocky terrain.

Köves had no chance to make any further observations. The plane touched down, and there was the usual flurry of activity: the unfastening of safety belts, a few quick tugs at crumpled clothing, but Köves was a little unsettled by the aptly brief parting word to the English travelling companion in the next seat—the Englishman flitted all over the globe as a representative for some multinational company, and during the flight Köves had seen the great value of that travel experience—it was, after all, the first time he himself had crossed continents, and moreover he was the only one disembarking at this place. Besides which it seemed as if the strains of the journey were hitting him now, all at once; he could hardly wait to be relieved of his luggage—even though it consisted of just a single suitcase that he might still have need of, he would come back later to reclaim it, with the help of his renowned and affluent friend—and to relinquish himself to the attentions of the staff.

He waited in vain, however; no one ran up to meet him, the airport terminal was dark and looked completely deserted. What was going on here? Were they on strike? Had war broken out and the airfield been blacked out? Or was it simply apathy, foreigners being left to puzzle out where to go? Köves took a few hesitant paces in the direction where he fancied he could see more solid contours in the distance, just possibly the terminal building, but before long he lost his footing—evidently he must have strayed off the runway in the dark—and at the same time he felt as if he had suddenly been smacked in the face: it was the hard beam of a searchlight, directed implacably straight at his face. Köves screwed up his eyes in irritation. At this, almost as if it were acknowledging his indignation, the spotlight slid lower and, giving him a full-body frisk-over so to say, ran before his feet, darting a few yards ahead on the ground before again returning to Köves's feet and starting all over again. Was this their way of showing him which way to go? A strange procedure at any rate; he could consider equally a courtesy as an order, and while he was pondering that, Köves caught himself already setting off—suitcase in hand—after the light beam dancing before him.

He had to walk rather a long way. The searchlight may have plunged everything around him into pitch-darkness, but Köves noticed that weed-overgrown soil alternated under his feet with further stretches of runway. These, however, seemed to be narrower, perhaps unsuited for jumbo jets of the kind on which Köves had arrived; perhaps, mused Köves, the runway for the latter had been constructed not long ago, which would explain why it had been laid farther off than these stretches. Or could it be perhaps—he pondered further—that the people here didn't want foreign travellers to see everything clearly straight away?

The pencil of light was then suddenly extinguished: evidently he had reached his goal. for Köves now found himself in front of a lighted-up entrance and a person. To be more accurate, the silhouette of a human form, standing several steps higher than him, because the lighting at the entrance was again angled in such a way that Köves was unable to see anything for the glare of light. At least it was at last a person, and the sole reason Köves did not hail him is because in the heat of the moment he could not think of the language in which to wish him a good evening.

Assistance was soon at hand, though:

"Just arrived, have we?" the person inquired of him. The question sounded more like a friendly greeting, and the hint of an overtone that was hard to decipher—malicious glee of some kind, perhaps—Köves may well have just imagined.

"Just now," he replied.

"Well I never!" said the man, and again with an overtone that—no doubt because he was unable to see the face addressing him—set Köves puzzling afresh. He was unable to decide if what he was picking out was derision, or even some sort of concealed threat, or just a plain assertion. That uncertainty is what may have triggered him into elaborating, though no one had asked him:

"I have come to see my friend," he said. "Only I didn't let him know in advance, so I could surprise him…"

"What sort of friend?" the man asked.

"Sziklai he's called … He later changed that to Stone … He's now known as Sassone, the world-famous writer of comedies and screenplays," Köves explained. Then, feeling the solid ground of facts beneath his feet: "You must have heard of him!" he added, much more firmly than before.

"You know very well that we cannot know of a writer by that name here," came the reply.

"No?…" Köves queried, and since there was no response, he remarked: "I can't say I did know, but I'll bear that in mind." He stood there in silence for a short while, the yellowish light pouring out of the entrance lengthening his shadow in an odd manner, displaying the suitcase dangling from his hand as an unshapely lump that was part of his body. Then, a good deal more quietly than before, so that after some introductory chat they might strike a more confidential tone, he asked, "Where am I?"

"At home," came the answer. It was now the man's turn to pause a little. Köves caught sight of the slight puff of condensation from his breath in the now-cooling spring night air—at last indisputable corroboration of the person's physical reality—as the man again spoke. This time he asked Köves with unmistakable amiability, almost a measure of sympathy:

"Do you wish to turn back?"

"How would I do that?" Köves asked.

The man stretched out an arm in a gesture of solicitation, as if he were making Köves a wordless offer. Köves turned round: a row of tiny portholes twinkled almost indiscernibly in the distance. It might perhaps have been the plane in which he had arrived. He was suddenly beset by a rush of homesickness for the guaranteed safety of its passenger compartment, the warmth of its air-conditioned atmosphere, its comfortable seats, its cosmopolitan passenger list, its smiling air hostesses, the unfussy, pull-down-table rituals of the meals, indeed even his bored and close-mouthed English neighbour, who always knew from where it was departing and at where it was arriving.

"No," he said, turning back toward the man. "I think there'd be no point in doing that. Now that I'm here," he added.

"As you please," the man said. "We are not forcing you to do anything."

"Yes," Köves acknowledged. "It would be hard for me to prove the opposite." He pondered a moment. "And yet you are forcing me," he resumed. "Just like the beam of light that was sent to meet me."

"You didn't have to follow it," the man instantly retorted.

"Of course," Köves said, "of course. I could have stayed out under a raw sky until day breaks or I freeze"—though there was perhaps a touch of rhetorical exaggeration in that, seeing as was spring.

He caught a swiftly suppressed burst of laughter from above him.

"Come on, then," the man eventually said. "Let's get the formalities over with." He stepped aside, and Köves was at last able to get under way and climb the few steps.

Certain preliminaries

He stepped into an empty, lighted hall; only now did Köves see how deceptive the evening had been outside, for here inside he did not find the lighting anything like as bright; to the contrary, it struck him more as gloomy, even gap-toothed here and there, and all in all fairly dingy. The hall itself was large, but in comparison with the arrivals halls of international airports—as witness the deserted desks, empty cashiers' windows, and all the other installations over which he cast but a cursory glance—it was provincially small-scale. Köves was now at last able to take a look at the man with whom he had been speaking up to now: in truth, he saw little more than a uniform. The man himself struck him as matching it so well and being so inseparable from it that Köves almost had the impression—obviously a false impression, of course, no doubt prompted by his tiredness—that this uniform had existed from time immemorial and would exist for evermore, and that at all times it moulded its transient wearers to itself. The uniform moreover seemed familiar to him, though without his recognizing it. "It's not military," he mused, "nor the police. Nor is it…" he caught himself in a thought that suddenly broke free, to which he could not have put a definite name. At all events, he therefore decided that he was dealing with a customs officer: when it came down to it, nothing—nothing so far, at least—contradicted that.

Meanwhile the man asked Köves to follow him. He showed Köves into a room which opened straight off the hall: all it was furnished with was a long table, behind which stood three chairs. The customs man, as Köves now called him to himself, immediately went around the table and took a seat facing Köves. Though it might have been an observation of no significance, it struck Köves that he did not occupy the middle chair that was naturally enough on offer, but one of those on either side. Köves had to hand over his papers and to place his suitcase on the table.

"Please be so good as to go outside, and take a seat," the customs man then said. "We shall call you when we need you."

So, Köves sought a nearby seat for himself; it was an armchair, though its uncushioned, fold-up wooden seat did not hold out hope of too much comfort. From this position he was able to see the entire hall, but while he had been in the office, something had changed out there—most likely in the lightning, it occurred to Köves: it was now darker, in the meantime some of the light bulbs had been switched off; maybe they were getting ready to shut down. Indicative of that was that in the far corners of the hall cleaning staff, with leisurely, listless movements, had swung into operation; a man in a cap and blue coat towed a vacuum cleaner along on the immensely long, worn-out, colourless strip of carpeting, but it was a machine of an antiquated kind that Köves had not seen around for a long time: its wheezy humming filling the whole hall with a monotonous drone. Now that nothing bothered him, or maybe because he was already getting used to it, the hall somehow seemed familiar to Köves. He was assailed by a sensation—absurd, of course—that he had passed that way once before, a sensation caused, perhaps, by all the fake natural stone—on the walls, the floors, every conceivable place—and the distinctive lines of the counters and other furnishings: the mark of a certain taste, one might almost say style, which in mid-century could still be considered modern, but which so easily became outmoded with the passage of fifteen or twenty years. Only this, and then the feeling of exhaustion which was again getting the better of him, could have produced the strange illusion that what he was seeing he had already seen once before, and what was happening had already happened to him once before.

For all that, he didn't know what was going to happen; Köves was suddenly gripped by a lightheaded, submissive, almost liberated feeling of being ready, all at once, to accept any adventure—come what may, whatever might snatch him, carry him off, and engulf him, whereby his life would take a new turn: Wasn't that why he had set off this journey, after all? Köves's life over there—somewhere into the night, or even beyond that, in the remoteness of limitless tracts, maybe in another dimension, who knows?—had, there was no denying it, hit rock bottom. As to how and why, Köves no longer— or for a goodish while at least—wished to think about that. He had probably gone to ruin bit by bit, doggedly, as if he were moving ahead, by imperceptible steps then: he had lived a certain kind of life, stumbled into certain situations, ditched his choices; and finally the colours of failure had emerged out of it all, it had been impossible to deny it any more. It may have begun at birth—or no, rather with his death, or to be more accurate, his rebirth. For Köves had survived his own death; at a certain moment in time when he ought to have died, he did not die, although everything had been made ready for that, it was an organized, socially approved, done deal, but Köves had simply been unwilling to satisfy the circumstances, was unable to withstand the natural instinct for life which was working inside him, not to speak of the good luck on offer, so therefore—defying all rationality—he had stayed alive. Because of that he had been subsequently dogged constantly by a painful sense of provisionality, like someone who is only waiting in a temporary hiding place to be called to account for his negligence; and although Köves himself, probably on account of the delicate structure of his mind—generally the mind—had not been fully aware of this, it nevertheless poisoned his further life and all his actions—even though he was not fully aware of it in point of fact and only saw the bewildering result. In short, he loafed around as a displaced person in his own anonymous life as in a baggy suit he had not been measured for and had been lent to him for some obscure purpose until, one fine day, enlightenment had dawned. This had happened in the shorter spur of a neon-lit, L-shaped corridor (where he had wound up through an utterly immaterial accident), in less than ten minutes (while he had been waiting for something utterly different), from which (having also seen to his accidental business in the meantime) he had stepped out onto the street with a fully formed task to accomplish. That task was essentially—much later, in the civilized, international ambience of the aircraft, for instance, in the company of the much-travelled Englishman in the neighbouring seat, Köves would have been ashamed to admit it even to himself—to write a novel. It had become clear all too soon, however, that Köves was not in possession of the prerequisites needed for the task: he had no familiarity with the practice of novel-writing, for instance; he saw only in big outlines, but not at all in the more precise details, what kind of novel he should actually write, and yet a novel is composed primarily of its own details; nor did he have a clue as to what a novel was at all, or as to why individuals would write novels, and why he would write one himself, or as to what sense that might have at all, most particularly for himself, and anyway who was he, in point of fact, and so forth— so many thorny questions, then, each on its own able to get a person snared for a lifetime. In the end, the novel had been completed in ten years, during which Köves lost touch with the world. The occasional income that he derived from the entertainment world—since writing the novel rendered Köves increasingly unfit to entertain people—had dwindled dangerously; his wife was forced into self-sacrificing breadwinning, and Köves was anguished to see her gradual acquiescence in a hard fate that she could do nothing to alter; meanwhile, he himself, staying shut up in his room—to be quite precise, the one and only room of their apartment—and lost in an abstract world of signs, practically forgot what life in the outside world was like. On top of all that, having used his last savings to get the novel copied by a typist with a reputation as the best in the business, then had it bound in a glossy folder, it was simply returned by the publisher. "On the basis of the unanimous opinion [of our readers], we are unable to undertake publication of your novel"; "We consider that your way of giving artistic expression to the material of your experiences does not come off, whereas the subject itself is horrific and shocking"; "The fact that it nevertheless fails to become a shattering experience for the reader hinges primarily on the main protagonist's, to put it mildly, odd reactions"; "For the most part your sentences are clumsy, couched in a tortuous form"—those were samples of what was said in the appended letter to Köves.

It was not this letter that exasperated Köves; he had completed the task he set himself, and—write to him whatever they liked— he was left with no doubts on that score; as to whether the novel stirred or didn't stir the reader, Köves regarded that as no more than an exasperating and superfluous matter that they simply wanted to foist upon him, though it had nothing to do with him. For all that, a concept like "the reader," along with the maniacal self-importance of the publisher's letter on the subject of this by no means clarified, yet—for him at least—completely abstract concept gave Köves no rest, and in the end made him conscious of a strange circumstance that suddenly appeared before him in an aspect of forceful absurdity, namely that he was a writer. Up till then, that had never occurred to Köves, or if it had, then in a different form; certainly not in the way in which he now, in the light of the publisher's letter, glimpsed himself, expelled from, and yet at the same time objectified in, this wretched line of occupation. There was no getting away from it, he had written a novel, but only in the sense that he would have flung himself out of even an aircraft into nothingness in the event of a terminal disaster, if he saw that as the sole possibility for survival; all at once it became obvious to Köves that, figuratively speaking, he could now only hit the ground as a writer or vanish into nothingness. This, though, awakened the most peculiar questions and thoughts in Köves. Before all else, whether this was what he had wanted, or to put it another way, whether it had actually been his goal, when he had set the task for himself as a result of the dawning of enlightenment, to become a writer? Köves no longer recalled; the years had washed away the memory of the moment, the experience of enlightenment had turned into wearisome effort, one might say a kind of slave labour, its purport continued to operate in Köves merely in the form of an implacable command spurring him on to accomplish his task. As a result, clarification of the question called for further reflection from Köves. He imagined, for instance, that the publisher had not written that letter, but exactly the opposite sort of letter. What was more—and Köves had heard that this sort of thing had happened in times past—the publisher's readers, the editor in chief at their head, would turn up at his home around dawn to assure him they had spent the entire night reading his novel in one sitting, passing pages from one to the other, and that the reader was indubitably going to be stirred to the core, so that they were going to bring it out right away. And then?—a sour note of scepticism resurfaced for Köves. What did one book signify, bearing in mind that at least one million book titles were published annually across the face of the globe, if not more? What could a reader's fleeting emotion signify (in his mind's eye, Köves saw the deeply stirred reader as, in search of a fresh stirred feeling, he was already stretching out a hand absent-mindedly to the shelf for a new book) as compared with the years that he, Köves, had dedicated to his task as he ruined his life, drained himself, and tortured his wife? And finally, how could he be reconciled to the practical outcome of his all-consuming task: a pitiful fee—to get to the bottom of all this, Köves had recently been making enquiries to this end—that could be earned within a few months in any branch of industry which was useful, unquestionable, and not subject to assessment by any publisher's reader?

Nothing became clearer to Köves than the fact that he had reached a dead end; he had irretrievably frittered away his time, what was more. He grew sick of novel-writing for good; indeed, sobering up as it were from an unbroken drunken binge which had lasted ten years, Köves was now unable to grasp with a clear head how he could have gone in for such a crazy undertaking. If he could at least be acquainted with the reason, then—or at least so Köves felt—he might find some solace in necessity. Like everyone else, he had naturally heard that what supposedly swept a person onto the novel-writing path was talent. For Köves, though, that term had signified nothing tangible. It somehow struck him in much the same colouring as saying about someone that his face flaunted a charming wart. That wart could later, no question, develop into an ugly inflamed lesion, even a malignancy, or it could remain as an attractive blemish—that was obviously a matter of luck. Except that Köves had never discovered on himself any irregularity of that kind; he had never considered himself to be the owner, whether privileged or unfortunate, of any kind of proud, innate distinguishing mark. The fault had to be lurking elsewhere, Köves reckoned, somewhere deeper down; in himself, in his circumstances, in his past, maybe even—who knows?—in his character: in everything that had happened to him, in the whole course of his life, to which he had not paid sufficient attention. If he could at least have his time over again, begin again from the beginning, Köves had daydreamed, everything would work out differently; he would know now where he ought to correct and change it. All of which, as he had been well aware, was impossible, and that was when he had decided on the trip. Not that he wished to leave his wife, home, and homeland in the lurch, but he had felt that he was in need of new inspiration, that he needed to dip his toes in foreign waters in order to be rejuvenated: he longed to be far away in order to get closer to himself, so that he might discard all that was old and lay hands on something new—in short, in order to discover himself and so begin a new life on new foundations.

Köves dreams. Then he is called for

Köves was also spurred on by a dream—the sort of constantly recurrent dream which visits everybody from time to time. It began with floating: Köves in nothingness. It was a twinkling nothingness, with minute points of light all around, like stars, yet it was a nothingness, and the many tiny lights led Köves astray more than they set him in the right direction. That was followed by anxiety, a bitter consciousness of a sense of his own confinement in big spaces; yet he was not afraid of becoming lost, that he would, as it were, be dissolved and vanish into thin air: on the contrary, even in his dream Köves distinctly felt he was apprehensive of coming across something. He was looking for something, but did not wish to find it; or to be more accurate, he wanted to find something, but not what he was looking for. His uneasiness kept growing, then all of a sudden scraps of things were being cast in front of Köves, as if they had been thrown aloft by the invisible jets of a diabolical fountain: faces and objects that were familiar to him. A face he loved, an object he saw, or made use of daily, a belonging he wore every day. He tried, but failed, to touch them, take them in his hands; he felt the objects and faces were somehow reproachfully watching his forlorn clawing after them, which was why they had offered themselves to him, so as to force him to struggle and, as it were, demonstrate that he was unable to grab hold of them. Köves felt that their distressing helplessness, their slipping past him, their sinking back down and dispersion, was his own fault: yes, he felt it was a fault that he was struggling in vain for them, that he was unable to hold in his hands things, each and every one of which was longing for the warmth of his touch. Köves sensed that desire clearly, including the clumsy yearnings of inanimate objects, which was why he was fleeing from them. He finally left them behind, or they disappeared, whereas he entered some sort of cavity: a cave or tunnel of some kind. It was nice there, because the tunnel was safe, dark, and warm; it would have been nice to stay there, to hide in the gloom, yet Köves was driven by an involuntary momentum, over which he had no control, to carry on further, onward, toward the light glimmering in the distance. The tunnel widened out all at once, expanding into a circular area, and Köves could see flaming letters as a kind of *mene, mene, tekel, upharsin* on the wall opposite. At first glance, he was terror-stricken by them, but then he noticed it wasn't so bad as all that; he was standing in a square that was well known to him—probably somewhere around the middle of the Grand Boulevard—and he was looking at the letters of a modern advertisement flashing in red, yellow, and blue neon, only these letters were varying their colours, indeed even their shapes, so quickly that in the end Köves, though he sensed they contained an extraordinarily important message of which everyone in the world, except him alone, was aware, was unable to assemble a single word out of them. While he battled with growing irascibility to make sense of them, the letters seemed to have suddenly gone mad, first starting to spin at an ever-crazier speed, after which the coloured lights blurred hopelessly together and faded, so that in the end Köves could only see a barely glowing sphere somewhere far below his feet, with himself again floating in nothingness. Only then did he notice how greatly the sphere resembled the Earth, with some sort of outline showing on it, though not one of the continents or oceans—rather a tangled contour, a peculiar shade which kept changing shape like an indolent marine jellyfish, assuming ever more dreadful forms. Köves sensed with horror that this incessantly moving shadow, these continually transforming lines, must resemble something, or rather: someone, moreover an inexpressibly important being, to whom Köves could not say offhand whether he was bound by fear or attraction, but who—and he was quite sure about this, by contrast—was projecting the dark, amorphous blot onto this milky-white globe. He had to puzzle out who it could be; straining every nerve, he racked his brains, then all at once, but in a voice which was almost earsplitting, he heard his own name called.

Only his dream could have intensified the voice so hugely, for it was the customs man calling him from the door, and in all probability he had been obliged to repeat the name twice or three times over until Köves at last grasped, with embarrassment, that he had fallen asleep while waiting, and he now leapt hastily to his feet in order to follow the customs man into the office.

Customs inspection

Although still slightly drowsy, Köves nevertheless noticed a number of changes inside the room. First and foremost, and it may have been an incidental circumstance, but it struck Köves with the very first breath of air he took, was that the room was now full of harsh tobacco smoke. He blinked in disgruntlement, the acrid air irritating him to cough: he was not used to tobacco like that—at all events, to something a cut better. Apart from that, there were now three people sitting facing him, with on each of the two outer chairs a customs man, one of whom was Köves's acquaintance, the other and also another—Köves could hardly characterize them better than that, because although obviously differed from his colleague in respect of personal features, through his uniform and the indifference reflected on his face, he looked exactly the same, and he knew that his customs man was who he was from the fact that he had just seen him take his seat on the chair to the right. The person seated in the middle Köves would have taken, at first glance, to be a soldier had he not quickly established that nothing supported that assumption, apart from the fawn-coloured tunic and the shirt and necktie of military hue: he carried no insignia of rank, nor belt nor shoulder strap by way of trimming, and so, Köves concluded, could not be a soldier, after all. In the end he decided that he too was a customs man, though clearly a different type of customs man—some sort of chief customs officer. Before them, in the middle of the table, he saw his suitcase again.

As he stepped into the room—on the principle that one should always be polite with customs men—Köves gave a friendly greeting of good evening, then waited attentively for their questions. Yet whether because they had not yet decided what to ask, or for some other reason of which Köves could not be aware, they asked nothing. One was smoking a cigarette, the second was leafing through documents of some kind, the third was scrutinizing him; they merged together in his blurred gaze in such a way that Köves finally saw them as a single triple-headed, six-armed machine, and it was obviously attributable to a brain confused by exhaustion that he suddenly caught himself on the point of racking his brains for an excuse, like somebody whom they had seen through and whose secret they had discovered—secret or offence, it came to same thing—which they were about to spring on him as a surprise, as Köves personally was not yet clear what it was.

"I wasn't given a customs declaration form," he remarked in the end, rather brusquely, in order to restore a due sense of proportion and order as it were.

"Do you have anything to declare, then?" the man in the middle said, immediately raising his head from his documents.

"I don't know what is dutiable here," Köves replied with icy politeness. A number of articles were reeled off; Köves mulled them over conscientiously, even reciting certain items to himself, in the manner of a respectful foreigner, who is showing he does not overestimate the local authorities precisely by showing his esteem, indeed even permitting himself a degree of persnicketiness in order to emphasize his goodwill, but at the same time also his rights, before replying that to the best of his recollection his baggage did not contain any of the articles that had been enumerated. But, he added immediately, if they wished, they should convince themselves of the fact. Whereupon he was given the answer that it was up to him to know what was in his luggage, to which Köves inquired whether they wished to inspect his suitcase.

"Should I open it?" he asked, and without waiting for an answer, with a strange zeal that even he sensed was excessive but was no longer able to keep in check, as if someone else were acting on his behalf, he leapt toward his case in order to snap open the locks. His efforts were superfluous, however: the case was already open. And when he hastily raised the top, although he found his belongings more or less in order, they were nevertheless not in the lovingly careful, painstaking order in which his wife had packed them for him.

He stared in astonishment into his suitcase, as if something indecent had been concealed in it.

"But you've already inspected it!" he exclaimed.

"Naturally," the chief customs man nodded. Without saying a word, he scrutinized Köves for a while, and Köves could have sworn he saw the shadow of a smile of sorts flit across the narrow, pallid face. "You are always acting as if you were surprised," he added, and Köves noticed that he exchanged a quick glance with his own customs man: he had to suppose that the latter had already briefed his boss on how he, Köves, had conducted himself in the course of their earlier conversation.

A silence descended. Köves irresolutely stood his ground; he was ransacking his brains for a question that he just could not put his finger on, so instead of that he finally asked:

"What do you intend to do with me?"

"That depends on you," the person in the middle replied forthwith. "We didn't invite you; you arrived here," and here it crossed Köves's mind that he had heard something of the kind already from his own customs man.

"Of course I did. But then why's that so important?" he asked.

"We didn't say that it was," came the answer. "But if it is important, then it's not important for us. You should quiz yourself, not us."

"About what?" Köves, grumpy from drowsiness, asked like a child.

"About what brought you here." That wasn't a question, nor was it an assertion, yet Köves still found himself cudgeling his brains for an answer, and like someone plucking an incoherent image at random from his fragmentary dreams, he finally muttered:

"I saw a beam of light, I followed that."

His rambling reason, however, must have stumbled on the right words, because his answer was evidently judged favourably:

"Carry on following it," the chief customs man said, nodding more mildly, indeed with a quiet, enigmatic seriousness that was suddenly transmitted to the faces of the two customs men on either side of him, the way these things do with underlings: somewhat exaggerating the original model, as a result of which an expression of some kind of rigid, implacable solemnity now appeared on the two outer faces, and Köves would not have been astonished—or at least that's how he felt at this juncture—if they had risen to their feet and saluted or started to sing. Without turning their heads that way, their gazes slipped over toward the chief customs man; he, however, did not move, and he now carried on, once more in his earlier manner:

"Your papers are in order. We shall treat you as if you had been domiciled abroad. Obviously you will wish to continue your original activity. In this envelope," and here he placed a brown envelope on the table before Köves, "you will find the key and the address of your apartment. Consider it an object that has been on deposit—as if you had left it with us and were now getting it back. Your suitcase will remain here. We'll let you know when and where you can pick it up."

He fell silent. Then in a tone which, apart from a certain conditioned mechanicalness, expressed nothing: no promise, but also no rejection:

"Welcome back!" and stretching out his arm he pointed toward the door.

CHAPTER TWO

On waking the next day. Preliminaries.
Köves sits down.

Although he had been allocated his home, Köves did not spend
the remaining hours of that night in his bed; as to exactly where
he did spend them, in the first moments of starting up from an, in
all likelihood, brief and light, yet nonetheless all-obliterating dream,
maybe he did not know either. The sky had assumed a glassy bright-
ness; his limbs felt stiff and numb, his shoulder blades were pressed
up against the back of a bench in the park area of a public square,
his neck felt as if it had been dislocated: it could be that as he was
sleeping he had simply laid it on the shoulder of the stranger seated
next to him, a basically well-built, tubby man wearing a polka-dot
bow-tie.

"Woken up, have we?" the stranger inquired with a friendly
smile on his moon face.

Since Köves was still staring at him wordlessly, and with the
confused gaze of someone who has been awakened suddenly, he
added by way of explanation:

"You had a good long sleep here, on my shoulder." From
which it seemed that they must have got onto informal speaking terms in the course of the night. But no, only now did Köves
recall that the man had spoken in a familiar tone from the very
start, had addressed him as if they were already acquainted—

obviously confusing him with someone else—and he, Köves, had let it pass, not being one to stand on his dignity. Köves also recollected that his new acquaintance had called himself a bar pianist, who had come from his place of work, a nearby nightclub (Köves had been utterly amazed to note to himself at the time that—whatever next!—the place even has a nightclub), in order to clear his lungs of the bar's smoky air here on the park bench.

How long could he have been asleep? A minute or an hour? Köves looked disorientedly around: the sparsely placed street lamps were still lit—green-flamed gas lamps on cast-iron posts with spiral ornaments, as in Köves's happier childhood days—and electric lights were glowing here and there in the windows of the grey, shabby houses surrounding the square. Köves could practically hear the bustling going on behind them, the rushed and hasty noises of waking up and getting ready, and was almost waiting for the as yet closed front doors to spring open and people to pour out of the damp doorways and line up in order to be counted. He must have dreamed something, his irrational ideas were mostly likely still being fed by that, yet Köves was nevertheless seized by a disagreeable emotion, a sense of having omitted to do something: he had already been put on a roll call somewhere, he was missing from somewhere, and an irreparable silence would be the response to the strident announcement of his name.

"I have to go!" he suddenly jumped up from the bench.

"Where to?" The pianist registered surprise, and it occurred to Köves just how often, over the past hours, this surprised, or at least surprised-sounding, voice had already held him back from leaving.

"Home," he said.

"What for?" With his eyes rounded and hands outspread, the pianist certainly looked like someone who was unable to make head or tail of Köves, again rousing the feeling in Köves that only at the expense of an unusual effort would he be able to convey his intentions, which even then would be left as some sort of ludicrous cavilling.

"I'm tired," he said hesitantly, as if offering an excuse.

"So, relax!" The pianist patted the broken planks of the bench with a podgily soft hand. Perhaps still not truly awake, Köves felt his resistance weakening; the earlier pressing urgency had been replaced within him by a pleasant torpidity.

"You can't put your head down now anyway," the pianist explained, as though to a child. "By the time you snuggle into bed and fall asleep, the alarm clock will be ringing. Or is it just that your mind won't rest unless you are rushing around after something?" Catching on slowly, as it were, Köves was now starting to be almost ashamed of himself, feeling he could be convinced of anything if he came up against the necessary patience or energy.

"Sit back down for a while," the pianist continued. "Look!" he produced from his coat pocket a flat bottle that was already rather familiar to Köves. "There's a drop still slopping about the bottom of this. That'll bring you round." So Köves complied again, as he had so many times during the hours which had passed. Those hours had now left in Köves's mind an impression merely of some sort of obscure struggle of which he himself seemed to be not so much a participant as merely the object—an object that he was soon happier to abandon to the enemy than quarrel over, because, or so Köves felt—right then it was just a burden to him. This mind-numbing exhaustion, the night's unclassifiable experiences, then to top it all those fine, fiery slugs he had swigged from the continually proffered bottle—that had to be the reason why even now, with his mind clearing, Köves was only able to summon up a few fragmentary details.

At all events, he had got into town from the airport by bus; Köves remembered how he had tried to stay alert, but his head had kept growing heavy with sleep and dropping onto his chest. His aim had been as clear as it was obscure: first of all, to reach a bed, in order at last to get a good sleep, with everything else taking its turn after that. He found the full address of his apartment in the envelope, at the top of a printed page, which had an official appearance: a registration form or a permit, in the dim lighting of the airport arrivals hall, and in his haste to reach the bus, Köves did not try to make head or tail of it, the one thing he managed to pick out being that he was obliged at all times to show it at the behest of any authority. Köves had a vague idea that he had already walked down the designated street—not here, of course, not one street of which he had seen as yet, let alone walked down, but in the place from which he had started on life's journey, his native city, Budapest; but Köves managed quite easily to gloss over this difference, despite the fact that it might have become a source of misunderstanding, because he was cherishing a hope that he would find his street here, too, and if there was no other way, then he would get into a taxi, his purse would stand that.

The bus, a decrepit rattletrap of a crate, shook the very spirit from him. Köves saw factories, endless dismal suburbs, neglected, tumbledown dwellings, then nothing, after which a jolt again startled him awake: they were snaking along barely lit side streets, the windows were dark, a reek of insecticide was seeping out of the houses, the streets were deserted. Köves recalled there being later on a broad, dark thoroughfare with vacant lots between the houses, then a sharp bend, and all at once he found himself in a square (as best he recalled he was asked to get off, because they had reached the terminus), where Köves in the first flush of curiosity looked around with a measure of inward approval, as though he knew exactly where he had arrived.

Yet he soon realized that this feeling of his ran counter to sound common sense and, of course—as became clear on closer inspection—counter to reality. All it came down to was Köves's hunch that he had seen the square somewhere before now, in the way that, arriving like this, in the middle of the night, at any central square of that kind, in any city, might have seemed familiar to him at first glance—from his dreams, from movies, from travel brochures, from illustrated guidebooks, from memories of unfathomable origin. The square to which it bore a likeness, or rather to which he likened it, Köves had last seen in Budapest before he had left on his travels: it was a quadrangular square, girded by proud buildings, in the middle of which was a diminutive park, in which stood an imposing group of statues. Now, this square too was unquestionably quadrangular, but of course differently: there were buildings here as well—even the dim street lighting revealed something of their original magnificence—yet what a lamentable sight they presented now! All maimed, senile war invalids. Köves was dumbfounded. Blackened walls, peeling plasterwork, pitting, and clefts everywhere. Were they bearing the traces of fighting? Had they been struck by some natural calamity? One of the houses, as if blinded, was lacking the entire row of windows on its uppermost floor, and in place of ornamental portals and elegant shops were mute gateways and boarded-up shop windows. In the middle of this square too Köves saw a sculptural group, the shoulders and chest of its main subject—a seated man—towering on a high plinth spattered with bird droppings, and he stepped closer in order to look him in the eyes (that sombre expression might, perhaps, put him on the right track), but the bowed head stared, sunk uncommunicatively, inscrutably, into darkness.

The square was deserted, with no sign of any taxi or night transport; Köves set off on foot with the peculiar assurance of a person led by memory, or by his travel experiences, although he could not boast of any travel experience, nor could memory have guided him in a place he had never been before. He left streets behind him, the houses bordered the line of his steps like decimated, lurching beggars, and Köves recalled that he had been startled when an infant had suddenly cried out from behind a window, as if he were surprised that children were also raised in this city. At street corners he was always gripped by the same shy hope: each time he hoped he had lost his way. Yet each and every time he came upon precisely the place he had known in advance, and at worst he did not recognize it immediately; for instance, in the place of a tall building he might now find a ruin or an empty lot; in place of a specific stretch of street that he would look for in vain, he would find one of a different character yet, in the end, exactly the same.

In Köves's memory, these minutes remained the most testing: he was going around a foreign city with whose every nook and cranny he was nevertheless familiar—a strange sensation. Köves did not know how to wrestle with it. His legs were leaden, as if he were walking not on asphalt but in sticky tar. At one point, he noticed by the edge of the pavement an advertising pillar, which was adorned with just one poster, and even that was a scrap, for the greater part of it had been ripped off or become detached due to the vicissitudes of the weather. CITY OF LIGHT, Köves read in big capitals. Was it an advertisement? A slogan? A cinema bill? A command? At all events the street was dark; Köves was reminded of how full of hope he had been on arrival, the unhesitating confidence with which he had followed that beam of light; though it had happened only shortly before, Köves still felt as if he had travelled an endless road since then, up hill and down dale, from the warmth into the cold, and the road he had covered had used up all his strength. The sense of wonder had quit him, bit by bit; he was seized by a benevolent weakness, and in the way he ran his hand over a scabby house wall or a boarded-up shop window, in the way his steps found their way in the already familiar streets, Köves was possessed by that unfamiliar, and yet at the same time relaxed, almost intimate sense of homelessness that was on the verge of suggesting, to an intellect sinking back into dull exhaustion, that he was, indeed, back home.

At this point, his recollections started to become disjointed, even undirected, like his steps; he again emerged into a square somewhere; he rambled along a dusty promenade among broken see-saws, abandoned sandcastles, heavy, ungainly benches that had been left high and dry from bygone days, and might have been taken for a wandering drunk—at least that was how the question, full of good-humoured support, and addressed to him from one of the benches, sounded to his ears:

"Whither, whither into the night are you going, old pal?" And he can hardly have dispelled that impression with his answer:

"Home," which had the ring of a gentle complaint. The man who had addressed him—Köves saw him in the murk of the spreading tree which overhung the bench more as an indistinct blob—was assuming a grave air as he nodded understandingly, like someone who fully appreciated that little good could be waiting for Köves back home.

"So is it far to go still?" he pressed his inquiries. In a rather doubtful tone, like someone who would not be surprised if he were to be informed that he was talking nonsense, Köves named the street, but the man merely said, with a renewed sympathetic nod:

"Well yes, that's a fair way off from here."

"But shorter if I go out by the bank of the Danube," Köves gave it another go, again rather as if he were counting on being rebutted, on having it explained to him, for example, that he was blathering, there was no bank of the Danube here, while nobody had heard of the street, yet the stranger merely disputed whether Köves would really be able to cut his journey in the direction he had indicated:

"Take a breather first, chum!" he proposed, and Köves slowly, awkwardly lowered his body to sit beside him—for just a couple of minutes, of course, in order to pull himself together—on the bench.

Continuation

But as to how they whiled away those few hours, sitting here next to each other, that—apart from his ever more uncertain attempts to depart (as if he did not just tolerate but frankly expected the pianist, each and every time to prevail upon him to stay)—Köves would have found it hard to say. Naturally they had talked; they had probably entertained themselves with funny stories, because Köves recollected having laughed. It had not taken long for the flat bottle to materialize for the first time from the pianist's pocket, and, turning it round and round in a hand raised on high, he had done his utmost to capture on it the dying rays of the moon descending onto a nearby house roof:

"Cognac," he whispered playfully in a respectful, all but reverential tone.

At all events, he soon took Köves into his confidence, relating that he played in a nightclub called the Twinkling Star:

"I'm acting as if you didn't know, being that you're one of our regulars," he said.

"Oh yes," Köves hastened to confirm.

"Though I haven't seen much of you recently." The pianist peered at Köves with a frown, looking suspicious all of a sudden: "Who exactly are you, anyway?" he asked, as if he had unexpectedly regretted having asked Köves to sit beside him, and, having scratched his head in vain to come up with some sort of explanation or justification as to his identity, all that Köves could say in his sudden confusion was:

"Who indeed?" and shrugged his shoulders. "I'm called Köves," he added; it was odd to hear his name sounding so insignificant that it rang almost disparagingly.

Yet it seemed this completely reassured the pianist: from the bottomless, satchel-like pockets of the overcoat that lay unbuttoned on his belly there now emerged sandwiches in paper serviettes.

"Life is short, the night is long," he said merrily. "I always stock up before closing time. Go ahead!" he offered them to Köves, himself taking a big bite of one. "In the Twinkling Star," he carried on with his mouth full, "you can come by exclusive nibbles, can't you, even in this day and age." The pianist at this point pulled a one-sided smile, as if he were speaking contemptuously about the place, about which, at one and the same time, in a manner Köves would have found hard to explain, he was nevertheless bragging. "When was the last time you ate any ham?" He winked at Köves.

"This evening," Köves gave himself away.

"Oh!" The pianist was amazed. "Where?"

"On the flight," said Köves. "That's what the stewardess brought round," he added by way of explanation, at which the pianist burst out laughing, as if he had finally made Köves out, and after some hesitation, and at first by no means as heartily but then all the more self-forgetfully, as if something had lifted inside him, Köves joined in.

"So, tell me now," the pianist said, slapping his thigh, "what else did you have?"

"Cold sirloin of beef, a peach, wine, chocolate," Köves recited, and both of them doubled up with laughter, so that even Köves had the feeling he was giving voice to distant fantasies, and childish ones at that, which were of no use at all other than for giving the grown-ups something to laugh about for a few minutes.

A bit later, however, the pianist again became long-faced; it seemed as if, behind the cheerfully glib words, he had continued to be preoccupied with disquieting thoughts, and he made ever more frequent references to his occupation and the nightclub, especially after Köves had remarked that it must be great to be an instrumentalist: he, Köves, supposed that a musician's life was a truly splendid, independent life, all it required was the talent for it, but that was something that he, Köves, sadly did not have.

It seemed, though, that he had said the wrong thing, because to all intents and purposes the pianist took offence:

"I'm well aware what you people think of me," he said, as if Köves belonged to a large circle of some kind who were all his adversaries: "He," and here he obviously meant himself, "he has it easy! He's got a good thing going for him! He plonks away a bit on the piano every evening, croons into a microphone, pockets the tips, and that's your lot!... Huh!" he gave an indignant laugh, so to say, to behold such ignorance.

"And it isn't?" Köves wished to know.

"How would it be?" the pianist burst out. "In a place where whiskey is also being purveyed!"

"Why?" Köves asked. "Shouldn't it be?"

"Most certainly!" the pianist said. "But I ask you ... Or rather not I, because it's of no interest to me, but..." The pianist now looked a bit flustered, as if he had become trapped in a sentence that could not be continued, and out of the shadow of the branches arching over his head he cast a swift glance at Köves, seated in the glimmering of the starry sky, before, having palpably calmed down on the one hand, but ever more agitatedly on the other, he carried on: "So anyway, as to who drinks the whiskey ... what pays for it?! And why whiskey, of all things?!"

Köves responded that he was in no position to know.

"And you think I ought to?!" the pianist heatedly rejoined, so Köves deemed it advisable to hold his peace, because it seemed to him that whatever he might say, right now it would only nettle him.

As it was, the pianist quickly calmed down:

"Right, let's have a slug!" He raised the bottle in Köves's direction.

The cheerfulness was restored for only a brief period, however:

"Then there's the numbers..." He fretted some more.

Köves had the feeling that this time he was only expecting to be prompted:

"What numbers?" he lent a helping hand.

"The ones I'm not supposed to play," the pianist replied straight-away, in a slightly plaintive tone.

"Banned numbers?" Köves pumped him some more.

"What do you mean, 'banned'?!" the pianist protested. If only they were, he explained, then he would not get the headaches either. What was banned was banned, a clear-cut matter: it was there on the list, and he wouldn't play it for any money. Except that there were other numbers, he continued, which were, how should he put it, tricky numbers; numbers which did not appear on any lists, so nobody could claim they were banned numbers; but then it was still not advisable to play them—and of course, they were the ones requested by most of the guests.

"Now, what can I say to them? That they're banned?" he posed the question, obviously not to Köves, but then it nevertheless seemed as though it were to him. "That would be slanderous, wouldn't it, even worse than my just playing them!" he went on to answer that himself. "How can I say a musical number is banned when, on the contrary, it is permitted, just tricky, and thus undesirable—though one cannot say even that about it, because if it were undesirable, then it would be banned..."

The pianist relapsed into a troubled silence, clearly rejecting the solution that, on the basis of what he heard, Köves too had to regard as inexpedient, but otherwise he accompanied the pianist's words with much nodding, feeling that he was hearing about interesting things, and even if he could not understand him in every respect, of course, he found that what the pianist was saying was nevertheless not entirely unfamiliar.

"Or," he levelled a fresh question at Köves, "am I to tell them that I don't know the number?"

Köves, tiring a bit by this point, felt it made a certain sense.

"But then what kind of pianist does that make me?" The pianist gazed reproachfully at Köves, and Köves conceded that, to be sure, he had not taken that objection into consideration. "I'm renowned," the pianist complained, or at least it sounded as if he were complaining, "for knowing every number in the book. That's what I make a living from, and I don't just make a living from it: I really do know every number in the book, I...," and at this point the pianist looked disconcerted, as if he did not know how he should express sentiments that he maybe did not wish to express in full. "So anyway," he carried on, "I won't budge on that. You could ask me why...." He glanced at Köves, but Köves didn't ask anything. "Even so, the only answer I have is that I won't give an inch." For a while he sat mutely beside Köves, presumably deliberating. "I won't let my good name be besmirched!" he announced abruptly, almost angrily, as it were against his better judgement. "Ah!" he then let fling. "How would you people know what it is like when an evening comes to the end, the low lighting is turned off, I shut the lid of the piano, and I start to ruminate about what numbers I have played, and who requested them, who was sitting at the tables, and who could that unknown chap be who..." The pianist fell silent, and for a long time he said no more, so Köves could only guess that he might be occupied with what he had just referred to as "ruminating."

As time passed, however, he seemed to forget that, too, and the good humour returned; yet the earlier weariness descended afresh on Köves's senses. The last words that he believed he heard were the following: "Don't ever feel embarrassed, old friend, just lay your head on my shoulder. If you want, I'll even hum a lullaby into your ear"—and maybe it was not the pianist who said them but Köves who dreamed them, because by then he was asleep.

Daybreak. Motor trucks. Köves speaks his mind.

So, Köves was still—or again—sitting there, and the fire of the last drop of the pianist's drink was coursing beneficially through his veins.

"How long are we going to stay?" he asked, to which the pianist tersely said no more than:

"Not long now," though he seemed in the meantime to be paying Köves hardly any attention. In the nascent light, Köves was now readily able to distinguish his slack and yet lively face: a new expression was displayed on that face—an expression which was abstracted yet at the same time uneasy. The ponderous body also shifted, with its limbs as it were rearranging themselves: the trunk which up till then had been turned toward Köves, was now leaning back; the feet, which had been slipped into shiny patent-leather shoes with old-fashioned pointed toes, were stretched out before him; the arms were outspread on the back of the seat—so long were his arms that one hand was dangling behind Köves from the end of the seat back—and he was visibly concentrating his whole attention on the street, as if he were awaiting someone who ought to be coming into view any time now. And Köves was assailed by a feeling—again an absurd feeling, just like he'd had the previous evening at the airport—that he too had been waiting all along, and was waiting now, for the same thing that the pianist was waiting for, even though he did not know, of course, precisely what it was they were waiting for, indeed, even whether they were waiting for anything at all in the first place.

So, he shifted his position, he too stretched out comfortably, lounging as if he were at home, so their arms were entwined, although they, like animals squeezed into a refuge, may not even have noticed this. Perhaps because his eyes had adjusted to it, but perhaps because his viewpoint had altered in the meantime, Köves did not judge the square as being so woeful now as he had done at night. The one thing that bothered him a little was a black firewall which was standing solitarily, looking as if a hurricane had blown the rest of the house away from it. Farther off extended a broad thoroughfare that Köves fancied he recognized, though in all probability this was a trick of the still uncertain light, because on closer inspection it proved not to be the street he had recognized, or at least that his eyes and his feet were used to. From that direction movement and scraps of sound drew Köves's attention to them: people were gathering in front of a pulled-down iron roll-shutter, mainly women, still in make-do clothing, sloppy, their heads bound in curlers. So they've started queuing up this early: no doubt it's for milk, thought Köves, seeing the cans and bottles that were dangling from the hands. From another direction there suddenly appeared hurrying, sullen-browed passers-by, so many silent reproaches as far as Köves was concerned; whether lugging bags or swinging empty hands, they were heading to wherever it was that for some reason—presumably obvious to them—they needed to be present. With heavy clattering, boxed-shaped trams began carrying their as yet sparse human cargoes hither and thither; cars whisked by, and Köves stared at them in bafflement at first, but before long he grew accustomed to their angular, cumbersome shapes. With a loud jolting on the even cobblestones, motor trucks also now appeared, two of them, one behind the other, and Köves may well have been daydreaming, because he was late in noticing their strange freight: people were seated on their platforms, men, women, and, so it seemed, even children. Their bundles and belongings, the odd piece of furniture, indicated that these were families who were moving house—all that was missing being at most any sign of joy or excitement or even anxiety, not to say vexation, at such a removal, at what was, therefore, some kind of change, a new circumstance in life. The lifeless faces, possibly still worn from an early wakening, passed before Köves's eyes in the dawn as if they were turning their backs indifferently on what they were leaving behind. Maybe because they were united in their sullen bad humour with those who were transporting them, Köves was slightly tardy in distinguishing the men squatting in the back of the trucks who were gripping a rifle between their knees: from their uniforms—he could hardly believe his eyes—Köves recognized them as being customs men, albeit shabbier-looking, commoner, or, as Köves would have put it, more pitiful than the customs men who had welcomed him.

He glanced at the pianist, but the latter did not return the look: hidden under the tree, he was watching the trucks with a keen, inquisitive gaze that now as good as pinched his normally soft, doughy features. He was watching them approach; when they got nearer, he almost stood on tiptoe in order to get a look into them, then turned as they passed and did not let them out of his sight until they had vanished in the distant bend in the road.

Then slowly, unfolding virtually every one of his limbs individually in the daybreak, rather like a genie in the process of slipping out of a flask, the pianist struggled to his feet off the bench. He flexed so violently that his limbs almost cracked, like a tree bending its branches; it was only now that it could be seen what a giant he was, with Köves (not himself exactly short) being practically dwarfed beside him when he too—involuntarily—got to his feet.

"We can go and get some shut-eye," the pianist said and gave a big yawn. "The day's done." Köves seemed to pick out from this something like a quiet satisfaction in the voice. However, it would have been futile searching for any sign of the affability he had grown used to: the pianist did not look at him any more, rather as though he had ended the service that, for some obscure reason, had bound him to Köves so far. His face was tired, worn, grey as the morning— grey as the truth, Köves caught himself thinking. A bit later (by then they were walking outside on the street, with Köves virtually not noticing that they had set off), the pianist threw in:

"Well, they won't come today then; they always come at dawn."

"Always?" Köves asked, most likely just for the sake of asking something; he was a bit confused, besides which he was forced to step on it, because it looked as though the pianist's trek had all of a sudden become urgent, and that he did not concern himself greatly with the fact that his own long steps were leaving Köves trailing behind.

"Didn't you know that?" The pianist looked down at him from the height of his shoulders.

"I knew about it as such," said Köves, but then, as though giving an answer to something different from, or maybe more than, he had been asked, he exclaimed: "Of course, I knew, I had to, how could I possibly say that I didn't!" whereupon the pianist gave him a surprised glance. "It's just that maybe ... how should I put it ... yes, it wasn't something I was ready for," he added, much more softly, still quite flustered but already starting to compose himself, though even so passers-by remarked it, albeit not as though they had been brought up short by curiosity, more in the sense that they hurried along still faster, fearing that even so they might unavoidably be obliged to overhear something.

"But you have to be ready for it," said the pianist, this time again looking more amiably at Köves, as if he were now striking up a friendship afresh.

"Now I don't understand," said Köves.

"What do you mean?"

"The bench."

"One of the best benches known to me in the city," said the pianist.

"It's because of the tree that you find it so pleasing," Köves nodded. "And also because I was there as well," he tacked on after some reflection.

"You got it! Two together makes it more entertaining." At this moment the pianist was quite as he had been, a broad smile wreathing his broad features, just as when he had taken Köves under his wing that night. "And more secure," he added.

Köves again pondered this.

"I wouldn't say that," he said eventually.

"One still feels that way; you'd have to admit that much at least." The pianist looked imploringly at Köves, in the way that one appeases the quarrelsome.

"Only for them to take the other one off along with you," slipped out of Köves's mouth before he had given any thought to the demands of good manners. "Do you know many benches?" he then asked in order to temper his words.

"Plenty," said the pianist. "Pretty well all of them."

By this point, the bustle through which they were proceeding was starting to pick up. At times they jostled among other people, at other times being held up by a red lamp.

"And do you imagine," Köves, in full stride now, turned his whole body toward the pianist, looking up at him as at a lighthouse tower, "do you imagine they're not going to find you on a park bench?"

"Who's saying that?" the pianist replied. I just don't want them to haul me out of bed."

"What difference does it make?" Köves enquired, and for a while the pianist did not reply; he paced mutely beside Köves, seemingly plunged in thought, as if the question had hit a nail on the head, despite the fact that it was unlikely—or so Köves supposed—he had not already put it to himself.

"The difference between a rat and a rabbit may not be great," the pianist eventually spoke, "but it's crucial for me."

"And why would they haul you out anyway?" Köves probed further. "Over the numbers?"

But the pianist merely smiled with sealed lips at that.

"Is there any way of knowing over what?" he then returned the question to Köves.

"No, there isn't," Köves admitted. They had reached a major crossroad, and as the morning light was reaching its fullness Köves looked around without any curiosity, feeling that he would now easily find his way: there was just a short stretch to go until he got home. "All the same…," he said haltingly, as if he were searching for the words: "All the same … I think you're exaggerating." The pianist smiled mutely—the smile of a person who was in the know, more than he was willing to let on. As though triggered by that smile, Köves burst out: "Is that what our lives are about: avoiding winding up as freight on one of those trucks?"

"That, indeed," the pianist nodded, and by way of reassurance, as it were, patted Köves gently on the nape of the neck. "And then you wind up on it anyway. If you're really lucky," he qualified with an expression that Köves this time felt was malicious, almost antagonistic, "you might even wind up at the back, at the rear end."

"I don't want the luck," said Köves, "nor do I want sit at the rear end, but in the middle." His agitation was in no way about to subside: "I think, he carried on, "all of you here are making a mistake. You pretend that all that exists are benches and those trucks … but there are other things …"

"Like what?"

"I don't know," and it seemed that Köves indeed did not know. Still, he did not let up:

"Something that's outside all this. Or at least elsewhere. Something," he suddenly came upon a word that visibly gratified him: "undefiled."

"And what would that be?" the pianist wanted to know, his expression sceptical yet not entirely devoid of interest.

"I don't know. That's just it: I don't know," said Köves. "But I'm going to hunt for it," he added swiftly, and no doubt equally involuntarily, because it seemed as if what he had just said had surprised himself most of all. "Yes," he reiterated, as if all he were seeking to do was convince the pianist, or maybe himself: "That's why I'm here, in order to find it."

But this was where the pianist now came to a standstill and offered his hand:

"Well, much luck with that," he said. "This is where I turn off, while you go straight on. Drop by to see me at the nightclub one evening. Don't worry about the money, you'll be my guest. As long as you find me there," he added with a wry smile on his big, mellow face.

Köves promised to pay a visit. The pianist then turned off to the right, while Köves went on straight ahead.

Dwelling

Köves lived in a long but in other respects not particularly distinctive side street; to the best of his recollection—though his memory might well have been playing tricks, of course—there had at one time been some fairly comfortable dwellings in this district of the city. By now, of course, the houses were deteriorating, showing signs of damage and defacement, some of them literally crumbling, with, here and there, a balcony that had once boasted sweeping curves now disfigured and hanging into space over the heads of passersby, with a notice warning of the threat to life, though evidently no one paid it any attention, and after the first few times of giving a cautionary glance up and dutifully walking round the warning sign Köves too passed beneath them with a nonchalant sense of defiance, and later on forgot even that. In the entrance hall he was greeted with a musty smell. Only a few of the imitation marble slabs that

155

had faced the walls in the stairwell had remained in place, the elevator did not work, and there were gaps and cracks in the staircase as if iron-toothed beasts were taking bites out of the steps by night. Since he could hear sounds behind his front door: movement, a rapid patter of short steps, a shrill female voice as well as a second, croaking one of more uncertain origin, Köves did not even attempt to use his key—that too he found in the envelope he had been given by the chief customs man—but rather rang the bell so as not to embarrass anyone.

Shortly after, a woman who was on the short side and well into her forties appeared in the doorway wearing sloppy men's trousers and a blouse of some kind, with what looked as if it might be alarm on her wan, peaky face, which disappeared the moment she had given Köves the once-over.

"So, here you are," she said, stepping aside to permit Köves to step past her into the hallway. "We were expecting you yesterday."

"Me?" Köves was astonished.

"Well, maybe not you specifically, but…"

"Who's come?" the previous croaking voice, presumably an adolescent boy, could be heard now, amidst a rattling of crockery, from one side, from the kitchen.

"Nobody, just the lodger," the woman called out and then again turned to Köves: "Or are you not the lodger?" and again cast a suspicious glance at him, even stepped back a bit as if she were suddenly regretting that she had let someone in who might be capable of anything.

But Köves hastened to reassure her:

"Of course," and if he felt a sense of some kind of irrational disappointment, he could only blame himself: by the sober light of day, naturally, he could not have seriously supposed that he had been accorded the priceless gift of a home of his own; as it was, they had probably done more for him than they had thought—most likely nothing more than a provision that was driven by the pressure of necessity, so they would not have to immediately start shifting him from place to place as a homeless person. "I couldn't come yesterday," he continued, "because I arrived overnight..." Just in time Köves strangled his explanation, for he had rashly almost disclosed his obscure origin, so, as it was, his sentence sounded unfinished, though fortunately the landlady helped him out:

"From the country?"

"Yes, from the country," Köves hastily acquiesced.

"I thought so right away." The woman did not hide her dissatisfaction in the slightest. "I hope you don't want to bring your family here, because in that case..."

But Köves interjected:

"I'm unmarried," at which the woman fell silent and now for the first time peered more attentively at Köves's face, as if with those two words—or the way he had said them—Köves had to some extent won her over.

"Can you play chess?" someone chimed in at that moment beside her: he caught sight of a chubby, bespectacled boy of thirteen or fourteen whose spiky hair, podgy physique, wobbly chin, and yet angular features reminded him of a hedgehog; he may have already been standing there in the kitchen door, watching them for a while, holding a half-nibbled slice of bread-and-butter in one hand, while two steaming teacups could be seen on the kitchen table behind him.

"Peter," his mother chided him, "don't bother...," and here she hesitated, and Köves was just on the point of telling them his name—in the confusion introductions had somehow been forgotten—but the woman had already carried on: "You can see he's only just arrived, he's probably tired."

"Well, can you or can't you?!" The boy seemed not to have heard the admonition, and the peculiar strictness manifested on his face made Köves smile:

"In that case," he said, "I can. Not very well, of course, just the way a person generally does."

"We'll see about that," the boy clenched his lips as if he were engrossed in turning something over in his head. "I'll get the chess board right away!" he announced and at that was already running out of the hallway toward a glass door—obviously the living-room.

Hi mother, however, nimbly jumped after him and managed to grab him by an arm:

"Didn't you hear what I said? Finish your breakfast instead or you'll be late for school and me for the office!" she reprimanded him. "My son," she turned with an apologetic smile to Köves, still gripping Peter's arm, "always sets his priority on pastimes before…"

"That's a lie!" The boy's seething anger, the palely clenched corners of his mouth and trembling of his lips genuinely alarmed Köves.

"Peter!" the woman rebuked him in a strangled voice, even shaking him a little as if to rouse him.

"That's a lie!" the boy repeated, though more as if he was over the worst of it. "You know full well that it's not a pastime!" at which he wrenched himself from his mother's grasp, dashed straight into the kitchen, and slammed the door behind him with a great crash.

The landlady looked embarrassed:

"I don't know what's up with him…," she muttered by way of an excuse. "He's so on edge…"

To which Köves said:

"It's hardly any wonder these days," and it seemed he had settled on the right words, because although the woman evasively said no more than, "Come, I'll show you the room," her expression relaxed, showing something close to gratitude.

Köves's room opened onto the other side of the hallway, diagonally opposite the kitchen: it was not particularly large, but it was enough for sleeping in and even gave a bit of room to swing a cat, the sort of place, Köves recalled, that back in his childhood had been called "the servant's quarters." It had obviously been designed to be darker, but since the firewall that would normally have overlooked the window—the whole of the next-door house was simply missing, its former site being marked by a dusty pile of rubble on the ground down below—the room was flooded with light; farther off was a disorderly yard beyond which was the back of another house, with its outside corridors, apertures onto its stairwells, its windows, indeed in many cases open kitchen doors with the figures that were bustling inside or before them, rather as if Köves had a view of its innards. The couch promised to be a good place to lie on—Köves was almost dying to try it out straight away—aside from which there was just enough room for a flimsy wardrobe, seat, and table, the latter being something the landlady seemed to be almost proud of:

"You can work on it, if you wish—not that I know what sort of a job you have, of course," she gave Köves a sidelong glance, and it struck Köves what a surprisingly clear impression her pale blue eyes made in that rumpled face—unexpected pools in a ravaged countryside, so that in the meanwhile of course he forgot to answer the implicit question he had been posed (or rather not posed), so that the woman, having waited in vain for a moment, carried on:

"It would be too small as a drawing table, say, but papers would fit on it, for instance."

Since Köves still said nothing—after all, he couldn't know what he was going to use the table for (not for drawing, for sure, but then who could know what the future might hold for him?)—the woman, now somewhat put out, added in the same breath:

"Right, well I won't intrude any further. I don't have the time, anyway; I need to set out for the office, and you no doubt have business to attend to..."

"I want to sleep," Köves said, halting the stream of words.

"Sleep?" the pools in the woman's face widened.

"Sleep," Köves confirmed, and with such yearning, evidently, that the woman broke into a smile:

"Of course, you said already that you were travelling all night. You'll find bedclothes here," and she pointed to the drawer under the couch, "and that's a wardrobe for your own stuff."

"I don't have any stuff," said Köves.

"None?" the woman may have been astounded, but not so much that Köves was obliged, and this is what he feared, to enter into explanations: it seemed that, being someone who ran a household in which there was a constant turnover of lodgers, she must have seen all sorts of things by now. "Not even any pyjamas?"

"No," Köves admitted.

"Well, that won't do at all!" she said so indignantly that Köves felt it was a matter of general principle, quite irrespective of himself personally—as it were, in defence of practically a whole world order—that she considered it wouldn't do for a person to have no pyjamas. "I'll give you a pair," she said with the excitement of one who had been spurred into action forthwith by this intolerable state of affairs. "As best I can judge, my husband's will be about your size…"

"But won't your esteemed husband…," Köves was about to start fretting.

Except that the woman curtly brushed that aside:

"I'm a widow," and with that was already out of the door then promptly back again to toss a folded pair of pyjamas onto the couch. "And what's your thinking," she asked, "about here on in, when you don't even have a change of underwear to your name?"

"I don't know," said Köves with his suitcase fleetingly coming to mind, though only as the flicker of a memory which barely impinged on him. "I'll do some shopping later."

"Is that right!" the woman said. "You'll do some shopping," and she gave a brief, nervous laugh as if she had been struck by an amusing thought. "It's no business of mine, of course. I only asked ... so, good night!" she got out quickly, seeing that Köves was already starting to take off his coat. "The bathroom is on the right," she said, turning back at the door. "Naturally, you are entitled to use it."

Köves heard them moving around for a while yet, the exchanges between the shrill and the more croaking voice—at times just whispering agitatedly behind the door, again bickering with each other, perhaps, like cats left to their own devices—and his head had just touched his pillow when the front door slammed, and with that silence fell. Köves now started to sink, and he was dreaming before he had even fallen asleep. What he dreamed was that he had strayed into the strange life of a foreigner who was unknown to him and had nothing to do with him, yet still being aware that this was only his dream playing with him, since he was the dreamer and could only dream about his own life. Before he finally got off to sleep, he sensed that a deep sigh had been torn from him—a relieved sigh, he felt—while his face was cracking a broad smile, and—for whatever reason—he breathed into his pillow, "At last!"

CHAPTER THREE

Dismissal

Köves awoke to a sound of ringing, or to be more specific, to having to open the door: it seemed that the impatient ringing, which kept on repeating, at times for protracted periods, at times in fitful bursts, must have pulled him out of bed before he had truly woken up, otherwise he would hardly have gone to open the door, given that there was no reason for anyone to be looking for him there.

He was mistaken, though: at the door stood a postman who happened to be looking for 'a certain Köves."

"That's me," Köves said, astonished.

"There's a registered letter for you," said the postman, and in his voice Köves picked out a slight hint of reproof, as if receiving registered mail in this place was not exactly one of the most commendable affairs, though it could have been that it was just the postman's way of taking him to task for the repeated futile ringing on the bell. "Sign for it here." He held out a ledger in front of Köves, obviously a delivery receipt book, and Köves was about to reach into his inside pocket when he became conscious of how he was standing there, in front of the postman: probably tousled, his face rumpled from sleep, in someone else's pyjamas—anyone might think he had idled away the morning, though that was his intention, of course.

"I'll get a pen right away," he muttered disconcertedly, but the postman—without uttering a word, as if he were only doing what he had been counting on from the outset—was already offering his own ready-to-hand pencil as if, merely for the sake of making his point, in the end he had delayed doing so up till now in order to make Köves feel ashamed.

In his room, Köves immediately opened the letter: it informed him that the editorial office of the newspaper on which he had been functioning up to that point as a journalist was hereby giving him notice of dismissal, and although, in compliance with the provisions of such and such a labour law, his salary would be paid to him for a further fortnight—"which may be collected at our cashier's desk during business hours on any working day"—they would be making no claims on his services from today's date onwards.

Köves read through the letter with a mixture of confusion, anger, and anxiety. How was this? Did life here begin with a person being dismissed from his job? Nothing of the kind, for of course Köves had not been working recently for the paper that had dismissed him; secondly, as far as that was concerned, he could, as it happens, have worked—now that he had been given the boot Köves felt truly drawn to this opportunity which had barely been dangled before him before it was being denied. And what if it was not his opportunity? How could he find out? The answer could only be given by experience; but then it was no longer an opportunity, but life—his own life. If he thought about it, Köves was not in the least attracted to journalism; it was possible, indeed highly probable, that he wasn't suited to the profession. Journalism—he felt deep inside—was a lie, or at least preposterous folly; and although Köves was not at all so bumptious as to consider himself the sort of fellow who was incapable of telling a lie, nevertheless—or so he believed—he was not capable of being up to every lie at all times: some of them were beyond his strength, others beyond his ability, or, as Köves would have preferred to put it, his talent. On the other hand, undoubtedly, he was clever with words, and it seemed that this was appreciated by people here—naturally after their own fashion; besides which—even though, of course, he was not there in order to be a journalist, or to cultivate any other idiotic profession—he had to have something to live off of, and journalism, leaving the lying to one side, was a cushy job which gave one a fair amount of spare time. Whatever the case might be, Köves decided in the end, his imagination could not latch on to anything other than what was on offer; the letter had turned him into a journalist, and more specifically a journalist who had been dismissed, so he had to follow up on that clue—and Köves was by now racing into the bathroom (the hot water—an unpleasant surprise for him, even though he somehow expected it—did not work) and at once started dressing in order to get to the editorial office as quickly as possible.

Köves's victories

As he hurriedly stepped out of the entrance, Köves literally tripped over a dog—one of those diminutive, long-bodied, short-legged, shiny-nosed creatures, a dachshund—which yelped loudly in pain, but instead of barking at Köves, sniffed around his shoes with a friendly wagging of the tail and even reared up to place its front paws on Köves's trouser legs and look up at him with bright eyes and outstretched pink, curly-tipped tongue, such that Köves, by way of propitiating the animal, scratched the base of its ears without breaking his stride. He then turned in order to press on ahead, only to almost bump into a white-haired, ruddy-cheeked, slightly tubby gentleman, dressed with slightly shabby gentility, who was holding a dog collar and leash in his hands.

"A dog owner too?" he hailed Köves with a friendly smile, and although Köves was in a hurry, the oddity of this encounter, or perhaps the even odder idea that he might be a dog-owner, pulled him up short for a moment.

"No, not likely!" he quickly responded.

"Still, you must like animals: the dog can sense that straight away," the elderly gentleman said with unruffled affability.

"Of course," Köves said, "But if you would excuse me," he added, "I have to dash."

"Do you live here, in the house?" The stout fellow, without showing any change to the amiability of his features, now cast a quick, sharp glance at Köves.

"Not long," Köves now replied, practically standing on one leg, and the old gentleman must have noticed the impatience:

"Then we shall no doubt have the pleasure another time." He finally let Köves go, in his old, somewhat porously woody-sounding voice and with an old-fashioned wave of the hand.

Köves rushed for a tramcar; it was getting on for noon, so he might have missed the "business hours" mentioned in the dismissal letter; he found the stop easily, though it was not exactly in the place he had looked for it, the former traffic island now being just a pile of grey paving stones that had been thrown on top of one another, from which direction came the intermittent bursts of hammering of sluggishly moving road workers, but as to whether the road had been torn apart by bombs, or ripped up to form a barricade that was now being repaired, or was just being widened, Köves was in no position to know. The tram—a makeshift assembly all three cars of which carried the stamp of different eras, as if, for want of better, they had been hastily dragged out of the dusty gloom of various depots—was a long time coming, and quite a crowd formed on the pavement around Köves, on top of which Köves, who supposed he ought to let a heavily built woman loaded with all kinds of bags and baggage get on before him, then—obviously in his surprise—did not resist the determined pressure of an elbow and, after that, a blatant shove accompanied by a curse, all of a sudden found that he had been left behind: it was not so much the strength but, presumably, more the will that he lacked, or, to be more specific, the disposition needed to will things, the necessary sense of desperation from which deeds might have sprung, and that—for all the difficulties, despite legs and elbows and countervailing wills—helped him up onto the second tram car.

He had to face further difficulties at the entrance to the newspaper office: the doorkeeper, a customs man with holstered gun, was under no circumstances willing to let him in without an entry pass (Köves would hardly have said he was surprised, deep down he had expected there would be some sort of obstacle like this, except he had been thinking of later on, already imagining himself caught up in easygoing simple-mindedness at the cashier's desk), which would be issued to him in the porter's cubicle a few paces away. Here, though, light was thrown on Köves's complete inexperience in not exactly immaterial questions regarding his own situation, being unable to give a straight answer to a single one of the porter's questions, nor as to where he was from, or for whom he was looking, or actually even who he was, in point of fact.

"A journalist?" he was asked.

"Yes," Köves declared. "I'd like to pick up what's owed to me," he explained.

"There's a fee due?"

"Something like that," Köves said. "In actual fact, my salary," he added, before he could be caught out misrepresenting the truth."

"Your salary?" The porter looked up at him disbelievingly from behind his desk, upon which lay a telephone, entry passes, and a list of names of some kind. "You mean you haven't picked up your pay packet yet?"

"No, you see…," Köves began, but the porter interrupted him: "Are you attached to the paper?"

"Oh yes!" Köves hastened to assure him.

"Then where's your permanent entry card?" came the next, loaded question, which would have done service in a cross-examination; a minute may have elapsed while Köves deliberated on his answer:

"I have been abroad for a while." This statement seemed to have an unexpected effect on the porter.

"Abroad? In other words, you handed it in for that time being," he said, now for the first time in the helpful tone of voice that, in Köves's view, a porter ought to speak. "May I see your ID, please?" he added with a practically apologetic look on his face for this intrusive yet manifestly inescapable request, pencil in hand to fill out the entry card without delay on the basis of the ID.

Resettling on it forthwith was not so much a look of suspicion as of crude and somehow hurt rejection when he glanced at Köves's ID:

"I can't accept a temporary entry permit." He pushed it away from himself toward Köves, who, far from treating it as a *fait accompli* that he himself, along with his papers, had been pushed aside so to say, did not pick it up, so that it remained at the edge of the table.

"I have no other papers at present," he tried to convince the porter, a scraggy little man, whose limbs on show above the desk were intact but whom, possibly due to something peculiar, whether in his features or his movements—he would have been unable to account for precisely why—Köves had from the very first moment taken to be disabled, and what was more: a war invalid—a totally arbitrary figment, as if one could only become disabled in a war. And in order to give authentic evidence of what he was saying, a brainwave so to say—fortunately he had stuffed it in his pocket before leaving home—Köves now produced and showed the porter the dismissal notice he had received that morning: "Here you are," he said, "You can see that I'm not lying: I am attached to the paper, I am a journalist, and I want to pick up my pay."

But all the porter said as his narrow, hard-mouthed expression ran over the letter was:

"I see!" in an unmistakable tone as he set the letter down on the table edge, alongside Köves's other piece of paper, with an even more unmistakable gesture. With that he had already turned to the next enquirer, for in the meantime several people, men and women, who were seeking admission into the building, had gathered in the small room: Köves had so far not even noticed them, at most feeling the pressure of some sort of silent weight on his back, even though in truth no one actually touched him, and it was only from the relieved looks on their faces that he understood how long they had already been waiting for him to be silenced and an end be brought to the fruitless struggle.

Now, though, wheels could turn, business resume; the porter was positively demonstrative in assisting all those who, unlike Köves, could lay claim to an entry permit, greeting some of them as old acquaintances, for others dialling a number on his telephone, while with yet others there was no need for even that, because they already featured on a list of names of those who were already expected somewhere upstairs. A cheerful activity, a kind of tacit agreement, developed around Köves and, as it were, against him—an impression hardly based on the facts of the matter, but more likely just on the undoubtedly exquisite sensitivity that Köves was displaying at that moment. Although no one paid any attention to him any longer, he nevertheless felt that all eyes were fixed on him, and the filling-in of each new permit seemed as if it were not an entry into the building so much as serving solely for his—Köves's—further humiliation. At all events, there could be no doubting that without the necessary will, and the appropriate expression of that will, just like he failed to get on to the tram, he was also not going to get into the newspaper office. The trouble being that in this respect Köves now found himself somewhat perplexed: he did not know what he was supposed to wish for. As regards what common sense would have made him wish, which was to enter the newspaper office in order to pick up his pay packet, Köves no longer wanted that; indeed, it had probably slipped his mind, and to the extent that he still wished to enter the newspaper office, it was purely in order to triumph over the porter and teach him a lesson. But even that he was only able to wish for if, so to speak, he puckered his brow, because what he really wished for was something quite different, and that would have been a breakthrough into another realm, a break with all sanity: Köves wished quite simply to strike the porter's face, and to feel with his fists how the sometime face was pounded into a slushy, shapeless mush—and meanwhile he merely beat himself up, as it were, for he was well aware that he wasn't going to do it, not out of compassion or discipline, nor even fear, but just because he was simply incapable of striking anyone in the face.

This anger which he felt, not so much for the porter as for himself, not to mention a confused urge, possibly vanity, not to abandon the arena without protest, without a trace, as if he had never been there—that, and not a purposeful rage, is what eventually exploded from Köves by the time the last of the applicants had gone, and before any newer ones had arrived:

"Right, so don't let me in, but then don't quote me the rules as being your authority, but your own rancour! This is my ID, there is no other, and you'd be amazed to know where I was given it and by whom! But now I'll take it back to them and report that you won't accept it—that you won't accept the ID papers they have issued!" he yelled, and he was astonished to hear his own voice almost screeching as he carried on: "In any event I have to receive my pay, and if by no other way, then they will send it via the postal service! Which, of course, simply incurs unnecessary added work and costs for the firm, but then don't worry! They'll learn who lay behind it: you, and your overstepping of your official sphere of authority!" With that he snatched up his papers from the table, and he had already placed a hand on the doorknob when the porter's voice caught up with him:

"Not so fast!" at which, slowly and reluctantly, Köves turned round: so was this how one achieved one's aim here, by gambling away all one's hopes?

"Just let me see that ID!" the porter urged, the features even surlier than before but now seeming as if they were covering up a certain hesitation. He looked in turn at Köves and the ID, as if he were comparing them, though of course no photograph of Köves was to be seen on the document; his hand also moved to reach for the telephone, but then he had second thoughts and instead suddenly snatched up his pencil to fill out Köves's entry permit in big, clumsy lettering, then quickly ripped the form off the pad; not one word was exchanged, they no longer even looked at each other, as Köves took the paper from him and hastened out of the room.

Continuation (a further victory)

Going up in the elevator—a continually circulating, endless chain of open boxes: a rosary, no: a paternoster, the name by which lifts of this kinds were commonly known suddenly occurred to him— Köves felt dull and tired, his heart was hammering, his eyelids kept on listlessly closing as if the victory he had just had gained had drained all his strength, although of course he was still in want of sleep and had also forgotten to eat breakfast. Was it always going to be like this? Would he always have to squeeze from himself such violent, self-tormenting passions each and every time he wished to move ahead? How was he going to control his emotions, and especially his sense of direction; after all, where was he actually headed? Which way was ahead? Still, Köves could not deny that his wretched victory—the wretchedness being precisely the fact that he felt it was a victory—had warmed his heart like a satin caress, nor was he able to suppress the quiet song of a vague satisfaction as though, within himself, he had stumbled upon hitherto unsuspected blind forces. He even forget to step out at the appropriate floor—as Köves was apprised by a notice board hanging in the vestibule, the cashier's desk was located on one of the lower floors of the building—he suddenly realized that he was being warned by a sign that he should alight or remain calm in the head of the elevator shaft, where the elevator would switch over and begin its descent; Köves preferred to alight.

It looked as though, instead of the cashier's desk, he had dropped in on the editorial office (if it was so hard to gain admission to the building, one would think they could take care that a person actually went about his business and could not wander around wherever he felt like, Köves supposed, with a measure of the scornful satisfaction of someone who has found a chink in a logic which went so far as to glory in its perfection. He found himself in an immensely long corridor illuminated by flickering strip lighting; from behind doors, which were in many cases wide open, could be heard the clacking of typewriters, snatches of voices, whether or excited or dictating articles, and a piercing ringing of telephones. His nostrils caught a whiff of the smell of fresh printer's proofs, and Köves, clearly through tiredness, was overcome by an indefinable feeling, a dizziness, like someone visiting the scene of a recurrent nightmare. People passed him or came hurrying the other way; Köves looked at them curiously: some were wearing boots which still practically reeked of a caking of soil and dung; others, wearing shoddy suits and bearing expressions which were sombre, troubled, or determined, looked lost as they clutched sheets of paper between fingers below the nails of which an indelible oily grubbiness had infiltrated; he encountered no more than a few lanky, balding, bespectacled, stubble-chinned, hurried men with nervously twitching eyes, most of them in shirtsleeves, a cigarette stub in the corner of the mouth, whom Köves took to be actual journalists. Toward the end of the corridor, he saw a door marked Editor in Chief ¨ Secretary's Office; on pressing down the door handle, he found himself in a light, airy room at the back of which someone was typing; near Köves a plump, blonde woman was seated behind a writing desk. Her haughty little double chin, well-groomed appearance, and trim clothing were the exact opposite of everything Köves had seen there up to this point, and, catching the whiff of an up-market perfume, he inhaled deeply, for the last time he had smelled anything similar was during his stay abroad. In response to the secretary's question as to what had brought him there, Köves without more ado announced that he wanted to speak with the editor in chief.

"Who shall I say is asking?" the secretary asked.

"Köves," said Köves, and the secretary leafed through a notebook.

"You're not down here," she said eventually.

"No, I'm not," Köves acknowledged, "But I still want to speak with him."

"What does it concern?" the secretary asked, to which Köves reacted, perhaps not entirely without acerbity:

"I've been given notice to quit."

"I see," said the secretary, exactly the same, though not in exactly same way, as the porter, looking at Köves not reprovingly but more with a degree of interest. "You're the one who has come home from abroad. We know about you," and at that, while the expression of curiosity on her face was extinguished just as incomprehensibly as it had lit up, she let Köves know that she would first have to come to an agreement with the editor in chief by phone, then the editor in chief would set a time point for an appointment, which he would inform her of, and about which she in turn would notify Köves—by telephone, if he had a telephone, and if he didn't, by mail.

"That way it's going to take a long time for my turn to come round," Köves considered.

"It could be," the secretary admitted, "but that's the way it works," adding that the editor in chief, unfortunately, was busy at the present moment.

"Doing what?" Köves asked, and the look that the secretary gave him was as if he had not arrived from abroad so much as straight from the madhouse.

"He's working," she said, "and he instructed me that he was not to be disturbed by anyone."

"I'm sure he'll make an exception for me," Köves reckoned, heading straight for a padded door—and if this careful insulation and the shining brass studs around it had left him in any doubt, the imposing plate which adorned the door's padding also enlightened him: Editor in Chief—at which the secretary shot out from behind her desk as if she had been stung by a bee:

"You can't be thinking of going in, surely?!" she yelled.

"Too right I am," said Köves, and kept on going, if not quite uninterruptedly, because he first had to get round the secretary, who now bobbed up between him and the door so as to block his path.

"Leave this instant," she shouted. "Clear off from here!" Evidently she had completely lost her cool. "Do you hear me?!" and it seemed as though Köves had indeed not heard her, because although he took care not to tread on the secretary's toes, he marched straight ahead with the secretary continually retreating from him (surely she's not going to grapple with me or pull out a weapon, Köves niggled to himself). "Even columnists are not allowed to go in unannounced ... not even the managing editor!" the secretary carried on, now with her arms outstretched as if to embrace Köves, although she was only defending the door with this desperate and, of course, useless gesture, as in the meantime the derrière she had thrust out behind her was almost touching the padding on the door. Köves was then again a witness to a turnaround that was the reward, so it seemed—always, or just at those rare, unpredictable moments of indecision, an operational glitch as it were—for extreme, indeed downright threatening stubbornness. Because on the drawn, quivering face of the secretary, who was by now practically crucifying herself on the door, there now appeared a hesitant look, then a smile of pained cordiality, and as if it had not been she who had shouted, indeed yelled at him just beforehand, in a sweet tone, albeit one still husky with agitation, she advised Köves:

"Take a seat for a minute, I'll announce you right away," at which she had already slipped behind the padded door, behind which—Köves noticed—stood a second door.

So he sat down. Something suddenly made him feel uneasy, and Köves puzzled out that it was the stillness: a typewriter which had been ceaselessly clattering in the background had fallen silent, and having only registered it in the way that one would, say, the rustling of tree boughs or the pitter-patter of rainfall in natural surroundings, which is to say he had not noticed it at all until now it had fallen silent. A tiny, high-pitched voice struck his ears from the same place; it seemed to be the sound of stifled female giggling, and he was just about to turn round when the secretary returned, and this time with the bland, official smile in place, as if nothing had happened between the two of them, she advised him:

"Be so kind as to go through," and at that moment, though perhaps somewhat less busily than before, the typewriter struck up its clattering again.

Continuation (a yet further victory)

As he stepped through the double door, Köves at first saw virtually nothing, and even later only a little; in the daylight that streamed in through the wide window, literally stabbing and unremittingly pricking his eyes, which already stinging from lack of sleep, all he could see behind an enormous writing desk was a compact lacuna, a dark form hewn out of the light as it were, that was nevertheless arranged in accordance with the forms of a human trunk, shoulders, neck, and head—obviously the editor in chief. The shadow was now augmented by an appendage, his outstretched arm, but due to the deceptive perspective caused by the light, Köves could not tell off-hand where it was pointing.

"Take a seat," he heard a voice which had a pleasantly deep ring but was slightly husky, maybe due to overuse or maybe heavy smoking. Since he saw just one chair on that side of the table, Köves sat down on it, although this chair was still facing the light, indeed, given that he was in a lower position through being seated, the source of the light was now apparent in the upper part of the window: the sun itself—albeit along with the editor in chief as well, of course. And because he had no idea where he should begin, what came to his lips straight away, even though, when it came down to it, there was nothing but the truth in its indecisiveness, was:

"I had to see you."

"Very sensible of you," could be heard from behind the writing desk. A tiny flame flickered then shortly after Köves heard this from behind a rising light cloud of blue-tinged smoke which within seconds had scattered in the light:

"My door is open to all," and on hearing this firmly resonant declaration the whole obstacle race that Köves had run in order to get to this room melted into thin air, like the cigarette smoke just before, and Köves was surprised to find something melting inside him into an obscure sense of gratitude which suddenly filled him with confidence.

It also coloured his voice:

"Because I've been given notice of dismissal"—an apology, almost a smile was hidden in that, as when men talk over among themselves some nonsense which has occurred.

"I know," Köves heard. "How can I be of assistance?"

"I've lost my bread and butter," Köves explained.

"Your bread and butter?" came back, somewhat shocked, at least to Köves's ears.

"What I mean is that I don't have anything to live off of." However much Köves might be embarrassed by his own words, it seemed he would have to speak clearly if he wished to be understood.

"I see, so that's what this is about." Now it seemed as if there was a touch of underlying impatience in the voice.

"Yes," said Köves. "I have to make a living, after all."

"Naturally, you have to make a living; we all have to make a living." The head moved about while it was speaking, so that Köves was now slowly able to make out the outline of a jutting chin and a forceful, imperious nose. "But then, ultimately it's not a matter of prime importance."

"It becomes a matter of prime importance if you have nothing to live off of," said Köves.

"Everyone in our country makes a living," and now Köves sensed in the voice something final, brooking no denial, as if he had been put in his place. "As far as your dismissal goes," the editor in chief went on, now with a somewhat more expansive intonation, "we weighed it up meticulously. To tell you the truth, we can't really see how we could make use of you. Although," and here the voice seemed to hesitate, but then continued all the same, "I won't deny that we received a serious recommendation on your behalf."

"From where?" the question seemed to slip out of Köves, but no doubt over-hastily, because it received no answer.

"We are not familiar with your work," the editor in chief continued. "Besides, so I hear, you have spent a lengthy spell abroad; you may not even be acquainted with the line our paper takes."

"But then," said Köves, "it's not just a matter of the line. With a paper," Köves became quite animated, "other types of work can be found."

"You're making me curious," he heard the editor in chief say, a remark that—not exactly hostile, but not too friendly either—again unsettled Köves. "What are you thinking of?"

"What indeed?" Köves tried to collect his thoughts as a suspicion was aroused in him that he was walking into a trap. "I can formulate proper grammatical sentences. I'm skilled at rounding out a story and supplying a punch line ... maybe," he added with a modest, self-deprecating smile, as if he wished to avoid the appearance of bragging, "well anyway, perhaps I also have some style."

"So." The word rang curtly, but Köves was unable to pick out any expression on the face haloed by the incoming rays from behind. "So in your view," the voice established rather than enquired, "a journalist's work consists of constructing proper grammatical sentences and rounding suitably pointed stories..."

"At all events," a strange defiance awoke now in Köves as in someone who knows he is right and has to defend his standpoint: "At all events journalism can't exist without that," and, without having a clue why, a recollection of how the pianist had talked that night about his numbers suddenly flashed across his mind.

"So." This now sounded even more curt and more assertive than before. Then, after a brief pause, Köves heard the following question, slow and precisely articulated:

"And you have no credo ... no persuasion?" and Köves suddenly felt like someone sizing up the depths of a chasm—and quite irrationally, too, since if he were going to jump, he would do better to jump with his eyes closed.

"None," he said. And then he almost shouted once again into the deafening silence which followed that word: "None!... How could I have any persuasion when I have never once been persuaded about anything at all! Life is not a source of faith, after all, life is ... I don't know what, but life is something else..."

He was soon interrupted:

"You're not familiar with the life we lead."

"I'd like to work, and then I shall get to know it," Köves said, in a low voice now, almost longingly.

"Well, work!" came back the exhortation.

"But I've been dismissed," Köves complained, despondently.

"You don't have to be with us to work," the voice exhorted further.

"But I don't know how to do anything else." Köves bowed his head, sensing he was behaving like a beggar.

"You'll learn: our factories are waiting with open gates for anyone who wishes to work!" chimed the voice, and Köves lifted his head again: the recognition, like a judgement, filled him with a calm, dull weariness, but in it he somehow regained his keen sense of pride.

"So, that's what you intend for me," he said slowly, almost whispering, searching in vain with his groping gaze for the purchase of any sort of face, as long as it was visible in the light.

"We don't intend anything at all for you," came back from over there. "That's just your misconception: it's up to you to find your alternatives." Then, seeming to make do with that for his lecturing, the editor in chief's voice turned warmer, almost congenial: "Work, get to know life, open up your eyes and ears, accumulate experiences. Don't imagine we have given up on you and your talent. This door," the arm swung straight out and pointed to somewhere behind Köves, obviously the door, "This door, you'll see, will open to you yet again."

"That may be." Köves jumped up: with his loss of hope (if there had been any) came that of his patience, his patience for everything which, being neither a constraint on him nor his freedom, was no longer of interest. "That may be, but I won't be stepping through it!" After which he was again outside in the corridor, he himself didn't quite know how, and with the abatement of his excitement while the paternoster sank downwards with him, obviously either for no reason, or just as a reaction to the excitements he had endured, but so unexpectedly he was almost frightened by it, he was veritably overwhelmed by a sense of relief, like some indescribable happiness. Everything had happened differently from the way he had wanted, and yet—probably only through being in the sort of worked-up state which cancels shades—he nevertheless felt he had got what he wanted. As if he had stood his ground for something, defended something—but what? The word occurred to Köves: honour. But then, he asked himself in perplexed amazement, like someone stumbling over an unforeseen obstacle, what was his honour?

South Seas

At the cashier's desk Köves was paid out what was owed him without a word—a laughable amount, although of course he had not yet informed himself about the prices, so his grumbling might just have been a sudden onrush of an employee's instincts, the eternal craving which always feels that whatever is tossed at it is a tidbit, swallows it with an unappeased muttering, and then is already opening his mouth wide for the next morsel, never asking whether even the previous one had been earned: as far as Köves was concerned, he had not put in a stroke of work for it, and as a matter of fact they had only made a payment to him so that he would not be in their way for two weeks, nor be able to pester them with his petty worries even that long, while they saw to it that they should also stamp his entry permit, for without that he would never be able to step out of the front entrance; and on getting out onto the corridor he passed a man who, Köves remembered, had happened to be picking up some money immediately before him at the cashier's desk and was just in the process of counting the bank notes yet again, for he too was visibly not very satisfied with the amount. As Köves went past, without raising his head, the man asked:

"They've kicked you out too?"

"Yep," said Köves.

"But why?" the man asked, though apparently more abstract-edly than out of genuine curiosity, as he stuffed the money into his pocket.

"I don't know." Köves shrugged his shoulders, perhaps a bit irritated, feeling sick and tired of his own affairs. "I wasn't even here," he threw out so as not to look grudging with his words.

"Aha!" said the other, a young man of roughly the same build as Köves, and now they trudged together down the long corridor toward the paternoster. "They sent you off into the country, and by the time you returned,

the notice of dismissal was waiting for you, right?"

"Right," Köves admitted.

"That's what they usually do," the other nodded. "We got out of it rather well," he added, as he and Köves stepped together into one of the descending boxes, which carried on sinking with them as its load.

"Why?" A spark of interest was kindled in Köves. "Have they kicked you out as well?"

"Darn right!" said the other.

"And why was that?" Köves asked.

"My face doesn't fit." Now it was his turn to shrug shoulders, just like Köves before. They were now in the entrance lobby. They handed in their permits to the customs man, then stepped out onto the street; the sunlight, the traffic, even the scanty, small-town bus-tle worked on Köves, with his all-accommodating and equalizing indifference, rather like an act of kindness. "These recent changes...," the previous voice caught his ear, and Köves snatched up his head in surprise: he had already forgotten that he was not alone.

"What changes?" he asked, more just out of politeness, as he had a shrewd idea in advance that the answer would be exactly what it was:

"Can anyone know?"

"No, they can't." Köves nodded, feeling that he was taking part with obligatory automatism in some ceremony then in fashion.

But then something came to mind, this time a genuine question, touching on the heart of the matter, which he really ought to have addressed to himself but which he posed to the other all the same:

"So, what are you going to do now?"

"What?" Köves's new acquaintance nonchalantly shrugged his shoulders. "I'm going to have lunch," and the self-explanatory announcement somehow resonated with Köves and cheered him up, like someone who, after a lengthy exile, feels he is slowly starting to return to the world of human society. "Come with me, if you can spare the time," Köves's new acquaintance went on. Köves could now see that he had dark hair, a bulging forehead, and a coarse yet, on the whole, still pleasant face which seemed almost to crack when he laughed, as if a boy were suddenly sticking out his head among the prematurely hardened features. "We'll go to the South Seas, you can always get something there," and if before he had merely cheered up, Köves now unreservedly rejoiced, because he gathered that what was in question was a restaurant, and he realized that this was the very longing which was lurking in him: to sit down in a restaurant and to eat and drink his fill without a care, even if it were to be for the last time in his life, with a good friend.

"Is it far?" he showed his impatience.

"Haven't you been in the South Seas before?" his new friend was genuinely astounded. "Well then, it's time you got to know it," at which they set off.

Washing of waves

A full belly, his thirst quenched with alcohol, even if it was weak, third-rate beer, the dense fug and the snatches of voices which would be cast up out of the constant buzz in the South Seas lulled Köves so completely that it was as if he were rocking on the backs of waves, at a detached remoteness from all the more solid certainties which were showing only indistinctly from a distance. When he had drifted in through the old-fashioned, glazed revolving door, it suddenly seemed to Köves that he was both acquainted with the place—a vast barn of a room, divided up into two or maybe more interconnecting spaces—and then again not, but at all events time had not passed by even the South Seas without leaving its mark: the velvet drapery showed signs of wear, a solitary piano on the podium, forlorn and shrouded in a cover—the whole thing gave the overall picture of a diner and coffee bar, gambling den and day-time refuge which had started to go downhill, where his new friend, Sziklai—on hearing the name something flashed through Köves's mind, nothing more than a vague memory in a world where the vagueness of memories vies with that of the present—plainly felt completely at home, so Köves relinquished all initiative to him as being someone who wanted, for the time being at any rate, release from a burden that could hardly be dragged a step further: himself. He was again overcome by tiredness, so he only registered events from the periphery of his consciousness as it were. His steps were initially hurried and then more hesitant as they penetrated the interior of the place, no doubt its hub, so to speak—Köves had that impression. They were looking for someone; then the wait-ress who hastened to meet them, neither young nor old, and who was given a tragic air by the two deep furrows which ran from her nose to her chin, in diametric contrast to her words and the casual gesture with which she pointed to an empty table covered by a tablecloth of a somewhat suspect shade.

"My editor friends should park their carcasses there," she said, from which it appeared that she already knew Sziklai well. Then there was their strange dialogue: Sziklai ordered fried fillet of pork for the two of them, at which the waitress asked:

"Do the gentlemen like half-cooked gristle?" Sziklai thereupon ordered Wiener schnitzel, at which the waitress, closing her eyes and pursing her lips, asked him:

"Tell me, in all honesty, when and where did you last see a Wiener schnitzel?" At this, Sziklai, seemingly exasperated, started to pick a quarrel:

"But it's here, on the menu!" he shouted.

"Of course it's there," the waitress retorted. "What kind of a menu would it look like without Wiener schnitzel?"

It struck Köves that they were playing some kind of leg-pulling parlour game with each other, to which distant shouts and the waitress's sudden impatience put an end. "Enough!" she said. "Our charming guests are already being kept waiting at other tables. You'll get potato hot-pot!"

And with that she was off, while Sziklai, his features suddenly cracking and the boyish smile surfacing among them, enlightened Köves:

"That's Alice, the waitress," which Köves cheerfully noted. That cheerfulness switched over to frank enthusiasm when it turned out that the potato hot-pot was actually not potato hot-pot, and under the mixture of potatoes and eggs Köves's probing fork prodded a fine slice of meat, whereupon he was just about to open his mouth when Sziklai intimated by vigorous head-shaking that he ought to keep his mouth shut (clearly they were being accorded a privilege of some kind). "You can always count on Alice," was all Köves was able to get out of Sziklai.

That was not the case with the other fidgeting, gesticulating or, to the contrary, sluggish or even mutely absorbed customers hovering near at hand or farther away in the sweltering half-light, about whom Sziklai seemed to know everything, with Köves taking in only a fraction of what he said about them. Regarding a fat, balding man, whose sickly-coloured face, despite the occasional mopping with a handkerchief as big as a bedsheet, was constantly glistening with perspiration and whose table seemed to be a sort of focal point, at which people arrived in a hurry, then settled for a while before jumping up again, whereas others stayed there for longer exchanges of ideas, a person whom Sziklai himself also greeted (the bald man cordially returned the nod), Köves found out that he was the "Uncrowned," and although who gave him that nickname was unclear, its import was easy to explain because he was the uncrowned king there, with half the coffee bar working just for him, Sziklai recounted.

"How come?" Köves enquired.

"Because," said Sziklai, "the chap was actually pensioned off as unfit for service." And when Köves asked what kind of service he had been engaged in previously, Sziklai responded: "What do you think, then?" and although Köves didn't think anything, being simply too lazy to think anything at all, nevertheless, pretending to take the hint, he dropped in an "Aha!", and it seemed that was precisely the answer expected from him. Now, he continued, "taking into consideration his previous merits" (and here Sziklai gave Köves a meaningful wink), the Uncrowned was granted permission to vend scarves and shawls to peasant women at provincial markets, as well as to take photographs of peasants and sell them the pictures. The permit was originally made out in the Uncrowned's name, authorizing him alone to sell and to take photographs. But then, for one thing, there was so much to do—peasants, normally the most mistrustful of people, Sziklai related, virtually turn into kids the moment someone wants to take a family photograph of them, so much so that it could happen there wasn't even any film in the camera (given that it wasn't always possible to obtain film in the shops), so they clicked the machine with an empty cartridge, took the deposit that had been agreed on, and of course the peasants subsequently never received the pictures that had been "taken," while the name and address given by the photographer, naturally, proved false—so much work that one man couldn't possibly get through it, besides which the Uncrowned was a severe diabetic and had heart disease. Also, there were plenty of people who needed "papers," said Sziklai. That was how they would come to be working for the Uncrowned: one way or another, he would obtain an official document for them, which stated that they were working for a non-profit company. That way they would not be open to charges of workshyness or sponging, nor could he be called to account for giving employment to what was maybe a nationwide network of agents. Because of course nobody, not even the Uncrowned, could give employment to any agents, could they; agents, on the other hand, could never work as agents without appropriate papers which certified they were not in fact agents, so they were therefore dependant on each other, said Sziklai, and the Uncrowned was respected not just as a boss but as their benefactor.

"What about him over there?" Köves gestured with his head toward a farther-off table by the street-side window, where he saw a silver-maned man, whose rugged face with its marked unruly features seemed to vouch for extraordinary passions that were held in check only with great difficulty. He wore spectacles with double lenses, the outer of which were dark-tinted and could be flipped up (as Köves could tell because they happened to be flipped up), and he seemed to be immersed in some occupation that could not be made out from where they were—Köves would not have been surprised if it were to turn out he was writing a musical score or painting miniature pictures. Sziklai's face, however, burst almost into splinters when his gaze swung across in the direction Köves was indicating:

"Pumpadour," he laughed. In his free time he, too, was one

of the Uncrowned's employees. To paint the dye onto the fabric intended for peasant women they used a spray device driven, or pumped, by a treadle, and that work is usually done by Pumpadour, which is the name given him by the Uncrowned, who incidentally appreciates the joke and is a fan of the theatre, and by way of a full-time job Pumpadour worked for the theatre across the street as one of the extras (Köves was almost surprised, this being the first he had heard that the town had a theatre), beside which he also took on repairing clocks and watches. No doubt that's what he was doing right then, repairing someone's watch, though while on the subject it often occurs that once he's taken a watch to bits he's never able to put it together again, and all the customer gets back is the dial, the metal case, and a heap of tiny springs and cogs, carefully wrapped in a sheet of paper, despite which he's never short of work, because the way he shakes a watch, puts it to his ear, opens its lid to take a look at the clockwork through those double-lensed spectacles—that inspires people with confidence time after time, not to speak of the low prices he charges.

All Köves could learn about a blonde woman—a striking figure, the way she propped her face, interesting after its own fashion, with the chin resting on her folded hands, staring with an empty gaze at nothing, an untouched glass of spirits on the table—was the name by which she was known in the South Seas: "the Transcendental Concubine," whereas it was Sziklai who drew his attention to a grey-templed, suntanned, conspicuously elegant gentleman, remarking that Uncle André was "the Chloroformist."

"How's that?" Köves laughed, and Sziklai related that once upon a time, when foreign countries still had links by international railways, Uncle André used to strike up acquaintances with rich ladies travelling first class, then by night press a wad of cotton wool, doused with chloroform, over their faces and then rob them; according to Sziklai, even now Uncle André knew by heart the timetable of all the express trains on the continent (if express trains were still running, that is, and the old timetables were still valid), even though he personally had been "withdrawn from service" on several occasions, indeed for long years at a time. As to what he did nowadays "to maintain standards," all Sziklai knew was:

"It's a mystery." To which he added shortly afterwards: "Women, you can bet it's women: that's all it can be."

There were, of course, other customers, respectable people, about whom there was nothing to tell, and others about whom there was, though Köves just listened without really taking it in, and he was not even convinced that he was hearing what he did hear: he both believed it and he didn't—ephemeral glimmers in a continually ebbing and rearranging wash of waves of voices, images and impressions, and people would have no doubt misconstrued his absent-mindedness, which was in truth a discovery, admittedly a somewhat gloomy, somewhat melancholic discovery, yet nevertheless sweet, like the taste of long-gone happiness, but all of a sudden he found he was being slapped on the shoulder by someone and urged "Chin up!"

"We'll get by somehow," said Sziklai looking pensively at Köves. "There are two ways," he went on: "the short and narrow, which leads nowhere, then the long and roundabout way, which leads to who knows where, but at least one has the sense of moving ahead. You should bear that in mind," he added promptly with a touch of care-laden anxiety.

"Why?" Köves asked, grumpily, like someone whose tranquillity is being threatened, yet with the faint smile of someone who has not yet given up all hope.

"Because," said Sziklai, "I reckon it's amusing and could be put to good use in a piece."

"What sort of piece?" Köves reluctantly posed the question, perhaps hoping that by posing it he would be able to elude it.

"That's precisely the point," said Sziklai. "I reckon a piece should be written," and Köves started to regain his senses, though only slowly, like a poison administered drop by drop.

"What kind of piece?" he inquired.

"That still needs to be thought over," said Sziklai, although it appeared that he may well have already thought it over, because he carried on at once: "A stage play would be gratifying, but tricky; the cloven hoof would be glaringly obvious straight away. I reckon it needs to be a light comedy: that's what will bring success."

"Success?" Köves questioned, hesitantly, as if he were getting his mouth round a strange, near-unpronounceable word in a foreign language.

"Of course," Sziklai looked at him impatiently. "One has to make a success of something. Success is the only way out."

"Out of what?" Köves asked, and for a moment Sziklai scanned his face mistrustfully as if he were searching for some secret.

"What a weird sense of humour you have," he eventually said, evidently brightening up, like someone who had come to some conclusion: "but you have a sense of humour. I don't, or at least it limps along when it's written down on paper. But on the other hand," he continued, his eyes constantly on Köves, and Köves became more and more ill at ease, because he sensed a demand in Sziklai's gaze, if nothing else, then at least for his attention: "On the other hand, I've been reading up on dramatics for some time. You can study it, you know," Sziklai gave a dismissive wave, "it's a load of baloney, only on my own I'm getting nowhere with the dialogues. I don't even have a really good idea," he went on, with the tension increasingly getting the upper hand over Köves, an ominous presentiment that he was gradually being sucked into something, a plan perhaps, that was being hatched far away from him yet still was going to claim his energies: "Old bean," he heard Sziklai's triumphant cry, "we're saved: we'll write a light comedy!" to which Köves said:

"Fine." Then, as if in self-defence, "But not now," and they agreed on that. First they needed to sort out their affairs; Sziklai signalled to Alice and, despite Köves's protests, he paid the bill, adding a big tip to the sum.

"What's this? Robbed a bank, have we, sirs?" the waitress asked as she buried the money in her apron.

"Marvellous character." Sziklai followed her with his eye, as if he were already seeing everything in the light of the light comedy to come, but then his face clouded over. "It's just such a pity," he added, regretfully.

"Why?" Köves enquired, at which Sziklai peered searchingly around:

"I can't see him here right now," he eventually said.

"Who do you mean?" Köves enquired.

"Her ... how should I put it, her guy," said Sziklai.

"Who's that?" For reasons he was unclear about himself, this time Köves would have been interested to be enlightened—Alice seemed to have caught his attention to some extent, but all Sziklai would say, evasively, was:

"There's lot of stories about him. And then," a melancholic insight appeared on Sziklai's face, "Alice is only a waitress, after all, and waitresses always need someone who can live off them."

"I see," said Köves. "Yes, I've heard about that sort of thing; the usual story, in other words," at which they made their way outside, with Sziklai nodding a greeting to a table here and there as they crossed the place. On the street, they shook hands and agreed that one evening they would, as Sziklai put it, "find each other" in the South Seas; indeed, they could leave messages for one another with Alice, now that Köves knew her, and as soon as their affairs were settled they would make a start on the light comedy.

"Until then, rack your brains for a good idea," Sziklai said by way of a parting shot, and with an easy smile, which may have been directed at the sunshine and the prospect of gratifying a sudden wish for solitude, Köves responded:

"I'll try."

CHAPTER FOUR

Permanent residence permit. Landlady, houseman.

Köves went off to the authorities in order to get his temporary residence endorsed as permanent and to obtain ID papers to that effect: Mrs. Weigand, the landlady, had reminded him for the second time that, insofar as he wished to carry on lodging with her, he needed to attend to his official registration as soon as possible.

"Of course, I don't know what plans you have," she said casting her clear little pools up at Köves, and Köves smiled uncertainly, as if he had less idea about those plans than even Mrs. Weigand.

"To be sure," he said, therefore, "I'm finding it very satisfactory here," as if that were the reason he was there, not anything else, to which the woman responded:

"I'm glad to hear it!" as she picked some invisible thread or crumb off the tablecloth. They were standing in Köves's small room—Köves had vainly offered Mrs. Weigand the sole chair as a seat, so he too remained standing—with the afternoon already getting on for evening, though not yet time to switch on the lights, and the landlady had just before knocked on Köves's door. Köves had initially flinched slightly, thinking the boy was going to burst in on him again, but before he called out "Come in!" it occurred to him that it could hardly be him as Peter was not in the habit of knocking.

"You didn't even mention that you're a journalist," the woman carried on, with a hint of mock reproach lurking in her voice and a timid smile appearing on her pallid, pinched face, as if she were in the presence of a renowned man with whom she ought to speak with restraint, and Köves, who had indeed mentioned nothing of the kind, was astounded at how well she was informed. How could that be? Did the grapevine work that fast there? Yet instead of asking for clarification, he considered it of greater urgency for himself to supply some clarification, as if he wished to dispel a disagreeable misunderstanding which almost amounted to mudslinging:

"Yes," he said, "only I'm not with a newspaper." Then, not caring what a letdown it might cause the woman (for all he knew she might have already been boasting that she had a journalist as her lodger), he swiftly tacked on: "They fired me."

But if she did feel any letdown, that did not show on the woman: it seemed as if she had, in some manner, become more relaxed; her face. cagey beforehand, now assuming a surprised, yet for all that, a warmer expression, and in a tone that Köves felt was more natural than before she quietly acknowledged:

"So, they fired you," and, head slightly askance, she looked up at Köves with interest, and, being a blonde, albeit possibly from a bottle, she now reminded Köves of a canary. "You poor thing," she added, at which Köves raised an eyebrow as though he were about to protest but didn't know yet what he should say. It was thus again the landlady who spoke next, now asking in a confidential tone, as if there was no longer anything to hide between them, and at the same time softly, as if she did not want others to hear them (although there was no one except themselves in the room, of course):

"And why?..."

Köves for his part responded:

"Can anyone know?"—an answer which now again seemed not to miss its mark:

"No," said the woman, slowly lowering herself onto the previously offered but at the time rejected seat, all expression being extinguished from her face, as if she had suddenly become aware of being inordinately tired, "one can't." They held their silence for a short while, and so as not to make the landlady feel awkward, Köves sat down too on his bed, while Mrs. Weigand, for want of more crumbs or threads, now started fiddling with the fringe of the tablecloth.

"I'll tell you what," she eventually spoke in the deep voice that Köves had heard from her only once before, on the morning of his arrival, "there are times when I feel that I understand nothing any more." She slowly raised her head to look at Köves, the unexpected pools among the zigzagging wrinkles now seeming to have shadows cast on them by dark clouds. "As a matter of fact," she continued, "I ought to be apologizing to you." Then, maybe taking Köves's silence to be incomprehension or perhaps expectancy: "On account of my son," she tacked on: "He's a nuisance, I don't doubt." There was no gainsaying it, Köves had been having trouble with the boy; already the very first evening, when Köves was getting ready to go to bed, having had practically no sleep for two days on end, the boy had simply opened the door on him, chessboard under his elbow: "I'm here!" as if, amid the myriad other urgent calls on his time, only now, at last, did he have the time to spare to meet a longstanding obligation toward the lodger. It was useless for Köves to look for a cop-out, in vain that he instanced his tiredness and bad humour, the boy had already spread out the board on Köves's couch and made a start on setting up the chessmen. "Black or white?" He glanced severely at Köves from behind his glinting spectacles, and promptly answered for him: "White. Your start." So, Köves started, then waited for his opponent to move, then again moved, hardly paying attention to the board, his hand pulling the pieces about mechanically, essentially independently of himself, in accordance with some dreamlike battle array that his fingers had somehow, no knowing how, retained a memory of, something that had entered them, perhaps, when he was still a boy himself—almost marvelling,

Köves smiled to himself at the thought: there had been a time, of course, when he too was a child, and he only snatched up his head in response to a hissing sound. It was Peter, lips contorted, head trembling, his face seemingly drained of the last drop of blood. "Such a cheap sucker trap ... a cheap sucker trap ... and I fell for it!" he was hissing, glaring at Köves with a look of hatred from behind misted-up spectacles. Then: "I resign!" whereat board and chessmen went flying in all directions, at which Köves, in his initial discomposure, began bending down to pick them up until it came to mind that he was dealing with a child who therefore should not be spoiled but chastised. "Pick up *now* the bits you've chucked around!" he rebuked him in the sternest voice he could manage. But the injunction was unnecessary: the boy was already scrabbling around on all fours on the floor, and just a few minutes later the board was already in front of Köves, with the pieces set in their places. "I'll hammer you now, thirty times in a row!" the boy informed him through clenched teeth, as if he were preparing to wrestle, rather than play chess, with Köves. He thereupon opened the next game. Köves most likely fell asleep several times while play was in progress, at which the boy would either nudge his knee or bawl out "Your move!" while Mrs. Weigand also popped her head round the door from time to time to enquire shyly: "Is the game not over?" and then disappear again, to which the boy paid no heed, except that once he remarked, evidently not so much for Köves's benefit as just for its own sake, out of petulance:

"I hate it most of all when she calls it a game!" "Why?" Köves was aroused by a spark of curiosity, "Isn't that what it is?" "No way," the boy snapped back curtly. "What then?" Köves poked further: "Work, perhaps?" "Got it in one!" It seemed as though the boy were glancing at Köves with a spot of respect. "I need a way of pulling myself out of this shit!" he added, but without expanding on that; teeth clenched, frowning, he was already pondering the next move, and his voice was already snapping brusquely, dryly, like a rifle shot aimed at Köves: "Check!" In the end, all her rational arguments—that it was late, for instance, or the lodger might be tired, and especially that it was long past Peter's bedtime, and tomorrow they both had school or the office to face—proved fruitless, and Mrs. Weigand had to literally drag her son out of Köves's room, yet for a long time still that evening Köves was able to hear the boy's hoarsely menacing and the woman's soothingly engaged voices.

"An odd boy!" Köves remarked.

"Yes, but you have to understand him." The woman was quick to get in her counter, and it was somehow well-drilled, as if it were not the first time she had used it and maybe—so Köves sensed— had to keep permanently on tap. "Things aren't easy for him," Mrs. Weigand went on, "and I have my difficulties with him. He's at just the age when he is in most need of his father…"

She fell silent, and Köves, out of some obscure compulsion, as if he had been called upon for some purpose, though he didn't know precisely what, followed that with:

"To be sure, he went quickly enough…"

What he said cannot have been clear, however, because Mrs. Weigand stared at him uncomprehendingly:

"Who did?" she asked.

"I mean," Köves chose his words carefully: he had strayed onto tricky ground, but now that he was there he could not retreat, of course: "I mean, he left you a widow at an early age…"

"Oh, I see," said the woman. She remained silent for a short while before suddenly hurling at Köves's face:

"They carted him off and he perished at their hands!" And, head held high, she stared at him almost provocatively, with a strange defiance, as if she were heaping all her sufferings at Köves's feet and was now waiting for Köves to trample on them.

Nothing of the kind happened, however. Köves nodded a few

times, slowly, with the sympathetic, rather long face of someone who, while of course not regarding it as right, also does not find it particularly unusual that someone, as Mrs. Weigand put it, was "carted off" and "perished at their hands," and who will make do with the dead without expecting further illumination as to the details; the woman's tense face, on the other hand, gradually relaxed and slackened, as if she had grown weary of the silence which had descended on them, or perhaps suspected him of harbouring a secret complicity woven between them, as it were, by their silence.

"Yes," she reiterated, this time languidly and even, it seemed, a touch listlessly, "they carted him off, and he perished at their hands! That's at the bottom of all this. There's no way he can accept it."

"How do you mean?" Köves asked.

"He's ashamed of his father," Mrs. Weigand said.

"Ashamed?" Köves was astonished.

"He says: Why didn't he stand his ground?" the woman feigned exasperation with upflung hands and head, as though she were now living, not with her husband, but with a question which was constantly coming up and to which she had now become just as accustomed as to her own helplessness.

"Child's talk," Köves broke into a smile.

"Child's talk," said Mrs. Weigand, "But then he's still a child."

"That's true," Köves conceded.

"He scarcely knew his father. And it's no use my trying to explain…," Mrs. Weigand fell silent, the sad little pools glittering moistly in the wintry landscape of her face. "Can one explain that at all?" she eventually asked, and Köves admitted:

"That's hard."

"So," the woman said, "Is my son perhaps right? Is it really shameful?"

"I suppose," Köves gave it some thought, "I suppose it is. Shameful. Notwithstanding the fact," he added with a shrug of the shoulders, "that one can't help it: one is carted off and perishes."

Once more they said nothing, then the woman exclaimed, again in her deep voice, though it still sounded brittle, like a wire which is about to snap:

"What perpetual pangs of guilt it causes: bringing a child into the world!... One never gets over it! And into a world like this, of all places..."

"The world," Köves tried to console her, "is always difficult."

Yet the woman may not even have heard him:

"I sometimes feel he hates me for it ... blames me," she said. "And I don't know," she went on, "I don't know if, all things considered, he might not be right ... what does he have to look forward to? What else will he have to go through?"

"And that ... that's his special pastime?" Köves put in quickly, fearing that he would find the woman breaking out in tears.

"The chess, you mean?" Mrs. Weigand asked. "He wants to be a contender in tournaments."

"Ah! In tournaments! Nice," Köves nodded appreciatively; it seemed they were over the hard bit, and he had managed to divert the woman's mind away from her futile brooding and into an easier channel.

"He's in training right now, preparing for some youth championship," Mrs. Weigand continued. "He keeps saying that he has to win the championship. He has to be a great player, really great," and one could tell from her voice that she was now citing her son's words, with a hint of playful hands-off-ishness yet also of hidden seriousness.

"I see." Köves was suddenly somehow reminded of Sziklai, and he could not help continuing with his words: "One has to make a success of something."

"Yes." Mrs. Weigand smiled the way mothers smile over their ambitious sons, sceptically yet with a degree of pride.

"Success is the only way out." Köves still had a good recall of what Sziklai had said, all the more as he had since heard it repeatedly from him.

"That's right," the woman said, nodding. "He says that with his physique it's no use trying in another branch of sport. There you are, see," she added. "He has powers of judgement … that in itself is something, isn't it?"

"Of course it is!" said Köves. "Let's just hope," and here he too broke into a broad, one could say jovial, smile. "Let's just hope he has the makings of a grandmaster!"

On that note, they took leave of each other, Köves putting on his coat and saying he was going to the South Seas to dine. The next morning, after the by then routine sounds of muffled squabbling outside his door, followed by the loud slamming of the front door, he promptly got up, his first foray taking him straight to the authorities. Getting his temporary residence permit endorsed as permanent, it seemed to Köves, was a pure formality; they had just copied his particulars from the one paper to another, and there was just one section to ask him about which—so it seemed—had not been filled out:

"Your workplace?" The question though, it was clear, was by no means as subsidiary as the manner in which it was put to him, like a conditioned reflex—ready and waiting for a notification that was foreseen and at most unknown as to its specifics—because when the female clerk heard the answer: "None," she raised her head with such a look of amazement at Köves as he stood before her desk that it seemed almost one of terror.

"You're not working?" she asked, to which Köves replied:

"No."

"How can that be?" In her astonishment, the female clerk may have forgotten for a moment about even her official position, her voice sounding just the way it would when one person asks something of another, simply because she had become curious.

"I've been dismissed," said Köves, and the clerk now stared at the half-completed ID, visibly racking her brains, as though some difficulty had cropped up in her work. Then, slapping down her pen, she suddenly got to her feet and hurried off to a distant desk, whispered something to the man who was sitting there, at which he too looked in amazement first at the female clerk and then at Köves, waiting farther off, before finally rising from his place and coming over to him along with the clerk:

"You have no workplace?" he asked, his censoriously knitted brow proclaiming that, for whatever reason, he was angry with Köves; Köves for his part repeated:

"None."

"What are you living off, then?" came the next question, undoubtedly apposite, so that Köves could at most have found its reproachful edge peculiar, even if he could not have expected in all seriousness, of course, that they might actually be concerned for him there.

"At the moment I'm still within the period of notice," he responded, and as if the fact that he had been fired now fell back upon him as his own shame, he added somewhat apologetically:

"I hope that I'll soon be able to find a job."

"So do we," was the retort, and all you could pick out of that too was a highly qualified severity, as if his hoping not to be forced into begging or dying of starvation were not convincing enough, and he therefore had to be given orders to that effect.

Not long afterwards, Köves also put in an appearance at the janitor's apartment in the house. Naturally, Mrs. Weigand had pushed for that as well: the fact that Köves had now become her permanent lodger, and therefore also the house's, had to be entered by the janitor into a register, Mrs. Weigand pointed out. "Indeed, it wouldn't hurt if the chairman got to know of you, although"—and

here it seemed Mrs. Weigand must have had second thoughts—
"that might be better left to the janitor." Köves, who took from this
only that it meant one less thing he had to attend to, didn't think
to ask who the chairman might be, or indeed the nature of the
chairmanship in question, when the woman mentioned that these
matters had come to mind in passing.

The janitor lived at the foot of the stairwell, where there were
two doors next to each other. As Köves approached, his eyes searching, one of the doors was suddenly flung open and a stocky man
with a bushy moustache appeared in the doorway in a grey work
coat but also huge boots, more suitable for ploughed fields, squelch-
ing in vivifying water, than for urban pavements, into which his
trouser legs were tucked baggily, peasant style:

"Me you're looking for, Mr. Köves?" he asked, to which, with
a sudden onset of irritation brought on solely by the rake-shaped
moustache, the fleshy nose, the thick, greying mop of hair growing,
wedge-shaped, low on the brow, the high-buttoned coat, and the
heavy boots—though it was absurd, of course, that a person should
get into such a lather by a person's largely random and temporary
external appearance—Köves replied with almost cutting sharpness:

"Yes, if you're the houseman."

"That would be me, who else," he chortled good-naturedly:
whether he had noticed Köves's irritation or not, the janitor had
plainly not taken offence. "Be so kind, Mr. Köves, please come right
in!"—the effect that the rasping yet somehow treacly voice had on
Köves was like stepping into a mushy, sticky material which had
suddenly welled up under his feet and had already gripped him up
to his ears as he entered a gloomy hallway swamped with a smell of
cabbage and warm vapours—behind a door, obviously that to the
kitchen, a shuffling of feet and clattering of heavy cooking vessels
could be heard.

"No doubt you came so I could enter you in the register." From somewhere the janitor got out a hard-covered notebook, a sort of large-format school exercise book, then switched on a tiny, yellow-shaded table lamp, the weak light from which illuminated only the notebook, the janitor's gnarled fingers, and—oh yes—a bit of the filthy tablecloth while throwing the room itself into, if anything, an even more Stygian gloom.

"How come you knew straight away who I am, before I even introduced myself?!" Only now was Köves struck by the janitor's sudden appearance—had he been waiting for him? maybe spying from behind the door?—and his irritation intensified to the point of nausea as he handed over the fresh bit of paper that he had been given by the authorities so that the janitor could enter the particulars in his register.

"My, my, Mr. Köves," there was a hint of good-natured reproach in the janitor's growling voice, and meanwhile a large pair of spectacles had appeared on his nose, which had a strange effect on his face, making it look frailer, and his ungainly fingers laboured over putting down the clumsy writing onto a notebook page ruled with both horizontal and vertical lines, "give me some credit, please! It's my business to know my residents ... so, you have no workplace." The wrinkles ran together on his low forehead as he glanced up at Köves over his spectacles, but Köves did not reply, and the janitor, while entering that negative piece of data into his notebook, muttered it over again to himself, though now just by way of a statement: "None." Then, putting the pencil down, closing the notebook and, so to speak, resuming his previous train of thought, he went on:

"That's a houseman's job ... that's what I'm paid for...," and, taking his spectacles off, he stood up and held the document out for Köves, who took it back. "Not a lot, of course ... one could not exactly call it a lot ... but I mustn't grumble ... and one does for the residents what one can...," and out of the murky words in the murky room, where only the janitor's gaze smouldered like glowing embers—Köves supposed, eagerly, almost peremptorily: it was most likely his disturbed senses that were making him see it in that way, for in reality it could only have been the little lamp flickering on the table that was being reflected in those eyes—Köves sensed a demand of some sort beginning to assert itself ever more explicitly, a demand that he soon understood and one to which he would, Köves decided, under no circumstances give in. But while he was coming to that decision, his hand, as if it were not even his own, was already breaking free and—Köves noticed to his great astonishment—reaching into his pocket, digging out a bank note, and pressing it into the janitor's palm, whereas the janitor, just incidentally as it were, as if this too were tied up with the conversation, accepted it and thrust it into his baggy trousers:

"Why thank you, Mr. Köves," he said, and at this point an indulgent cordiality crept into the rusty voice, "Honestly, that wasn't my reason for saying it. Nice coat you have there." He immediately perked up. "It seems to be made of a good material," and, before Köves knew what was going on or could move, the gnarled, yellowed fingers were already pawing his overcoat. "Foreign by any chance?"

"Right, foreign," said Köves, as if he were only telling the truth out of disdain.

"Do you regularly get parcels from abroad perhaps?" the janitor inquired, and Köves, who had meanwhile come to his senses, now replied with unconcealed sarcasm:

"If I do, you'll know soon enough from the postman!" And with that he was on his way to the door when the janitor's response—

"My, my, Mr. Köves, so what if I do? It's not a secret, or is it?"—caught up with him more or less on the staircase, and as he made his way up from the basement the chuckling also gradually faded away, so that all he carried with him, on the folds of the overcoat that had been praised shortly before, was the cabbage smell.

The man with the dog

One noon—or might it not rather have been getting on for evening? Since arriving there, time seemed to have become somewhat disjointed, with his having left the old tempo behind but not yet having found his way into the swing of things in the new place, so that it was as if it were all the same to him what the time was, the part of the day, and even what day, obviously as a result of the lazy way of life, which would change as soon as he found work and it imposed order on him, although, he mused, might it not be all the same to him precisely for that reason?—Köves set off at an easy pace to the South Seas. No doubt it was a Sunday, with an unwonted sluggishness reigning over the city; sounds of jollity could even be picked out here and there, the sleepy stillness broken by the racket of children, a strident burst of music and the odours of Sunday lunches streaming from open windows; only the ruins looked even more inconsolable than at other times—maybe the absence of the otherwise constant sound of hammering and the sight of workers scrambling around on buildings—as if they were unable either to be built up or destroyed and now wished to stay there forever the way they were, stubbornly holding out in the midst of perpetual decay as it were, though tomorrow, of course, the hammers would ring out anew, goods trucks do their rounds, people yell. Peter had turned up in the room already early that morning, when Köves was still in bed, and the boy had wanted to set out the chessboard on the bedspread, on his stomach, but Köves told him in no uncertain terms that he was unwilling to play. "See if I care," the boy said in response. "I was fooled by you once, but you know diddley-squat about the game. And anyway, I hate you," he added from the doorway, leaving Köves hoping that the hatred would spare him thereafter from playing chess. Later on, Köves went for a walk, looking around the city—having a bite to eat at a stand-up buffet en route, whatever they were selling as long as it was cheap—and looking at shop windows in particular, at least those that were not boarded up. He had already procured for himself one thing and another, but shopping did not proceed anything like as easy as Köves had, if not imagined, in any case would have liked; a crowded throng packed most of the shops, and in many cases he was greeted by a line of people stretching outside the doors, and by the time he had reached a counter it turned out that he had to buy something other than what he had wanted to buy, in the best case at least something similar: a nightshirt instead of pyjamas, for example, but even then only in a much larger size than his, more of a fit for some potbellied giant, although Köves couldn't stand nightshirts, so in order that he would be able to return her husband's pyjamas to Mrs. Weigand, he chose to sleep in the buff, though he bought a nightshirt nevertheless, and—with exchange in mind—not just one but two, for when he was about to leave he had spotted an unaccountable dash of joy in the saleswoman's expression which suggested, Köves reasoned, that nightshirts must be a scarce commodity there, so it would not be smart to pass up this good fortune; in the end, it emerged that Mrs. Weigand did not insist on hanging on to the pyjamas at all, as she herself had no use for them and they were, as yet, too big for Peter.

He was already at the corner when the sounds of wheezing and a hurried scrabbling of the claws of tiny legs struck his ears, and as he turned the corner a little dog flew like a brown projectile, hurled with great force, at his lap, flinging its tiny head and its shiny nose this way and that in its ecstasy, sniffing, lapping with its lolling tongue at Köves's hands, fixing its sparkling button-eyes expectantly on Köves, then from farther away a porously woody-sounding voice blared:

"Here this instant, you little rascal!" It was the elderly gentleman and his dachshund, whom Köves had run across not long before. "A shameless flatterer, you are, nothing else!" the elderly gentleman's grouching sounded more like an expression of affection as he bent down and attached the leash in his hand to the dog's collar. "There's no escaping him once he's formed a liking for someone," he continued, apparently still grumbling but in truth with barely concealed pride. "But it's rare for him to form a liking for a person at first sight, take it from me, Mr. Köves!"

"I see you already know who I am," said Köves, somewhat surprised, "so there's no need for me to introduce myself."

"Certainly I know who you are." The elderly gentleman was jerked vigorously by the end of the leash, as the dog suddenly pulled away in his excitement so as to bless a house wall with a cocked rear leg. "In a certain sense it's my duty to know. Keep still now!" he scolded the little dog, which was again leaping around like crazy, getting entangled with their legs. "I'm the chairman, you see." He again turned his head with its fine white hair, ruddy-cheeked face and amiable smile toward Köves.

"Ah! I see," said Köves. "Chairman of what?" and, to make the question sound airier, even more casual, Köves bent down to stroke the animal, which in gratitude immediately jumped up at him.

"The one that you too, for example, elected." The elderly gentleman's smile now beamed broadly and at the same time took on a somewhat impish look. "Come now, Mr. Köves!" he said in a quieter, confidential tone, "let's not play with words!" and Köves, perhaps less at a loss than before, reiterated:

"I see."

"We already met the other day," the elderly gentleman went on, "but you were in a hurry then."

"I had something to take care of," explained Köves.

"That goes without saying," the old fellow hastened to assure him, "but you may have more time now. We're taking a constitutional." He glanced at the dog, which, after the initial paroxysms of delight, had now, it appeared, suddenly grown bored with them and was straining at the leash after some scent or other, its muzzle pressed to the pavement: "If you would care to join us, please do. How do you find it in our house?" he then asked. Köves replied with an easy little half-smile:

"Couldn't be better," saying it like someone who meant it, make of it what one might.

"Splendid!" said the elderly gentleman. "Mrs. Weigand is a fine, decent lady; you couldn't have a better place to stay." He glanced askance at Köves, who, because he could not tell offhand, and he could not discern from the face which was turning toward him whether was he was expected to agree or protest, held his peace. "I gather you're a journalist," the old fellow went on. "I know you're not with a paper at the moment." Quickly, almost in anticipation, as if seeking to cut Köves short, he raised his free hand (with the other he was trying to restrain the dog, which, on spying the small park in the middle of a square which had suddenly appeared before them, was all for scampering toward the strip of wan grass). "I imagine that has nothing to do with your talents. Nowadays…," the elderly gentleman was getting nowhere with the dog, which was on its hind legs, straining at the leash with all its might, so he bent down and released it: "Scoot! Off you go and take your poop, you rascal!" only after which did he continue the sentence he had begun: "Nowadays," and here his face, up to that point sunny and bursting with health, darkened slightly, "it's not easy to live up to one's profession. Could you explain to me, Mr. Köves," he said suddenly, turning his whole body toward Köves, "why I've become the chairman, for example?"

Köves, surprised as he was by the question, and having even less clue what the explanation might be, and he chose to respond at random:

"Obviously they trust you."

"Obviously." The elderly gentleman nodded, strolling along the gravelled path of the square's garden, hands clasped behind his back. "I myself can think of no other explanation. They trust me, but they serve someone else. After all," the elderly gentleman spread his arms as they walked on, "that's people for you. The battle's not yet over, and already they're lining up on the victor's side. Yet," and here the elderly gentleman came to a halt to raise a stubby, well-manicured index finger on high by way of warning: "victory is far from assured, and what will decide it is precisely the fact that they already think it's all over. A strange logic, Mr. Köves, but I'm old now and nothing surprises me any longer," and with a shake of the head he set off again, Köves at his side: what he had heard may have been enigmatic, but it interested him all the same, and he had just formulated a question in his head when, with a sharp about-turn which ended up as just a half-turn, such that Köves sensed his gaze on him, although he was not actually looking at him, the elderly gentleman got in first:

"Have you seen the houseman yet?" his voice may have been dry, yet it still sounded as if it were concealing a sneaking excitement.

"Yes, I have," said Köves.

"And did he not say that you should come up and see me?" The customary affability was now lacking from the elderly gentleman's smile; it was somehow more of a gash, the corners of the mouth trembling slightly as if he were rubbing salt in his own wounds.

"No. Or rather…," and Köves was suddenly reminded of Mrs. Weigand's strange hesitation when she had mentioned the chairman the other day, as well as his own visit to the janitor, about which he now thought back, he himself knew not why, with a degree of bewilderment. "If I omitted to do something," he said, "then I would ask you to excuse me."

"The omission," the elderly gentleman now began visibly to regain his previous, amiable poise, "was not yours. Just look!" he pointed to the middle of the little park, "Wouldn't you know it, but that rogue has again found something to amuse himself with," and indeed the dog was leaping around a young boy's ball, then

scampering after pieces of gravel that the child threw for it to fetch.
"And it's not the first omission that has been perpetrated against me,"
he then went on; they had already crossed the square's garden and
had now set off around its perimeter. "Being the chairman, I ought
to protest, of course. Only I'm completely unsuited to the role, Mr.
Köves."

"Come, come," said Köves, "people didn't elect you because they
saw you as unsuitable…," he was slowly beginning to understand
the old fellow, and as he understood him his distress provoked a
smile: that was all it was about, a storm in a teacup, he thought.

"But it's true," the old fellow kept plugging away, casting the
occasional solicitous glance at his dog farther off as they carried
on walking. "I can't keep a secret, for instance. Then, I'm incapable
of the requisite objectivity: what counts with me is always what I
feel sympathy or antipathy toward, that's all that matters, there's
nothing I can do about it." He spread his arms. "If two people call
on me to ask about someone whom I have taken a liking to, then I
can't say anything about that, even though I'm well aware that I'm
making a mistake, a mistake, and in a double sense: first of all, I'm
contravening the need for official secrecy, then, secondly, I'm throwing myself on the mercy of the person they were warning me about."
He fell silent; with his puckered brow and long, trouble-laden face
he now oddly resembled his dog. "What I have to do is no picnic,
Mr. Köves," he sighed. Köves, more as a mechanical courtesy than
anything else, remarked:

"It's no picnic for anyone conscientious."

The old fellow, however, truly pounced on the remark:

"That's what it's about, precisely! Conscientiousness and sympathy! I didn't warm at all to the two strangers who came round
to see me—and I suppose they also dropped in on the janitor—
though I'm well aware that duty binds me to them. All the same,
my sympathies are with the person they were asking about. Yes, yes,
we're still here, you little scamp!" he called out to the dachshund,

which was rushing toward them only to race off again. "I wouldn't take it too much to my heart if he were to find himself in danger," he eventually added.

"All the same, the person in question can only be grateful to you, in my view," Köves said, by now undeniably fed up with the role that had been forced on him, but not judging the moment as propitious to part from the old fellow.

"Grateful!" The elderly gentleman raised both hands in the air. "Have you any idea how much I've done for other people?! And it was never so that they would feel grateful to me but so that I should be able to sleep soundly at night."

"Maybe it's to that you owe your prestige," Köves said, cracking a smile, like someone bringing the conversation to a close. He came to a halt, thereby forcing the old fellow to stop short. He was just about to hold out his hand when, fortuitously it seemed, something else came to mind:

"And what did the two men enquire after?" he asked; his smile had not yet vanished, only become set as though it were only there still out of forgetfulness.

"The usual things." The elderly gentleman shrugged his shoulders. "When the person in question comes home, whether he has any visitors, then does he have a job, is he working already," the old fellow would have liked to resume his walk but, since Köves did not move, he nevertheless remained standing there.

"Were they customs men?" Köves asked, his voice unquestionably faltering a little bit.

"I don't know what you're talking about, Mr. Köves." The old fellow, paying no heed to Köves, set off after all, so compelling Köves, if he wanted to hear him, to do the same. "Were they customs men, I wonder?... They didn't wear any uniform, and I have no idea why customs men should get involved in such matters. You see how much I put myself out?" He looked reproachfully at Köves.

"We're already discussing things that one should not speak about, because how do customs men come in here, and why would we look with suspicion, or maybe—even worse—fear, on a body that upholds the law?…"

"I understand," said Köves. "My thanks to you, Chairman."

"For what?" the old fellow asked, patently astonished. "I didn't say anything! But I can see how much you want to go, and I won't hold you up. We'll stay a little longer. Here, rascal!" he called out to his dog. He did not offer his hand either, as if he had forgotten to do so or had taken offence at Köves.

The South Seas: a strange acquaintance

He may have got there too early, though of course it was also a Sunday: Köves could not see a single free table in the South Seas. He had already spotted Sziklai beforehand—to Köves's considerable surprise he was sitting at the table of a man with a grey moustache and some kind of uniform—not a military or police one, nor even anything like that of the customs men: rack his brains as he might, the only other bodies among Köves's acquaintances whose members might wear a uniform were railway workers and firemen—but in any event he did not get beyond his own arbitrary guesswork as he was approaching the table. Sziklai was appearing not to recognize him, and it was only the vigorous shaking of a hand dangled under the table which gave Köves to understand that he should not take a seat there for the time being, nor even greet him. There was the usual hum in the place, the usual smells, and great merriment at the Uncrowned's table: as he passed, the way regulars do with one another, Köves gave an easygoing nod, while the Uncrowned, his thighs wide apart, his waistcoat unbuttoned over his belly, and in mid-guffaw (evidently someone had just told a joke or funny story) good-humouredly called over to Köves: "Good evening, Mr. Editor!" Sitting at a table further away, in a tight, outmoded suit, with a strangely cascading necktie and a rakish stuck-on moustache (it could only have been stuck-on because a day ago not so much as a bristle had been sprouting on the spot), was Pumpadour: there must have been an interval between two acts at the theatre and he had popped across in his costume for a drink, or perhaps because he had an important message for the Transcendental Concubine, who, chin resting on her hands, was listening to him impassively, her gaze emptily fixed, maybe on transcendence, maybe on nowhere (three empty spirits glasses were already lined up before her). Toward the rear was a noisy crowd: the table reserved for the musicians (as Köves had learned from Sziklai some time before), who would later be dispersing to go to the nightclubs where they were engaged. Not long before, Köves had spotted among them a conspicuous figure, his physiognomy, over a polka-dot bow tie, broad as the moon: his acquaintance, the bar pianist, who in turn noticed Köves and joyfully got to his feet in order to greet him, so that Köves abandoned Sziklai for a moment.

"Well now!" exclaimed the bar pianist, sinking Köves's proffered hand into his own huge, soft fist, "Have you found it yet?"

"What?" Köves asked, having no idea offhand what the pianist could be asking him to account for.

"You said you were looking for something."

"Yes, of course, of course," said Köves; the musician evidently had a better recollection of his words than he himself did: "Not yet," at which the pianist, for whatever reason, seemed satisfied, as though he had been fearing the opposite and was now relieved.

"Where did you meet Tiny, the pianist?" Sziklai asked, when Köves sat back down at their table, and Köves, glad that he was at last able to say something new to Sziklai, told him about the bench and the pianist's dread. "How do you mean, scared?… Him of all people?...," Sziklai's harsh features began to crack bit by bit from the smile which spread across them.

"Why?" Köves asked, finding Sziklai's amazement somewhat unsettling, "Is that so incredible?"

"What do you think," Sziklai countered. "Who do you suppose plays the piano in the Twinkling Star?"

"Aha!" Köves responded, whereupon Sziklai's "You see!" carried the air of didactic superiority of someone who had managed to bring order to Köves's confused frame of reference.

In the "Rumpus Room," the name given to a low-ceilinged, windowless parlour, illuminated only by the nightmarish glow of neon tubes, in a wing right at the back of the restaurant, card games were going on amid a cacophony of sounds clattering back off the walls, with slim, grey-templed Uncle André, the Chloroformist, a bored, man-of-the-world smile on his lips, was walking from table to table, stopping every now and then, behind a seat, to take a peek at the cards, and Köves was just debating inwardly whether he should leave and come back later when Alice, as she rushed by, took his fate in her hands:

"Come," she said, "I'll give you a seat with my partner," and with that was around him and making her way toward a table in the corner—in point of fact, a sort of service table, stacked with tableware, glasses, and cutlery, from which Alice laid the tables—at which a well-built man sat beside a pile of plates, his head bowed as if he were sleeping, only the balding crown of his head showing, in front of which Alice, with Köves a few paces behind, now halted and, leaning across the table, gently, yet loud enough for Köves to hear clearly, asked him:

"Are you thinking?...," at which the man slowly lifted up his face and sleepy-looking, grave expression to Alice—a fleshy oval of a face, were it not for this expression, accusatory even in its plaintiveness, irritated even in its wordless sufferance, and, taken as a whole, somehow crippled—whom Köves had of course seen a number of times before in the South Seas, though up till now only from farther off, when he had given an impression that was more genial, friendly, and, one might even say, cheerful.

"I'm going to seat the editor here," Alice went on. "He won't disturb you." The woman's voice surprised Köves: breezy as she always was with strangers, himself included, the bravado seemed frankly to desert Alice in front of her "partner." He was even more astonished by the murmured entreaty that she directed at him:

"Try and amuse him a little," as if she were entrusting a seriously ill patient to his care, at which, on taking his seat at the table, nothing more amusing coming to mind at that moment, Köves for a start told him his name, and the man in turn informed him of his own, in a high, strident voice, like an operatic singer:

"Berg!"—snippily, sternly, and yet somehow still sonorously: it was already known to Köves, of course, along with the usual dismissive waves of the hand and expressions of commiseration accorded Alice by common consent, whenever the South Seas' regulars mentioned the name—if it was mentioned at all—among themselves.

"What am I going to have for supper tonight?" he said and then turned to Alice, clearly complying with her entreaty beforehand by giving a smile that was more intimate and ready to joke, and it seemed the waitress too immediately played along with the game:

"Cold cuts," she said.

"What's that when it's at home?" Köves enquired.

"Bread and dripping with spring onions," Alice replied. Then, turning to Berg, who did not seem to be in the least amused, and maybe had not even heard their banter (his head was bowed as if he had dozed off to sleep again), she asked him in a softer voice which sounded almost anxious:

"Would you like a petit four?" at which Berg again lifted his lethargic, accusatory expression at her:

"Two!" he said. On that note, the woman went off, while Berg, turning to Köves, who now felt for the first time the gaze of that distracted, yet somehow still discomfiting look being directed at him, commented:

"I'm fond of sweet things!" in a sonorous, matter-of-fact tone from which Köves nevertheless reckoned he could pick out an apologetic note:

"I'm quite partial to them myself," he found himself saying offhand, and idiotically of course (it seemed that some of Alice's incomprehensible discomposure must have rubbed off on him).

Still, it seemed as though this had aroused in Berg some interest toward him:

"Journalist?" he asked.

"Yes," said Köves. "But I've been fired," he added promptly, to preempt any possible misunderstandings as it were.

"Well, well!" Berg remarked. "Why was that?"

To which Köves, breaking into a smile, responded:

"Can anyone know?"

"One can," Berg said resolutely in his high voice. So that Köves, plainly surprised by an answer of the sort which was so uncommon there, said, shrugging his shoulders with a slightly forced lightheartedness:

"Then it appears you know more than I, because I don't know, that's for sure."

"But of course you know," said Berg, seemingly annoyed by the contradiction. "Everybody knows; at most they pretend to be surprised," and here a distant memory was suddenly awakened in Köves, as if he had already heard something similar here before.

Their conversation, however, was interrupted for a while by Alice's return. She set down the petits fours in front of Berg, whereas Köves was given rissoles, two sizeable discs, with potatoes and pickled cucumber, Alice clearly being of the opinion that Köves could stuff himself cheaply on that. Although not slow in responding with a grateful smile, in reality Köves could hardly wait for them to be left alone:

"Could it be that you too were kicked out?" he asked, because he seemed to recall having heard something of the kind about Berg, though he did not remember precisely, of course, for in the South Seas, as Köves had begun to notice bit by bit, people knew everything about everybody and nothing about anybody.

It seemed, though, that Berg, too, was sparing with accurate information:

"You could put it like that," was all he replied, nibbling the pink icing off one of the petits fours and placing the pastry base back on the plate.

"And"—it went against his practice, but this time Köves, for some reason, did not wish to concede the point—"do you know why?"

"Of course I do," Berg said coolly, resolutely, indeed even raising his eyebrows slightly as though exasperated by Köves's obtuseness. "Because I was found to be unsuitable."

"For what?" asked Köves, who in the meantime had likewise tucked into his supper.

"What I was selected for." Berg bit into the second petit four, which was chocolate-coloured though of course it did not contain chocolate, just a paste that resembled it.

"And for what were you selected?" It seemed that Köves, in his bewilderment, was unhesitatingly adopting Berg's curious ways with words.

"What I am suited for," came the answer, with the same effortlessness as before.

"But what are you suited for?" Köves kept plugging away.

"You see," Berg's face now assumed a ruminative expression, not looking at Köves, almost as though he were not talking to him but to himself: "that's the point. Probably for everything. Or to be more precise, anything. No matter. Presumably I was afraid to give it a try," and, returning to the real world as it were, Berg now looked around the table with a searching gaze until his eyes alighted on the serviettes, on one of which he proceeded to wipe his fingers, which were clearly sticky from the petits fours. "And now we shall never know," he continued, "because I have been excluded from the decision-making domain."

"How was that?" Köves asked.

"By recognizing the facts," said Berg, "and the facts recognizing me."

There was a clattering: Alice carried away a number of plates and sets of cutlery from the stock piled on their table, with Berg closing his eyes, as though the woman's scurrying around and the attendant skirmishing were a cause of physical agony, while Köves made use of the opportunity to ask for a glass of beer from Alice, who, leaning over the table and articulating as if she were speaking to a deaf-mute, asked Berg:

"Aren't you thirsty?" to which Berg shook his head, his eyes still shut, his face anguished, now somehow childishly imploring, merely held up two fingers, at which Alice hesitated a bit:

"Won't that be too much?" she asked, at which Berg folded one finger down, to leave just the index finger raised beseechingly upright.

"Fine," the woman said after some further reflection; "You'll upset your stomach," as she hurried off. Köves, who by that point could hardly wait to make a remark, was at last able to trot it out:

"That all sounds very interesting, but I don't quite understand."

"What was that?" Berg opened his eyes, having visibly forgotten what they had been talking about before.

"What do you mean," Köves was growing impatient, "by the facts recognizing you?"

"I said that?" Berg asked.

"You did," Köves urged, rather like a child waiting for the next instalment once a story has been begun.

"No more," said Berg, and now cracking a smile, as if he were seeking to tone down his words with the smile, "than that I am just like a certain gentleman who tasted vinegar."

Impatience was gradually beginning to curdle into irritation for Köves. "I don't know who you're talking about."

"It's not who I'm referring to that matters," said Berg, "but what he said."

"Well then," Köves pushed, "what?"

"That all this be accomplished." Berg smiled, whereas Köves, in whom the last vestiges of politeness were swept away by this smile, contrived in its raggedness, and this way of talking, with its riddling and quackery, and who was now aroused to unconcealed exasperation, remarked almost aggressively:

"It's all very well that the person in question said that, but you—forgive me!—you are sitting here, on a comfortable café seat, and you're not sipping vinegar but scoffing petits fours, and with great relish too, as I can see."

Berg, though, was not perceptibly in the least put out by Köves's irritation, if he even noticed it:

"Don't blame me for that," he said, almost appeasingly. "They seem to have forgotten about me."

"Who has?" Köves regained his self-control, all that was left of his irritation being an unspoken aversion, though that aversion was somehow still thirsting to be satisfied. His question, however, was succeeded by silence, and Köves had given up on an answer—he had also nearly polished off his supper and was hankering only for the beer that he had ordered—when suddenly, in a sonorous tenor voice, his head bowed so that Köves could hardly see his face, Berg started to speak after all:

"In the room where they run through the list of names, from time to time, and they reach my name, which is quite soon, given that my initial is B, someone will cry out: 'What! Is he still around?! Let's get rid of him.' His colleague will just wave that aside, saying, 'Why bother?! He'll snuff it of his own accord anyway!'" at which point he looked up suddenly, though not to look at Köves but at a small dish Alice had set down in front of him, this time with a white-coated petit four on it, while Köves got his beer and promptly emptied it in one draught. Whether it was because of the drink going to his head, or because the question, against his will, had been ripening in his head and now wanted to pop out, he asked smilingly, like someone who, purely for the fun of it, of course, was going along with the game:

"And what they will decide in that room about me, for example, do you suppose?"

"You see, that's the big mistake people generally make." Berg too now smiled, and all at once everything strange now peeled off him (or maybe it was precisely his strangeness which had now become familiar to Köves), though he was suddenly struck by the queer, albeit possibly deceptive hunch that Berg was also a foreigner—who knows, possibly an older compatriot who had fetched up there longer ago and therefore knew the ropes better than he did. "It's you who has to decide," Berg went on. "Here they merely give you the opportunity, and then what they do in the room is take cognizance of your decision."

"And do you suppose," the scene that Berg had, as it were, painted for him seemed rather incredible, yet—possibly through its very vividness—it still gripped his imagination, "do you suppose that such a room really exists?"

"It may be that in reality it doesn't exist," Berg shrugged his shoulders almost absent-mindedly, "But the possibility exists. And the worry is: What if it exists after all, and adding to that the uncertainty over whether it does, indeed, exist?—that's enough."

"For what?" Köves asked.

"To permeate every single life."

But Köves was not satisfied with that answer:

"It's not enough for me," he said. Then after an interval, pensively and showing his puzzlement in confidence to Berg, he noted, "I don't see any method here."

"That is precisely what is methodical about it," Berg countered immediately, his face twitching slightly as if he were offended by Köves's doubts.

Köves, however, resolved that he was not going to be won round as easily as that:

"The fact that I don't see it," he asked, "or that it is unmethodical?" Berg's response to which:

"The two together"—only dissatisfied him even more.

"That is just an assumption, he said, "empty words, no evidence. It lacks something…," Köves searched for the word. "Yes," he eventually said, "it lacks life."

"Life?" It was now Berg's turn to look surprised. "What's that?" Köves was frank in quietly admitting:

"I don't know." But he added straightaway: "Perhaps no more than that we live." Glimpsing in the corner of his eye that the man in the uniform was taking his leave of Sziklai, and Sziklai was already searching round for him, Köves suddenly got up from the table:

"I'll see you!" he said, to which Berg nodded without a word, plainly not seeking to hold him up, whereupon he hurried over to Sziklai and beheld, with a warm, cosy feeling, the way his friend's face was transformed by the laughter which was wrinkling his countenance:

"I've joined the fire brigade!" Sziklai relayed his news.

"How's that?" Köves joined in the laughter as Sziklai related that the "guy" with whom he had been "negotiating" just beforehand was the city's deputy fire chief, whom he, Sziklai, had got to know quite some time before:

"When I was with the paper, I did him a few favours," he said. "At the fire brigade they have now woken up to the fact that fighting fires is actually a daring, hazardous and heroic calling that the public at large, and even the firemen themselves, are not fully alive to: they just put out fires, but in effect without being aware of what they are doing. In short, every trick of the letter, the word and conceptual impact has to be mobilized to awaken a sense of self-esteem in them, and public esteem toward them, to which end they would be willing, moreover, to allocate a substantial sum of money, if they were able to find an appropriate expert."

"Which would be you?" Köves enquired.

"Who else?" Sziklai laughed. "Born for it, I was." The guy, he related, offered him the rank of lieutenant, but he would only have to wear the uniform on official and festive occasions.

"I have a hunch," he mused, "that for him I've come at just the right moment."

"How's that?" Köves asked.

"Because I've been fired and it's the only chance I've got," explained Sziklai. "Don't you see?" he looked at Köves, at which Köves admitted:

"Not exactly."

"Get away with you!" Sziklai fumed. "They need the publicity, they have the cash for it, money to burn, but he can't get at it directly, so what do you think he wants?"

"Aha!" Köves said, just to be on the safe side, and:

"There you are!" Sziklai too finally regained his composure. "Now all we have to do is find something for you," he continued.

"Me?" said Köves, "I'll find a job tomorrow."

"Where's that?" Sziklai was surprised, with Köves replying:

"Anywhere," and recounting that two men had been asking

after him. "They were from customs," he added. Sziklai scratched his head:

"Yikes!" he grimaced. "Let's try to think it over," he suggested, though Köves reckoned:

"There's nothing to think over," and Sziklai had to concede, albeit grudgingly, that he was right.

"All that worries me," he fretted, "is that you're going to vanish, that you'll be lost to me in the depths of somewhere."

And as if the smile with which Köves had greeted his words were bearing out his anxieties even more emphatically, he exclaimed:

"And what's going to become of the comedy?!" Yet evidently, even now, he could not have read anything encouraging from Köves's expression, because he went on: "I won't forget about you; I'll definitely find something for you sooner or later," he hastened, agitatedly, to assure him. Köves expressed his thanks, and they agreed that "whatever might happen" they would continue to meet there, in the South Seas, after which Köves said good-bye, saying he wanted to get up early the next morning, paid Alice for his supper, then came to a halt for a moment by the exit, because at that very moment the revolving door spun and in came Tiny, the pianist, who greeted Köves with an expansive and overdone gesture.

"Which bench," Köves asked after returning the salutation, "will you be gracing with your presence tonight?"

"None," the pianist said: he looked more uncared-for than usual, his face shone greasily, his polka-dot bow tie was missing, and Köves caught a sour whiff of alcohol.

"Are you not worried any longer about being taken away?" asked Köves.

"Sure I am," the musician replied, "but I'm even more worried that I'll get rheumatism!" at which, mouth open wide, he laughed long and loud at his own joke—if that's what it was and he was not speaking in all seriousness—as if he never wished to stop, during which Köves noticed that there were a number of gaps between his long teeth, which was a rather belated observation, or so he thought, considering that he had once spent a whole night in his company.

CHAPTER FIVE

Matutinal intermezzo

One morning when Köves hastily pulled the front door to behind him (in reality it was closer to dawn, as nowadays Köves was working in a steelworks, and the factory was far away, so Köves always ought to have set off from home earlier than he did), he was brought to a standstill by an unusual clamour in the normally still stairwell. Sharp, explosive sounds prised at and reverberated against the walls: the innocuous barking of a dog, but magnified to an intolerable pandemonium by the resonant stairwell, and in the turn of the stairs above Köves there now appeared a ruddy-cheeked face in a frame of snow-white hair. Köves's first sensation—no doubt the product of ceaseless dashing around, which was gradually making him blind to his surroundings and view every chance event, whatever its nature, as representing merely another obstacle—was one of frugal grouchiness: he would now have to waste some of his precious time on unavailing courtesies. Even so, the old fellow's garb almost brought a smile to his face: although the promise of a sweltering day ahead had already crept into the closed space of the stairwell, the elderly gentleman was wearing heavy walking boots, thick woollen socks, shorts, and a windcheater, with a large rucksack pressing down on his shoulders, a heavy suitcase in one hand, and the other clutching his dog to his chest, and on spying Köves the dachshund instantly started barking again, while his tail, that animated spokesman of canine delight, drummed like a rain shower on the windcheater's fabric. Köves was just about to move on, a perfunctory greeting on the tip of his tongue, when two other men attracted his attention. They were behind the old fellow and were young, each of them also carrying a suitcase, doubtless not their own but the old fellow's— they were travelling cases of sorts, flaunting on their sides the faded remains of gaudy stickers; Köves was sent off into a daydream on spotting on one of them surf and the sun-shaded terrace of a bathing resort hotel—clearly assisting him, forming a single, cohesive group, so that Köves might well have taken them for the old fellow's porters had he not noticed the uniforms they were wearing and their sidearms.

It was too late for Köves to hurry down the stairs in front of them as if he had not seen them, or perhaps to give voice to some degree to what he felt, along with a disapproving shaking of the head; nor could he jump back into the apartment (the idea of doing so fleetingly crossed his mind, but Köves would have considered that bad manners, for want of a better phrase on the spur of the moment); then again, of course, the paralyzing effect of surprise could have played a part in his just standing there, frozen, rooted to the spot.

The old fellow, who at first, it seemed, had wanted to pass him without a word—and that would have been the best as Köves, with hardly any loss of time, would have been able to hurry down straight after them and race out of the entrance hall and on to the tram stop, in blind haste, so to speak—all at once now came to a standstill after all, and partly by way of an explanation, partly just a little, perhaps (although quite likely it only came across like that to Köves), by way of an apology, yet also, at one and the same time, as if he were calling on Köves to act almost as a witness to his case, spoke in his wooden voice, which was even less sonorous than usual:

"So, it's come to this, Mr. Köves."

Köves was just about to ask something (though as to what, he didn't know, of course, as this was hardly the place for questions: he might at most have wished the old fellow good luck, if that had not sounded absurd even before he could get it out), but instead one of the customs men broke the silence, and although Köves didn't make a precise note of his words the gist of them was that the old fellow should stop "loafing around" and "get a move on." He even raised a free hand, and Köves became seriously alarmed: for him to become a passive onlooker to an act of violence was something which—or so Köves felt, at least at that moment—would be too much for him.

Yet nothing happened, whereas the old fellow, as though suddenly awakening to the strengths residing in his defencelessness, went on unperturbed:

"Fortunately, I've been permitted to bring my dog along," and he gave a wry smile, as though that were now the sole concession granted him in life, and he should be thankful for even that. The dog, as though sensing they were talking about it, started to wriggle in the old fellow's arm, barking to be set down on the ground, wanting to get at Köves's feet, while the customs men looked impatient (they may have feared that the yapping might draw people out of the apartments, on top of which it could not have been fully in line with regulations for them to be hauling the old fellow's luggage after him like servants: no doubt they had been constrained to do it solely by their haste, for who knows what sort of night, and how much work, lay behind them, or who may have been hurrying them along in turn, as a result of which the second customs man, in irritation, which seemed to be intensified by his inability to do anything with Köves present, told the old fellow off for speaking when he was forbidden to do so, while the first one, by way of underlining the point as it were, swung round to address Köves:

"And who are you?" At which Köves started slightly: he was suddenly beset by a vague feeling that his negligence could land him in trouble, even though he had no idea what act of negligence he may have committed—besides being there, of course.

In the manner of someone in whom resentment at being intimidated finally prevails over the fear in itself, he flung his reply back at the Customs man in such a way that he himself was unsure whether he was on the attack or defence, or simply telling the truth:

"Who am I? Nobody!" He was just about to add that it was sheer chance that he had stepped out of the door at that moment, but, even though it fully accorded with the truth, he vaguely felt that would be a form of betrayal vis-à-vis the old fellow, as if he were meaning to say that he, Köves, had nothing to do with the whole business, though as far as that goes it was again no more than the truth, of course.

He therefore said:

"My name is Köves." Tossing in, with an added disparaging edge: "A worker," even though he himself did not know what the reproach covered, or to precisely whom it was addressed, so that in all likelihood it went unnoticed.

After that Köves was further held up on the steps for long minutes while he fumbled uncertainly in his pockets, as if he were searching for something that he just could not lay his hands on—his cigarettes, perhaps, although of late he had given up smoking—and in the meantime the whole stairwell around him was filled up with quiet rustling: it may have been his fraught imagination playing tricks on him, but Köves fancied he could pick out a quiet clicking of keys in locks, a cautious clumping of windows being shut, until he heard from the street the dull thuds of suitcases being tossed up onto the back of a truck, followed by the rumble of a truck engine, at which Köves was finally able to scurry down the stairs and sneak out of the entrance hall, and warily at that, lest the janitor notice him and happen to suppose he had seen something.

Accident. Girlfriend

That morning, Köves made his way alone along a by now deserted street from the tram toward the steelworks; at the gates, the head gatekeeper asked him sternly, as if he had never seen him before (which might have been the case, of course, given the number of workers in the factory), who he was looking for, while Köves, perhaps in the irrational hope that he might sneak past without attracting attention, tossed out while he was still in motion:

"A worker from the machine shop," flashing toward the gatekeeper the entry permit with his photograph that he had been given not long before.

"You're late, you mean," the gatekeeper stated, blocking Köves's path and taking his card away from him so as to note down the details for the report he would have to file on Köves's late arrival, whereas Köves—well aware that lateness was treated severely, almost more severely, in his experience, than work itself, as if some general inclination (or its lack) could be deduced from it—tried pleading, albeit without much conviction:

"Not by a lot," which only obliged the head gatekeeper to look at the clock.

"Three minutes," he said, stepping into his glass box and sitting down at the desk, whereupon Köves, who remained standing in the doorway and rested against the frame as if he were already tired out, badly and massively tired, though the day had not even started, remarked, more due to his overwrought state than in any hope of pulling a fast one on the head gatekeeper:

"It wasn't my fault," though he immediately regretted it, because in response to the head gatekeeper's question:

"Whose then?" he was not really in a position to give an answer that would have dispelled any doubt. There is no denying that at that moment Köves would have been hard put to say whose fault it was that he was late: perhaps himself most of all, since, from the head gatekeeper's point of view, he, Köves, should undoubtedly have been honour-bound to push aside—whether politely or rudely, but in any event citing the punctuality expected of him—all those standing in his way, shake them off, cut his way through them, and set off for the factory, having given deeper weight to the thought that the head gatekeeper was hardly going to appreciate the emotions that had nonetheless been surging through Köves to detain him in the stairwell. What weighed still more heavily in the scales was the fact that Köves felt he was unable to set forth his reasons, would simply have been unable to relate to the head gatekeeper that morning's events, at least the way they happened—there, by the head gatekeeper's desk, where everything was impelling him to the crucial and the rational, Köves suddenly saw that this story was simply untellable. If he were to come out with it all the same, he would probably lose the thread, being forced into all sorts of evasions in the course of which his true feelings would come to light (those feelings now appeared to Köves as if it were not he who was feeling them and they were only importuning him like some evil-minded gang in order to make him their accomplice, although Köves was guilty of nothing, of course, unless of being late), so what he said in the end was:

"I got caught in a traffic jam," but fortunately the head gatekeeper did not notice his discomfiture (he had very likely had a shrewd idea what the answer would be, having heard a more than a few excuses of that kind over the years), and now that he had finished writing, he got up from the desk:

"You need to be prepared for that. The next time set off half an hour earlier," he advised Köves and handed back his pass.

Not much later, Köves was standing by a workbench and trying to file the upper surface of a lump of steel level, filing—so it seemed—being the key concomitant of the machine fitter's craft, for Köves had signed on at the steelworks as a machine fitter, even though he was not a machine fitter, and if he were to be a worker, he had no wish to be a machine fitter; Köves had his own notions about that, until of course he came up against the reality of it. In his mind's eye, Köves had seen a big, clean space and, in a well-lit place at one of the workbenches, himself, possibly in a white overall, surrounded by minute tools and tiny precision machines, where, possibly with a magnifying lens in one eye (the spectacle of Pumpadour, whom he had seen so many times in the South Seas, may have been somewhat instrumental in this), as he fabricated some tiny device that would then move, tick, whirr, or spin. It turned out, however, that it was useless his hankering after that sort of work, the factories in the city were mostly steelworks, and a steelworks devours manpower, so they were always taking people on, and at the employment office Köves was advised to sign on as a machine fitter. Köves was none too eager, on the grounds that if there were fitters, what was the point of a machine fitter, why not a locksmith, who—Köves imagined—produced locks, keys, fastenings, that kind of thing, and for whom a day would come when he could set off on a stroll round the city, or so Köves imagined, and from time to time peep into the entrance to an apartment block, maybe even walk round the outside corridor, and have the modest satisfaction of being able to tell himself that he had made this or that lock, or whatever, but there they were: those were objects that preserved, albeit anonymously, a trace of his handiwork. Köves had barely any idea about machine fitting, or at most no more than he had acquired once, a long time ago—long, long ago, it seemed to Köves, when he was still a small child—at a railway station, that having been a time when Köves took an extraordinary interest in locomotives, and at the station two black men (everything about them was black: their clothes, their tools, their faces, and their hands) had banged on the wheels of a locomotive with big hammers, prompting Köves to ask his companion (no doubt one of his parents) who they were and being told: machine fitters, and henceforth whenever machine fitters crossed his mind (and of course they rarely did cross his mind) he would visualize them as, so to say, fairytale monsters of that kind, a sort of cross between a giant and a devil. It soon became clear, though, that this was the only opening on offer at the employment office: what had been brought to Köves's attention at his first word, as a piece of good advice, proved, as such, to be more of a command for him, he only had to sign a bit of paper that—to Köves's amazement—was already waiting for him, completed, as if the office had already been counting on his coming by: of course it is possible that it was just some impersonal form onto which they would subsequently enter the precise particulars (Köves did not see clearly what they thrust in front of him then snatched away immediately after). Afterwards, he even haltingly brought up the objection that he knew nothing about the craft: never you mind, they had replied, they'll teach you within six weeks. Köves had left the office with mixed feelings (he was supposed to report early the next day at the steelworks); he felt a degree of incredulity over the notion that within six weeks he would become proficient in all the ins and outs of a craft which could hardly be simple, on top of which he shuddered at the thought that he might have to serve an apprenticeship among trainee kids.

As luck would have it, there was no question of that; the people around Köves learning the machine-fitting craft were all adults, some learning for one reason, some for another (in most cases the exact reason never emerged, and making enquiries, for which Köves had neither the time nor the inclination, seemed to be frowned on there), but in any event next to Köves a slim man with a moustache and a pleasant outward appearance was filing, engrossed in his work and silently, in shirtsleeves and a peaked cap of a kind that at most Köves might have seen abroad, had he been interested in equestrian sports, as well as gloves that an expert eye would have been able to recognize, despite the wear and tear, the stains and holes, as being made of buckskin. Had he been fired from somewhere? Or was some guilt burdening his conscience (like Köves's, too, in all probability), and had he become a machine fitter as a punishment or, for that matter, out of clemency? Or had he perhaps originally had an occupation which had now simply lost relevance, become unnecessary, like that of the sluggish, slightly burly figure who was filing away a bit farther off, whose closer friends would sometimes, within earshot, call "Mr. Counsellor?" Köves had no way of knowing.

People of all sorts were there, though, from the mysterious to the simple, from those who were upright to the more slovenly, indeed uncouth; there were even a few female machine fitters—on Köves's other side, for instance, there was a girl filing away, and highly competently too: Köves would occasionally watch enviously, yet at the same time with a tinge of smiling acknowledgement, how in her eagerness her lithe body would quiver all over, her headscarf would slip away from the glossy black hair, tiny beads of sweat would appear on her upper lip, and the girl would sometimes catch him looking, smiling the first time secretively, later on more boldly, and by now sometimes throwing out the occasional remark to Köves, to which Köves, his attention wandering, yet still like someone withstanding the challenge, would toss back some repartee. At other times, he would fasten his gaze on a pair of identical men—at any event both were stocky and balding, both were wearing brand-new blue overalls, which in Köves's eyes unaccountably looked like the external mark of some resolve, not unlike new penitents who don a monk's cowl yet, out of old habit, still get it made by their own tailor, filed away with dour assiduity: they were there in the morning, they disappeared in the evening, and they spoke not a word either to others or to each other; Köves heard that they had been dismissed from somewhere, but they considered that this had been a blunder and were now waiting as machine fitters for light to be cast on that blunder, and the reason they were so guarded was that they were afraid a fresh blunder might befall them, or even that they themselves might commit one.

In short, Köves was making do there (to some extent, being present as if he was not present at all, or as if it was not he who was present: an illusory feeling, since it was he after all), and he had already been touched to cheery wonder by the obscure minor delights of a worker's life: those of the lunch hour, the end of the shift, even of a job of work well done, though the latter was not entirely unalloyed, given that, to tell the truth, Köves had little success with the file; he would never have believed that to smooth a lump of steel immaculately level could be so beyond his powers. Köves regarded filing as almost a matter of honour, and it had got to the point that he now dreamed about it: he stood transfigured at the workbench, iron filings falling from under the file in a flurry of grating, scraping noises, but to no avail, as the foreman—a stout, flaxen-haired man who walked up and down good-naturedly, though somewhat lethargically, among the people bent over their vises and from time to time, with a gesture that was patient but showed little in the way of encouragement, would make an adjustment to the way Köves was holding his elbow or hand—with the aid of a tiny, gallows-like measuring tool was always able to point to some bump or hollow, disfigurement or crookedness on the lump of steel on which Köves had laboured with such furious care.

Köves derived some solace from drilling: that went well for him, one might even say splendidly, as unlike others he never snapped the bits, while he was also able to look forward to plate-shearing with definite confidence—they had tried it out that afternoon, with the gentleman-rider taking a turn at the metal shears before Köves and the girl after him, with the girl calling something across to him with a smile (Köves did not understand it: it sounded as though it were meant to encourage or spur, even urge him on, but in any case

Köves had thrown back some facile comment while he set the metal plate in position, then gave a self-confident heave on the steel handles of the shears, heard a cry and was astonished to see the girl's horrified expression, only after which did something warm pour down his forehead: it seemed he must have stood the wrong way at the machine, and as he had heaved it toward himself the handgrip had banged on his head.

As to what happened to him and around him after that, Köves was only able to follow it with a docile absent-mindedness, like someone who has laid down his arms and allows himself to be swept along by events (which are none too important anyway). Out of the hubbub which arose around him he could again clearly pick out the girl's appalled yet almost boastful exclamations of "it's my fault it happened, my fault for telling him to get a move on," after which a white handkerchief was held to his forehead—more than likely that too was the girl's. Köves stained the handkerchief quite profusely with his blood, then they lay him down on a bench to staunch the flow, and after that they got him to his feet after all, when they decided that he needed to be taken to the factory's doctor. As well as he could remember, Köves did not see the girl among those who accompanied him, having sought her in order to return the handkerchief, so he stuffed it in his pocket, even though in doing so he had no doubt daubed blood all over his pocket. They crossed various courtyards before finally reaching the surgery, where the factory doctor pronounced that, the shock aside (though he was not in the least bit of shock), there was nothing seriously wrong with Köves, at which the escort (somewhat disappointed, he thought) left Köves to himself with the doctor and the nurse working alongside him. With rapid, skilled movements, they carried out several procedures on his head (Köves caught the pungent smell of disinfectant and felt some stinging), as a result of which a plaster, rakishly slanted and not too large, ended up on Köves's brow, directly under the hairline. The doctor told him that he had "stitched" the wound and, enunciating clearly so that Köves, being a simple worker, should be able to understand him, made him promise not to touch the plaster and to come back for it to be treated in three days' time. He could return to work the next day, he added; the wound did not justify his being put on the sick list. Köves was then allowed to lie for half an hour on the surgery's couch, and by the time the half hour was up, the shift had also ended.

Köves nevertheless went back to the locker room, partly in order to change, but mainly so as to get a shower: he was able to wash down every day in the steelworks shower room, and there were times when he was in low spirits and felt that the only reason it had been worth getting a job there was for the sake of its shower room, though now of course he had to twist his head about so as not to get the wound wet. While he was dressing, several people patted him chummily on the back, after which he was soon joining the human flood pouring out of the factory.

At the gate, or maybe even before (he was unsure), Köves found that the girl had appeared beside him. Everything that happened to them after that Köves accepted, without any particular surprise, assent or dissent, as a well-organized and self-explanatory process, as a fact that had long been decided and only needed them to recognize it so they might submit to it, even though to some extent that still depended on them, and to that extent Köves might have been mistaken all the same. It began with some teasing (what lodged most in Köves's memory was the girl's opening remark: "What an elegant plaster!"), after which somehow neither of them boarded the tram but instead they wandered around in what, for Köves, was the unfamiliar realm of the outer suburbs, where they came to some sort of park, then all of a sudden Köves found he was strolling with a good-looking, dark-haired girl under the leafy boughs of an avenue of trees, and from far away, with a somewhat astonished yet indulgent smile he was beholding a strange and unfamiliar thing happening to him—precisely the fact that he, Köves, was strolling under the leafy boughs of an avenue of trees with a good-looking, dark-haired girl. He was nagged by a vague anxiety, perhaps a presentiment of imminent danger, but defiant urge kept welling up in boiling waves to give way to her and perish.

"Don't you have a home to go to?" the girl asked, and Köves, coming round from his dreams as it were, could only echo the question:

"Home?" as if he were surprised by the savour of the word, as well as the thought that he ought to be going home to somewhere. "No," he then said, and the girl, averting her eyes as though she were not even addressing the question to Köves but to the trees lining the street:

"Don't you have a wife?" she asked; that, it seems, is what interests girls everywhere and at all ages equally.

"No," he replied, and the girl now fell silent, as if she wished to be left on her own for a while with Köves's answer.

A little later she said:

"It's still early."

"For what?" Köves asked.

"To go up to my place," the girl responded, and the promise implicit in those words was distant enough for Köves to win time, but on the other hand sufficiently enticing to make him restive and spur him to some sort of action: Köves felt his arm moving and encircling the girl's shoulder.

Later on, Köves recalled a restaurant, a kind of beergarden where a third-rate Gypsy band squeaked and squealed stridently as a clutch of shirtsleeved men at some table or other defiantly bellowed some song, their faces red as lobsters, while at other tables solemn, overweight families sat stiffly, wordlessly, stricken in their incommutable presence as it were; it was here that Köves—his head now starting to throb, which may well have made him somewhat preoccupied—learned that the girl had come to the city from somewhere farther afield, against the will of her parents, who had intended their straitened peasant fate for their daughter, but she had run away from her parents and the future that had been lined up for her by starting work at the factory:

"You have to start somewhere, don't you?" she said, and Köves keenly approved, even though every nod he gave sent a pain shooting through his head. They later got on a tram which jolted along, taking them farther out of the city, where they alighted somewhere and the girl led Köves among squat, newlybuilt housing, which, in the uncertain glimmer of the sparsely sited street lamps already—perhaps on account of all the planking, sand heaps, and unfilled holes that had been left there—looked like ruins, until they turned in at a gate, climbed a dark set of stairs, and the girl groped with her key to open a door and in the hallway signaled Köves to remain quiet, which he, although not knowing the precise reason, accepted as self-explanatory, as if there was no way of reaching the place he and the girl were approaching other than stealthily. In the end, they slipped into a tiny side room, where the girl switched on a table lamp with a pink shade and Köves cast a fleeting glance across the objects which, so to speak, consummated the room's perfection: a cracked mirror, a rickety wardrobe, crocheted doilies, a grinning rubber dog sticking out its tongue under the lampshade, a line, discreetly strung up in a dark corner, from which hung a few pairs of stockings and items of underwear, an artificial flower poking up from a chipped vase, a chair, a table, and, above all, a fairly broad but springy bed which would presumably be squeaking later on, while his nostrils were assailed by the smell of poverty, cleanliness, some cheap perfume, and adventure, though he had a hunch that the latter was the sole volatile scent among all the other durable odours.

After which, the next thing Köves caught himself doing was making love—despite everything and over and beyond everything that he had shared in there, how was it possible that he had been made to forget that he was a man? All at once, he now awakened to his insatiable primeval thirst: it was as if he were seeking to douse his throbbing, burning member, yet finding it had plunged into bubbling lava, which burned it even more, with the girl, to start with whispering but then aloud, as it were, egging him on, Köves, like someone in whom a protective concern had suddenly awakened with the passing of the initial half-hours of recurrently erupting self-oblivion, so to speak, asked the girl:

"Aren't you worried about having a child?"

The look the girl gave might have been, if anything, more worrying for him:

"Why should I be worried?...," she asked, but she was unable to follow on as she had heard a noise (Köves did not notice it), and she now bid Köves to be quiet, quickly slipped out of the bed, her body white before Köves's eyes as she bobbed down here and there to search for an item of clothing, which she then draped round her shoulders before dashing out of the room, though her nimble feet soon brought her back, as if she did not wish to leave Köves on his own for too long in the bed, lest he be overcome with loneliness or a fit of absurdity and fear, and she uninhibitedly discarded her negligee, leaned over Köves, and switched off the lamp before nestling up to him with a total confidence which t slightly astonished Köves, like a discreet assault, yet at the same time also disarmed him.

"It was the old lady," he heard the girl say in the dark.

"Which old lady?" he asked.

"The old lady," the girl repeated.

"I see," Köves murmured.

"She was thirsty," the girl said, then after a brief pause added: "She has cancer; she's dying," the girl's voice rang firmly, almost optimistically, and on hearing her Köves himself did not know why he winced a little. The girl, though, as if she now wanted quickly to interpose herself between Köves and the questions that were assailing him:

"Don't worry, she's already gone to sleep. She won't disturb us any more," she whispered, and after some wavering hesitation

Köves meekly sensed that he was again gradually being suffused by a wave of ardour.

Köves is summoned. Forced to have second thoughts

Köves was called in; he was just in the middle of filing away when the foreman came over to him to say that he was urgently wanted upstairs, in the office. What sprang immediately to Köves's mind was his recent lateness, and although the foreman insisted that he should drop everything and get his skates on, Köves—who after all was merely a worker there (he could hardly sink much lower than that), but then it was precisely through this that he had attained his freedom, even if that freedom did not consist of much more than not having anything to lose—reckoned he was in no hurry to be hauled over the coals. First of all, therefore, he put down the file he was holding, shook the iron filings from his trousers and shoes by stamping a few times, wiped his hands on an oily rag with a few big, easy movements (the way he had seen real machine fitters in the nearby workshops do it), and only then, having as it were disposed of the more important matters, did he set off out of the workshop at a leisurely, ambling pace, responding to the girl's questioning look only with a wink of the eye: since the first time, Köves had several times spent the night at the girl's place, reaching the point that they had breakfasted together in the pocket-handkerchief kitchen and set off together for the factory, with the girl delighting in covering the short stretch from the tram to the steelworks hand in hand, although Köves usually found some pretext (such as an urgent need to blow his nose) for withdrawing his hand from the girl's. In the meantime, Köves learned that the old lady, whom fortunately they never encountered, was some distant relative of the girl's; the old lady had taken her in, and the girl looked after her in return, and when she died the girl would get the authorities to hand over to her the big room in which the old lady was presently living, and in point of fact, it would be possible to obtain the whole apartment, or at least there would be a greater chance of that if the girl had a family, and especially a child; to all of which planning Köves listened with approving nods, but always in the manner of a well-disposed outsider who, although of course not indifferent to the girl's life, was nevertheless not, by any means, a part of it, and yet it seems that this did not dampen the girl's spirits: she just smiled at Köves, as if she knew something better than he did. The previous night, indeed, Köves had not spent with the girl, excusing himself on the grounds that he needed to pay a visit on an uncle, but tossing and turning in his bed, unable to get to sleep, he had been surprised to find himself missing the girl. Yes, if he was a worker, then (so it seemed) he needed a wife; but then, on the other hand (it crossed Köves's mind), if he had a wife, that would turn him into a worker for good, not that it made such a big difference (he was already one as it was)—Köves no longer knew, in his restless half-slumbering state, where he stood even with his own affairs. In the end, the girl would be right: if she gave it time, that would tie him, without his noticing it, to the girl's life, and that in turn to the works and promotion, as they waited for the cancer-stricken old lady's death, and meanwhile along came children, one after the other.

Köves was supposed to look for the shipping department (the head of the department wanted a word with him), and for a while he wandered uncertainly along various corridors, until he finally spotted a group of men who, with laboured care, were lugging heavy crates out through a door, but the female clerk sitting inside (who, having first asked Köves if he was a truck driver, had found out he was not) informed him that he was in the wrong place: this was the haulage department; shipping, she said, was something different), at which Köves begged pardon, remarking that he hadn't known that.

"No?" the clerk was amazed. "Oh well, you'll learn," and with that gave directions to Köves, who, in another corridor, indeed on another floor, finally spotted, hanging one of the doors, spotted a sign that read SHIPPING, with below it, in smaller lettering: CUSTOMS MATTERS – PERSONNEL MATTERS – MATERNITY BENEFIT. Slightly nonplussed, especially by the "Maternity Benefit," Köves entered a relatively plain office, where, apart from the customary female clerk, there was a man with the outer appearance of a machine fitter, pacing up and down, hands in his pockets, with obvious impatience, though when Köves took a closer look, of course, he immediately noticed it was only his clothing that made him look like a machine fitter, more specifically the unbuttoned, faded-blue overall jacket, and especially the peaked cloth cap that, for whatever reason, he was wearing indoors in the great heat; under the jacket were a white shirt and a necktie, and though sagging slightly and wrinkle-creased, and despite the thick locks of greying hair peeping out from under the cap, he had a soft, youthful-looking face, his piercing blue eyes glinting at Köves as he stepped through the door:

"Köves?!" he shouted, and on receiving an affirmative answer almost set upon him: "Where have you been all this time?!" at which Köves, acting the dumb worker, shrugged his shoulders, having come when he was told to and being there now, but when it came down to it, of course, he could answer for himself in his own way.

"Right! Come along anyway, come!" The man seemed to relent, ushering Köves with a cordial gesture in through a side door marked, HEAD OF DEPARTMENT, which he carefully closed after them, then offered Köves a chair while he himself sat down behind a desk, directly in front of Köves. He stayed silent for a while, running his gaze keenly over the piles of paper and bundles of documents which were heaped on the desk, pulling out one or another to look at, only to toss it back testily:

"Well then," he eventually spoke, abstractedly, as he was doing that, and to Köves's astonishment in an undeniably friendly, if not downright intimate, tone of voice. "How are you finding it here, with us?" Köves, who on the spur of the moment did not know whether he should consider the cordiality inherent in the question an aberration, or suspect a trap in it, or even whether he should take the question seriously at all, hesitated a little before replying, as though he thought the formalities could be dispensed with and wanted to get straight to the point.

As nothing happened, however—the man was still hunting through his papers and seemed to be waiting for an answer—Köves said:

"Wonderfully," so as to say nothing, yet still break the silence.

"Wonderfully!" the man repeated the word, even Köves's intonation, while he pulled out one of the desk drawers and leaned over to take a look in it. "And here I am, unaware of how wonderful it is to be a machine fitter with us," which shut Köves up for good. "You're a shrewd one…," the man went on, pushing the drawer back in irritation and straightening up again: "Very shrewd…," and now his face suddenly brightened, but only so to speak incidentally, and just momentarily at that: most probably he had come across the document he had been looking for, and on the desktop after all, and he now immediately became engrossed in it:

"With your talents…," he went on, he was all but griping. "With your knowledge…"

Like someone who had suddenly concluded his dual activity and wished to devote his attention solely to Köves from now on, he now slapped vigorously on the desk and flashed his piercingly blue eyes at Köves:

"How long do you intend to laze around here?!" he almost snarled. "Did you think you would be able hide from us?! Tell me frankly, are you really satisfied here?!" at which Köves, who had been fidgeting on the seat in growing astonishment, was genuinely stunned. What was this? Was this a joke? He gets kicked out of everywhere to find they are only willing to take him on at a steel-works, forcing him, a mature adult, to become apprenticed as a machine fitter, and then they have the nerve to throw it back in face, as if it had been his idea to become a machine fitter? Had he not been driven there by necessity, in the face of duress? Had he not come here because he couldn't go anywhere else? And now here they were, all at once pretending that among all of life's boundless, rich parade of options he, Köves, had happened to choose this, as it now turned out, the very worst of all, and on his own whim at that? In what way could he be satisfied?... Köves had hardly given any thought to that so far; indeed, it had not occurred to him (he had not come to the steelworks in order to be satisfied, after all); but now he was being asked, even if it was hardly in all seriousness of course, and possibly was even expected to answer—for which he would still remain in their debt, of course—Köves felt that the entire time he had spent there was a single day, with its mornings and evenings maybe, but still a single, long, monotonous day, running constantly in the grey colours of dawn, that he kept scraping away at with his file as at an unerodable piece of steel, with its alternations of boredom and the deceptive relief of the end of the shift, and with the fleeting distraction that the girl offered, for which he had to pay with a feeling of belonging together. Köves had supposed that he was now going to live his life like that—in truth, of course, maybe he didn't think that, in truth he more likely thought that he would only have to live that way temporarily, for today, tomorrow, and then maybe the day after tomorrow, because it wasn't possible to live that way, though it had occurred to Köves to ask himself: Does man not live in a way he is not supposed to live, and then does it not transpire that this was his life after all?—at all events Köves was, in a certain sense, undeniably calm, and now that the department head was poking around at his composure, as he had been with his documents just beforehand, a hunch vaguely took shape in Köves that in that composure he had, to some extent, lighted on himself, perhaps more than in anything else before.

Now, therefore, he enquired, sharply, coolly, like someone whom emotion had made to forget he was a machine fitter:

"Why? You know of something better for me, perhaps?"

The department head, however, did not seem to be put out in the least by Köves's manners.

"Yes, I do," he smiled. "That's why I summoned you."

Casting a swift glance under the now part-way raised palm of his hand, which had been resting on the document that had been located with such difficulty, he continued:

"You're a journalist. From tomorrow you'll be working for the press department of the Ministry of Production, the ministry which supervises us," and he had maybe not even got the words out, or Köves heard them, when, slipping out of Köves, brusquely and harshly, as if his life were under threat, came a:

"No!"

"No?" the department head leaned over the desk toward Köves, his face unexpectedly softening and sagging, his mouth opening slightly, his eyes staring confusedly at Köves from under the cap: "What do you mean, 'No'?" he asked, so Köves, who by then had visibly regained his poise, although this seemed to have reinforced rather than shaken his determination, repeated:

"No," like someone shielding something tangible against some kind of fantasy. And so as not to appear like the sort of uncouth bumpkin who could not even speak, he added by way of an explanation:

"I'm unsuited for it."

"Of course not." The department head too had meanwhile calmed down and plainly resigned himself to the utmost patience he could muster in order to acquaint Köves with one thing and another. "Of course you're not suited: we are quite clear of that ourselves." There was a momentary pause as a slightly care-laden expression flitted across his face, then, overcoming his doubts as it were, he slowly raised his blue gaze and trained it straight on Köves: "That's precisely why we're posting you over there," he went on, "so that you will become suited," and now it was Köves's turn to lean forward in his chair in surprise.

"How can I become suited for something I'm unsuited for?!" he exclaimed, making the department head crack a smile at his bewilderment.

"Come now, don't be such a baby!" he soothed Köves. "How would you know what you're suited for and what not?"

"Who but me?" he yelled, even more vociferously than before, "Surely not yourselves!" in his excitement he seemed involuntarily to take over the use of the plural from the department head, even though there was just one of them sitting facing him.

"Naturally." The department head's eyes rounded and one eyebrow shot up almost to the middle of his forehead at the sight of such ignorance. "Look here," he said, an unexpected tinge of gentleness creeping into his voice. The free hand which was not covering the document moved, stretching forward, and Köves was now beset with a vague feeling that the department head might be seeking to grasp his hand, though of course it could only have been his confused imagination playing tricks on him, it was too far away anyway, so nothing of the sort happened. "Look here, I could tell you a great deal, a very great deal, about that. Who could know what he's suited for and what not? How many tests do we have to go through until it becomes clear who we are?" The department head was warming to the task, gradually bringing the colour of more briskly circulating blood to his pallid features. "Upstairs," and at this point the hand which, just before, had been reaching forward was now raised, fingers spread, as if he were raising a chalice above his head, "in higher circles, they've come to a decision about you. How do suppose you can defy that decision?"

"But it's about me, after all," Köves interposed, somewhat unsure of himself, though not at all as if he had been persuaded, more because he was interested in what the department head was saying, yet he again seemed to be astonished:

"About you? Who's talking about you? What role are you marking out for yourself, apart from doing what you're told?!" And with his face now flushed like someone incapable of containing his enthusiasm, he called out: "We are servants, servants, each and every one of us! I'm a servant, and you're a servant too. Is there anything more uplifting than that, more marvellous than that?"

"Whose servants?" Köves got a word in.

"Of a higher conceptualization," came the answer.

"And what is that conceptualization," Köves got in quickly, as if he were hoping he might finally learn something.

The question must have been over-hasty, however, because the department head stared mutely at him, as if he could not believe what he was hearing, and then he again glanced at the document that he was warming under his palm:

"Of course," he spoke finally. "You've returned home from abroad."

All the same, he answered the question Köves had asked, though by now in a much drier tone:

"Unbroken perfectionism."

"And of what does that consist?" Köves, seeming to have already accepted that he was a journalist once again, yet was not to be deflected.

"Our trying ceaselessly to put people to the test." The department head at this point indicated, with a brusque flip of the hand, that they had exhausted the subject and should revert to practical matters. "Consider it a piece of good luck," he said, "that you've been noticed," and it seemed that his words had a sudden sobering effect on Köves as well.

"I don't want good luck," he said, now in the same dry, determined tone and with a feeling he had already said that before to someone, even if then he may have been even less well-armed against luck than he was now. "I want to be a worker," he went on, "a good worker. If I understand something, then...," he hesitated slightly, but then he must have decided there was little risk to laying his cards on the table: "then you can't trifle with me so easily."

The department head, however, evidently appreciated his openness, his expression now all goodwill, his voice ringing warmly:

"A good worker," he said, "is the last thing you'll be. Either you leave here or you won't come to anything. After all, you haven't even learned how to file yet." He fell silent, looked at Köves with his head slightly tipped to one side, then, with a friendly smile to balance, as it were, the harshness of what he had to say, he carried on: "In point of fact, we could dismiss you. You simply don't come up to the requirements, after all. However," he swiftly tagged on, "naturally we would prefer it if you were to accept our offer of your own free will," and here Köves was all at once overwhelmed by a bottomless weariness which had actually never left him since he had arrived there.

They exchanged a few more words, with Köves most likely also signing something, after which the next thing he noticed was that, as on so many occasions already during his stay there, he was leaving an office with unsteady steps, without knowing anything more than he had when he entered, and he thought, with a certain amount of shame, of the girl's beseeching, then uncomprehending, and finally, no doubt, astonished expression when he later packed his things together and left the factory without saying a word.

CHAPTER SIX

In a South Seas refraction

That evening, Köves turned up once more at the South Seas, spinning in through the revolving door and making a beeline for Sziklai's table, where he was sitting in exactly the same pose as when he last took leave of him, and a broad smile now brightened and then cracked the hard face into tiny shards, as if all he had been waiting for ever since was Köves's arrival.

"What's 'my literary talents' supposed to mean?!" Köves waded in, throwing himself down on one of the chairs without even asking, and the smile froze slightly on Sziklai, who had no doubt been counting on a more cordial reunion.

"What it's supposed to mean?... I don't understand...," he mumbled, his face still reflecting, on the one hand, the joy of seeing Köves again but now also, on the other, a touch of disappointment, whereupon Köves related what had happened that morning:

He had been handed his papers for the job at the steelworks and told to present them at the press department of the Ministry for Production, and without delay moreover, lest the greater part of the remainder of the working day be lost, and in order that Köves might be set immediately to work at the Ministry, should they see fit. Köves had rushed from one tram to another—the Ministry was near the city centre, a long way from the factory—as if he had been handed some extraordinarily fragile public property: his time, which he had to deliver perfectly intact to its destination, taking care, above all, not even to dream of pilfering any part of it for himself. This near-missionary feeling, as if it were not him who was arriving, or rather it was him, except representing himself, so to say—that easiness had helped him through the usual stumbling blocks with which he had to grapple at the porter's lodge in order that, ID card in hand, he should then make his way between the two customs men at the main entrance. Köves had raced, panting, up stairs and along corridors until he had, at last, found the press department, where it had turned out that he would have to wait as the press chief just happened to be dealing with something else. "He's in a meeting with the current chairman of the Supervisory Committee," disclosed the typist—herself busy now clattering at her typewriter, now reaching for ringing telephones—in a voice that switched to a more confidential tone after she learned from Köves what had brought him there. "I see," Köves commented, somewhat dazed, his face but then gradually recovering an intelligent expression, as though he were suddenly sobering up from a bout of intoxication and, with some primitive instinct, which seemed all at once to resuscitate the torpidity of his original nature, was already settling himself on what was, presumably, the most comfortable chair in the room. Now, of course, it would not occur to him, Köves smiled to himself, to rush the padded door; or if it did (as it had indeed just occurred to him), then not in the least with any disposition to act, at most the glint of a memory, an almost painfully exquisite memory that he had preserved of himself. What a child he had still been back then, Köves reflected, as though musing on times long gone. When had that been? Yesterday? Twenty years ago, perhaps? Ever since arriving in the country, Köves had always had a spot of trouble with time; while living it, it seemed interminable to him, but when he thought about it as the past, it seemed practically nothing, with a duration that might have fitted into a single hour, in all likelihood, the thought crossed Köves's mind, an idle hour at a twilight hour in another, a more real, one might say a more intensive life, somewhere getting on suppertime, when a person has nothing better to do, nor does it does matter anyway, and ultimately, it fleetingly occurred to Köves, an entire lifetime was going to pass like that, his life, on which he would eventually be able to look back with the thought that he could have seen to it within the space of a single hour, the rest being a sheer frittering away of time, difficult living conditions, struggle—and all for what? At that moment Köves would have found it hard to say what; it was more just the sense of struggle that lived in him, of effort, without being able to see more exactly, or at least suspect, the object, let alone the purpose, of that struggle, though of course it could have been he was just tired, as usual, his intermittently failing reason maybe only indicating his exhaustion, the toe-curling boredom of the struggle. Maybe his mind was wandering, although it did not escape his attention that a woman and, immediately after her, a man hurried out from behind the padded door and crossed the room heading straight for the door—so Köves noticed that she was a good-looking woman who, through her hair and probably also her dress, left him with a fleeting impression of the yellowish-reddish-brown coloration of ripe chestnuts, whereas the man, diminutive, dapper, and with a moustache, whose jerky movements seemed as to be explaining something, striving to detain the woman, who was hurrying off wordlessly, without looking back and, improbable as it was, he appeared to have a flower adorning the buttonhole of his jacket—Köves continued to keep his eyes on the half-open inner door, waiting for the press chief and the current chairman of the Supervisory Committee, who, for whatever reason, he imagined as being an elderly, sturdy, bald or silver-haired man. It seemed, though, that he was wrong: after accompanying the woman to the door, it was the fastidious manikin himself who returned and, for the first time, cast a distracted and, outwardly, in some way drawn gaze first at Köves, then at the typist, who now announced in a soft, impatient voice that this was Köves, "the new colleague," at which the man, a spasm of pain flashing across his face, asked Köves to "be patient for just a little longer," and then vanished behind the padded door, which meant Köves had seen the press chief after all, and therefore the woman who had departed just beforehand could only be the current chairman of the Supervisory Committee. Shortly after, the handset on the typist's desk buzzed. Köves looked at the typist, she at Köves, and Köves got up from the seat and headed for the padded door with the happy yet unsettling feeling that "their eyes met and they were in accord." The press chief, his lineaments by now fully composed, with conspicuous affability invited Köves to take a seat and, while Köves established that he really was wearing a flower in his buttonhole, in point of fact a white carnation, told him that he was delighted to be able to welcome him among his colleagues, which Köves heard with well-founded scepticism. He instructed Köves to see to take whatever steps were necessary to ensure that his personal details were placed on file at the office—the typist would be of assistance there—and there was time enough to assume his new sphere of duties the next day: "We arrange for articles to be reprinted in the press," he said, and a doleful smile appeared on his face, making Köves think at first that maybe it was the "reprinting" that distressed him, possibly he felt it was unworthy, but he could have been wrong about that, because the press chief's long, brown, moustachioed face, seemed to carry some secret sorrow which nevertheless, at least in this mute form, sometimes sought to emerge, whereas at other times that smile lurked on it, even as he went on: "But what am I doing explaining all that to you, of all people, when I've heard all about your outstanding literary talents?" at which Köves jerked his head up like someone who had been roused suddenly from a long and tranquil dream with some frightening piece of news. "My literary talents?" He grew alarmed. "From who?" he asked. All the press chief said, this time substituting a mysterious smile for the doleful one, was "From our mutual friend; I can't say more than that…," yet Köves instantly guessed all the same whom he should suspect.

"Don't tell me you're not pleased about it?" Sziklai laughed out loud, but whether because he wanted to avoid giving a straight answer, or because he was curious about something else, Köves asked instead:

"So, you know him?"

"Certainly I know him," Sziklai replied, his eyebrows raised in amazement, as if surprised at Köves's ignorance. "All the same…," he carried on but then broke off what he had to say so as to order two beers, no: "two shots" in celebration of their reunion, from Alice who had hurried up to their table and, for her part, likewise shared their delight, commenting that "We've been missing our Mr. Editor badly"—"All the same…," Sziklai then picked up the thread of their conversation again, "How do you think you got out of the meatgrinder into such a classy job?"

"How?" Köves inquired curiously, but like someone already harbouring forebodings.

"By my organising it for you," Sziklai wised him up.

"You?!" Köves was astonished. "You mean it wasn't an arrangement from higher up?" He gave himself away, like a child who, driven by his own curiosity, starts taking a doll apart in order to see what is speaking in its belly; and having got going, he also related to Sziklai how he had been dismissed from the steelworks, and Sziklai laughed so hard that a tiny tear welled up in one eye and lodged, twinkling, in the thicket of wrinkles which had formed at the corner of the eye.

"An arrangement from higher up!" he choked. "Well of course it was an arrangement from higher up: I arranged it." He finally calmed down, adding that the press chief was an "old client." He had already known him during his journalist days, but he had "renewed contact"

with him at the fire brigade, he said, at which point Köves asked par-
enthetically how, now it had come up, Sziklai felt being with the fire
brigade, at which Sziklai gave a haughty dismissive wave:

"Superbly! I have them eating from the palm of my hand." Now,
he went on, the fire brigade was one of the Ministry for Production's
biggest clients, with all its orders for motor vehicles, pipes, fire lad-
ders, helmets, and whatnot, in large quantities, and of course—as
tends to be the case—goods at knock-down prices for the most
part don't come up to scratch, and then it was his—Sziklai's—job,
on behalf of the fire brigade, to raise the threat of public exposure,
whereas it was the press chief's job, on behalf of the ministry, to dis-
suade him from doing that, to reassure him with all sorts of prom-
ises, and the two of them generally managed to find ways of coming
to terms with each other.

"If you know what I mean," Sziklai said, winking meaningfully
at Köves.

"Sure," Köves retorted hurriedly, so as not to hold Sziklai from
telling his story, because his own case was of more interest than
any disputes between the fire brigade and the ministry. So anyway,
Sziklai continued, during one of their talks it had come to light
that a vacancy had arisen in the press chief's department, and even
though filling the position was not exactly of great urgency, still, if
Sziklai happened to have a possible candidate in mind, the press
chief would of course give serious consideration to offering the job
to the person in question, and needless to say, said Sziklai, he had
"jumped at the opportunity."

"I told you I wouldn't forget about you, didn't I? That I'd find
something for you without fail!" The one thing he hadn't known, he
anticipated Köves's next question, was where Köves was to be found,
given that he didn't have his home address:

"Which is absurd, old friend. Give it to me right away!" at which
Köves nodded vigorously as though that was precisely his intention,

he was only deferring doing so until later in order not to interrupt Sziklai; and Köves had also forgotten to inform him, Sziklai upbraided him further, where he had gone to work. Now, discovering his place of work was by no means as difficult as Köves no doubt supposed, he went on; he had simply donned his fire officer's uniform, gone off to the employment office, and enquired whether they had, by any chance, recently placed in employment anywhere an individual by the name of Köves, whom the fire brigade had reason to be interested in, and of course they had immediately been of service. Köves himself, however, Sziklai had not wished to notify for the time being.

"You were behaving so oddly when I last saw you that I was afraid you were quite capable of standing in the way of your own luck!" Consequently, he had merely given Köves's name and workplace to the press chief, and the press chief "set the matter on an official footing," which subsequently, having done the rounds from one department to the next, had eventually arrived at the steelworks in the form of a categorical order from higher up.

"Do you get it now?" Sziklai asked.

"Sure," Köves replied with a thin smile, like someone who admittedly might have been slightly taken in but was nevertheless not entirely oblivious to the funny side of the situation. After which Sziklai once again got Köves to repeat what the head of the shipping department had said, the things about higher conceptualisation, unbroken perfectionism, and putting people to the test, the whole situation as they had sat opposite each other and debated things in all seriousness, when he, Sziklai, and the press chief had already talked about and arranged everything ages ago, and having again laughed at the whole thing as if he were hearing it for the first time:

"You see, old chap, now that's a true comic situation for you!" his raised index finger drawing, as it were, the abiding lesson for the two of them.

Literature. Trials and tribulations

One evening, Köves bumped into Mrs. Weigand, the lady of the house; to be more accurate, as he was about to leave he was standing in the hallway when the woman called out to him from the opened kitchen door to please excuse that morning's events, though Köves— his hand already on the door handle—could think of nothing off-hand which had happened that morning (it had been a hard day at the ministry), but then it came back to him. It had concerned the boy, Peter, of course, or in truth more the fact that nowadays, since he had been working for the ministry, Köves had adopted a number of customs which pointed to being pampered; so, for example, he had taken a fancy—perhaps implanted by the girl—to having a break-fast before leaving the house, and the previous evening he had been in a shop to purchase some tea for this purpose, if not tea consisting of genuine tea, of course, at least not of the type whose fragrance or residual aroma Köves, at the moment of purchase, could almost sense shooting up from the depths of some distant and maybe non-existent past. In the morning, then, Köves had appeared with the tea in the kitchen: he seemed to have forgotten that he no longer had to get up at daybreak, as when he had been at the steelworks, so he had caught the members of the household in the kitchen just as they were in the middle of their own breakfast, so, mumbling some sort of apology, he was about to withdraw immediately, had indeed already mentally abandoned his plan, as the idea of not breakfasting alone but in company had not figured at all among the fantasies he had woven about breakfast, yet Mrs. Weigand protested so strenu-ously, invited him so warmly, making space for Köves's tea on the gas stove, that he could hardly back out without causing offence. In the end, breakfast was consumed in a tense atmosphere. Peter, who had in front of him on the table, a pocket-sized chess table with small holes in the middle of the squares into which fitted the pins of the pieces and, holding a nibbled slice of bread in one hand, moved the chess pieces with the other, only raised his eyes to the others to signal how much of a nuisance they were to him (though even so Köves noticed that behind the thick lenses of the spectacle the boy's beady eyes were red from strain, or sleeplessness, or possibly both), so that Mrs. Weigand gradually gave up talking, only whispering to offer Köves the sugar and the mud-pie-like bread, and was finally reduced to simply gesticulating behind her son's back to apologize and indicate her helplessness, to the point that Köves at times felt on the verge of laughing out because it looked almost as if the two of them were the children, with the forbidding and feared head of the family ruling over them with fickle despotism.

"I can't do a thing with him," Mrs. Weigand complained, spreading her hands then letting them drop again in a gesture of helplessness, uncomprehendingly shaking her pallid, peaked face, tipped slightly to one side, its pools now quite without lustre. "Since the chess competition got under way I simply can't do a thing with him," she reiterated to Köves, who recently had sometimes found himself trying to stitch his ministerial press briefings together at home (as a result of which the time had duly come, after all, when he made use of the table to which the lady of the house had drawn his attention with such pride on the day he arrived there, which, long ago though it had been, had nevertheless remained fresh in Köves's memory) and was forced to slam his pencil down angrily, he was so disturbed by the constant squabbling between mother and son which filtered into his room, especially the shriek of the boy's breaking voice, like steam whistling through a valve under high pressure, though who could tell whether Köves might not secretly have been glad to be disturbed and whether he was not seeking, by that whole business with the indignation, the gesture of throwing down his pencil and leaping up angrily from the table, not only to conceal from, and justify to, himself his relief, for there was no denying that the moment a person began to write, at least in Köves's experience, he would instantly find himself becoming mixed up in a whole tangle of unclarified and unclarifiable contradictions.

"Is it, perhaps, that the game's not going well for him?" Köves inquired, with a hint of gloating, it could not be denied.

"Not as well as he would like." The woman was still shaking her head as though to indicate that she herself disapproved of what she was saying: "Apparently, nothing has been decided yet, but one game has been adjourned and it's now a life-and-death matter that he wins the next match…," the woman fell silent, her pools hesitantly seeking Köves's gaze.

"Life-and-death?" Köves cocked an eyebrow in amused astonishment.

"That's what he says," the woman complained, seemingly already a little bit calmer for being able to talk.

"Child's talk." Köves broke into a smile.

"Child's talk," said the woman. "But then he's still a child." Köves was assailed by a sensation of a conversation held long, long ago being reprised.

"Well then," he therefore brought the conversation to an end, "if it's that important to him, then no doubt he'll win it," and if Köves, once he was on the stairs, felt it was exceedingly doubtful whether this really had been the appropriate solace to bestow on the woman, it was time for him to set off for the South Seas, partly in order to dine, but partly also out of duty, so that he and Sziklai might continue to turn over the matter of the light comedy, though as far as that was concerned, their brain-racking so far did not have much to show for it, comedy writing proving, at least for Köves, an onerous, depressing, and not in the slightest bit joyful labour. As in the past, when their friendship was as yet free and easy, unclouded by any common interest, Köves and Sziklai would sit every evening at their regular table in the South Seas, trade jests with Alice—although the waitress was never at a loss for a snappy retort, it seemed as if recently this had come at the cost of some effort on her part, with the tragic furrows around her mouth also apparently more deeply set than before, so it was sometimes on the tip of Köves's tongue to ask her why he never saw her "partner," Berg, around in the restaurant these days, but for some reason he did not put the question to her, with Sziklai's presence making him feel ill at ease on one occasion, while on another he would feel it was not opportune, and then again, who knows, maybe he feared what the answer might be—and amuse each other with their fire-brigade and ministry yarns, or single out a guest or party for comment, yet from the very first moment the comedy which was awaiting their attentions cast a shadow on their spirits.

"So," Sziklai's brow would darken on his arrival, for instance, an event that although expected nevertheless seemed to come as a surprise to him. "Given it any thought?!…"

"Too right I have." Köves would pull himself together, as though he had been waiting all along solely to be able to impart at last all the innumerable thoughts that he was aching to get out.

"And?" Sziklai's hard face gazed questioningly at Köves: "Have you come up with anything?"

"It has to have love as the starting point," Köves declared adamantly.

"Fine," Sziklai concurred, "let's take love as the starting point. Then what?"

"There's a boy and a girl," Köves offered apprehensively, as though that was about as far as he was willing to push it at that moment and was worried—most likely with good reason—that it would be far from enough to satisfy Sziklai.

"What happens to them?" he could already hear the impatient voice. "What stops them from being happy?"

And since Köves subsided into silence with an expression

which was intended to be pensive but in truth was more just dark, as of someone in whom murderous passions were already being stoked against the imaginary loving couple whom they were supposed to steer into a safe haven of happiness over the course of the comedy.

"Right, so you've no idea," Sziklai established, as Köves admitted with his continued guilty silence.

"There, there! No need for hanging the head," Sziklai relented. "We need to think up a good story," he opined.

"Indeed," Köves agreed.

"Let's try to think," Sziklai would propose, at which a longer-lasting, facilitative silence would settle in between them, and all Köves had to take care of was to preserve, like some sort of theatrical mask, a haughty expression of brightly musing yet simultaneously expectant communicativeness appropriate to light comedy, as though he would speak the moment the brainwave came to him, which could be in only a matter of minutes now. His gaze and his attention, however, would be freed to go their own ways, flitting about the room, coming to rest, every now and then, on a table or face—the Transcendental Concubine over there, behind her drained glasses of spirits, resting her elbows on the table and her chin in turn on her folded hands, her empty gaze seeming to be trained on Köves but without seeing him. Did she really not see him? Köves was somewhat troubled in dragging his gaze away from her: in truth, he had a tie to her through a rather embarrassing affair, though he had only himself to blame for that, if not the girl at the factory. There was no denying that memories of the girl kept flaring up in Köves; it was far from merely a taste for breakfast that the girl had quenched in him, for she had also awakened in him a wild animal in search of game. Yes, there were times when Köves longed for a woman's warmth, and not in the abstract but very much the practical, palpable sense of the word: longed for a woman's body-warmth, a woman's silkiness, a woman's sleekness, and not necessarily the girl's (whom he could have located and placated, of course, had he not considered that too big a price), for Köves's longing had no object; or to be more accurate, it was impersonal; or to be even more accurate, Köves longed for a woman, but no woman in particular, and that longing, or rather torment, might yet drag him into danger, Köves reflected. Perhaps it was precisely this that he was musing on that evening, Sziklai having gone away early, because he would have to get up the next day at dawn, because the fire brigade were holding an exercise, leaving Köves to linger solitarily over his beer, and while doing so he noticed that the Transcendental Concubine seemed to be sending him some message, first with her eyes, then by a slight quiver of a shoulder and hand; but when, with the deceitful smile that he laid out like a lawn, so to say, to cover his twinges of crude voracity, Köves got up and went over to the woman's table, she appeared to be outraged all of a sudden:

"What's the idea?!" she asked in her strangled, hoarse voice. "That you can simply come over here and take a seat at my table just like that?!" thus forcing on Köves a cheekiness he was reluctant to affect:

"Why, anything against it?" he asked provocatively. At bottom, there wasn't, so Köves took a seat; he even ordered several rounds of slivovitz and got slightly tipsy as he listened to the woman's somewhat halting disquisition about how the world, themselves included, did not exist, and existence was taking place somewhere else, the world was just an obstacle to existence, so it had to be done away with, because it was not reality, only appearance, to which Köves— his wit sharpened by the drink, apparently—commented, after a time, that it would no doubt be necessary to pay for the slivovitz in reality, whereupon the woman gave a sharp laugh and familiarly placed a warm, dry hand on Köves's thigh. And although the woman's proximity did much to ease Köves's burning torment (as though by now he no longer saw in her a stimulus, more an obstacle to the realisation of his longing for women), maybe the disconcerting incongruity manifested between her blonde hair, her softly contoured chin, and her determined, impudent nose nevertheless induced him to follow the woman on the night-time tram, then a series of streets right up to her dwelling. This was another side room, like all the other rooms on which Köves had paid private visits so far, and although it was true that this time he was not enjoined to be quiet, all the same the stuffy gloom of the hallway intimated the presence of sleeping people somewhere, but rather, on entering the room, veritably to freeze in horror, for in the glimmering semi-gloom (the room gained its mysterious illumination, as he later discovered, simply from the light of a street lamp on the other side of the road) there were phosphorescent eyes staring at him from every side, and Köves even fancied he could hear the heavy breathing of the beings to which they belonged, until the imagined sound was broken by a squeal of laughter from the Transcendental Concubine: "Bet that scared you!" she choked with laughter, toppling over onto her half-made bed. "Dolls' eyes," she eventually got out, but then her high spirits seemed to be replaced in a trice by a despair which seemed to be just as bottomless. "Yes, indeed," she complained in an odd, frail, baby-talk tone: "My landlady constructs dolls' eyes...," and it was only now that Köves noticed the innumerable as yet sightless dolls and teddy bears lying on the floor, shelves, and table. "For that ugly, fat man...," she carried on, her mouth set to whimper: "The Uncrowned ... You know him?" she looked up at Köves from the bed, the setting with all those fixed glass eyes revealing her to be particularly talkative.

"Of course," Köves replied.

"Then come closer," the woman burbled, and when Köves complied, once again, as in the restaurant, he felt her fervent hand on his thigh, only now a little farther up.

"Where's the bathroom?" he inquired, perhaps to win time, even if he could not know for what.

"What do you want from the bathroom right now?" The Transcendental was evidently none too willing to let him go, but since Köves, almost incomprehensibly even to himself, like a drunk clinging irrationally to an obsession which has occurred to him out of sheer whimsy, dug his heels in, it was again the accustomed, slightly hoarse voice which irritably snapped out: "So, go if you must! You'll get to it in the end!" In the bathroom, a trap stuffed full with towels, tooth-glasses, and a blotchy mirror, Köves—who, it seemed, really had drunk more than was good for him—deliberated on whether he should spend the night there by locking the door on himself, or preferably slip unnoticed out of the dwelling, but in the end, like an escapee who remorsefully returns to the site of his sins, he stole back to the room, where the woman—and it was more just her outlines stretched out on the bed that Köves saw in backlighting which was filtering in through the window—betrayed by the even, slightly whistling sound of her breathing that she had in the meantime—more than likely just as she had been: fully clothed—had fallen asleep. Köves waited around longer, in case she woke up (although, admittedly, beyond waiting, he did nothing to facilitate that), then on sobering up, somewhat offended and slightly relieved, yet at the same time ashamed at seemingly not having the strength to give way to his own weakness and in the end, having so stingily and fruitlessly preserved what had been there to be squandered, he left the dwelling nice and quietly, and the next day the Transcendent seemed not to recollect a thing: the usual spirits glasses in front of her, she herself with her usual distant gaze, was listening to what Pumpadour, flowingly silver-maned and passionately rugged of face, was obviously saying with some force, leaning close to her face, and she returned Köves's cautious greeting with no more than a fleeting, preoccupied, and totally disinterested nod. Köves likewise soon tore his gaze away from the musicians' table if it accidentally strayed that way, almost out of habit, in the hope of coming across his old friend, the pianist, whom he had not seen since the day he bumped into him here, in the revolving door of the South Seas. One evening—an evening when Sziklai happened to be running late—Köves was unable to put up with it any longer, so he got up and went over to the musicians' table and, having first begged pardon for the disturbance, inquired of a bald, slightly puffy-faced man with drooping bags under his eyes (Köves seemed to recall once hearing that he played a wind instrument, maybe the saxophone) whether he knew anything about the pianist. To Köves's great astonishment, however, the saxophonist seemed to have not even the slightest inkling who he was enquiring about, even though the pianist's appearance was hardly what one would call unobtrusive, on top of which Köves seemed to recall having seen him and the saxophonist many a time in earnest conversation, from which he had deduced that they must be good friends, or at least close acquaintances.

"He plays piano at the Twinkling Star," Köves tried to jog his memory.

"At the Twinkling Star?!...," the saxophonist registered surprise. "But there is no pianist there. The Tango String Band plays at the Twinkling Star!" As though to forestall any incredulity on Köves's part, he turned to his neighbour, a gaunt, dark-haired man whose shaven face carried a hint of blue and who exuded a whiff of hair oil: "Does the Twinkling Star have a pianist?" but the man was just as amazed as the saxophonist had been.

"How could it?! The Tango String Band plays at the Twinkling Star!" he said, looking at Köves with something that verged on indignation.

"There, you see!...," said the saxophonist, as though that had served to refute Köves definitively, so Köves quickly thanked him for so obligingly setting him straight and went back to his seat; he still saw the blue-shaven man passing some irritable comment to the saxophonist, who in turn spread his arms, pulling a face and shaking his head as if by way of an apology, and Köves sensed it was most likely on account of his importunity. A minute later, Uncle André, the Chloroformist, in his elegant dark suit, a long cigarette in his hand, passed by Köves's table, gracefully bowing his grey-templed head at Köves's greeting. Then, as if something had suddenly sprung to mind, stopped short and, with an urbane smile somehow at odds with the confidentially hushed tone of his voice, said:

"I heard you were asking about Tiny, the pianist, just before."

"Yes," Köves said, startled: he did not recall having seen Uncle André around when he was speaking with the musicians, though of course it could well be that he had not taken a hard enough look around. "Does that mean you know something, perhaps?"

"I do indeed. He was a very good friend of mine." Uncle André nodded, and although he had not given a precise answer to what Köves had asked, on contemplating the receding slim back, Köves was nevertheless left with the feeling that he had indeed received the answer to his specific question and could now only trust that everything was going as the pianist would wish and that he had not been hauled out of bed.

In short, as for stories—he only had to look around—there were plenty of those: he even related one or two of them to Sziklai, and at these moments they would chat in complete agreement, almost forgetting why it was that they were sitting together, until it would again occur to Sziklai:

"Anyway, let's get back to the comedy!"

"Let's," Köves would concur, resuming his sedulous expression.

"Let's at least figure out a decent girl," Sziklai encouraged him, and he explained that if he had a decent female lead character the comic writer would find that the "battle has essentially been won." In Sziklai's words, the girl needed to be a little ditzy but exciting, at once "unbearably capricious and adorably attractive," but by then it was usually getting to be late in the evening, so the girl would, as

Sziklai put it, be "put away for tomorrow," when they would assure each other, now beyond the revolving door in the darkness and stillness of the night, that they would meet up anew in the same place, the South Seas.

Continuation

Köves had better success with literature in the ministry, albeit not in what was strictly his field of work: Köves had no need of any literary talents for his work, though as to what talents were actually needed he never managed to find out. Köves spent his first days at the ministry almost exclusively reading, and more specifically reading the writings of his colleague, the other staffer, or to be more correct (this being his official title): the senior staffer, the press chief, with a somewhat pained smile and now with two flowers in his buttonhole, being of the opinion that these writings would serve Köves as a better introduction into the scope of duties that were awaiting him, and at one and the same time an example to be followed, indeed, he might say—and here the press chief's glance searched out the typist's, as if the two of them knew something to which Köves was not yet privy—he might say, an ideal example. Köves therefore began reading these written creations, which seemed at times to be some sort of report, at other times an article or perhaps an essay of some kind, all of which opened as if frenziedly seeking to inform the outside world about some piece of news, an event, or maybe an item of information which, in the course of the article, the author must either have forgotten all about or that Köves quite simply did not understand, and all the less so because right after the opening sentences his eyes would begin darting here and there, ever lower and lower, until they slipped right off the paper and Köves—to his great horror—all of a sudden caught himself having nodded off. Besides which, or so it seemed to Köves, the senior staffer—an aging, balding figure as it happened—had very likely started writing in early childhood and had been writing incessantly ever since, because carbon copies of his works, held together with paper clips, filled entire shelves and desk drawers, and if Köves's tormented gaze accidentally strayed onto the typist, perhaps to be cheered up by the sight for a fleeting second, she would instantly spring to her feet and, unbidden, pile up more and still more towers of the senior staffer's oeuvre onto Köves's desk, only to scurry back to her typewriter, on which she would be typing the senior staffer's dictation or copying one of the senior staffer's compositions that she had been handed to make a fair copy of. Even so, of course, the reading did leave some impression on Köves, a vague but at least uniform impression that, taken as a whole, reminded him of something Sziklai had said on the evening he had "joined the fire brigade." Essentially, or so it seemed to Köves, what they were concerned about here was much the same, with the appropriate modifications, of course: more particularly, it was as if people in the Ministry for Production had woken up to the fact that production was, it seemed, far from the natural activity that for a long time they had thought it was, but was actually an extraordinary, heroic undertaking, indeed vocation, that the public at large, and even the workers themselves, were not fully alive to; they just did the work, but effectively without being aware of what they were doing, and it was the senior staffer's duty—that is to say, now his as well, it dawned on Köves with a shudder—to awaken a sense of self-esteem in them, and of public esteem toward them.

There is no denying one day Köves realized that he was now not just reading but writing the senior staffer's reports, articles, and essay species (if indeed that was what he succeeded in doing, about which Köves was far from sure, as he usually did not understand, and therefore could not judge, the compositions that he wrote with his own hand, indeed brain). An unbroken stream of announcements came in to Köves or the senior staffer, to the press chief himself or the typist, about which, if they impinged on his sphere of duties (and everyone except Köves appeared to know precisely what Köves's sphere of duties was) Köves would be informed without delay. Köves would then have to go out to the locality (usually one of the steelworks) in order to check for himself the veracity of the announcements, which would concern some invention or performance, possibly the latest exploits of some paragon of production, and then to put in writing the outcome of that inspection—or to be more accurate, to put in writing what he ought to put in writing, though Köves was far from invariably clear what that was. It would not be so bad if he had to write about an invention, Köves considered: after all, an invention was a precisely circumscribed, readily describable fact of indisputable content, provided one was convinced of the genuineness of that fact and understood its objective essence. Except that it was far from sufficient, Köves had to realize before long, for him to be convinced of the genuineness of a fact, when that fact otherwise did not accord with what was considered there as being a desideratum, indeed requirement, of the fact (and facts in general); no, a fact, Köves recognized, was not something one could simply be satisfied with, and although he had heard much in the press office about the importance of the facts, he quickly realized that a fact was the least important aspect, much more important was how he viewed the facts, or rather how they had to be (or ought to be) seen, and what was more, what fact was viewed as a fact at all—generally it was here that Köves went off the rails, losing his control over a piece of his writing. For Köves these pieces of writing were a little like filing had been for him at the steelworks: the task appeared simple, nor was he lacking in endeavour, but all the same he was unable to do what presumably simpler-minded beings than he—a girl or a senior staffer, for instance—were able to accomplish without difficulty. What made Köves's position all the

265

worse was that whereas in the steelworks there had been the fore-man, who at least showed with his instrument where, how, and by how much he had gone wrong, there in the ministry he was totally reliant on himself: the press chief displayed such blind faith in him that Köves thought it would be hazardous, not to say the greatest folly, to shake it with his perplexities and questions, whereas the senior staffer took very little notice of Köves, and even on the rare occasion when he had to exchange any words with Köves, his gaze would wander off somewhere past Köves's head, as if he regarded Köves as some kind of transitory phenomenon that he did not con-sider worth closer inspection.

Consequently, Köves lived in a constant torment of uncer-tainty: almost every day he would produce a piece of writing, longer or shorter, which, as best he could, would be fashioned along the lines set by the senior staffer in respect of its syntax and an out-wardly meaningful obscurity, or rather he would keep on amending it until in the end he himself did not understand it, for as long as he was able to understand it even he could see it was meaning-less and therefore could not be good, or to be more accurate, could not serve its purpose—a purpose about which Köves was the least clearly aware of all, of course, though by the time it had been com-pleted Köves would be unable to decide whether or not it was suit-able, because he would not understand his piece of writing, and even less what purpose it served. So that when, one afternoon, the press chief, who had just returned to the office, whence he had left post-haste roughly an hour before—averring to the typist in passing that if anything urgent or of especially high priority were to come up, he could be contacted at the office of the current chairman of the Supervisory Committee, where he would be holding important talks—stopped behind Köves's back, casting his eyes over him just as he was toiling on that day's composition, Köves was startled like someone for whom the moment of truth had just struck. And when the press chief placed a hand on his shoulder and said to him, albeit in an undeniably amiable tone:

"Would you be so good as to step into my room for a minute?"

Köves got up from his desk like someone who, after much anguish, was almost relieved that he was finally going to hear sentence passed.

The press chief gestured obligingly that he should take a seat on the chair in front of his desk, but before complying with the tacit request, Köves, like a dying man who, with his last ounce of strength, is still thinking of his obligations on this earth, placed that day's piece of writing on the press chief's desk.

The press chief literally started back.

"What's that?" he asked.

"A totally new manufacturing process," Köves kicked off in a slightly lugubrious tone, "that…"

But the press chief immediately cut him short:

"Come off it!…," sweeping Köves's creation into one of his desk drawers. Then on seeing the look of amazement on Köves's face, an effortless little smile appeared in the general area of the moustache and, leaning forward slightly over his table, and in a voice that was lowered in friendly fashion as it were, he asked Köves with a conspiratorial wink:

"A new manufacturing process? Who's interested in such nonsense?!" leaving Köves, who on the spur of the moment didn't know what he should do with his face, the naked, uncontrollable thing which was constantly seeking to bring about his ruin (he would have best preferred to hide it in one of his pockets, or under his clothes, and then surreptitiously throw it away on the street, as one does when getting rid of a shameful, inconvenient belonging), broke into a faltering smile, but at any rate drew his eyebrows gloomily into a frown ready to be scandalized, as it were.

Yet the press chief now leaned back in his chair, adjusted his necktie, then with just a trace of a long-suffering smile and, his head tilted slightly to the side, came out with:

"I'd like to read out a poem to you."

"A poem?" Köves was astonished.

Then, as if to intensify Köves's surprise still further:

"My own," the press chief smiled as he produced a folded sheet of paper from the inside pocket of his jacket, which once again was freshly adorned with a small white-petalled bloom, and slowly—to no little horror on Köves's part—began to unfold it.

Turning-point. Passion. Back to earth

One morning, perhaps more midmorning, Köves stepped out of the front door and set off with a whistle, though there was no reason for that, the weather being overcast, with a cool wind blowing, and over the streets rose a cloud of dust (constant, yet at first glance it came merely from construction sites, with their proliferation of ruins, scaffolding, and obstacles of every kind) mingled with pungent smells, as though possibly (it was not out of the question) heralding the approach of autumn, conjuring up in Köves romantic images of bygone (perhaps never-were) real autumns of reds and yellows and crackling hearths, and awakening a whimsical longing for a light, soft, yet warm overcoat into the upturned collar of which, in one of those familiar acts, he might bury his chin—but anyway he set off with a whistle to his workplace, the Ministry for Production. To tell the truth, that morning Köves was not going to be exactly on time (the previous evening, he and Sziklai had spent a little too long weaving the still-nascent plot of their prospective light comedy, so in order to clear his head Köves had gone by foot across the city, which by then was sunk into a muffled night-time hush broken only, now and again, by an unexpected noise of scuttling, creaking, murmuring, or groaning, as if of audible scraps of a restless collective dream of those asleep behind the darkened windows, as a result of which he had got to bed late and simply overslept, though in view of the intimate relationship that had been built up with the press chief Köves could consider himself—unquestionably with good reason—as being in the rather privileged position of someone who would not get his head chopped off right away if he took certain liberties, provided he did not overdo it, of course. For notwithstanding the fact that Köves had barely an inkling about poetry (apart from an obviously critical year in his distant childhood, he had never written, or even read, any poems), the press chief seemed to trust in his judgement, because, after the first occasion, he read out his poems to him on a more or less regular basis; indeed, the previous afternoon there had also been a short story, or as the press chief himself styled it: "more of a prose ballad." No question, Köves's judgement was usually favourable: insofar as he was able to discern, the press chief's poems were mostly lyrical verse, and Köves generally did not understand much of their content, since they were either too short, so that they had ended by the time he had started to pay any attention, or else too long, so that by the time he was able to form an opinion about them the press chief's singsong voice and the sonorous rhymes would have lulled him into a pleasant, half-sleeping trance, as a result of which it was with a clear conscience that he was able to praise their allusiveness, their melancholic mood, their enigmatic atmosphere, and so forth. Even so, it struck Köves that there was a regular, one might say maniacal, recurrence of certain images in the course of these poems, for instance, the "fleshy calyx" of, as a rule, a "carmine" blossom which "thirstily imbibes" a dewdrop or raindrop "quivering" on it, or the fountain the jets of which "shoot" on high, sometimes irresistibly, sometimes like a rainbow, and goodness knows how else though always, at the end of a poem replete with rain, dew, drizzle, and every other conceivable kind of moisture. Undeniably, the task of listening to and, above all, discussing (or to be more accurate, praising) the poems represented extra work for Köves (the press chief would normally call him into his room "for a little chat" at the end of the regular working day, when they could not be disturbed by either the senior staffer, or the typist, and there was little likelihood of things that unexpectedly had to be attended to intervening), while on the other hand the press chief's confidence, which, whether justified or not, was in any event seemingly unqualified, inspired Köves too with courage, so that he would now set his diligent compositions down on the press chief's desk with a surer gesture, even if the consequent fate of those written works continued to remain a mystery to him, perhaps (he reflected once, with a touch of superior cheerfulness) the day would come when new recruits following in his footsteps would be edified by them, in just the same way that he had learned from the senior staffer.

He was therefore all the more surprised when, on getting to work that morning, he found the press chief, the senior staffer, and the typist all in the office (they were standing in a group as though they had nothing else to do that day other than, for instance, wait for him), and then his own expansive good morning was met, instead of by the expected reciprocation, by a frigid silence lasting several seconds, finally broken by the question with which the press chief greeted Köves:

"What time is this?"

Köves told him approximately, and not without some misgiving, whereupon the press chief—that morning again with a white flower in his buttonhole—asked:

"When does the working day start?" to which Köves (what else was he supposed to do?) specified a time-point roughly an hour and a half before.

"Where have you been up till now?" was the press chief's next question, to which Köves, who had of course not for the first time

officially set off for some steelworks (in reality he simply expropriated the time for himself, employing it for sleep or pottering about,
possibly even for private purposes, with no-one having reproved
him so far for doing so, the press chief least of all), replied that he
had gone off to one of the steelworks the first thing that morning on the matter of some extraordinarily important performance
results, or to be more accurate: he ought to have visited it, but he
had been prevented from doing so by certain reasons, very serious
reasons at that, in point of fact the matter of his health, as he had
awoken that morning to find that he felt dizzy and queasy, and he
may have had a fever as well.

"And are you feeling better now?" the press chief asked, and
after some hesitation Köves considered that even if he was not yet
feeling absolutely fine, at any rate it was better than earlier on.

"In that case," the press chief now brought out the hand that up
till then he had been hiding behind his back and which was clutching a sheaf of paper, and Köves, if he was not mistaken, was horrified to recognize his own writings, all the many, many assignments
he had written and handed over to the press chief since arriving
there—"in that case, try to devise some useable communiqués out
of this dog's dinner," with which he tossed the entire bundle onto
Köves's desk (for he had a desk of his own in the ministry), but he
misjudged the swing, or maybe he deliberately released the bundle
from his hand prematurely, so that the unclipped sheets drifted
and wheeled and flittered in all directions about the room, obliging
Köves virtually to give chase and gather them one by one.

While he was doing that, the press chief set off to see the current chairman of the Supervisory Committee for the purpose of
holding important talks, as he averred to the typist, whereas the
senior staffer likewise informed the typist that he was awaited in a
locomotive works on a matter that would brook no delay, and Köves,
who had by then been seated at his desk for a while, staring at the

untidy stack of papers that had piled up on it, all of a sudden became alive to a distinctly stimulating sensation coming from behind the nape of his neck—not a touch, more just a gentle puff, warm, exhilarating and fragrant, like an insinuation of the proximity of a female body. Köves hesitated for no more than a moment—it was not really a hesitation, just a cautious, as yet incredulous recognition—before raising his arm and, without even turning round, with unerring accuracy seized a soft, little hand which, in the midst of strange, and even to his ears alien, hiccuping and lonely sounds—it seemed the press chief's incomprehensible manner of treatment must have been telling on her a little, after all—she started not so much kissing as more like tearing and mauling him, like a hungry animal would a prey which has unexpectedly come its way. And while a light arm snaked round his neck from behind, and a pliant, warm, living weight fused to the nape of his neck, Köves practically sensed with his hair how sounds are formed within a female chest and rise ever higher as tickling vibrations:

"Poor darling!…," the typist said, or rather whispered in a deep, emotion-laden voice.

It still took a long time before Köves, that afternoon, was able to hold this creature who had been hiding all the while, up till then, behind a wall of taciturn industry, whom he had mentally compared every now and then to a smart, graceful, nimble little squirrel, but who, with a single act, so outgrew that humble simile that for the rest of the day Köves could only be amazed at his own blindness; nor did he remember anything else of that day—at most its length as they strove to avoid, rather than seek out, each other's looks, like people who have already reached agreement on the one essential matter, and now all that was important for them during these dreary hours until the time was their own was to spare each other, to quell their painfully mounting impatience, for they barely existed, and even if they did, they were never able to feel they were alone.

So that by the time he was able to take her arm—this was in a side street into which they each turned separately on the way from the ministry, hurrying along the pavement, keeping their distance from each other like strangers, until the woman finally looked round, slowed her steps and allowed Köves to come up alongside—the reined-back feelings had well-nigh cooled and died in them, rather like a limb going to sleep.

"My room's not far from here," Köves spoke almost morosely.

"Then let's go to my place, I have a whole apartment," the typist responded in roughly the same tone that Köves had so often heard her using on the telephone on office business.

Once the door had closed behind them, however, they had only just enough time to swiftly get out of their clothes, but not to make the bed as well: they sank onto the gaudy, threadbare carpet, snatching, tumbling about, panting, moaning, as though all they had been doing for centuries, no, millennia, was wait, wait and endure, oppressed and, even under the blows which battered body and soul, concealing within themselves, secretly and as it were slyly, a hope, however preposterous, that their torments would one day, just once, be obliterated by rapture, or if it came to that, that all their torments would one day melt into rapture, from which they would groan just as they had from their torments, for throughout their lives all they had ever learned, ever at all, was to groan.

As a result, in respect of the whole day and the night that later greeted them, Köves precisely recalled certain words, moods, touches, and various situations, but much less their sequence and connections.

"What actually happened between the two of you?" the girl asked, but whether that was in the office, in the street, or in bed, Köves couldn't say, because later on they did, after all, let the sofa down and got into bed in the slowly gathering twilight, as into a castle moat or a ship's cushioned casemate, perfectly safe from the outside world, and flinging their intertwining bodies about over and over again were nevertheless able to get even for the ill treatment they had suffered. "Did he take you into his confidence? Let you in on his secrets?"

"What secrets?" Köves asked.

"That's his way," the girl said. "First he pours his soul out to you, then he murders you..."

"All he did with me is read out a short story," Köves protested.

"What was it about?"

"It was nonsense. I couldn't even tell you if I tried," Köves shrugged his shoulders.

"Try," the girl implored, so Köves did try, though it wasn't easy, of course, because at the time he had not paid sufficient attention, and so now he was unable to remember much; what he was able to sketch most vividly, to the girl's great amusement, in which Köves fancied that he could detect some hints of impatience, almost of deterrence, if he was not mistaken, was his own alarm when, on the afternoon of the previous day, he was summoned by the press chief into his room on a matter that Köves had no doubts about for even a second and yet, instead of the usual folded sheet of paper, had this time pulled a whole bundle from his desk drawer.

"I've written a short story," he announced to Köves with a modest yet somewhat defiant smile.

"Oh good! A short story!" Köves enthused (in reality, of course, he was aghast).

"Perhaps," the press chief amended his previous words with a somewhat meditative expression, "I might better call it a ballad, a prose ballad."

Köves then related to the girl how the press chief had put on the eyeglasses that he rarely used, set them straight on his nose, pulled down with a few vigorous wriggles of his outstretched arms the cuffs of his shirtsleeves, which, it seems, had ridden up, smoothed the sheets of paper, cast another scrutinising glance at Köves, cleared his throat, then finally launched into reading out in an oily, sentimental voice, while he, Köves, who had by then acquired sufficient practice as to how to adopt the role of attentive listener, settled down with his elbows placed on the chair's armrests, the palm of one hand cupping his chin and over his mouth (thus allowing him to discreetly cover any yawns that welled up), and was mainly preoccupied with weighing up the quantity of sheets of paper lying in front of the press chief and meanwhile thinking uneasily about the promise made to Sziklai to meet up that evening at the South Seas at an earlier time than usual. He had consequently abjectly failed to catch the title of the short story, and likewise its opening lines: all he remembered was a fogginess about when the story took place, the total absurdity of its location, and the antiquated, tortuous, indeed (or so Köves considered) defective language of the tale. In short, it was about the press chief, or rather not the press chief, not a bit of it: the protagonist of the story, a "Wanderer" of some sort (Köves tried to call him to mind) who was roaming around a desert of some kind and all at once arrives at a tower of some kind (as to why precisely a tower, or what sort of tower, the typist should not ask, because that never became clear, Köves explained), and in the tower he spies a marvellous woman (come to think of it, it was more than likely the woman's singing which had drawn him to the tower in the first place, it occurred to Köves), who now came down to him and led him into her garden, though of course no indication had been given that a garden was to be found there at all. That was then followed by a lavish, one might even say lush, description of the garden, Köves retailed, the lawn with its bushes, the mirror-smooth little lake, the fragrant, carmine, fleshy-petalled blossoms which thirstily imbibed the dewdrops quivering on them, not to speak of a fountain which boldly shot up its jets on high. Anyway, he carried on, while the woman is leading him along these paths, the press chief, or Wanderer (though Köves could only ever imagine the latter amidst the garden scenery in the form of the diminutive, immaculately dressed press chief in some outrageous costume), notices that the woman has heavy shackles on her hands and feet. He remarks on it, promising the woman that he will secure her release from them, but all the woman responds, oddly and brusquely, is: "I like the shackles." Then they sit down somewhere, at the foot of some tropical plant (sadly, on the spur of the moment, Köves was unable to recall its splendid, resounding name: maybe a magnolia, though possibly a eucalyptus), the moon rises, and in its light the press chief notices weals, scars, and signs of whiplashing on the woman's shoulders and breasts (quite why was unclear but, somehow or other, the woman had disrobed, it seems). "Do you like being whipped?" the press chief asks the woman, but this time she remains silent and merely looks at him enigmatically with deep, dark eyes "like the water of nocturnal wells," Köves recited. The press chief is then overcome by a disagreeable presentiment, except that by now a sense of compassion, to use a mild and by no means accurate word for it, has been awakened in him, and this has stifled more sober considerations, so that he starts to kiss the woman's wounds, and she, in an enigmatic manner, stands up, takes the press chief by the hand, leads him back to the foot of the tower and there, on the moonlit lawn, submits to his passion. At this point there ensued certain details (Köves inferred that, rather than the expected fulfilment, the press chief, or rather Wanderer, had experienced some sense of let down, as if he had found the woman's ardour too little: grim light was soon to be thrown on this, as well as his presentiments. Because a horrifying cry resounds, and a strapping, sinister man in black appears in the doorway to the tower, a cat-o'-nine-tails in his hand—the man of the house and the woman's husband, who in all probability has seen everything from one of the tower's windows. There now followed

painful scenes of betrayal, cruelty, and fornication, Köves warned
the girl, with misgivings that he jokingly exaggerated somewhat.
The man of the house "sets his servants and hounds loose" on the
press chief. The woman pleads for mercy, first for the two of them
but, as the man raises the lash on her, forgetting the press chief, for
herself alone, at which the man pulls the woman up and clasps her
to his chest. The press chief, who in the meantime has been struggling with "the servants and hounds," now catches the woman's
glance, reading compassion from it and something else: "stolen rapture". His strength then fails him, and he yields to "the servants
and hounds". He possibly even dies, or at least the woman and the
man suppose so. Nevertheless, he can still see and hear. He sees the
woman's smile, the gesture her hand makes as she strokes the mus-
cles of the man's arm and chest, even his lash, and he hears her voice
as she extols the man's strength, and he sees the man eyeing with
grim delight the press chief's corpse and his living wife. The woman,
for her part, elatedly returns the man's gaze. The sinister couple now
sink to the ground and try to make love on the lawn, glimmering
in the silver of the moonlight, right next to the press chief's corpse.
The man might have triumphed, but to no avail; the woman tries
out in vain all the tricks and secrets of love that she has just learned
from the press chief, so in the end they clamber to their feet on the
turf and stand there, broken and overwhelmed with shame, tears
glistening in their eyes. "Not even now?…," the woman asks gently.
"Not even now," the man replies, his head lowered. In despair and
anger, he is about to grasp the lash again, but the woman knocks it
from his hand with a single blow. She takes the shackles off herself
and uses them to fetter the man. The woman, indeed, goes further
by attaching smaller chains to the man's nose, lips, and ears, with
the man submissively, mutely enduring all this as though he had
been vanquished. Taking the chains in her hands, the woman then
leads the man into the house and up the tower, and the mortally

prostrate press chief hears the rattle of irons from up above, from the man's window—presumably he has been chained to the wall.

At this point, having spoken ever more haltingly for a while, Köves fell silent for good, it seemed, indeed for a moment he might even have dozed off, because he started up at the sound of the girl's insistent:

"And then...?" to which Köves replied that that was essentially the end of the story. The man was clapped in irons, the woman goes up the tower again, and the press chief hears her striking into song again: Ah! So this woman never sleeps, he thinks in horror, quickening his steps, for in the meantime he has somehow pulled himself together and, evading the vigilance of servants and hounds, made good his escape, and with his "lacerated wounds" he is now moving around outside anew, in the desert maybe, but free at last.

"Free!" the typist's unexpected, unduly shrill exclamation brought Köves round, almost making him jump. "The wretch!... He'll never be free," she added bitterly, leaving Köves, who felt his reason was beginning to slip away again (his exhausted, contentedly tingling senses demanded a break, sleep, a deep, unconscious dreaming, as if he were inebriated) and, offhand, maybe could not even have said whether it was still the dying evening or already the first glimmer of daybreak which was shimmering in the window, asked with a thick tongue:

"Of what? And who won't?"

"Do you really know nothing?" the typist asked, and it really did seem that Köves knew nothing, nothing at all. "The current chairman of the Supervisory Committee!... The bitch!...," the typist's voice shrilled like an alarm at night, and Köves felt a warm, moist touch from the girl's face on his fingers—in the dark she seemed to have buried her brow and tear-filled eyes for a second in Köves's hand, but then she immediately snatched it up with an impetuous movement, as if she were seeking to throw far away the pain burrowing within it, shaking her head several times, making her swirling hair swish silkily, fragrantly, on Köves's shoulder too.

"How long have you been working at our place?" she said, her voice still choking, like someone swallowing her tears, "and you still go around as if you had nothing to do with us, as if you were a foreigner: that's what the boss was saying this morning, and I'm saying it too."

"I can't help it," Köves muttered. And like someone whose tongue is loosened by approaching sleep or some other stupor, he added with uninhibited, cheerful determination: "None of you were of any interest."

"I can believe that. There isn't anything interesting about us," he heard the girl's quiet, bitter voice, and although she was now— it seemed like a long, long time already—lying wordlessly, stiffly beside him, Köves, even if he did not come completely to, also did not fall asleep; instead, on some unconscious compulsion, he moved and stretched out his hand questingly until the palm was caressing the at first bristling, but then ever-less-resisting, ever-more-melting female skin, and as if the warmth of the caressing fingers were also loosening her throat, the girl started talking quietly:

"The current chairman of the Supervisory Committee … you'd think, wouldn't you, that was just one of those temporary titles, lasting only until it's somebody else's turn: that's what you'd suppose from the name, isn't it?"

"Indeed," Köves agreed, even nodded, though probably pointlessly as it was dark and the girl wouldn't have been able to see it.

"Well, it isn't!" the girl cried out, as it were rebutting Köves's assertion in a sharp tone of triumph. "Not a bit of it! She is permanently the current chairman of the Supervisory Committee; by pure chance she is always the current one, her, her, and no-one else, it's been going on like that for years, and it will go on like that for still more years!… Who is going to dare stand up to her husband?"

"Why? Who's that?" Köves asked, more due to the pause that had ensued, which seemed to be demanding his voice, confirmation of his presence, rather than out of any genuine curiosity.

"The minister's secretary," the girl retorted with the same bitterness as before, though this time it carried a near-exultant ring of delight at being well informed.

"You mean there's a minister?" Köves marvelled, but here it seemed the girl was almost angry at him:

"You can't seriously be asking that," she said, "when there's a photograph of him hanging in every room, including ours, and right above your head at that." Köves did, of course, remember the photographs perfectly well, though on the other hand, perhaps precisely because he had seen so many of them, he remembered the face itself only vaguely, like the sort of faces one recalls because they fleetingly pass before one's eyes in specific places, at specific times, time and time again, but never recalling them for themselves, merely for those specific places and specific times, so he sensed that the girl had misunderstood his question, though as to what sort of doubts he wished to express thereby, maybe he himself had already forgotten, and therefore in order to preserve his authority all the same, he merely remarked:

"That's not in itself proof he exists."

"Oh," the girl mocked, "so you're an unbeliever! You need proofs, because if you aren't suspicious, you feel stupid, and perhaps you even brag about your lack of faith, but meanwhile you have no idea about the real world, no idea about anything!"

With that dressing-down, Köves clammed up, and he listened without saying a word to the girl's easy-flowing voice and fluent words as to the simultaneously refreshing and soporific patter of warm rain.

The minister—he existed all right, he was all too real! And even more real was his power, power in general. A ramifying thread which interwove everything and twitched everyone to do its bidding. There might be some individuals whom he did not reach, or who even did not see him—Köves for one, who therefore did not have the foggiest idea about him. And not through any stupidity: the girl had been watching Köves for a while and was convinced that he was not at all stupid. But then what could Köves be after? she had fretted, and she confessed that, to this day, she did not know. It was valid to ask, of course, whether it was possible to live like that, at least over a protracted period—outside the circle, that is. One thing for sure was that he was not going to get very far in life, though perhaps he would manage to preserve his intellectual independence, and at this point, after some groping in the dark, the typist squeezed her fingers over Köves's lips as though she had concluded from his breathing that he was about to fly into a rage on account of her scathing words. Because, she continued, undeniably there was also something appealing about that independence: Was any further proof needed than the fact that Köves was in her bed right now? Of course not. Köves probably had not the slightest idea how weak, how vulnerable, how exposed, how defenceless he was. That morning, when "the humiliation occurred"—that, by the way, was bound to happen sooner or later, everyone knew that, everyone was waiting for it except Köves, of course—well anyway, that morning when all that happened in the end was what was bound to happen, she had nevertheless felt real pain, yes, literally physical pain, a sickly feeling, and, strange as it may sound, that sickness had told her what in fact she thought about him.

"And what would that be?" Köves asked, in a sharp, sarcastic tone, as though he were protesting not so much at what the girl was thinking about him but the very fact that the girl should be thinking about him; and the girl answered only after a pause, as if she had needed to wait until the hostility in Köves's voice had died away everywhere, even in the room's farthest recesses.

"That you are innocent," she said.

"What do you mean?!" Köves rejoined promptly. "You think that someone who has committed no crime is automatically innocent?"

"Not at all," the girl replied. "The way you live is already a big enough crime: your innocence is the same as a child's—it's ignorance," and this time Köves maintained a silence, as if he were searching for counter-arguments, but so long was it taking that in itself it threw doubt on any refutation. Köves was not even aware, the girl continued, that his situation ... and here she hesitated as if she were trying to find the appropriate words with which to alert Köves to his situation: his situation was the most precarious, the most fragile, in the department, he being the only person who was completely dispensable. The press chief, she enumerated, was indispensable, not just because he was the boss but because he was the minister's speechwriter; it would not surprise her if Köves was unaware of even that. You see, she chortled, of course he was unaware. He might not even have heard the minister speaking as yet, might even be unaware that the minister occasionally gave speeches. Well then, it was actually the minister's secretary who was supposed to write the minister's speeches; however, he got the press chief to write them for him. Even if no one actually said it in so many words, that was basically the reason for maintaining the press office, even if there was also a certain amount of work with the press—but then the senior staffer took care of that. That was why he, too, was indispensable, because, to be honest, Köves did not do much to make the senior staffer dispensable. As far as she was concerned, every department always had need of a typist, though it was just the post that was indispensable, not herself personally, and she had no doubt that "some people would be glad to get rid of me," she wouldn't go into the reasons for that now, if ... well, if it didn't happen that it was actually she who wrote the minister's speeches. She realized that Köves would now be pulling

an incredulous face in the dark, but he should believe her that it
didn't call for any wizardry; the minister's speeches were always
constructed after the same pattern, one only had to recognize the
pattern, though anyone was capable of that: it was pretty much like
filling in empty boxes in a printed form. A speech was still a long
way from being ready with just that, of course; the typist merely
produced the "initial draft," or in other words "collected, arranged,
and outlined the material," which she would then submit to the
press chief, who would make his comments, then on the basis of
those comments, she would reword the draft and again hand it over
to the press chief, who would make any corrections that were seen
as still necessary in his own hand and pass this on to the minister's
secretary. He, in turn, would read the whole thing through, likewise
make comments and give it back to the press chief, the press chief
back to the secretary, and the secretary now to the minister, who
would make his own comments, give it back to his secretary, the
secretary to the press chief, and he possibly again to her, after which
it would again go on its way up the chain, possibly getting stuck
for a longer or shorter interval, oscillating back and forth between
secretary and press chief like a trembling compass needle, before
finally reaching the minister, and it was possible that it would then
be set off once more down, then again up ... at this juncture the
girl laughed out, in a deep, hoarse tone, as if she had never before
dared to see the operation in the light in which she was now seeing it, in the dark: the purposeless and ridiculous shuttling up and
down the official hierarchy, which the next day she would again be
seeing in the colours of unrelenting seriousness, because that was
how she had to see it; indeed, wished to see it: in just the same way
as she would arise from a bed disordered by lovemaking to put on
her clothes, another face, the inviolable armour of the secretary—
and at this her naked body touched Köves's, as if this fundamental
insight had awakened in her a sensual desire that she had to quench

rapidly, with rapid breathing. In short, she picked up later on, the department's work was completely attended to by the three of them. Köves had only been taken on because there had been a need to do a quick favour for someone—the fire brigade, perhaps, as best she could recall.

"Yes, the fire brigade," Köves confirmed.

"And you still did nothing to consolidate your position," the girl chided him.

"What was I supposed to do?" Köves asked, like someone who was finally starting to take some interest in his own affairs, albeit belatedly of course, and therefore not so much with an eagerness to do something about it as out of the idle curiosity of a resigned regret.

"Open your eyes and find your way around the chain of command!" she girl told him.

"Is that so?" Köves muttered, as though the idea of doing that dispirited him even in retrospect, even undone. "And what would I have gained by going that?" he inquired nevertheless. For instance, he would have understood the press chief's novella, the girl answered. He would have known what everyone knew: that a power struggle was going on between the press chief and the minister's secretary, and also who was the instrument of that rivalry. She would be curious as to whether Köves was aware of that, at least, but of course he wasn't. Well, it was the highly esteemed current chairman of the Supervisory Committee, and at one and the same time the minister's secretary's bitch of a wife, yes, her!—through her each kept a tight grip on the other, they literally clashed with one another over her body. On the surface, of course, the secretary's position was incomparably the more favourable, both as the woman's husband and as the minister's secretary, who could simply stamp the press chief underfoot, pulverize him; but then, on the other hand, and the three of them were well aware of this, he didn't do that precisely because he could. She could guess what sort of face Köves was pulling in the dark: an ignorant face, because he wouldn't understand this, his mind worked on different lines—she wasn't saying that disparagingly, but, quite the contrary, appreciatively, in some respects with outright admiration for Köves's turn of mind, but it was still true, that's what power was like, that's how it operated: if it could not be exercised, then it wasn't power. Ah! What did Köves know about that sort of thing: nothing, less than nothing! One fine day, for example, the press chief would receive a cold, unmerciful break-up letter from the woman which cruelly trampled in the dust all the feelings they had hitherto professed for each other. He had no clue what had happened; for days he had roved around the office pale as death, incapable of hiding his pain, wincing from the suffering and humiliation, trying to call the woman up, or to get calls put through to her, but not reaching her, finding she was not available, by pleading sickness, maybe not setting foot in the ministry for days on end, until, let's say a week later, there would be a telephone call, or a letter would arrive, in which, for instance, the woman would inform him that every word of the previous letter had been dictated to her by her husband, the secretary, because he had come across something—a telltale piece of paper had popped up, or some fresh rumour had reached his ear—so, out of dreadful necessity, she had put down what had been dictated purely in order to avert the momentary threat, but with every word she had written she had suffered agonies of pain. Which was all very well, but in the meantime the press chief had been put on the rack: although this was not the first time it had happened—oh, by no means the first, nor even the second—he had nevertheless believed every word of what was in the letter, imagining he had been betrayed, deserted, indeed conspired against, and any moment might find himself struck down by the secretary's avenging fury; pictured them in the marital bed as, for the sake of their spent love, they wring new stimuli for themselves out of his existence, so to say, and maybe at the climax of their pleasure they vilified his name; indeed—though he could not seriously have believed it, yet there were precedents—he even imagined they would murder him; yes, he had even played with that thought, had voluptuously pictured for himself a scene in which the secretary returned home with bloody hands, confessed to his wife, and the woman merely said: "Thank you." That was the sort of thing he dreamed up, so it was genuinely painful to see him in such distress, torturing himself. How downcast he looked sometimes, destitute, that one was left not knowing what to do, how to console him, how to pull him round, when ... when it was just power, a power game, nothing else. That was how it went, these were its laws; that was what it looked like when it was exercised, and she, the typist, would be mighty curious to know whether the press chief really did love the minister's secretary's wife in the way he himself imagined he did, or rather, as she herself, the typist, now thought, as a result of much head-scratching and her ruminations during many a sleepless night, the prey that the woman's person represented for him. Otherwise what would the woman be worth to him if he did not have to claw her away from the minister's secretary; and similarly, what would the wife be worth to the minister's secretary if there was not the constant suspicion, if there were no cases of her being caught red-handed; if he could not order her to heel like a whimpering dog time and time again; and if he could not always use those occasions to give the press chief a kick. As to the woman, what would all this mean to her if she could not feel that she had two men in her power; in other words, all three of them had become so intertwined that they no longer knew who was controlling whom, who was on top and who the underdog, and why they were doing it at all—they were just doing it because they started doing it at one time, and now they were unable to do it any other way…

That, then, was how things stood, and anyone who did not know that, and was unsuspectingly fooled by appearances, or by the press chief's words, like … well, like Köves by that novella:

"No doubt you made some pronouncement about it," the girl queried, or rather asserted.

Certainly he had, Köves replied, since the press chief expected that of him; that's why he had read the story out to him.

"And what did you say?" the girl wanted to know, and Köves, who no longer recalled much, it seemed, replied that it had been nothing in particular, little more than empty phrases, stock words of praise, like how interesting it was, how original, things like that.

"Nothing else?" the girl was unconvinced.

"Oh, yes!" it seemed that Köves now recalled more. "I told him that I considered it to be a symbolic story, but it still showed the mark of a lived personal experience."

"There you are," the girl's voice was all gentle, comforting triumph. "He must have believed that you knew his secret, and now he has surrendered for good, put himself in your hands for good," the girl spoke in an almost caressing tone, her hand finding Köves's face in the dark and stroking it as if he were a little boy. "Oh dear, that's ignorance for you," she reproved him.

"Yes," said Köves, "it seems that I don't nurture the same interest in him that you do," and the hand now stopped on the face, then pulled away, as if by making the remark Köves had withdrawn himself from their joint concerns and joint subjection to step onto a separate path and had thereby possibly offended her.

"How much you know about him," he went on, all the same, his voice revealing not surprise so much as almost wonder. "You know him in the way that a person can only know her tormentor," he added.

"My tormentor…? Why would something like that occur to you? How dare you say anything like that?" the girl asked indignantly, in that almost injured tone of voice people use who are offended only by the truth.

"And what if it were the case?" she said later with the liberated, almost scornful confidentiality that, it seemed, their ineffaceable hours of intimacy had precipitated within her. "Should I put up with it? Accept being walked all over, trampled upon?"

But it was most likely daybreak by the time this took place, when the light seems to bring with it a restoration of the order which will sunder them and soon direct them to their distinct, widely separated places, and they eye each other strangely, almost with hostility, like people who by the sober light of day are counting the cost of a venture predestined to come to nothing—it was something like this that Köves felt, still dazed from the sudden awakening and hurried dressing, while the girl stood before him in an immaculate dress, a cloud of fresh scents around her, radiant and cool as (it crossed Köves's throbbing head) a drawn sword, and urged him to get going, so they did not arrive at the ministry together.

"You're horribly ambitious," he said, or rather complained, as he searched for some final item of discarded clothing, maybe his necktie, maybe his coat. "You're eaten up by ambition. What do you actually want?" he asked, probably not driven by any curiosity, more simply to occupy the awkward moments until he had finished dressing.

But the girl must have misunderstood him, because she gave him an answer, overstrung, irascibly, in confidence and scornfully, like before:

"Him," she said. "I want him back," suddenly turning her back on Köves, and he saw her shoulders heaving, followed a moment later by a choking sound that was instantly stifled. Yet when he tried to approach her: "Don't touch me!" the girl exclaimed, then "Get going, go!" she added in a sudden fit of anger that Köves felt he did not deserve as he had done nothing to upset the girl, or if he had, then it was not deliberate: "Just so you don't get the idea that

I'm going to walk arm in arm with you to the ministry where your notice of dismissal is waiting!"

"Notice of dismissal?" Köves was astonished, not so much at the news in itself, more at its unexpectedness, startled solely by the setting, the timing, and the occasion. "How do you know?" he asked a little later, and of course he had not the slightest intention of setting off.

"I typed it yesterday morning." The girl now turned round to face Köves, her voice milder, a look of almost embarrassed sympathy on her face.

Köves then soon found himself in a strange stairwell, then on the street, where he pondered for a few seconds which direction he should now take.

CHAPTER SEVEN

Change of direction

Not much later—it must have been midmorning, getting on for ten o'clock—Köves was standing in another stairwell and pushing once, twice and, finally, a third time on the bell of a battered door, which had no name-plate and had clearly seen better days, until an ill-tempered stirring could be heard from behind it and a bald, oval head, fleshy face, and morose pair of eyes appeared in the peephole, and then a high-pitched, brassy voice resembling a trumpet hooted at him:

"You?!…" Berg was amazed. A key then jangled, a lock clicked, and Köves found himself in a gloomy space—some sort of hallway it must have been, for one of his shoulders immediately bumped against one of a pair of cumbersome entrance-hall wardrobes of disparate sizes—from which he stepped through an open glazed door into a lighter, somewhat more spacious room. It was an odd room at first glance, and its oddity was not caused by the paler and darker blankets laid on the floor, which obviously served as a carpet, nor even by the two rush-bottomed armchairs and a stool which were fraying around the wooden frames, or the two bed-settees, already sagging like potholes, which were set alongside the middle of the wall, it was more something that was missing: it was only then that Köves saw that might have been meant to be among these things was the table he now spotted in front of a tile stove, which was standing in one of the far corners of the room and on which he could see a decrepit office desk lamp, which was shining even in the light of the morning, sheets of paper, a sharp and a blunt pencil, a red pencil sharpener, as well as a small metal tray, and on it, in single-file as if heading toward the stove, a green, a white, a pink, and a chocolate-coloured petit-four, along with a glass of water, then, in a recess between the table and stove, another rush-bottomed seat without a back—in all probability the one from which Berg had jumped to his feet, when Köves had started ringing at the door.

"To what do I have to thank for the ... How did it come to mind that ... How do you know the ring to give?" with great difficulty Berg got out his questions, evidently none too pleased at having to receive a guest.

"The same way that I knew the address." Köves smiled tentatively, by way of an apology, as it were.

"So, you've come from the South Seas?" Berg asked.

"Yes," Köves nodded, still a little uncertainly, as if he too were surprised by it. There was no denying that although he had started off from the typist's dwelling with the initial intention of going to the Ministry of Production, if only to pick up his notice of dismissal, he had changed direction en route, it seems, because not long afterwards he found himself sitting in the South Seas and asking Alice to bring a substantial breakfast. One word led to another, and all at once there slipped from Köves's mouth—due to sleeplessness, the experiences and unordered thoughts that were still whirling confusedly about in his head: in short, inattention—the question which had anyway long been on his mind: "How's your ... partner?" to which Alice had responded that if he was really curious, why didn't he pay a visit? "Where?" Köves had asked, perhaps less surprised than the surprising suggestion would have justified. "At home," Alice replied as unaffectedly as though Köves was a close friend who was constantly dropping in on them, and from the look she gave Köves seemed to discern a mute plea. He then recalled that Alice had complained for a long time, relating how Berg had not set foot outside his home for weeks, perhaps months now; and if she did not take home, and set down before him, his lunch and supper he would not eat but just die of hunger; and it was useless her telling him to get out sometimes, come down to the café, see something else than the four bare walls—all her talking was to no avail, for it was hard to get even a word out of him; he was more and more wrapped up in his thoughts. "About what?" Köves asked. "His work," the waitress answered evasively and with a touch of uncomprehending nervousness over an activity somewhat alien to her, which on the spur of the moment put Köves in mind of Mrs. Weigand's agitation in the way she was used to complaining about her son. To his dubious question as to what she was expecting him to achieve with a visit, all the waitress was able to say, with an unsure smile of unclear hope, was, "What a nice chat he had with you the other day...," but still, he was there after all.

"People are worried about you," he said, perhaps partly by way of explanation, with the hint of a smile, as if being simply the faithful bearer of that concern, but also with the required solemnity of one who was thereby fulfilling his mission.

It appeared, however, that Berg was not deceived:

"Some people may be worried," he said in ringing tones, "but that's not what brought you."

"No," Köves admitted; then, as though he were loath to admit it: "Cluelessness," he added, with a slightly forced smile. "Am I disturbing you?" he asked next.

"As you can see," Berg cast a sullen glance at the table, "I'm working," placing a hand on his papers as on a restless animal. Making his way round the table, he dropped his heavy, but not disproportionate body down onto the stool and, like a gaoler over his prisoners, ran his eyes, fleetingly, but severely and appraisingly, over the petits-fours:

"You're writing?...," Köves asked after a short lull, quietly and, involuntarily, with a degree of sympathetic tact.

Berg, spreading his arms a little and grimacing, made the irritated admission:

"Yes, I'm writing," like someone who had been caught in a shameful passion that he himself deprecated.

"And what?" Köves probed further, after allowing another considerate pause to go by, to which Berg, in wonder, raised a glance, as it were, looking past Köves:

"What?...," the question came back, as if this were the first time he had thought about it. "The writing," he then declared, and now it was Köves's turn to be surprised:

"What do you mean?" he asked.

"What would I mean?" Berg shrugged several times in what amounted to serene helplessness, any pretence at making an effort suddenly peeling off him, as if Köves were no longer making him feel uneasy: "One is always writing one's writing," he carried on, "or at least always should be writing it, if one writes."

"Fair enough." Although Berg seemed to have forgotten to offer him a seat, Köves nevertheless set himself down in the armchair diagonally opposite Berg, cautiously smoothing down the rush ends sticking into his thigh from its frame. "Let me put it another way: What's the writing about?"

"Mercy," Berg responded promptly, without a moment's hesitation.

"I see," said Köves, although he couldn't really have seen as he followed it straightaway by asking: "And what do you mean by 'mercy'?"

"The necessary," came the answer, as swiftly as before.

"And what is necessary?" Köves plugged away, as though sensing that the moment was favourable and wishing to make use of it.

"You're again posing the question badly," Berg motioned, his hand suddenly dropping, like an irrevocable decision, cutting a swath through the petits-fours, his glance darting over the table, most likely in search of a serviette (there was no way of knowing, but maybe he imagined he was in the South Seas), which of course he did not find, so he was only able to clean his presumably sticky fingertips by fastidiously rubbing them together. "You should ask what's unnecessary."

"Right," Köves conceded to Berg, as though it were a riddle he had posed: "What's unnecessary?"

"To live," Berg supplied the answer, with a frosty little smile playing around his mouth, as though after a cruel act, carried out with ruthless purposefulness, although—at least as far as Köves could ascertain—all he had done was polish off a petit-four.

"I have never heard of a single living soul asking whether it is necessary to live," Köves objected, perhaps more sharply than he intended.

"The fact that people don't pose it doesn't mean that it's not a valid question," Berg said and shrugged his shoulders.

Maybe," Köves pondered, "I would understand what you are saying better if I could get to know what you are writing."

"And how could you do that?!" was Berg's response, with a smile that bore a hint of an almost cocky excitement.

"I know one way," Köves ventured. "You could read it," he blurted out, a suggestion that was followed by a prolonged silence.

"To tell you the truth," Berg finally spoke, "I was preparing to do that very thing when you rang the doorbell. You see," and he seemed to hesitate, "...you see," he carried on nevertheless, "one section has been completed and I ... ah! What do I care what you think!... I like to try out how it sounds when read aloud. But I had not been expecting," he added, "to have an audience as well..."

"Maybe it would be more natural that way…," Köves offered.

"How do you mean?" It was Berg's turn to be flummoxed.

"I mean, if you're already writing," Köves tried to explain, "then it's natural that … in short," he broke into a smile, radiating jaunty reassurance, "it's natural for an artist to have an audience…"

But he had slipped up, it seemed, because Berg's face clouded over, as if the effect of the reassurance had been rather to put him out of humour.

"The natural instinct for man to be an artist is not at all natural any longer," he muttered. Köves did not respond, whereas Berg launched into a series of little moves, not every one of which was familiar to Köves but which he recognized, in totality, as preparations for giving a reading, so he continued to hold his tongue. Finally, Berg broke the silence, though not at all in order to read:

"Would you like a petit-four?" was all he asked, in a dour voice, which, unusually for him, was trembling a little from an attack of stage fright.

"No thank you," Köves declined. "I had breakfast just before."

Berg then seemed to be struggling but in the end only took a sip of water, then, without taking any notice of Köves, articulating clearly in his sonorous voice, began reading very clearly, starting with the title, which in itself was slightly disconcerting, even startling:

I, the executioner…

Writing, Ladies and Gentlemen, that strange and inexplicable desire to give form and expression to our lives, is a seductive but dangerous temptation. We cannot, in any case, decipher the dreamy secret of our lives, so we would do better to observe a modest silence and step aside quietly.

Nevertheless, something impels us to put ourselves forward, out into the limelight of public attention, and as greedy buskers we strive to grab a scrap of approval and understanding. What can what has happened and what has yet to take place do to change that?

I may, perhaps, count on your kind indulgence when concerns like this are used to preface my book, which will, in due time, comprise the true story of my life—or at least the authentic story of an interesting and instructive life. Every life, of course, is interesting and instructive. But it is not given to every life to be laid out before the world in a carefully considered analysis, with its contents enhanced by generalization. That, at any rate, is how I intend to speak about my life: this is what I decided during those sterile days when the idea—I might say: the compulsion—to write first arose within me, though I was still struggling and kicking against the temptation. An entire week went by like that, a valuable, irrecoverable week: having definitively resigned myself, I am beginning to value time now that I have so little of it at my disposal. That week—most likely last week, since today is Monday—was the week of decision, then, and with its throes it insinuated eventful variety into my life. But maybe I needed this week of lively hesitations and internal excitements, which set it off from the indifference of recent months and years, for my work, and my internal resistance to writing may have been merely a natural protective instinct, the desire to preserve my sure and, in its own way, comfortable mental attitude, from the siege of expression, which, against my inclination so to say, compels me to view everything vividly and freshly, at a high emotional temperature, and to live through again—even more vividly than in reality—things which have already happened once. That is what I said previously was a seductive but dangerous temptation.

And yet all the same, as you see, I am buckling down to it. I feel a little bit as though I were commencing everything afresh, even though I cannot move forward with any of the excitement of a new beginning, just the resignation of unalterability, on a path already trodden once—otherwise my writing could not lay claim to the moral credence of *this is what happened* and *this is how it happened*, and so of reality, but would be just as irresponsible a flight of fancy as any novel. I have to say, however, that the self-assured defiance which precisely this unalterability awakens in me means too much for me seriously to consider, even for a second, any other eventuality my life might take. No, I am not of a mind to change matters that have been settled—and that seemingly lazy expression is, on this occasion, very accurate, because I really do have no mind for it. Not that looking back offers so much joy: my life has not been joyful, but it is a life that has been settled and solved, indeed exemplarily solved. A life that is worth speaking about, or at least so I feel, though the right to the final word necessarily lies with the Reader. Because, Ladies and Gentlemen, in order for us to be able to speak about our lives, we need to know how to appreciate our fate, to wonder with childish enthusiasm over the career that we have taken. My book is the fruit of that wonderment, of the childish amazement that was won back during the tranquil months of my arrest and detention over what has been my life and what now, during the nebulously melancholy time of my captivity, affects me with such a peculiar magic………

Let us, then, take courage in both hands.

It is perhaps unnecessary for me to indicate the exact

date; at all events, it is autumn, the sky is very likely covered by grey clouds, as shown by the tiny square of the horizon I can see from the pocket handkerchief of the window of my diminutive room, or, more properly and more accurately: my cell, my punishment chamber, and this leaden glimmer superbly matches my meditative frame of mind. I am in the favourable situation that I do not have to, indeed, it is expressly forbidden for me to step out onto the street, for that is precisely why I am locked in here, under a strict confinement which takes from my shoulders—albeit with punitive intent—responsibility for the further course of my fate. At least for my part, that is how I view my present form of life, and I would deeply deplore it if that were to be laid at the door of my depravity with the unbending prejudice and regrettable lack of comprehension which are so sadly typical of the world.

So, due to the fact that I have been isolated from the world with benevolent strictness (I could never stand rainy weather, and especially not the wind, the biting, dank wind, one of the curses, among others, of our draughty city, which always made me depressed and irascible) in my pleasantly temperate cell, without the disturbing irritation of outside influences, I can freely give myself up to my pastime of putting down on paper a thing or two, whatever I happen to see fit and necessary, as a refreshing counterbalance to interrogations, with their worn statements and proceedings in court, where I can only respond to what I am asked, and I can only show myself in the light that is forced upon me. Vanity, you will say, and of course you will be both right and wrong, as usual. Because in my opinion, and I speak as a man of some intellect and culture incidentally, or maybe not even incidentally since following the closing of my career in this world, you see, I am returning to intellectual pursuits—in my opinion, then, anyone is worthy of attention who wishes to show himself in a more complete light, thus supplementing the picture the world has built up—always one-sidedly—about him, and such an aspiration cannot simply be dismissed with a reproving word and blindly taken for nothing. At all events, it is fortunate that I still have the time and opportunity to devote to this belated and, no doubt, surprising need of mine, and this points to the advantages of civilized prisons, as opposed to *our* prisons, which have disadvantages practically to the exclusion of all else.

I must apologize in advance if, during what follows, I am a little whimsical in the approach I adopt to my own portrait, mixing it, from time to time, with thoughts that are seen as necessary and, after all, belong to the portrait, because, although a man of intellect and culture, I am not a literary man, at least not in the everyday sense. There is nothing to do but to throw myself on my natural talent, my strict sense of form, and my special sensitivity toward the phenomena of life; in a word, on my cultivation, innate and acquired. That is no small thing either, because even if, as I say, I am not a literary man, in the field of confessions and autobiographies the beginner is confronted with wonderful examples, more enlightened, indeed entrancing examples from the Enlightenment era, or even those of great penitents and confessors—examples that I feel called upon if not to outstrip, at any rate to take courage from their finely-nuanced accuracy, their heroic honesty, their gratifying endeavour to strive constantly to draw a lesson.

You have every right to shake your heads disapprovingly at the mention of these lofty models, to upbraid me for my rash tactlessness, and to regard as sadly typical the brazen unabashedness with which I dare to construct a link with the aforementioned blessed geniuses, I, a gaolbird, as it has become clear from what I have said; even if you know who I actually am, although I have already alluded to that in the book's title. And even if on top of all that you were to recognize my name, the rightly infamous name that I shall disclose to the Reader in one of the ensuing paragraphs! No matter what I might have to say for myself against such reproaches, I would again only be able bitterly to attribute to the fact that the world places greater weight on the immutability of its notions of morality than on admitting the truth; that it manifests more feeling for condemnation than for judgement, and instead of looking to the bottom of things it thinks it better to dispose of them with a few time-honoured commonplaces. I, who will stand before the court accused of causing the deaths of 30,000 people, am able to transcend my fate, and to my pleasant surprise—obviously to the world's surprise as well—I still feel that much responsible interest toward life as not to be ashamed of spending my last days and hours with moralising—rather appropriately and not unskilfully, you have to admit. Even if I cannot expect you, against your convictions, to respect the moralist in me first and foremost, at least pause before the phenomenon with the astonishment that it deserves. Because, see here, even in my peculiar career I have been able to preserve my original conviction, based on my upbringing, my spiritual and mental culture, as if nothing had happened, or rather as if everything which happened happened by accident, as if I were not giving it my full attention and commitment, or in point of fact, my consent, solely from the necessity of the recognition that I could not refuse the duty that had been assigned to me, the order and the mission marked out for me by a higher place, however regrettably it might have run counter to my own way of thinking and inclinations.

Would you believe that this fact, publication of which will probably serve merely to unleash a further outburst of general horror and indignation upon my head, instead of being able to sway you to a little more sympathy toward me (which is not my aim, by the way; I have no aim with you): would you believe that this fact is welcome least of all in my eyes and bestows on me far more bitterness, punishes me with burdensome reflection, instead of my being able to take a quiet satisfaction at this steadfastness of my nature? You can believe that I have done everything, grasped every opportunity in my peculiar career, to coarsen myself, to make myself bestially insensitive, primitively dull-witted, but, sadly, I didn't succeed. My spiritual refinement was too high, my mind too civilized, and the havoc that was accomplished in others, and to which, out of the necessity to accommodate (and maybe also out of a certain curiosity, a desire to find out about myself), I also contributed with my own efforts; in the end, it was unable to destroy the fundamental determinacy of my character, and that character, in the event, coming to a sensible compromise with the circumstances, gave in merely to appearances, even though those appearances probably became hideously intermingled with reality. Now, here I stand (or rather sit) with the burdensome consequences of all this, and I am overcome by an ever more urgent need, by fleshing out the false reality—my acts, in other words—to furnish a more complete picture of myself; this, in my view, extraordinarily noteworthy need that you called vanity earlier on, but which, you will nevertheless have to acknowledge, is the most salutary form of vanity, socially speaking.

And here I come to your disapproving shaking of the head and small-minded reservations. I take the liberty of asking whether we should ascribe a lower value to the self-revelation of one man, who has gone through certain depths of life and is prepared, without any showing-off, to put its lessons at the disposal of the world, than another, who has moved within more innocuous extremes, assuming the former sees and interprets his life on the basis of the same morality and possesses as much human grit and happy creative power, even if in respect to form and artistry, he may leave more to be desired for want of the necessary practice and adequate time. All the same, it is precisely in the name of morality that you protest against my being allowed to speak out, as I have become someone who has forfeited the right to do that; someone who should not be allowed to speak out, only interrogated; someone who is unworthy of your sympathy and cannot supply any useful innovation or self-awakening lesson. Because I am, perhaps, not mistaken if I assert that your interest in grand confessions is attracted not so much by the excessively strange or wildly individual as by what is common, general, manifested in even the most extreme excesses, which pertains to yourselves, too, and which you happily discern, for instance, in the words of an aristocrat of sensitive soul who was blessed with a gift for expression and a vivid imagination, but was otherwise unexceptionable, who was made great by his talent and innocuousness and who in your mutual recognition of each other deliciously satisfies the dreams you weave about yourselves. Under no circumstances, by contrast, do you have any wish to have anything in common with me; you would most happily see me as some kind of savage, a strange wild animal; in any case as a person who is utterly foreign to your nature, with whom you can have nothing at all to do at the level of living contacts, and you derive satisfaction from the fact that the false reality created by my acts serves such assumptions perfectly, because you are not in the least curious about the fuller reality—I understand that endeavour, yet I still make so bold as to furnish the information that it is nothing more than self-delusion, which is not worthy of you. And now that I am modestly but categorically declaring my right to my human condition, my relevance to the general, you wish to have nothing to do with me; you avert your gazes from me in the name of morality lest I impel you to even the slightest bit of understanding or sympathy for me—that is to say, lest in me you should recognize yourselves to even the slightest degree.

I believe I see it clearly now: you fear my confessions. That is of no interest to me, though; far from putting me off, if excites and stimulates me. I am familiar with the fear aroused in people by our appearance alone: that jackbooted, pistol-on-belt, formidably overpowering appearance, in which there was also, against your will, a trace of reluctant, nauseated pleasure, precisely because it was against your will—oh yes, I am familiar with that feeling, which set me off on my career, and which I subsequently, out of revenge for myself as it were, pursued with ever-growing passion, trembling from the desire that others should also experience it; that it should enslave others, eat deep into their souls and stir up in them a licentious freedom, the abominable, soul-destroying pleasure that they live through in their fear—as I say, I am familiar with the fear, which this time I wish to transplant into you as a moral lesson, not by means of my aggressively real but my magical appearance; that is, by the representation of myself through words and language.

And this is the point where I feel, distinctly feel, that I have no reason to blush before the aforementioned blessed souls as far as my intentions go; that in respect of its blessedness my self-revelation is in no way inferior to theirs, assuming you have the courage, in the course of unfolding my excessively and wildly individual career, to recognize what it is in me that is blessed for yourselves. Which is, first and foremost, the fact that it was me who went through my career, not you.

I have the feeling that this way of formulating what I have to say is somewhat abstruse and might give rise to misunderstandings that will then invite your deliberate misunderstanding. I need to speak clearly, like all those who have the aim of struggling against the stubborn resistance that the world has displayed to implacable truths. But then, why should I beat about the bush? My blessedness lies precisely in my implacability, in which all of us should spot our selfish motives, as you shall see later on. So, what was it that I wanted to say? Nothing other than that you should recognize your salvation in my excessively wild fate, inasmuch as it might have been your fate, and inasmuch as I lived it, not despite, but instead of you.

Now that I am saying these words—I first said them to myself before writing them down and then saying them again, to my liking, out loud, which I would suggest the Reader do as well—I am seized by an unprecedented excitement, because I feel that I have finally managed to capture the essence of the thoughts and emotions which are churning confusedly inside me; indeed, the essence of my fate, the essence of the feeling that basically determined my career, which has made me so responsive to the will of my surroundings and is so typical of my covertly intimate relationship with the world. Now, that last sentence of the preceding paragraph is what this strange sensitivity of mine dictated to me. Yes, when I committed my definitive act—the first act of murder, which subsequently proved to be an irrevocable choice, just because it had happened, and because *it could have happened*—that is, the opportunity was presented to do it, and in point of fact an opportunity was not presented to do anything else—so when, under pressure of external compulsion, I committed my definitive act, that pressure of external force, as you will see in the course of the ensuing plot, was not present at all—it did no more than simply accumulate within me, became an inner compulsion, which is to say that it returned to its original form. Because the external compulsion was merely secondary, nothing more than a projection of a genuine will, which comes true if reality favours it. And the loose strands of an external compulsion which were not the bonds of a genuine will could easily be torn asunder by the world. But no, the world did nothing; it awaited events with bated breath; it wanted to see what would happen, only then to be horrified by it— horrified by itself. When I set off on my career, and steadily worked my way through it, all that happened was that, with my extraordinary responsiveness, I had understood the will of the world, your will—or if you prefer: the will you have conceived against your consciences—and, by the reality of my acts and career, I redeemed and returned to you your consciences. You, however, with an inconsistency typical of the world, will not hear of it, and the more you recognize the vitality of the relationship between us, the more you will deny it, and all the more I shall be seen by you as loathsome.

I, on the other hand, stick to my guns, and like a conductor who, at the end of a concert, will point to the orchestra with a sweeping gesture as a way of indicating that the source of the success is to be sought in their common effort, so I point to yourselves—but then, of course, you will know that it is actually me you must applaud; that is, me you must string up.

In itself, though, that would be in order; that is the role which has been reserved for me in the game and which I have taken on, albeit not without some reluctance, and not exactly with good grace, since, as a result of the foregoing, I have a refined sense for ceremonial games; and no charge would distress me more than to be called a spoilsport of such fastidious games, though you will have no reason to do so, I feel, given my performance. There is just one thing I bridle against, which is that people will try to ascribe the moral composure, to which my every word bears witness, to my depravity, though it is nothing other than true inner peace.

I can already hear the question: How can that be? Surely this can't be someone who wishes to sing the praises of a career which flouted the general consensus so blatantly and deviated from the world so profligately that he has ended up before the tribunal of the court? Yet that is precisely my intention. Because if I were not to do that, I would be misleading the Reader, who otherwise would never understand the strange grace in which I partake.

Yes, grace, I said. Because if someone can look back on his life with composure—burnt-out and weary, immensely weary, maybe, but still with composure—that is grace and, in itself, a victory. For I have to admit that I am as amused as much as I am saddened by the world's propensity, stemming partly from simple-mindedness, partly from deliberate prejudice, to interpret my career as a failure, as a failure primarily in a practical moral sense, and to force that notion on me with self-important fuss. At the same time, I sense an eager longing in this pushy attempt, an urgent but basically clumsy entreaty, as if it depended on me, on my keenly and anxiously awaited words, for the world to be given back its childish faith in its ideals. Everything here turns on one question, and in this the world now displays what for it is an unusually fine discriminatory power, and that is on whether I feel guilty. Because the fact of my guilt has already been decided, otherwise I would not be locked up in here, subjected to the hassles of interrogations. But that is not what is important here, and, to my greatest amazement, those who have undertaken to be my judges are on the right track when they make a distinction between crime and consciousness of guilt. Because the moral significance of a sentence, the liberating effect to which every sentence lays a claim, if it considers that it is founded on morality, in my case depends solely on me, stands or falls on me, on my endorsing it, on my transfiguring it, on my raising it to an intellectual plane through my consciousness of guilt. How great the sympathy, how great the compassion, and then again how great the contempt with which I view this unfortunate demand, which simply underlines now shaky the ground is on which the world's moral balance rests!

It is not me, then, who is the spoilsport: it is you. You, who disown me, who wish to hear no word about a tacit agreement existing between us, and fastidiously turn up your noses just on hearing about that possibility; when you now wish to see my fate, which we have transformed into what it has become, by common consent, merely an excessively wild individual, which has nothing to do with what is in common, and which it would be best to be rid as soon as possible, and then, after the obligatory shuddering, quickly forget all about.

You will have to realize that it's my duty to protest against a bogus solution like that—my duty, for one thing, out of self-awakening, philanthropic unsparingness, for another, in the interests of preserving my dignity, which cannot tolerate being cheated so treacherously for the sake of cheap peace of mind.

If you are inclined to look more deeply into yourselves, you will understand me. Because, Ladies and Gentlemen, we have been hopelessly locked up together with one another in this world in miserable camaraderie; everything which happens carries such significance that we can no longer disperse it, nullify it, deny it from each other. We have to accept one another and our stories, and, even in the most extreme case, we have no other choice than to weigh up how, in the given situation, we can get away with even the mildest of our past deeds. And if everything that I shall relate to you further on is perceived by you in this way, then both parties, yourselves and I, will be able to get something out of it, although in the final analysis I truly do not know, in this respect, who will have the simpler task: you, who will be living on under the burden of my fate, or I, whom, through my likely removal from your midst, you will charitably excuse from further life. At all events, I draw my composure from the thought that my educationally-intended autobiography has in this way taken sweet vengeance for my fate on a world which allowed, tolerated, and thus wished for, this fate—sweet vengeance, I say, and ultimately I have striven to prepare your minds so carefully in order to make them sensitive to that vengeance.

Grounds, objections and a sad final conclusion

Having let the final sheet of paper drop onto the table, Berg looked up at Köves, who now shifted position on the creaking and uncomfortable seat (he had not dared bat an eyelid during the reading), and asked in a tense, eager tone:

"And then?...," like someone who was not looking for a breather but rather expecting it to go straight on.

Berg, however, spread his hands slightly:

"That's it," he smiled.

"What do you mean?!" Köves spluttered. "You didn't even get started!"

"To be precise, you heard the preface," Berg informed him. "That's as far as I have got. The rest has yet to come."

"All of it, in other words!" Köves seemed disappointed, if not actually annoyed. "All I've heard so far is preaching, a pile of assertions that I can either believe in or not, because...," Köves searched for the right word, and, it seems, he had not graduated from the hard school of Sziklai's tuition for nothing, "...because there is no plot underpinning it!" was how he finally phrased his stricture, which was not exactly tactful, and Berg's brow appeared to darken for a moment, but then he perhaps realized that Köves's impatience, at root, must have been fed by approbation, or at least involvement. "At least give me an idea what happens over the course of the plot," Köves grumbled. "Who is that fellow, anyway? Who did he take as his model?"

"Who would I take it from if he were foreign to me?" Berg responded to the question with a question.

"You mean to say," Köves was incredulous, "you are that fellow?"

"Let's just say that's one of the possibilities," Berg replied. "One possible path to grace."

"And what other paths might be possible?" Köves wanted to know.

"That of the victim," came the answer.

"And then?...," Köves pestered further.

To this, however, Berg responded:

"Only two paths are offered here." A short pause ensued, with Berg groping like a blind man in the direction of the petits-fours, alighting upon the green one, grasping it, then putting it back and instead raising the chocolate-coloured one, but promptly dropping that too, hastily, resolutely, as if he were responding to a pledge that had been resuscitated from forgetfulness.

"And writing?" Köves piped up again. "Isn't writing grace?"

"No," Berg's high voice snapped back as a curt yelp.

"Well what, then?"

"Deferment. Ducking. Dodging," Berg itemized. "The post-ponement—impossible of course—of the election of grace."

"In other words," Köves asked, "you are either executioner or victim?"

"Both," Berg answered in a slightly impatient tone, like someone who is required to provide information on matters that have long been known. His glance skimmed over the table until it stopped on a slip of paper, which he now lifted up from amongst his papers. "'It might perhaps be pleasant,'" he read off it, "'to be alternately victim and executioner.'" Berg put the slip down and again glanced at Köves. "That's what the writing says, and I am its realizer," he said.

"What writing is that?" Köves inquired. "Did you write it?"

"No," Berg replied. "When it was written the time had not yet come. The time," his clear voice chimed out as if he were not speak-ing but singing, "is here now."

He fell silent, leaned back against the tile stove and, perhaps to stop them from being able to move, folded his arms on his chest and bowed his head. A little bit later he spoke the same way again, head bowed, as if he were not speaking to Köves, just as he had done in the South Seas when they had got to know each other:

"For a long time man was superfluous, but free. It was up to him to beg for what was necessary, or in other words, for grace—as I have already said, they are the same thing. Now, though," he raised his voice, "man is just superfluous, and he can only redeem his superfluousness by service."

"What sort of service?" Köves asked after the passage of what he judged to be a decent pause.

"The service of order." Berg again raised his discomfiting gaze.

"What sort of order?" Köves was a rather timid about putting a further question, fearing that Berg might get sick of the conversation before it was time, but he could not miss out on a chance to possibly learn something.

An answer came back, however, even if it bore a noticeable touch of irritation:

"That's a matter of indifference; it's enough for it to be order." Berg again hunted, and this time he took hold of a scribbled sheet. "Here we are," he said in doing so, "a few words that were left out of the preface but will definitely have to be fitted into the work somewhere else," and then started reading: "Because, Ladies and Gentlemen, if things go on like they are, life's demands will soon exceed the bounds of man's moral capacity, and believe me: man will only be redeemed by order, by setting those demands into an enthralling system..."

It seemed it was now Köves's turn to lose his patience:

"You're constantly using words that," he didn't even wait for Berg to stop speaking, "that I never hear anyone else using. 'Moral capacity'!" he exclaimed. "What do you mean by 'moral'?"

"Sensitivity to crime," Berg replied.

"Crime!" Köves fumed on. "And what's a crime?"

"Man," said Berg with a short, cool smile.

"Man!" Köves reiterated. "And what is man's crime?"

"That he is accused," said Berg.

"Accused of what?" Köves dug in.

"Of being guilty."

"But of what does his crime consist?" Köves wouldn't give way.

"Of being accused," and although this had brought them full circle, Köves cried out as if there must still be some way of breaking out of this:

"But what's the good of that?"

"Of what?" Berg asked.

"Of accusing man!" and here a cold, bloodless smile again appeared around Berg's fleshy lips:

"To make him understand his superfluousness, and, having understood his superfluousness, to yearn for grace in his misery."

"I see." Köves fell silent for a while, though it seemed he was far from reconciled to the answer.

He then suddenly asked:

"Does there exist another world, besides the one in which we live?"

"How could it exist?!" Berg appeared to be truly hurt. "It is not allowed to exist," he added severely, as if he were forbidding it.

"Why not?" Köves enquired.

"Because it would complete our spoliation. Plus it would make even our superfluousness superfluous."

"In that case," Köves now posed the question, "who is your 'executioner' addressing all along?" In so doing he may well have touched on a sore point for Berg, because only after a protracted and visibly difficult struggle did he commit himself to answering:

"Even if it seems that another world comes into existence while one is writing, it is only on account of the blasted demands of the genre that it seems so, on account of the blasted demands of the game, the blasted demands of irony … anyway, it can only seem that way because the other world doesn't exist," he said in the end.

"But it must still exist in our hopes all the same," came Köves's quiet objection.

"It can't exist, because there is nothing in which we can hope," was Berg's instant retort.

"Yet you write nevertheless." Köves was doubtful.

"What do you mean by that?" Berg asked.

"That you hope all the same," Köves asserted.

"In other words," and a faint, affronted smile appeared on Berg's lips, "you're accusing me of deception?"

"You draw the boundaries too tight." Köves strove to avoid giving a straight answer. "Something," he faltered, "something is missing from the construction…"

"Yes," there was a glint of mockery in Berg's eyes, "I know what you're going to say now: life."

"Precisely," Köves agreed. "You speak about order, and you confuse that with life."

"Order," Berg spoke, "is the terrain, the battlefield on which life takes place."

"That may be, but it's still not life," Köves countered. "You're banishing the accidental and all other chance…"

"The accidental?" Berg gaped. "What do you have in mind?" He smiled in the way one smiles at a child.

"I don't know," Köves squirmed uneasily, and in all likelihood he didn't know, although their conversation reminded him of a conversation he had had with someone else in the dim and distant past, at the commencement of his arrival there, and thus of his life, as it were, during which he had argued in similar terms: he had not learned much since then, it appeared. "The way you talk," he finally grasped for the words in his helplessness, though this time there may also have been a touch of asperity from knowing he was right, "it's as if all of us get totally bogged down in the mess, whereas you, I notice, have somehow managed to find a way out, if you please."

"Harsh words." Berg was astonished. "Provide some evidence to back that up," he demanded grimly.

It seemed, however, that Köves was not going to take the opportunity:

"What is that...," he began a question with a pensive look on his face, "that definitive first act that, if I rightly recall, the hero commits under pressure of external compulsion, yet nevertheless without the external force being present at the time?"

"Yes," Berg started as though bringing his mind back from dwelling on other things, "that's a decisive, I might almost say crystal-clear passage in the construction. Still, what the act is I don't exactly know as yet—it's something I still have to work out," he said, and brushed it aside.

"In that case," Köves was curious, "how does he know that he's going to commit it?"

"He has to commit it, because, as I say, the construction is ready to hand." Berg was growing impatient. "The opening and the end for sure; it's just the path stretching between that I don't yet see quite clearly."

"Yes," Köves said, "and that path is life itself." Then with a smile, as if he had just noticed them, he remarked: "You have some fresh petits-fours."

"As you see," Berg got out in a somehow strangled voice, his gaze veritably looking daggers at Köves, "I am trying to refrain from that pleasure."

"Oh yes," Köves hastened to acknowledge, "I see."

Then next thing he knew he was asking:

"And love...," here he wavered for a moment as if, now that he had got it out, he himself were looking back in astonishment at the word that had popped out of his own mouth, as at an obstacle he had thought was unjumpable. "Is love not grace?" he went on to pose the question nevertheless.

This time, though, he seemed to have violated some concealed boundary, because the storms of emotion that swept over Berg's face were such as to truly scare Köves.

"What's that got to do with me?!" erupted from him, and he almost jumped up from behind his table. "Even if it is grace, it's not mine; I'm at best its victim ... Yes," he carried on, "they tolerate me, like this, as I am—you can see what I'm like, can't you—and by way of, indeed on the pretext of taking care of me—well, I can confidently say they tyrannize me, even though it is, no doubt, experienced by them as suffering ..."

"Why suffering?" Köves's curiosity, it seemed, got the better of his initial horror at having rattled Berg so thoroughly.

"Because a tyrant always suffers." Berg seemed to have been somewhat mollified by being able to expound his reasoning. "Suffering," he went on, "partly from himself, partly from his unachievable ambition, since he can never rule absolutely over others, that being impossible as there is always an ultimate, unassailable retreat, into madness or death, if nowhere else—so he ends up turning against himself. You know, I sometimes think that martyrs are the most perfect tyrants. At least, theirs is the purest form of tyranny, before which everyone kowtows..."

For a short while, he seemed to be brooding before suddenly and alarmingly exclaiming "Oh!" and then so much plaintiveness sounded in his expressive voice that Köves felt obliged to lower his head in shame and out of respect, so to say, as Berg went on: "how terrible it is! We long for love, to be loved, but at the same time how it humiliates us! What a victory love is! What tyranny! What slavery!... It forever eats away at the conscience like the disgrace of the bloodiest crime..." After the first, alarming cry, Berg's voice slipped ever lower, so that Köves barely understood the final words;

even after that, Berg whispered something he did not pick out at all. After sufficient time had elapsed for it no longer to look like impoliteness, Köves cautiously got to his feet, remarking that he was very tired, he had not slept much the night before, which after all was true, just as the claim to be feeling exhausted was not an outright excuse, so he would have to take his leave, at which Berg glanced up at him as if he had only just noticed he was still there. Then he too got up with unwonted affability—this rather disconcerted Köves, because it was a little as though something in Berg had broken and he had somehow flopped together more in a heap, and moreover without having noticed, or at most with an awkward shyness, one might even say with humility, moving onto his face—and accompanied Köves to the door, where, hardly giving clear expression to what was on his mind (if indeed his thoughts were dwelling on Köves and on the words intended for him) he declared:

"I'll be glad to be at your disposal another time," and with that Köves, to his undeniable relief, was once more outside, first in the stairwell, then down below in the street. He set off homewards on foot—the fresh air could do no harm, then back at home he could finally have a good sleep: if he had been sacked, he would at least enjoy the advantages of his regained freedom—and it seems his mind must have still been on the conversation with Berg, because on getting close to the house he noticed merely that he had landed in the middle of an excited crowd. He had to push his way though mostly old people, women, and sick people—idle or retired people with time to spare—in order to reach the front door, registering only as much of the words which were flying about around him as were absolutely inescapable: "from the chandelier," "the end of a rope," "had to smash the door in," "monstrous," "by his own hand," and "they telephoned her at the office," he heard while, coming to the house, he noticed that a dark, angular automobile with its doors closed was parked in front. Then two men in caps and some indeterminable uniform stepped out of the house, and on the stretcher that they slid into the load space through the rear door, and swathed from head to toe in some sort of sheet, lay a figure which seemed, from the size of the shape protruding from beneath the linen, to be the body of an adolescent boy. At that moment, an almost implausibly sharp, irregularly broken scream shattered the hush which had suddenly descended just beforehand, almost as if by magic, before Mrs. Weigand appeared in the entranceway, though to Köves—of course, it was just his tiredness, to say nothing of his astonishment which must have shown her in that absurd complexion—it seemed it was not Mrs. Weigand herself, but rather someone or something else who was screaming out of her throat and waving her head and arms about, a foreign being that had taken up residence in her and to which she was completely surrendering herself in her shocked and uncomprehending defencelessness: inconceivable pain.

CHAPTER EIGHT

Köves returns. Changes. The drowning man

One fine day, Köves turned up again at the South Seas; he had
not been there for a long time, he had been in the army, because
the same post as the dismissal letter from the ministry had also
brought a demand that he immediately discharge his deferred military service, at which the army had sniffed him in and swallowed
him up, until the day came when even it could stomach him no
longer and one morning—it happened to be during the solemn
moments when general orders are read out—he dropped full length
on the floor, almost knocking over a chair and two fellow squaddies
in the process, then showed no inclination to return to his senses,
despite being disciplined, punished, taken to task, and pilloried, so
he was finally carted off to hospital, where he was surrounded by
suspicious doctors who cross-questioned him, took samples of his
blood, tapped his limbs, thrust a needle into his spine, and—just
at the point when he was fearing he would be unmasked, with the
attendant, none too promising consequences—abruptly and most
unceremoniously, so he barely had time even to be surprised, though
there was plenty of reason for that, he was discharged, because one
of the checks had shown that one of his thighs was an inch thinner
than the other and, even though Köves was unaware of it, he was
probably suffering from muscular dystrophy. Sziklai's face split into
a thousand pieces from laughter when Köves told him the whole
story:

"They could hardly wait to get rid of you, old chap!" he slapped
Köves on the thigh in question and put the fortunate outcome of
the affair "solely down to the changes."

"What changes?" Köves was amazed, being up to date on

nothing since he had been recently preoccupied with rather different matters.

Yet Sziklai did not appear to be much better informed than him:

"Can anyone know?!" he almost reproached Köves for his tactlessness, and it had been so long since Köves had heard the question that, for the first time since he had been discharged from hospital and the army, he was almost seized by a feeling of having found his way back home.

"In any event, one can sense winds of change," Sziklai went on, half rising from his seat to scan round the coffeehouse, as though searching for someone. "Just look over there." He nodded before long toward one of the distant tables. "Do you know the gentleman who is ensconced at the head of the table?" The aging, stout man with the prominent chin and vigorous nose whom Köves glimpsed in the direction indicated, and whom, under other circumstances, might have struck Köves as imperious, was very likely someone he had seen before somewhere; nevertheless he had to wait until Sziklai enlightened him:

"Don't tell me you no longer recognize our all-powerful editor in chief?" At which, suddenly cottoning on, Köves was veritably flooded with grievances which had by now melted into distant, as good as forgivably sunny memories of a long, long bygone age, and now he fancied he also recognized the two thickset, balding men seated on either side of the editor in chief: they seemed to be identical people from the factory, though he was far from certain about that and, with the table standing so far away in a gloomy room, there was every chance he was mistaken.

"He was sacked," Sziklai grinned.

"Sacked?...," Köves was astonished.

"No kidding: times are like that now." Sziklai again settled comfortably on his chair. They had even sought him out, he related, offering him a job back on the newspaper, as a columnist at that, because it turned out that what they had done to him was not just against the law but flew in the face of common sense, as Sziklai had been one of the most outstanding people they had.

"They woke up to it a little too late," Sziklai said, shrugging his shoulders. "I'd be crazy to go back to being a reporter when I've settled down so brilliantly with the fire brigade." But no doubt they would take Köves back, he hastened to add; he had already put out feelers along those lines, and...

Köves, though, writhed on his seat as if he had been suddenly stabbed:

"I'm not going back to the paper!" he protested as though tormented by bad dreams.

"So you already have a job, then?" Sziklai enquired.

"I'm not going to get a job!" Köves declared so adamantly and, with such a cold repugnance, that it was as if he were not speaking for himself but maybe on behalf of someone else with far more important, far more pressing things to attend to than to fritter away his irreplaceable time in any mere job.

"And what do you intend to live off of?" Sziklai was curious.

"I don't know," Köves declared, this time in a tone of grave concern: he appeared only now to have woken up to his hard and seemingly extreme decision, as if he had not taken it himself but rather had been impelled by some external force, and at that moment one had the impression that he himself was, perhaps, even less prepared for the implications of this than was Sziklai, who assessed these things from a practical standpoint and considered that Köves could make a living without having a job. In his opinion, they would just be happy that Köves did not "come forward with any claims against them," in return for which they would clearly offer—Sziklai "would have a thing or two to say about that too"—to take him on as a special correspondent: if Köves was smart and industrious, he might be able to "place an article with them" every week.

"Besides which," Sziklai smiled, "the Firefighters' Platform is naturally waiting for you with open arms, old chap," and he related to a happily dumbfounded Köves that while Köves had been away in the army, he, Sziklai, had not been "loafing about" either. It may have taken time, and it was not without its difficulties, but he had managed to get "the managers" to understand that rather than using their own amateur-dramatic society, the job of gaining the fire brigade mass appeal would be done much more effectively and successfully by well-known professional actors who were beloved by all, insofar as he could persuade them to place their talents in the service of the fire brigade, at least for one night. Now, one could not expect professional actors "to play any old role," so that meant professional writers needed to be won over, like the actors, to the idea of placing their skills at the fire brigade's disposal and each put together an evening of entertainment which, at a professional level, skilfully and effectively blending tragedy and comedy, was drawn from the subject matter of firefighting, or at least somehow touching on it. Consequently, since they were talking about professionals, it would not do to forget about the customary fees which would be owed them; indeed, it would do no harm—given that they had to be won over to a line of duties which was out of the ordinary, not to say special—to offer something a touch over the customary. That was how the Firefighters' Platform had come into existence: a small touring company which played in towns and villages alike, and every other month presented a new programme, generally consisting of a compering role and "sketches."

"The compere's lines are always written by me," Sziklai pointed out with an obdurate expression on his face, as though Köves might have some idea of denying him, "and I always write one of the sketches, as does my boss, the deputy commander ... seeing as how he has lately discovered the inner writer in himself ... you know how it is," he winked at Köves, "...and from now on you will write one of them, and then we could even do yet another one as co-authors, under a pen name, though we'll actually write all three of them together, of course, old chap." Provided he could make do with little, then, Köves would be able to make a living from sketches and newspaper articles—that is, until the light comedy was completed, of course, when they would be dealing with success and never again be tormented by financial concerns, Sziklai spurred him on before raising an arm to ask Alice over to their table, more than likely wishing to anoint their high hopes with a higher-class hooch, except that in Alice's place a greasy-faced, flat-footed, paunchy waiter waddled over, for one fine day, to the great sorrow of all the South Seas' regulars, Alice had vanished from the coffeehouse.

"Where to?...," Köves was astonished, but he asked Sziklai, and later others too, in vain. She had handed in her notice one day and just vanished, and her post had not been filled since: obviously at the back of it was that dubious, disagreeable, and freakish character, likewise not seen since, on whom Alice had wrongheadedly squandered her time, her attractions, and, no doubt, her earnings as well—that was about all he managed to find out, though when he probed a bit more thoroughly it immediately became clear that this was all just speculation, the only certainty being that Alice was no longer in the South Seas.

Another face that, although once so familiar, had been missing even longer now, rather like Köves, turned up again out of the blue. This face had changed, everyone agreed on that: it had become longer and yet somehow wizened, a bit decrepit, but it was still the same face that, even so, looked down on the others from a towering height from over a bow tie of uncertain colour: it was Tiny, the pianist, and his appearance, as Köves was able to observe with wonderment, was by no means greeted with joy on all sides, more with a certain amount of embarrassment. There was a rumbling in the South Seas, rather like the rumble of a wave suddenly dashing on a rocky channel, and that was how backs and heads moved, rising and falling in alternation on the wave, though only a few people—at the musicians' table, for example—stood up to welcome him, and rather hesitantly at that, with a cautious, somehow crooked smile on their faces, whereas others carried on their momentarily interrupted conversations as if nothing had happened, particularly a large male group, all in black tails underneath which each wore a red silk cummerbund: the members of the Tango String Band, until all at once there was a scraping of a chair being pushed back, though with a noise more befitting a throne than a mere chair, and from it, with the assistance of nimble hands placed under the elbow, the Uncrowned staggered to his feet, threw his stubby arms apart, and with much puffing and blowing, sweating profusely, embraced the stupefied musician (or to be more precise, leapt at his neck), and however strange the spectacle offered by the embrace of these two portly men—the smaller one and the giant—the South Seas regulars were nonetheless able to regard the Uncrowned's act as constituting some sort of solemn proclamation, so to speak, an authorisation, indeed invitation, because, as if waiting for a signal, all at once now almost everyone jumped up, so that they too might hug the pianist or shake his hand, or at least touch the hem of his jacket, pass him from hand to hand, to celebrate and ask him about his sufferings.

Later on, though, he became the centre of endless, heated debates: Köves could only wonder at how much excitement, emotion, and passion which, lacking a specific object, must have been seething hitherto in the South Seas, nebulously like cigarette smoke, for it now all to condense suddenly around, as it were, the magnetic personality of Tiny, the pianist, and coil around, bubble like a maelstrom in the form of sharp reproofs, embittered outbursts, indeed veiled accusations and barely concealed mutual threats. There were cases where, with arguments running low, or when people tired of reasoned argument, they simply hurled short slogans tersely from table to table (by then the musicians had split between two tables, with Tiny's supporters at one and their opponents, the Tango String

Band to the fore of course, at the other, though there were some who sat today at one and next day at the other, indeed, even some who did not take a seat at all, but scampered between the two tables, perhaps unable to make up their minds, perhaps mediating conciliatorily or, on the contrary, further fuelling the antagonisms, who could tell)—battle cries like, for instance, "Tiny to the piano!" which would elicit the response, "You can't blackmail us!," even though Tiny had no wish to sit down at the piano, so there could be no question of any blackmail either, as gradually became evident to Köves at any rate. The hefty disputes, the most serious arguments, of course, were aired at the Uncrowned's table, and Köves, who caught only snatches of what was said, gathered it was about whether Tiny, who as a result of the changes everyone knew about—or, to be more correct, that no one at all knew about precisely, and yet were still obvious to everyone—had, from one day to the next, been released from the agricultural labour to which he had been carted off, and whose carting-off moreover was judged as "lacking any legal foundation," notwithstanding which he had not been given back his job ("the piano he was hauled away from"); so, whether Tiny should be satisfied with whatever work he could get, and resign himself to possibly having to play in some out-of-the-way dive or not compromise and hold out—through the courts if need be"—to regain his original position, currently being usurped by the Tango String Band.

Or rather, an elderly, leather-jacketed marketeer raised his index finger—among the Uncrowned's dyers, marketeers, photographers, and all sorts of other employees, as it now turned out there were also some advocates and barristers, though nowadays, of course, they were not pursuing their original occupations—or rather, the leather-jacketed marketeer corrected them with a pedantic smile:

"Gentlemen, let's not throw hasty expressions around: instead of "usurpers" we would do better to accept … let's say the formulation "those currently having legal title," because that objectively reflects the facts," which met with prompt agreement from the leader of the Tango String Band, a man with burning eyes, whose oily black hair was plastered sleekly to his brow. The Tango String Band, he explained with his burning eyes, and with his bony, yellow hands scything the air, the fingers spatula-shaped through constantly gripping his string instrument, nails clipped to the quick—and he could safely assert that all the members of the band shared this view, could only be delighted that the unmerited vilification of a "fellow musician," and what was more "a fellow musician of such great attainments," had been ended, but might he be permitted to ask why "an innocent band was now being mucked about as live scapegoats" when their only "sin" was that, certainly, "they were tied by a legal contractual relationship to the nightclub," and, certainly, did not intend to break that contract until it had "legally" expired. To which one comment was that, if the Tango String Band really were so delighted about an artist, "without exaggeration, a great artist," regaining his freedom, then instead of continually protesting about a "legal contractual relationship," they should consider it "their moral duty" to give up their position to the person to whom it "rightfully belongs." Out of the general tumult unleashed by these words the index finger rose up once more, and its owner, the elderly marketeer, made the observation that although he would not like to be looked on by anybody as the sort of person who was "indifferent in respect of moral questions," nevertheless he did not think it appropriate to shift discussion onto "a solely moral plane" because:

"Don't forget, gentlemen, that a 'moral duty' may be a moral duty, but that doesn't make it a legal concept," he reminded the rest of the table with a subtle, clever smile.

It seemed his words had little effect, however, as the discussion had irretrievably shifted solely to the moral plane and carried on that way, with references to "Tiny's sufferings," and in response with great insistence initially, to the "innocent band" and the "legal contractual relationship" but later on with the counter-accusation of "blackmail," and in the midst of the ensuing general uproar Köves's ear also picked out the word "revenge"—to his uneasy surprise, most likely out of the mouth of the baggy-eyed saxophone player, who, together with the blue-chinned musician (who still reeked of hair oil), as Köves was somewhat bewildered to notice, was most vocal in springing to the pianist's defence. Köves would hardly have ventured (nor of course did he wish to) to remind them of that long-bygone, rather unfortunate conversation that he'd had with them when he had been enquiring about Tiny.

Yet the fact that the pianist had an opinion of his own about his own affair, and moreover one that differed from everyone else's, Köves only got to learn at last late one evening, with the coffeehouse almost empty except for some musicians on their day off, a few incorrigible regulars, along with Köves himself, of course, who were still loitering around the place (Sziklai was not in the South Seas that day as the Firefighters' Platform happened to be presenting their new show out of town), when the musician, grasping a half-emptied small glass of cognac to which the Uncrowned had treated him quite a while earlier, strolled over to Köves's table and asked:

"May I?" at which Köves of course was delighted to invite him to take a seat, having not seen him in the coffeehouse, it now occurred to him, in point of fact for days on end, although it was precisely during these days that the passions raging around his figure had been at their most ferocious pitch, as if the absence of the subject of the disputes not only did not disturb the disputants but was considered to be practically a condition for the disputes to proceed undisturbed.

"What do they know?!" the pianist said to Köves with an indulgently disdainful smile, gesturing vaguely with his head at the virtually empty tables around the place, and went on to tell him that they had made him carry out farm work—digging potatoes, feeding pigs. "I had to get up at the same time as I used to go to bed ... I could tell you stories, but what's the point?" he continued. "I have a sound constitution, I stuck it out." In time, they got to know at HQ that he was a professional musician, and the officers had ordered him to play something. They had procured a violin for him to start with—that being the commander's favourite instrument: he wanted to hear his much-loved songs on the violin, and had become truly furious at him for not knowing how to play that instrument, even doubting whether he could be a musician at all if he couldn't. In the end, they had procured a piano (in reality, an out-of-tune upright pianino), and he had to play on that. By way of a reward he would be given a helping of special rations and exemptions from some tasks, as well as having poured into him the sour local vino, on which the officers used to get smashed. Later on, he was also allowed to play at village dances, then there was an occasion when he had to accompany a third-rate scratch Gypsy band, sawing away on their beat-up fiddles and wheezing through their clarinets—one could just imagine how that sounded. He had cursed the day when he admitted to being a musician a hundred times over; even feeding the pigs was more respectable work than that.

"And now I'm supposed to start all over again?" the pianist smiled hesitantly, dubiously. "There was a time," he mused, "when if I could not play for two days running, I would be itching, raring to go so badly I would almost go nuts. And now?… I'd be happy not to see a piano. I've burned out, old chum. Here," and with the tip of a crooked middle finger, looking almost as though he were intently listening inwardly, he cautiously tapped on his chest as though on a closed gate that he had already been asking to be let in through for quite some time in vain, "There's no more music inside here…," and it was useless for Köves to reassure him that, once he had rested himself and got back to a normal life, he would see, the inclination would return, the musician mournfully shook his head in doubt.

In recent days, the South Seas regulars had also been preoc-cupied by another case, likewise the subject of widespread debate among themselves, though this time engendering merriment rather than dissension. Köves learned from Sziklai why it was he had not seen Pumpadour around at all recently, and the Transcendental Concubine only rarely, and even then not with the customary schnapps glasses, but totally sober, her vaguely dreamy gaze now replaced by a slightly crabbed look, like someone who has been rudely wakened from a prolonged sleep by cold reality, and who was always in a hurry, always laden with parcels and shopping bags, which had never been the case before.

"She bakes and cooks," Sziklai chuckled.

"How's that?" Köves marvelled, and Sziklai, who—at least "until events took a tragic turn"—now knew everything "first-hand," from Pumpadour himself, for whom Sziklai had of late been securing regular appearances with the Firefighters' Platform, told Köves that "things have started to look up for her," with Pumpadour suddenly deciding to ask the Transcendental to marry him, and she, bridling at the idea, in a nonexistent world, of becoming the nonexistent wife of a nonexistent person, who was not even an actor but a repairer of clocks, though more a repairer of lighters than of clocks, became so infuriated that she declared she never wanted to see Pumpadour again. Time passed, but the Transcendental showed herself to be unbending, declaring roundly to Sziklai, who "tried to mediate," that she "simply didn't understand how our relationship could have degenerated to this," whereas Pumpadour complained to Sziklai that the woman was his "last fling," and that if he did not win her hand, "life would have no meaning." In the end, he had written her a letter asking her for "just one final meeting." The woman had consented, promising to pay a visit at the specified time, while for the occasion Pumpadour cobbled together a device out of all sorts of wires, an acid of some kind and an ordinary battery and taped this tightly to his body under his jacket—the device being intended to blow up and "kill both of them" the moment they embraced. Either he miscalculated, or the device was not foolproof, or maybe a combination of the two: perhaps the Transcendental disentangled herself from the hug before Pumpadour was able to activate the device, or maybe the batch was too weak, or the tightness of grip, "the two bodies clinging together," that Pumpadour had reckoned on for a detonation was missing—but in fact Pumpadour alone experienced the explosion, the outcome of which, apart from the scare, was nothing more serious than some bruising and burns to the chest. The Transcendental had immediately run to call a doctor and ambulance, while Pumpadour, overacting as ever, Sziklai said, had fainted, was carried off to hospital, and although his injuries had healed quickly, had meanwhile been discovered to have stomach ulcers, so now the Transcendental visited him regularly, taking in his meals for him, since he had been put on a special diet.

"How's it all going to end?" Köves cheered up, and Sziklai, likewise laughing, suggested:

"I fear the same way as our comedy: a happy end!" because, after many vicissitudes, interruptions, and fresh beginnings, the comedy had, indeed, now begun to take shape, with Köves usually working on the dialogue in the South Seas, so that at least when he was trying to write a comedy he was not haunted by the depressing spectacle of mourning perpetually accorded him by Mrs. Weigand since her son's suicide, her eyes long not the limpid pools that Köves had once seen them as, but now covered by frozen sheets of permanent ice, his ears catching through the walls, night after night, the stifled sound of her sobbing. Besides which, Köves anyway found it easier to write a light comedy in the racket of the coffeehouse than in the loneliness of his own room, where he was constantly in danger that his attention would wander and escape his control, with foreign figures intruding onto the stage out of nowhere, such as an old man with a little dog tucked under one arm and a suitcase in the other hand; or else he was supposed to be hammering out the comedy's ditzy, exciting, flighty, and adorable female character, but suddenly into her place other girls would push forward on whom he did not recognize those characteristics, at most their dearth—the factory girl, for example, who had been waiting for the death of her aunt from cancer and, for all he knew, might still be waiting now. Images would come vaguely to mind, memories lurk in waiting, all images and memories which had no place in a comedy and, as Köves thought, would probably not have come to mind if those empty white sheets of paper were not staring up at him, and if he did not have to sit there facing them. In his excruciating dreams (Köves had recently been sleeping poorly, indeed having bad dreams), like an alluvium which was continually sinking only to keep stubbornly resurfacing, he would sometimes make out a word, a word that, although not written down anywhere, he could nevertheless almost see, somehow starting with the letters of his name, but longer—*követelés*: "demand"? or maybe it was *köte-lesség*: "duty"?—and then, if he looked closer, was not even a word but a drowning man, tumbling around amidst the waves, and Köves felt he ought to fling himself in after him to rescue him from the current before he drowned. Then, all at once, he was seized by a fit of rage: "Why me?" he thought in his dream, but it was no use looking around, he was on his own, facing the drowning man. He almost jumped, though he feared it would be a fateful jump, and the drowning man would pull him down into the maelstrom—then, fortunately, he would wake up in time, but the unpleasant atmosphere of the silly dream would trouble him for the whole day.

Letter. Consternation

One afternoon, Köves was sitting at the table in his lonely room—not long before, a late-summer light shower swept over the city, so, as he had no wish to get drenched, Köves had set to work at home—and probably even he thought he was debating whether he should make a start on the sketch that needed to be delivered for the Firefighters' Platform, or should he write the newspaper article that was due, or should he get on with the light comedy, when, all of a sudden, he caught himself writing something that seemed most likely intended as the opening lines of a letter:

> Lately, I have been thinking of you constantly. To be more specific, not so much of you as of what you read out; or to be even more specific, not so much of what you read out as of... You see, it's precisely about this that I want to write. How can that be? That's simple. Because I have picked up certain experiences which will certainly come in very handy for you, whereas I don't know what to do with them. In short, I want to be of assistance to you, because you can't deny that you are stuck. I believe you when you say that "the construction is ready to hand," but there is something looming up between the "man of intellect and culture" and 30,000 corpses—maybe it too is just a corpse, but in any event the first, and thus the most important, because the question is whether it can be stepped over or ultimately presents an insurmountable barrier. Yes, that definitive first act which subsequently "proves to be an irrevocable choice," if I rightly recall, just because it happened, and because it could have happened, indeed nothing else could have happened, and although it happens under the pressure of external compulsion, it does so in such a way that the external compulsion happens not to be present at the time, or is present merely as a circumstantial factor (with your permission, I would tag on the latter). It is governed by a purely helpful intention, then, though possibly also a little by one of protest; no, I can't think of a better word for it at present

than "protest," though I don't know what it is I am protesting against. I bow to your superior learning, but as I have already said many times, your learning lacks the colour of life, which usually shades into grey. You see, how precisely you visualize the extremes, but you get stuck on the simple, grey, absurd motive which leads to the extreme, because you are unable to imagine the simple, grey, absurd act, and the simple, grey, absurd path leading to that act. Just between the two of us, it's not easy to do so; indeed, I'd go so far as to say it's almost impossible.

So listen!

Let's start with me being called up by the army. I was reluctant to comply with the call-up order, in the way one is always reluctant to fulfil one's personal destiny, all the more so as one usually does not perceive it as such. Every possible and impossible get-out crossed my mind, even including the idea of jumping off a high point in such a way that I would break a leg, but a friend (a fire officer) informed me that there was no sense in that, because they would simply wait until the fracture had mended, then whisk me off to be a soldier.

So, I went off, dazed and apathetic like a lamb to the slaughter, and, before I knew what was what, I was being fitted up in a uniform. You can't expect me to fill you in on the horrors of barracks life, which may be rather well known, but still strike one as new if one experiences them personally. What I might say about them, perhaps, is that it is a complete absence, indeed denial, of one's uniqueness, coupled with the incessant and intensified delights of physical being. It's not true that one's personality ceases to exist; it's more that it is multiplied, which is a big difference, of course. And incidentally, to my no small surprise, when it came to physical performance I held my ground splendidly, often in the most literal sense, which as time went by filled me with almost a sense of self-satisfaction, as though the space vacated by my uniqueness had been occupied by the soul of a racehorse, which, in the intervals between being disciplined and made to run around, spots a good breather in the collective dormitory, in the steaming body-warmth, the loosening, eerily familiar atmosphere of frivolity and banishment. The barracks town was situated in some unknown part of the country, on a desolate plain, where the wind whistled incessantly and bells from the distant settlements tolled incessantly, and I well remember one dawn, when I was standing in line in the open air, in front of the kitchen, holding a mug for coffee: the sun had just risen, the sky was hanging dirtily and shabbily above us; my underpants (in which, just beforehand, I had been performing physical jerks to orders that had been barked out through megaphones) were clinging, clammy from rain and sweat, to my skin when, all of a sudden—through an indefinable decaying stench, compounded of ersatz coffee, soaked clothes, sweaty bodies, fields at daybreak, and latrines—broke a memory, though it was as if the memory was not mine, but somebody else's whom I seemed to remember having seen once in a similar situation, some time long ago, somewhere else, a long way away, in a sunken world lying far beyond the chasms of all prohibitions, dimly and by now barely discernibly, a child, a boy who was once taken away to be murdered.

If you don't mind, I won't supply any further details.

Yet what a filthy dream I woke up to once! I am standing in a room by a desk, behind which is seated an obese, hormonally challenged bonehead, with matted hair, rotting teeth, bags under his eyes, and a sneer on his face: a major, and what he wants is for me to put my signature at the bottom of a piece of paper and accept a post as a prison guard in the central military prison.

So…

I tell him—because what else can I say?—"I'm not suitable." And what do you think the jackass with the overactive glands and the rotten-toothed grin replies? "No one is born to be a prison guard"—that's what he says, by way of encouragement. Look at it this way, others had signed up, meaning the rest of them, my fellow squaddies, because the whole platoon had been singled out for the job. "But I'm a man of intellect and culture," I try once more. (You don't by any chance know why precisely that phrase should have come to my mind?) To that he says: "Do you like the people?" I ask you, what answer are you supposed to give to that, if life is sweet to you, even if you happen not to like the people, since who on earth could have room for enough love to go round an entire people, and anyway the sonofabitch isn't asking you to sign up as a god, just as a prison guard. So I say, "Yes." "Do you hate the enemy?" is the next question, and again, what answer are you supposed to give to that, even if you have not seen hide nor hair of the enemy, and as to hating, it's at most just this major you hate, and even him (human nature being what it is, its attention soon distracted and quick to forget) only in passing. "Right then, sign here!" he says, and he stabs a disgusting, stubby, flat-nailed, nicotine-stained index finger at the piece of paper. So, I take the pen from him and sign where he is indicating.

I'm trying to think why. Whichever way I look at it, I can see only one real reason: time. Yes, and this is something you may find a little curious, but only because, as I say, you are not familiar with the colours of life and don't know that what we later on view as an event of major significance always appears initially in the guise of little curiosities, but it was mainly due to time that I signed. In the end, no pressing reason came to mind, and I couldn't just stand there for an eternity, pen in hand. You might say there was no need for me to take it in my hand. Well, yes, but then the whole thing seemed so unreal that I did not feel my signature was any more real. I personally was completely shut out of the moment, if I may put it that way: I took no part in it, my existence went to sleep, or was paralyzed inside me, or at any rate it gave no twinge of unease to warn me of the importance of the decision. And anyway, was it a decision at all, or at least my decision? After all, it wasn't me who chose the situation in which I had to make a choice, moreover a choice between two things, neither of which I wished to choose: I didn't wish to become a prison guard, of course, but nor did I wish to be punished, for although it's true that no one threatened punishment, that is something one takes for granted from the outset and is usually not far wrong about. Then again, there were a few incidental factors which played a part: I have the sort of nature which prefers to try to please people rather than pick a fight, so I would have to say that I was also driven to some extent by courtesy, but maybe also, in some way, by curiosity to see what a prison here is like, though in such a way that I was safe. So you see, any number of reasons relating to the spirit of frivolity and eerie familiarity that I have already mentioned were being impressed on me by my surroundings.

This is sounding as though I were making excuses, when I am merely bearing you out, for I stepped onto the path of grace—or at least what you call grace.

Not long after that, I found myself in the prison. I shall never forget my first impression: solid wooden doors lining a cool stone corridor; alongside the walls, widely separated, men standing with hands held behind their backs, foreheads pressed to the wall. They were clothed in worn-out military fatigues, without insignia, belt, or indication of rank. Armed guards were standing about at both ends of the corridor. Every now and then, a soldier hurries the length of the corridor; his glinting boots, coloured collar-patches, pistol jiggling on his butt, his supreme indifference, a true provocation. Otherwise, endless time and perpetual, suffocating stillness. And a particular odour; there is no better term for it than a prison stench.

I landed there, then, and it was not long before I was looking around with an eerie sense of familiarity. What else could I have done? I am being careful not to portray as simple what was apparently simple: for instance, you won't hear a word from me about force of habit, or anything else which presents the reality as reality just because it is the reality; not for a second did I consider it as being natural to be there, and on the other hand not a second could pass that I did not consider as being natural, since I was there, after all. So, nothing struck me straight away: I saw no torture chambers, nobody starving to death. Admittedly, there were some nights when executions took place in the courtyard but, for one thing, I didn't see them, for another, they were wrapped in a shroud of legality: death sentences passed by a court of law. There was generally an explanation for everything. Nothing went beyond the bounds and scale that, so it seems, I was able to accept. The military prison wasn't the worst of prisons either; its inmates had either been sentenced for ordinary transgressions or breaches of service regulations, or they were waiting to be sentenced, unlike "over there," as people, somewhat enigmatic expressions on their faces, referred to the customs service's prison, which was separated from ours by an impenetrable wall.

Enough of this, though! It's starting to sound as if I wanted to describe the circumstances—or in other words, again offer excuses—and as if the circumstances could be described anyway. They can't. I long, long ago resigned myself to the fact that I shall never know where I am living and what laws I am governed by; that I am reliant on my sensory organs and my most immediate experiences, though even they can be deceptive, indeed maybe them most of all.

It's funny, but before anything else I had to attend a school, a sort of course, where, along with my fellow squaddies, I was given instruction in what a prison guard had to do. I recollect the smile I had when I took my place on this course: it was the smile of the damned, of one who was, by then, ready for anything in the spirit of the contract, with the scrutiny of that bitter smile being the only reservation.

But I had not expected what happened next. What did I expect? I don't know exactly; how could I? Essentially something along the lines that they, in their own crafty way (about which again I can have had no precise notion), would put my brains, my soul, even my body to work; would instruct and bully me, din into me, some crude, savage, and blind consciousness; in short, prepare me for my sinister job. Instead of which, what do I hear? You'll never believe it: they are perpetually going on about the law, about rights and duties, regulations, records, procedures, official channels, health regulations, and so on and so forth. And don't think this was done disingenuously, with a hideous,

337

hand-wringing grin on their faces: not a bit of it! With the straightest imaginable expression, not one word out of place, not one collusive wink. I couldn't get over it: Could this be their method? They pitch me in among prisoners, then leave me to myself? Are they relying on my duties to transform me, to break me in? Well, I thought to myself, if they have picked me out for their ends (and of course it was useless to rack my brains as to what sort of mystery could have guided that choice: some sort of educational intention, perhaps, or—and after a while this seemed the likeliest to me—merely blind, impersonal chance), they must also know what they're expecting from me; but then, it suddenly occurred to me, did I myself know?

In a word, I was scared. As a prison guard, I was terrified of the prisoners. Or rather, I was terrified of coming into contact with prisoners in the capacity of a prison guard. It seemed unavoidable, though, since that was why I had been stuck in the post. The hormonally challenged, dog-breathed major's question as to whether I hated the enemy kept resurfacing like a nightmarish dream, and I was seized by fear a thousand times over that they would delegate some miserable authority to me and force me to live up in practice to the word I had given. (How many times I regretted it now!) Because I naturally, or perhaps I should say: instinctively, took as my starting point the idea that a prisoner was just a prisoner, and wrong can only be lying in wait for those who exercise authority over them. On the course, naturally, I heard umpteen times over that the basis of the administration of justice was the law, so the prisoners were transgressors of the law, whom the law had sentenced to imprisonment for their wrongs. I also saw that one or another of the pretend prison guards among my companions jumped at this sort of reasoning, as if the fact that they were facing criminals directly threw light on their business; extreme necessity might have compelled even me to try my hand at the method, but it has always been my experience that it is pointless for me to pursue my luck down this path. For whatever reason, I completely lack the propensity to act as a judge over others, and I have had the feeling there is no crime on earth which could adequately justify, at least in my eyes, the job of prison guard.

That, then, was the belief with which I entered service as a prison guard in a prison.

But they must have spotted something about me that, with due care (or cowardice, if you prefer), I myself undoubtedly hurried to get spotted at every turn, because in the end I was assigned to duties against which even my eerie sense of familiarity could have found nothing to object. You know, the six-storey chasm of the military prison is a canyon whose nether regions have been turned upside down: the sixth floor was a secure area, blocked off from the stairwell by grey-painted iron walls, its inmates, unlike those on the lower floors, wearing an outfit of coarse cloth or striped prison duds, their supervision (what luck!) entrusted solely to a handful of old-hand career NCOs specially trained for the purpose, who, like wood lice, only felt truly at home in the gloom of the prison, not to speak of the nearest drinking den. Moving down, each floor loses a bit of the general bleakness, so that the second floor was no more than a sort of purgatory, inhabited solely by prisoners who worked on the outside, along with those who had the privilege of working in the internal units like the kitchen, the laundry, and the tailor's, cobbler's, and repair shops, such as the cooks, the barbers, and the clerks in various offices, while the prisoner doctors and pharmacist had a comfortable cell there; here was the surgery and hairdresser, and this floor also provided access to the legal block, with its lawyers, and the corridor leading to the court—named, so I was told, as in every prison in the world, "the Bridge of Sighs."

Well, that was where I was assigned to duties, and I have to say I didn't have to overexert myself. I went on my shift in the morning, and that was roughly also the end of the day's work. The large cell spaces were practically all empty, their inmates did whatever they had to do, each in his particular workplace. During the evening hours, I would open and lock doors, more in the manner of an obliging lackey than a surly prison guard, for the groups of prisoners returning from their work, perhaps, needless to say, neglecting to carry out the virtually mandatory frisking. After the evening meal, I would settle down for a bit of a chin-wag in the medics' cell, then count the prisoners and report the number by internal telephone to the duty officers at the main gate; after lights out, I too would stretch out on my iron bed and sleep peacefully until reveille the next morning, if allowed to. In our prison, you see, I was the decent guard. If you get really bored some day, ask me to tell you about all the things I did for the poor prisoners. Heaps, if that is any saving grace. For some I even smuggled letters in and out—only for the most reliable ones, of course, as that was a fairly risky enterprise. During the day, too, I would occasionally poke my nose outside my room to run an eye over the prisoners waiting along the wall to cross "the Bridge of Sighs" for some reason, and if I spotted signs of dejection or exhaustion in any of them, I would call him out and take him to the toilets so he got a chance to move around and at least rest for a few minutes, and there's no denying it, I greatly enjoyed playing the role of mysterious Providence's local vicar, who suddenly bestows on a prisoner, hey presto!, the thrill of a good deed as unexpected as it was suspiciously unjustified.

That is how I lived, then, resentful about my fate having discarded me there, yet as comfortable as could be in that discardedness, with twenty-four hours on duty alternating with twenty-four hours off, and I supposed that army service would eventually be over and the duties come to an end.

Looking back on it, I can find no explanation for that eerie sense of familiarity. If I try to summon it up, it's as if I were trying to inspect the life of a stranger with whom I never had anything to do, and about whom I would prefer, if possible, to hear nothing more. The snag, though, is that he is constantly being talked about, and the person doing the talking is me. Do you remember our first conversation in the South Seas? You asked then the question, What was man was fit for? You were right, I too see that now: that really is the question, and an exceedingly awkward question at that, I sense.

One morning when I went on duty, I was greeted by my fellow guard—a swarthy, stocky, short-legged, and, to all appearances, spruce manikin, except that the prison-guard vocation had taken up residence in him, squatting there like a hideous reptile—with the information that one of the prisoners in solitary confinement was refusing food. I should note that several cells for solitary confinement were installed even on this purgatory-like floor, on side corridors off the ends of the main aisle, though they were not used, as in the nether regions on higher floors, for prolonged seclusion, let alone punishment; at most, unfortunates would spend the first few days of their detention there until they

341

had got through their first questioning by the examining magistrate and been assigned to a shared cell. There was therefore a speedy turnover in their inmates, so by the time I had registered a face, the next time it would be another looking at me when I opened up or, like it or not, checked through the spyhole. Of all my prison-guard duties, I found that shameful procedure perhaps the most difficult of all to accustom myself to—and if I'm complaining, just imagine what the person whom I was obliged to use it against would say! The very first time—I remember I was still in training for the job on the course—I had to be literally ordered to do it. My heart was in my mouth, I was so frightened of the spectacle that would unfold before me. In the end, it was different from what I had expected; not horrible, but perhaps something even worse: forlorn. Through the hole I could see a cell: a bunk, a toilet bowl without seat, a wash-basin—oh, and of course the man who had to live there. Later on, I tried to look at this as if it were not me looking but a prison guard, but of course it was not long before I had to resign myself to only being able to look as a prison guard, but in particular a prison guard who, sadly, just happened to be me. In no way could I accustom myself to that damned spyhole, through which it was possible to watch the prisoner in his cell at any time, possibly even the most inappropriate moment. It was explained to me that that was precisely the purpose: to be able to inspect the prisoner, check that he was not sick or harming himself or to catch him red-handed doing something prohibited. It was just that I had no wish catch anyone red-handed, and there was nothing at all that I wanted to inspect which might be repugnant or would displease me—I had no wish to know what a person gets up to behind the door, if he happens to have been locked up in a solitary cell. It was not hard to guess, of course: he is scared and bored, and from certain signs that were eventually distilled, almost involuntarily, as a conclusion within me, I observed, to my astonishment, that even if the prison guard did not enter the cell from time to time, it seemed for some prisoners that this would only fulfil their sense of abandonment. I devised several obvious techniques, such as stamping as I made my way along the corridor, so they could hear that I was coming (which was against the rules: the ape-faced chief warden used to slip felt overshoes onto his boots and approach the coolers like a hyena which had been famished for months; before entering a cell, instead of knocking, I would fumble for a long time with the key on the iron door, as though I was having trouble finding the lock; and although the doors, fitted as they were, with sordid expediency, with a sort of drop-down window hatch, through which the unfortunates were given their food, I always opened the door, so that they would get some air, the noise of rattling dishes, a somewhat cheering glimpse of busy comings-and-goings. As I say, in our prison I counted as one of the better guards.

Well anyway, this prisoner wasn't eating, says Short-arse. Maybe he's sick, I tell him. The hell he is: he's up to no good, says he. Chummy, says I, there's no need straight off to … Fine, says he, he's already put in a report, I should make reports about further developments otherwise he would be obliged to report that I am neglecting to make reports. Screw you, I retort in friendly fashion. Just bugger off home, I'm the one on duty now.

We chatted something along those lines, and then I quickly forgot all about it. What did I find, though? He really didn't want to eat. Neither at noon, nor in the evening.

I waited until lights out, and when the stillness of the night had descended on the prison—a special kind of tranquillity this is, a lit-up, timeless night, the everlastingness of the nether regions, filled with dull, mysterious, muffled hissing and bubbling underwater murmurs, so to say—I open up the solitary cooler rather like an inflamed wound, with a degree of indistinct hope. 'So, tell me why…,' I kick off, something like that, not really able to see his long, thin face, as it is covered by a long, wispy beard which ends in a long, wispy, ruffled tip (they'll soon shear that off when they stick him over in a shared cell, I thought to myself with my supercilious prison-guard gloominess). He tosses out in a flip way something to the effect that his principles demanded it—and I very specifically recall him using the word "principles." "What principles are those, then?" I ask with a kind smile, because I had the feeling then that there was no principle on earth that I couldn't refute. "That I'm innocent," he snaps, and you see, I don't even have to refute that, for which of us is not innocent, and anyway: what does it mean?

I said it out loud, or maybe only thought so to myself, I don't know, but anyway I entered his cell, as it were dropping whatever prison-guard reserve I had. I soon had to realize, though, that my efforts were completely futile: he wouldn't listen to my arguments, didn't budge when I ordered him, indeed, did not utter a single word after that. He just kept running that dark, obdurate look of his over my face, like a blindly groping hand. Like someone who doesn't allow himself to be deluded for one second by deceitful words, he searched about like a cornered animal which was ready to dive under the bunk or scurry away between my legs at the first suspicious sign. I could see he was ready for anything, looking on me as his enemy, or rather not even his enemy: a prison guard, a screw, a person with whom one does not enter a debate. His eyes were burning, with red blotches over his cheekbones; it was the second day that he had not eaten ... I talked and talked; in the end I don't know what annoyed me more: the look which obstinately banished him from the world of being understood and making himself understood, or the situation he had forced on me and which was slowly making a prisoner of me too, locking me in that cell, along with this prisoner, and all of a sudden, before I could escape, time would draw in on us and the night carry us away.

"Do you have the slightest idea what you can expect?" I asked him in the end—and, whatever the rules may say, I had long been addressing him in the familiar form, not out of any contempt, not at all, but driven purely by fraternal irritation, to be precise.

"You're not eating?" I continue. "It's just they won't allow you that luxury here," I laugh, though not out of any amusement. "You can starve, but only if they starve you. And if you don't eat, they'll make you, I can assure you. They'll take you into the sickbay, push a tube down into your stomach, if possible scratching your gullet in the process—I've seen it happen," I lie, though forgivably, as I had heard about what they did but, of course, had taken good care not to be party to such a spectacle. "And if you vomit it up," I went on, "they run it in up your backside, or else they strap you down on a bed, stick needles into your veins, and push the nutrients in that way. And don't go thinking that this somehow just happens, as if you were not there or not taking part in it. Or that you can sail through the whole thing without being tarnished by it. You'd be wrong, very wrong!" I exclaim, and perhaps even I am not aware what sorts of fragmentary memories my own words are reopening within me, or what images are welling up from the depths, as from the cellar of a ruined house when the wind whistles through them. "No one who is tortured," I yell, "No one can remain untarnished—that's something I know all too well, and don't ask me how. Afterwards you won't be able to speak of innocence any longer, at best of survival. And if you should have a wish to die, that isn't permitted either. You think they'll feel any pity for you? They'll bring you back from death's door seven times over, don't worry! Dying can only happen in the permitted manner: with them killing you."

That's how I spoke, and my words appeared to be ineffectual. "Is this what you want?" I had another go. "You are doing nothing more than inviting them to commit these outrages, don't you see?"

All of a sudden, something came to mind; I don't understand how it had not occurred to me before, or could it have been precisely this that was secretly guiding me all along?

"Apart from which," I carried on, "you'll be dragging others into disgrace along with yourself. I'll have to write a report on you," slipped from my mouth before I had a chance to think better of it. "Do you give any thought to other people's innocence?!" I can hear my own reproachful voice. "Here, I've never lifted a finger against anyone...," I stutter and, for all that I'm a prison guard, I might even have got round to begging the prisoner had something not pulled me up. What was that? Now, pin your ears back, or keep your eyes open, because you'll hear, or rather read, the most disgusting and, at the same time, most obvious thing,

I might well say a flash of genius took wing here. Anyway, the beard covered up a lot, of course, but it seemed to me as though I spotted a scornful smile flitting over the prisoner's face, at least briefly.

I have tried any number of times soberly to analyse that moment, and may I say in my defence that both analysis and sobriety have always turned out to be my downfall. The way I would like to remember it, the smile infuriated me to the point that I suddenly flew into a temper. However hard I try, however, I don't recall that I was overcome by anger, especially an anger that would have deprived me of, or even just clouded, my judgement. No, all I felt was disgust, sudden despondency, resentment, and again disgust, which included this gaol-breathed prisoner, with whose, for me, all at once so extraneous wretchedness I had been locked together by the moment, through an equally extraneous series of causes, just as it included me. It was all, all, sweeping me toward the simplest solution, of course insofar as I can consider it a solution, to rid myself of that moment, with panic-stricken haste, and in the simplest possible way, as it comes. But I sensed a resistance, a stubbornly aloof, last-ditch, irrational resistance which is incomprehensibly and unfairly standing straight before me, when all I want is the light of reason, I am undoubtedly right as well; and then, abstractly as it were, I also sensed the disparity of incommensurable forces which pertains between a convict who is being stubborn and a prison guard, who, with the sleeves of his shirt rolled up to his elbows, shoulder belt running diagonally across his chest, pistol dangling on his haunch, and trousers thrust into soft top boots, may be the very image of high-handedness and terror, should his whim so will it.

For whatever reason, I took a step forward. A tiny

little step only, and I immediately stopped again. Clearly, though, the prisoner may well have misunderstood—or, as I preferred to think at the time: misinterpreted—the movement, because he instantly flinched. But there wasn't much room, and his leg was immediately caught against the bunk, so he could only lean his upper body farther back, and that was how he faced me. That was when I raised my hand and struck a defenceless prisoner in the face, causing him to drop onto the bunk, from where he looked up at me, not without a trace of fear, yet still with a smack of satisfaction, if I wasn't mistaken, indeed, so it seemed, even a touch of surreptitious defiance.

I no longer paid him any heed. I backed out of the cell, with my trembling hands locked the door with great difficulty, then slowly, as if I were trooping to the dead march at an execution, I set off down the corridor to my room. ...

That, then, is the letter as you may wish it. The "crystal-clear act" (I remembered that right, haven't I?), the wound that never heals.

If you wish, by the way, it may even open up the route to the 30,000 corpses.

Purely for the sake of order and continuity, I would add that as far as I am concerned, the following morning, at that breathtaking sublime moment when general orders are being read out, I simply fell down flat on the floor, then for weeks and months on end, even in my dreams, I stubbornly hung on to a new being, summoned up out of some illness which was no doubt not properly pinpointed, whom I became, or wished to become. It was a madman, no question about it, the sole refuge available to me at the time—the other, so that I might, so to say, provoke my arrest, and I don't know if that was not what I really wanted, even if only in secret, so even I would be unaware of it, as I can't have wanted that, after all. I will spare you the details of how many jails I did time in, how many punishments (I almost wrote humiliations, as if I could have been humiliated still further) I was subjected to, until in the end, I landed in hospital where my games, arbitrary as they may have been, but still following a definite logic, were now carried on under the crossfire of expert eyes. After all, everything depends on the firmness of our will, and in my experience a person can cross over into madness with terrifying ease, if he wants that at all costs. I had to see, however, that I could not consider this a solution. Not that I thought it was cheap, more because my normal life was no more foreign to me than madness. Then the investigations suddenly came to an end, and for a while they left me in peace, and then, on some spurious pretext, I was released from hospital and discharged from the army—thanks to the changes, as I hear from all sides nowadays.

So, now here I stand (or more specifically, sit) with my story, which I shall hand over to you, not knowing what to do with it myself. When all is said and done, nothing irremediable happened: no one was killed, and I personally did not become a killer; at most, all links broke down, and something—maybe I do not even know precisely what— has been left lying in ruins. I am striving ever harder to crawl under those ruins so they cover me completely. What else can I do? I was unable to set off down the path to grace that you denoted; all I was capable of is what I have told you, and in the end my strength cracked doing even that. I know there is the other possible path, but I can't truly pull even that off, I have missed the opportunity, so to say, at least for the moment. At this protracted, difficult moment, I am obliged to notice, destiny is taking a rain check. As a result,

I live concealed in the crowd, in protected—I almost said: happy—insignificance. I write newspaper articles and light comedies; if I try hard, I can undoubtedly make some sort of success with that. I can tell no one else what has happened to me: either they will considerately excuse me or sternly condemn me for it, though I need neither, because they will do nothing to move what is immovable. Something else is needed, and again all that comes to my mind is a word of yours, though not in the least in the sense you use it: grace. But I feel that is farther from me than anything else. From time to time, the dull, rummaging rustling of my perplexity is drowned out within me by the savage voice of fear. It is not fear of fear or cowardice, but rather something else, and occasionally I feel that my fear is all I can rely on, as if that was the best thing about me and might, in time, lead somewhere—no, I'm not putting that well: which might lead me out of somewhere, even if it leads nowhere...

But that is of no interest to you. You have simply got the upper hand over all this with a judgement and have locked yourself, with an eerie sense of familiarity, into the world of constructions, from which you deny every living thing every living way out in the name of the sole possible grace, which in reality, of course, is some form of damnation, and which, I admit, you are absolutely right about, even if, from another angle,, you are not right, because it is not as easy and simple as that, even if from yet another angle it really is that easy and simple..."

At this point Köves suddenly stopped writing, as he may well have felt he was becoming bogged down in a confused line of thought from which he would have a hard job extricating himself at present (he was probably a little tired, on top of which his patience suddenly failed him), and he remained sitting for a while longer, bent over the filled sheets of paper, as if he were pondering whether to run through it again, but then he swiftly gathered the sheets, folded them in two and hesitantly looked around as though searching for an envelope (fruitlessly, of course) before finally stuffing them into his pocket and setting off from home in a hurry.

Köves was getting close to his target, having decided that he would slip the letter in person under the addressee's door, when something in a narrow, busy street brought him up sharp. Neck craned, he was looking for a gap in the crowd: as he had thought, making her way along the other side, was a woman who was neither young nor old, her clear, agreeable face, long unseen, creased by two deep, tragic furrows. Beside her, or in fact more behind her, constantly falling back, a robust man: his bald, oval head, his fleshy face—of course Köves recognized him instantly, and yet somehow he did not recognize him but just stood, rooted to the spot, motionless. For something was missing from the face, precisely the thing that had made him so recognisable and unmistakable, but as to what that deficiency was it took several seconds for Köves to mutter to himself, his lips chilled in alarm: intelligence.

At that very moment, the man suddenly came to a standstill before a shop window (it was some sort of bakery, with a display of sweet pastries, cakes, and petits-fours adorning the window). The woman took another pace, and only when she must have sensed that she would be unable to drag the man along any farther did she stop and turn round. Köves saw her saying something and also nodding—maybe encouraging him to come on, but the man perceptibly dug his heels in, squatted and, arm extended like a child, pulled the woman back toward the shop window, until she finally relented and, with a mild shake of the head, entered the shop with him.

Flabbergasted, Köves stood at the kerb for a brief moment longer in the bustle and then quickly turned on his heels and, devastated, bewildered, shot off toward the city as if he were hoping that perhaps somewhere in the streets he would be able to rid himself of the spectacle, as of some burdensome and unpleasant object, but meanwhile the feeling pressed in him that, on the contrary, he ought to preserve it and bring it out from time to time in order to come to understand its import.

The letter stayed in his pocket.

L

Köves was given an assignment to make enquiries and write an article about why the trains were running late: the trains always ran late, but it seems they only found it unusual now, when everyone had, at long last, got used to it, though Köves, who knew very little about railways (he was not even in the habit of travelling, so the fact that the trains ran late was to him, no denying it, a matter of some indifference), was by now on the second day of trotting from one office to the other in order to collect the basic information needed for the article lest, when the time came for him to come forth clad in the expected superiority and irrefutability, he should find himself accused of not being fully informed. He had even put in an appearance in the inner offices of one of the railway stations to inspect with interest exceedingly complex point- and signal-switching apparatus, listen somewhat dozily, but with encouraging nods, to various high-ranking railway officials, who expounded on the state of rolling stock, the difficulties of freight transport, and the like, apologetically as it were, then finally found himself in the office from whose rooms, they explained to Köves, they directed all the trains that sped along (or, if it came to that, were held up) on the distant rails, and since the high-ranking official with whom Köves was due to talk happened, at that moment, to be right in the middle of directing, among various complicated charts and audio-visual devices, numerous trains, Köves was asked to be so kind as to wait a little until they called him.

It seems, though, that they must have forgotten all about him, or possibly unforeseen problems had cropped up inside while they were directing the trains, but in any case Köves had spent long enough time strolling up and down a deserted, windowless corridor, illuminated by no more than the nightmarish light of neon tubes (at one end the corridor ran into a blank wall, while at the other end made a right-angle turn into a passage which promised to be quite a lot longer than the one he was in, so it was likely that Köves was located on the shorter limb of an L-shaped corridor) himself to have forgotten (or at least not to have thought about for a long time) what he was actually doing there, for whom and what he was waiting, even whether he was actually waiting or simply happened to be there, in the same way that he might be anywhere else. Besides which, Köves was in a somewhat strange mood: at once lively and pensive, inattentive and keyed up—like everyone nowadays, so it seemed to Köves. He had hit the road that morning from the South Seas (he had a big breakfast beforehand), and there he had been welcomed straight away with excitement and a babble of voices: at the Uncrowned's table (even that early he had taken his seat at the head of the table in person) they were in the middle of unrolling some fabric or other, a long sheet of the kind which is secured at both ends to poles and held up high (that was what they were trying out at that moment: it was embellished with the words WE WANT TO LIVE! in fancy, coloured embroidery), so that one of the waiters was obliged to hasten to the table and on behalf of the manager (who had no time to go himself and passed on well-disposed greetings) asked the gentlemen "for the sake of everyone's comfort to please be so kind as to avoid making any stir." While he was subsequently making the rounds of the offices, Köves's ear had been caught, every now and then, even on streets which seemed to be a bit busier than normal, by the slogan that he had first come across in the South Seas, but signs of excitement were also being manifested by the high-ranking officials, who, despite the rather disquieting nature of their thoughts as far as the subject matter went, would crack an occasional smile while making their expositions, would lose the thread of their thinking or fall silent for a moment, all ears to the street sounds that would drift in through the window from time to time, and even if it could not have been put into precise words, all that had an effect of Köves, of course.

This elation, this state of readiness which couldn't make its mind up what to be ready for, and therefore probably magnified every tiny thing inordinately, may well have caused Köves, all at once, to hear the tramp of marching feet in the corridor. Tens or hundreds of thousands, or millions?—Köves could not have said. In reality, of course, it was just one person, and not near at hand but in the longer limb of the L-shaped corridor, which Köves could not see into from where he was—clearly an official who had clearly stepped out of his room and was now clearly hurrying to another room, his footsteps echoing in the narrow corridor, and Köves was no doubt perfectly aware that this was the case, it was just that his present mood simply would not tolerate him taking into account such trivial and dreary facts. He merely sensed something: the vortex of those echoing steps, the pull of the marching—this truly made him dizzy, enticed him, induced him to join, dragging him off into the flood, the ranks of the unstoppable procession. Yes, out into the multitude, because Köves now did not just hear the tread of a single official as the tread of many, he could almost picture the multitude as well: warmth, security, the irresistible, blind tide of incessant footsteps and the twilight happiness of eternal forgetting were waiting for Köves—not for a second was he in doubt about that. At that very second, though, he also saw something else in the corridor: a vague apparition which resembled the drowning man haunting his dreams. Of course, he only saw the drowning man in the way that he did the multitude; in other words, not at all, yet meanwhile feeling that he saw it better than if he actually saw it: it was his uniqueness which was writhing there, his abandoned, ownerless life. At that moment, Köves sensed, with almost piercing clarity, that his time there had come to an end and had simultaneously been accomplished: whether to make the jump or not, he had to choose—indeed, with an obscure sense of relief, he felt he no longer even had to choose. He was going to make the jump simply because he could do nothing else; make the jump even though he knew it would be a fateful jump, that the drowning man was going to carry him along, and who could know how long they would have to struggle in the depths, and who could know whether he would ever be able to find his way up into the light again?

How long he stood there in the corridor, and how long he experienced the strange and evidently destined to be far from transient mood which overcame him like a sudden shock from the outside, as it were—Köves would have been hard put to keep an eye on, to be sure. The fact is, the footsteps which had induced this almost feverish state of stunned elation had not even died away when the door opened and he was called for, and Köves went in and behaved as though he were Köves, the newspaper correspondent, who was interested in nothing else but why the trains were running late, looked at charts, listened to explanations and, who knows, maybe even posed a few questions of his own, nodded, smiled, shook hands, took his leave—none of this disturbed him in the least, did not even impinge on him, as if it were not happening to him, or rather exactly as if it were happening to him alone since—he realized all at once, as he raced down the stairs and stepped out onto the street—it was precisely in this respect that some irrevocable volte-face had happened to him: everything which had happened and was happening

355

had happened and was happening to him and could no longer happen to him without the incisive consciousness of this presence. He may still have been living, but he had virtually lived his life already, and all at once Köves glimpsed that life in the form of such a closed, complete, rounded story that he himself was lost in wonder at its foreignness. And if it was hope that this spectacle elicited from him, that could have pertained only to this story; Köves could only hope that if he personally was beyond saving, his story could still be saved. How could he have imagined he could hide away, detach himself from the gravity of his life like a stray animal from its chain? No, this was how he would have to live from now on, with his gaze riveted on this existence, and to watch for a long time, fixedly, wonderingly, and incredulously, watching on and on, until he finally spotted something in it which very nearly no longer belonged to this life; something which was palpable, confined to the essential, incontestable, and accomplished, like a catastrophe; something which would gradually become detached from this life, like a frost crystal that anyone can pick up and gaze at its final configurations, then pass on to other hands for inspection as one of Nature's marvellous formations...

That was how Köves roved the streets, now dawdling, now breaking into a dash, aimlessly and yet, most likely, setting himself an aim as he was going, and of course he noticed that he was sometimes stumbling into obstacles, having to make his way round people, whole groups of people, there being many out on the streets and making quite a racket; he even saw a march, this time a genuine one, with the slogan WE WANT TO LIVE! on the banners raised on high amid the ranks of the marchers, and Köves felt a brief sense of cheerful, absent-minded advocacy at the sight, in the same way that he advocated sunlight, for example, even if his solitary occupation, of course, gave him little chance to devote particularly close attention to it. It was probably getting late, though it was still daylight when he turned into the street on which he lived, and he seemed to hear his name being called out among the other cries, though he started only when someone plucked at his arm: it was Sziklai, who, it became clear, had just dropped in to see Köves and had even left a note for him with his landlady, then he had stuck around for a while longer, running up and down the road, and had just decided not to wait a moment longer when who should he at last happened to see but Köves.

"Old chap!" he exclaimed, evidently extremely excited, his hard, olive-tinted face, and the sharp lines etched into it looking like a veritable wood carving, "Get your things together. We'll be coming for you tonight with a truck!"

"What sort of truck?" Köves asked in a daze, as if he were not entirely sure that it was he who was being spoken to, and whose arm had been grabbed, and whether the person who was nevertheless being spoken to and whose arm had been grabbed really was himself. In the end, on tenterhooks and annoyed as he was, and laughing nervously at Köves's amazement, Sziklai was obliged to tell him what had happened: the whole city had been stood on its ears, the fire brigade had been disbanded, the soldiers had gone home, the South Seas had closed, the borders were rumoured not to be guarded by anyone, and a group of people—including Sziklai—who had been waiting long, long years, knowingly or not, for a chance to escape from this city, which denied all hope, this life which belied all hope, had now got together and rustled up a truck, on which they would be setting off under the cover of the night, taking Köves with them.

"Where to?" Köves asked, at a loss to understand, and Sziklai came to an irritated standstill, having meanwhile set off almost at a run, and although he had little idea where he was going Köves more or less mechanically tagged along with him.

"Does it matter?" Sziklai fumed. "Anywhere!..." He set off

again. "Abroad," he added, and in Köves's ear the word, at that instant, sounded like a festive peal of bells.

He walked on for a while without a word, head sunk in thought, by Sziklai's side.

"Sorry, but I can't go," he said eventually.

"Why not?" Sziklai again came to a stop, astonishment written all over his face. "Don't you want to be free?" he asked.

"Of course I do," said Köves. "The only trouble is," he broke into a smile, as if by way of an apology, "I have to write a novel."

"A novel?!" Sziklai was dumbstruck. "Now of all times?... You can write it later, somewhere else," he went on. Köves continued smiling awkwardly:

"Yes, but this is the only language I know," he worried.

"You'll learn another one," Sziklai said, waving that aside, almost tapping his feet in impatience: it looked as though other urgent matters were calling him.

"By the time I learn one I'll have forgotten my novel."

"Then you'll write another one." Sziklai's voice by now sounded almost irritated, and it was more for the record than in hope of being understood that Köves pointed out:

"I can only write the one novel it is given me to write," for which Sziklai could no longer come up with, and maybe did not even look for, a counterargument. They stood wordlessly, facing each other in the street, a storm of shouts of "We want to live!" around them, then—was it Sziklai who made the first move, or perhaps Köves?—swiftly embraced. Sziklai was then swallowed up in the crowd, whereas Köves turned on his heels and set off back, at a shambling pace, like someone who is in no hurry as he already suspects in advance all the pain and shame his future holds for him.

CHAPTER NINE

We reach the end

though there is no end, because—as we know—nothing ever comes to an end: one has to carry on, onwards and onwards, confidentially, and with nauseating volubility, the way two murderers chat together. Even though what we have to say is as drably objective as murder is psychologically simplified to another statistic which is just as superfluous as, let's say, the fact that years wore on and Köves did write his novel. He had it fair-typed too, and submitted, like a petition, to a publishing house. One fine day, the postman delivered a bulky package, and just from the feel of it Köves instantly recognized that it was his novel. Ripping it open, he found a letter appended to the manuscript bundle: it informed him in a few frosty lines that his novel had been considered unsuitable for publication.

Köves becomes of interest to us once more, and not for long either, at that moment, like a descent on a precipitous slope which plunges into darkness, in that caesura of his life. He is still standing there in the hall, novel in hand, an aggrieved but all-suspecting smile on his face: it is a grimace he usually maintains for destiny. He probably imagines that a severe, maybe irreparable blow has befallen him. For a short while, before resolving to step onto his downward path, to take a breather as it were, he draws back into his fiasco like a sick eagle to its nest, its wing broken but still with a sharp enough gaze to be able to scan the ravaged domain of truths and self-justifications for prey. Finally, the hour strikes, so to say, and he has to go. If he keep his eyes open, by the side of the road, he will, for all that, spot a few usable flowers which, even if they do not, of course, compete with edelweiss, he can nevertheless certainly pluck for himself. He tries to decide, first and foremost, whether the publisher might be right: Has he written a good or a bad book? He quickly realizes that from his own point of view (and it may be that it is faulty, but it is the only point of view from which he can look at the world), it's all the same if he personally considers that the book was exactly what it could have been. Because, even more important than the novel itself, he comes to realize—and this realisation, to be sure, comes as an unexpected surprise—was what had been lived through by his writing about it. That was a choice and a struggle, and precisely the kind of struggle that had been given to him. Freedom had set against himself and his fate, strength had drawn from the circumstances, an assault which subverted necessity—what else was a work, every human work, if not that?…

The rest? A happy end is in store: by the time he gets to the bottom of the slough he will learn that they have decided to publish his book after all. He will then be pierced by a painful longing, and with the sorrow of nostalgia he will insatiably taste the sweet memory of his fiasco; the time when he lived a living life, when he was consumed by passion and nourished by a secret hope that a future old boy, standing before a filing cabinet and thinking, will no longer be able to share. His unique adventure, his heroic age, will have come to an end once and for all. He had changed his person into an object, diluted his stubborn secret into generality, distilled his unutterable reality into signs. What was for him the only possible novel will become a book among other books, which shares the mass fate of all books, waiting for the chance that the glance of a rare customer may fall on it. His life will become the life of a writer who goes on writing books until he has picked himself completely clean to leave nothing but bare bones, freed of all excess frippery. One must imagine Sisyphus happy, the tale runs. Most assuredly. Yet he too is threatened by grace. True, Sisyphus (and labour service) is timeless, but his stone is not immortal. On its bumpy path, through being rolled so many times, in the end it wears down and, all of a sudden, it occurs to Sisyphus that for a long, long time, whistling to himself as he is lost in thought, he has been kicking a grey lump of stone before him in the dust.

What is he supposed to do about that? Obviously, he bends down to pick it up, thrusts it into his pocket, and takes it home—it's his, after all. In his empty hours (and now there are only empty hours in store) he will undoubtedly take it out from time to time. It would be ridiculous, of course, for him to buckle to rolling it uphill, onto the heights of the peaks, but with his senile, cataract-dimmed eyes he contemplates it as if he were still pondering the weight, the grip. He curls his shaking, numb fingers round it, and no doubt he will be clutching it still in the final, the very last moment, when he slumps down, lifeless, from the seat facing the filing cabinet.

ABOUT THE AUTHOR

IMRE KERTÉSZ was born in Budapest in 1929. At the age of fourteen he was imprisoned at Auschwitz and later at the Buchenwald concentration camps. Upon liberation in 1945 he worked as a journalist before being fired for not adhering to Communist party doctrine. After a brief service in the Hungarian Army, he devoted himself to writing, although as a dissident he was forced to live under Spartan circumstances. Nonetheless he stayed in Hungary after the failed 1956 uprising, continuing to write plays and fiction in near-anonymity and supporting himself by translating from the German writers such as Joseph Roth, Freud, Nietzsche, and Wittgenstein. He remained little-known until 1975, when he published his first book, *Fatelesseness*, a novel about a teenage boy sent to a concentration camp. It became the first book of a trilogy that eventually included *Fiasco* and *Kaddish for an Unborn Child*. Subsequent titles include *Liquidation*, *Union Jack*, and *The Pathseeker*. He was awarded the Nobel Prize for literature in 2002 for "writing that upholds the fragile experience of the individual against the barbaric arbitrariness of history." He lives in Berlin.

TIM WILKINSON is the primary English translator of Imre Kertész (his titles include *Liquidation, Kaddish for an Unborn Child, The Pathseeker*, and *The Union Jack*) as well as numerous other significant works of Hungarian literature. His translation of Kertész's *Fatelessness* was awarded the PEN Club Translation Prize.